Broken Ground

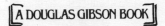

Jack Hodgins

⟦A DOUGLAS GIBSON BOOK⟧

M&S

Cloth edition published 1998
Trade paperback edition 1999

Canadian Cataloguing in Publication Data

Hodgins, Jack, 1938–
Broken ground

ISBN 0-7710-4184-5 (bound) ISBN 0-7710-4183-7 (pbk.)

I. Title.

PS8565.03B76 1999   c813'.54   c98-931296-8
PR9199.3.H63B76 1999

We acknowledge the financial support of the Government of Canada
through the Book Publishing Industry Development Program
for our publishing activities. Canadä

We further acknowledge the support of the Canada Council for the Arts and the
Ontario Arts Council for our publishing program.

This is a work of fiction. Characters, places, and events
are the creation of the author's imagination.

Cover design: Kong
Front cover silhouette based on photo of Canadian troops in France, 1916,
by William Ivor Castle (National Archives of Canada c46606).
Cover photograph courtesy of Courtenay and District Museum,
McPhee Collection.

Set in Goudy by M&S, Toronto
Printed and bound in Canada

A Douglas Gibson Book
McClelland & Stewart Inc.
The Canadian Publishers
481 University Avenue
Toronto, Ontario
M5G 2E9

1 2 3 4 5   03 02 01 00 99

ACCLAIM FOR

Broken Ground

"Jack Hodgins is in serious danger of becoming a cultural icon, in the fine tradition of Margaret Laurence or Robertson Davies or Farley Mowat."
— *Edmonton Journal*

"Spanning much of this most bloody and turbulent of centuries and balancing different points of view, both male and female, young and old, Hodgins tells a uniquely Canadian story which is not only powerful but ennobling. As such, *Broken Ground* is a profoundly moving affirmation of life and a resounding declaration of faith in a century that has severely tested humanity's spiritual resolve."
— *Kitchener-Waterloo Record*

"He is, after all, one of this country's great virtuoso writers, and *Broken Ground* is one of his best."
— *Vancouver Sun*

"Sparks immediate memories of W.O. Mitchell's knack for capturing the pain of growing up. Here Hodgins matches Mitchell in sensitivity and perception. . . . A significant and good book."
— Montreal *Gazette*

"Splendid. . . . A terrific story. . . ."
— *Calgary Herald*

"It may be Hodgins' best novel yet, mingling moments of magic and lyricism with visitations from the Inferno – the latter represented by scenes of trench warfare and a horrific fire that sweeps through the community. Hodgins' evocation of the fire, in particular, is one of the few scenes in Canadian history that deserve to be called 'epic.'"
— *Toronto Star*

"Hodgins builds up a sense of connectedness and shared experience, stories told and retold as the fibre of the community."
— *Globe and Mail*

"Jack Hodgins always goes after the hard stuff: precision, honesty, wit, morality and a good, energetic story. *Broken Ground* might be his best book."
— *Ottawa Citizen*

"It is a powerful novel, a complex and deeply moving novel."
— *Canadian Forum*

BOOKS BY JACK HODGINS

FICTION

Spit Delaney's Island
The Invention of the World
The Resurrection of Joseph Bourne
The Barclay Family Theatre
The Honorary Patron
Left Behind in Squabble Bay
Innocent Cities
The Macken Charm
Broken Ground

NON-FICTION

Over Forty in Broken Hill
A Passion for Narrative

for my parents
Reta and Stan Hodgins

I

Voices from Portuguese Creek

1922

Charlie MacIntosh

He entered the settlement on horseback from the wrong direction. At least it seemed like the wrong direction to me, since that old logging grade came down from nowhere but a few scattered farms and the timbered lower slopes of the mountains. This was in June, while the air was still blue with the smoke that wouldn't leave.

I was in the attic window again, rolling one of my clover-and-newspaper cigarettes and keeping an eye on things. Across the road, Mrs. Seyerstad sat halfway up the staircase on the outside wall of the Store pretending to read a book, though she was really watching my Uncle Archie in his blacksmith shed. Her gaze was so steady that anyone but my uncle would have felt it. But Uncle Archie didn't even glance her way. He dismantled an engine and washed its parts in gasoline and set them out on the tarp on his gravel floor. She might as well have been upstairs marking arithmetic tests for all the attention she'd ever get from him.

Then this fellow came riding down the old logging grade on his clay-coloured mare, looking as though he'd been dragged through a fire just slowly enough to scorch his clothes. His wide-brimmed hat was baked and curled at the edges. His long coat was eaten up with so many black-edged holes that it fell in ragged shreds around the tops of his roasted boots. He might have been another

fire-fighter down from the mountains, worn out from battling the
blaze that filled the sky with rolling clouds of smoke. But he
wasn't anyone I'd seen before.

Mrs. Seyerstad stood up to watch him dismount outside the
blacksmith shed and speak with Uncle Archie, leaning against
his horse like someone too tired to stand on his own. His hat was
cast at a slant that put most of his face in shadow.

Stuffing my unlit smoke into a pocket, I scrambled back from
the window, dropped through the trapdoor hole, and skidded
down the wall-ladder as fast as I could. If my dad needed my help
with the chores he could whistle me back. I had to get over across
the road to see what was going on.

By the time I got there, Matthew Pearson had come out of the
Store with the newspaper in his hand, heading for the blacksmith
shop himself and leaving Mrs. Pearson and Elizabeth to wait in
the Model T. He took two last bites off a dill pickle and licked his
fingers. "Well, Charlie," he said. "Spying again?" His eyes shone
like happy wet dark stones, brown with yellow flecks. He poked at
the sticky smear on my overalls – our ceiling joists leaked pitch.
"You planning to be a sniper?"

"No sir," I said. "But I seen him coming down the old logging
grade."

"Good. Then you've had time to figure out if he's friend or foe.
What do you think? Will we need to run him off?"

Matt Pearson's face was mottled with pale freckles right to his
hair, even out to his ears. It was as if he'd managed to scrub off a
coat of rust, leaving only a stain.

"I think he's been fighting fire," I said.

He put a hand on my shoulder. "I was thinking the same
myself. Let's find out."

Matt Pearson had been up there fighting that fire like nearly
everyone else. If he was like my dad he found it hard to close his
eyes once he got home, in case the wind changed direction
while he slept. Twice they'd put out the fire, but it had only gone

underground along the roots to smoulder awhile and then burst
roaring wild as ever into the timber again.

Al Hueffner had already gone across to look over the man's
horse, which was cropping weeds in front of the slant-roofed
blacksmith shed. She might not have gone through fire but she'd
gone through something. Swamp, maybe. Her legs were caked
with dried yellow mud up to her knees.

"Quiet horse," Hueffner said. Being from Texas, Hueffner
claimed to know horses. He and his wife had come up from San
Antonio to run the Store, where Leena Hueffner did most of the
work while Hueffner talked about digging the Panama Canal.
Sooner or later he would find an excuse to tell this stranger how
he'd lost his arm.

"Been up in the woods, have you?" Matt Pearson said. He
winked at me to show he was asking for us both.

The stranger tilted his head. "Just got here this morning from
Owen Sound."

"Where's that?" Hueffner said.

Matt Pearson answered for him. "Georgian Bay." The Pearsons
had moved out here from the Ottawa Valley. "Hueffner still
thinks this country's the empty space he saw on his Texas maps."

"Where's Georgian Bay?" Hueffner said. My dad believed that
sometimes Hueffner was stupid on purpose.

"North of Dallas," Pearson said, to make it easy for him maybe.
Then he said to the stranger, "You rode that horse all the way
from Ontario?"

Before answering, the man thumbed back his hat and looked
here and there around us. Tall snags, black stumps, fallen tangles
of brush left behind by loggers. That was just about all this place
had been when we moved out to Vancouver Island after the War.
For three years my dad had been clearing land. Everyone else had
been doing the same. Tall donkey-piles of charred roots smoul-
dered in every field, curled about with thin blue ribbons of smoke.
The air was thick with the taste of burning pitch.

Then he looked at Matt Pearson again. "Whenever she got tired she decided to go lame for a while. Mostly when it rained. She probably thought it a waste of effort to chase across the country after a woman."

"A woman?" Hueffner said. "You mean we should be locking up our wives?"

Sandy MacKay had come out of the blacksmith shop in time to hear this. He sometimes used Uncle Archie's tools. "You might want to take that coat off first," he said, serious as any hangman. "You smell like a campfire that's been doused with horse's piss."

I turned away to hide my grin and watched a little red-striped garter snake come sliding out of the grass behind the mare. It wriggled across the gravel and passed so close to my naked feet I could feel a tingling in my toes. Then it disappeared beneath the stack of railroad ties that had been lifted from this logging road before we moved here.

Uncle Archie worked on his engine and paid no attention to this. Mrs. Seyerstad had moved to the top of her staircase where she sat on the landing with both hands under her chin, her usual station for watching the road from town. Behind her, the wall of the Store was as white and glaring as a movie screen. I didn't know if she could hear what was said.

The stranger knelt and re-tied the leather thong that bound his right sole to its boot. When he stood up again he didn't take off his coat, he laid a hand on his horse's mane as though he might ride off without another word.

"That's all right," Matt Pearson said. "Just name the woman you think would welcome you dressed in an outfit like that."

"I didn't leave home like this," he said. "I got caught in that little downpour this morning. By the time I rode up her lane I looked like someone who'd slept for a while in a ditch."

We waited for the name of the woman he'd come three thousand miles to find, but I didn't get to hear it. My dad hollered just then from across the road. I knew what he wanted. He'd told me at breakfast. He was ready to blow another stump.

I ran for home. "The big one this time, Charlie!" he said when I'd climbed the slab-wood gate. He laughed. He knew I wouldn't want to miss this. Better than any stranger on a horse. His Powder Monkey was what he called me. Black Villains was what he called the stumps. Today's villain was as big as a chicken coop, big as a lighthouse in the Outer Hebrides. "Yon black-hearted fiend's about to meet his Maker – old God o' Stumps in the sky."

Some of the men had put a stop to their blasting when fire broke out in the mountains, but my dad would not be put off. "Yon blaze is ten miles away, it disna' even know we're here. We've a job to do, laddie, and we'll do it now!" He didn't even ask about the stranger across the road. My dad had such a good time being himself he was never all that curious about anyone else.

He put a hand on my arm and steered me off across the hayfield towards the torn-up clearing – dirt and rocks and splintered wood. Today's stump sat in the farthest corner against a stand of alder and dead skeletal snags. This was the biggest one so far. Four spring-board notches high meant loggers had had to go up a dozen feet to cut above the pitch. I'd climbed it once and stretched out across the top, but couldn't reach the centre with my toes to the edge.

"Start trembling," Dad shouted. "Ye've met your match in the Mackinaws."

Mackinaw was what he sometimes called us, instead of MacIntosh. He called the Korsakovs the Horsey-Coughs. Howard Stokes was Hard Strokes. Al and Leena Hueffner were Huff and Puff. He made a joke of everyone's name, he behaved as if the people of this Returned Soldier Settlement were all old friends, though they'd never heard of one another before the War.

He dug with a long-handled shovel, down between the roots. "Right down to the middle, Charlie," he said. I stayed on the upper side of the creek and squatted on my heels to watch. "We'll crack 'er in four perfect quarters, just you watch. *Snap*, like a nice crisp apple."

He laid bare two roots as thick as his legs, and kept on digging in the gravelly dirt between them, his shovel blade flashing sunlight with every arc. He took off his shirt and threw it to me and dug until he was far enough down to dig under the stump itself. Sweat ran down his back, but he didn't quit until he'd made a cave the size of a woodstove oven. Then he came up for his shirt and rubbed it over his streaming chest while we walked across the dirt field to the barn, where he'd set the boxes out on the weedy green patch of buttercups and clover. "You bide here. This is where we'll watch 'er."

The wooden boxes were the same as the boxes he'd nailed to the kitchen wall for dishes, all with dovetail corners, "Canadian Explosives Ltd." stamped on their sides. There were some in our living room, too, that Mother had covered with crocheted cloths to make small tables for photos and coal-oil lamps. These on the grass behind the barn were filled with paper tubes.

Off went Dad with a box under each arm, the rolled-up fuse hanging in loops from his belt, the blasting caps tucked in his grey wool shirt. He saluted Dolly and Jim, who hung their horseheads over the gate to watch. Then down into the hole he went again, to shove the sticks of powder into his cave. "Ninety-five, ninety-six, ninety-seven!" He raised his voice to shout. "Did y' know I could count this high, Charlie? Hundred and eight, hundred and nine."

Now he inserted the fuse into a blasting cap. Poked a hole with an awl into the end of a powder stick, then slipped the blasting cap into the hole. He packed dirt against the powder sticks, and stood up to run the fuse a few strides out across the dirt and cut it with his knife. Then he lit a match and held it to the fuse. He whooped, to warn Mother in the house, and came running.

"Heads down!" He skidded in to drop to the ground beside me.

You'd never heard the air so silent. A tiny voice, a girl's, came through the woods from the direction of the Pearson farm where Major Burgess had built his slaughterhouse before moving farther away. I put my hands to my ears and felt the earth humming up through my bones. Somewhere, a cow bawled.

"What the devil," Dad said. We waited. "Dammit, Charlie, did y' go and put a hex on me again?" He pushed back his hat and scratched his thinning hair. His chest was pale as porridge but his neck was the colour of bricks. Below his throat was a V of coarse red skin.

The last time this happened, my dad had waited a good long while before running down to yank on the fuse to pull it out. Then he'd danced around and acted silly for a while before he set a new one and came back. Mother gave him the dickens for it. "You think I want you with your fingers off? You think you'll be any good around here without a leg? Don't do nothing stupid like that again, you fool. Just leave it."

"I canna' leave it, Ellen," my dad explained. "Suppose the lad is out there a week from now and she goes off."

Mother had no answer to that so my dad leaned down and kissed her nose.

"There's a length o' time ye're to wait," he reminded me now. "D'ye remember what it is?"

"The length of the fuse in minutes instead of feet, then double it," I said.

"Ye're counting?"

I started to count.

Then I interrupted myself. "How long'd you make the fuse?"

Dad shrugged. Maybe he didn't know.

"Dammit, Charlie," he said. "Some poor devil could walk through while we're eating. Ahlberg's cow could break through the fence. I will not pay for one o' his stupid Jerseys."

We waited. My dad put on his shirt and buttoned it up to his neck. "Some wee child could take a shortcut through to the creek and get blown to pieces," he said. "Now mind – stay where ye are."

He was up and running again. He went at that stump in a kind
of a circle, as if there were a terrible beast beneath it that had to
be caught by surprise. Crouched over, making himself as small as
he could, he came at it from the side – hand out, to yank on that
fuse. That was how they snuck up on the Germans, he'd told me.
Just in case the scoundrels weren't dead. He'd only delivered mail
and supplies in the War but he knew what others had done. You
couldn't be sure the enemy was dead until you nudged him with
your toe, he said. You might have to use your bayonet.

By the time I knew enough to holler, it was too late. The great
black-hearted villain rose, straining to pull itself free of the
ground and take all of the field along with it. But it fell back right
away, shivering, into its place. Dirt and rocks and splinters of
wood shot out in every direction, a dark rough whistling fountain
spray from deep in the earth, driving my father back, his arms
flung wide like a scarecrow's, to fold up and roll over in a clumsy
heap on the dirt. Stones and chunks of wood came raining down.
The noise came later, *whoompf*. The shocked earth shuddered
beneath me.

My mother ran screaming out of the house, "Mac! Mac!" and
across the hay field and then across the torn-up soil of the newest
clearing to where he lay. The stump had settled in tilted sections,
split four ways up the middle just as he'd promised. I didn't
move. I waited for Dad to stand up and laugh. I waited for Mother
to holler, "Why d'you do these things, you fool, driving me mad
with your tricks!" Dolly and Jim stared from the gate, twitching
their ears. In the fenced-off pasture, five grazing Ayrshires did
not raise their eyes from the yellowing pasture grass. I didn't
know that Mrs. Seyerstad had come across the road until she
was there beside me, holding my shoulders, "Are you all right,
Charlie?" pulling me in against the shining material of her blouse.
Uncle Archie went running past with his long thumping strides,
with the stranger in the scorched clothes right behind him,

stirring up a wind that smelled of fire and ashes, hurrying down to my dad.

Matthew Pearson

Within fifteen minutes of the explosion people had already begun to gather at the Store, as if there'd been something in the sound itself that sent out a signal announcing that this one was different, or even that this one was what we'd been listening for without even knowing it.

When we first set eyes on this logged-off stretch of second-growth timber we were expected to turn into farms, some of us were taken with the extravagant beauty of the green Pacific world – snow-peaked mountains, thick underbrush high as your waist, salt water so close you could smell it. But we had come from every corner of this wide dominion and a few of us were scared off right away by the unexpected. Forest fires, mountain lions, and rain. Some of us, on the other hand, were so pleased with the distance we'd put behind us that it took a while to see this place would kill us with the sort of work it required. Mac could be only the first.

By the time Ellen and Archie had set off for town with Mac in their wagon and we'd started to cross the field and the road again to the Store, the gravel space in front of the building had already begun to fill with men on horseback and families in trucks, as well as individuals who had come out from inside to stare at MacIntoshes' place with their arms folded across their chests. We walked apart, not talking, most of us with our heads down, the fellow in scorched and tattered clothing bringing up the rear. I tried to think how I might convey to Maude what I felt about this.

But I had only to shake my head for her to know. As she got back into the car with young Will in the crook of her arm, his blankets spilling down against her skirt, I saw in the set of her jaw that she was getting herself prepared.

But I didn't get into the car myself. Charlie Sullivan had just arrived on horseback. "Mac," I explained. "Surprised by a delayed explosion."

He spat juice to one side, and raised his long melancholy face to watch the wagon heading south, then lifted his tweed cap and refitted it with a little twist. "Any hope?"

"Too late for that." Unless they knew someone in town who could raise the dead, Archie was only saving the cost of a hearse.

Sullivan's eye caught mine for a moment before he leaned away to spit again to the side. Like Maude, he knew what I thought. This was the sort of reward they gave you for spending three or four years of your life being shot at for the King. This was your recompense and thanks. We were farmers who'd never farmed land like this before, or cleared land like this before, or for that matter even *seen* land like this before the War. We were risking Mac's fate every day of our lives.

"If we can do nothing to help we should leave," Maude said, pained that I'd needed reminding.

But Sven Ahlberg had pulled up in his McLaughlin-Buick taxi, back from town with merchandise for the Store. "Poor ol' Mac," he said, when we'd filled him in. He took the matchstick from his mouth to say it. "I thought if anyone could make a go of it –"

"Young Charlie'll find it hard," said Howard Stokes. He held tight to the ankles of his own small son, who sat on the back of his neck and held onto his hairy ears like a pair of reins. Stokes was nearly seven feet tall, with shoulders as broad as a door. "He thought his father was a god."

"Johanna Seyerstad took him up to Reimers'," I said. "That boy will need watching now."

Elizabeth jumped down from the car and leaned against my leg. Taking my hand, she placed it on her shoulder so that she could rest her head against my hip while we watched the others come straggling back from the MacIntosh place, including the scorched and ragged stranger. She would have his crayoned portrait all over the house before the day was through – sharp angled limbs and exaggerated dress.

The hat shadow and dark whiskers gave a smokehouse look to his pointed face. In those clothes he might have been some derelict wretch out of a poem by one of the wilder romantics, I thought. Or an escapee from a public burning. You would not be surprised if he'd started proclaiming lunatic prophecies, except that instead of madness in his eyes you could see only a deep, settled calm.

I had noticed this placid composure earlier, when he'd first arrived at the blacksmith shed and we'd quizzed him about his costume. In a voice that suggested he saw nothing remarkable in this himself, he'd told us he had crossed the country in pursuit of the woman who'd broken a promise to marry him. The lady's name, he'd said, was Nora Macken.

Sandy MacKay raised his bushy eyebrows at the rest of us. The Mackens had arrived from Owen Sound two years before in the family Overland, with Nora and nearly a dozen brothers perched high on a stack of furniture. They'd moved onto a hundred acres spread one mile behind the Store that a surly fellow named James Connolly had abandoned to return to Saint John. We knew the Mackens.

So we could have stopped him right there and told him he'd wasted his time on this chase, but he went on to tell us she'd been so attached to her brothers that when the family decided to move she couldn't bear to stay behind. "But I'd started to hope she might have changed."

We could have advised him on that, too, but he seemed determined to tell us about their reunion, which had taken place just an hour or so before this conversation. "When she opened the door she didn't even look surprised to see me, she just ordered me out of my clothes."

"What's that?" said Sandy MacKay, wiping the back of his hand across his giant moustache. "My girl usually waits until I've ate her shortbread first."

"No, wait!" The stranger laughed. "She meant so they could be dried. She pushed me into a bedroom first."

"A bedroom too," said MacKay, his small blue eyes eager to see us laugh. "Next time I go calling I'll take a swim in the horse trough first."

She opened the door just wide enough to hand him a shirt and a pair of trousers belonging to one of her brothers. She gave him socks she'd darned herself, then put his clothing into the cookstove oven with her mother's bread, and stoked up a blaze in the firebox.

Brothers had gathered to stare so he stepped into somebody's gumboots and went out with Nora to walk the trail to the barn. But there were brothers there as well, shovelling manure, so they walked the trail from the barn through cattle pasture and stumps until they came to a narrow creek. "On the bank of the creek she told me she'd met this fellow who owned a farm behind the school."

"Herbie Brewer," said Hueffner. "Latour's old place."

"Latour was another Returned Soldier who decided he'd returned to the wrong location," I told him. "Hated the kind of trees we've got around here, said that even when they're felled they block his view. He went back to Manitoba."

"More than just met him," the stranger said, shifting his gaze to something distant. "Married him too. As you gentlemen would already know."

"I was wondering if she got around to telling you that,"

Hueffner said, with his weak eye closed against the smoky air.
"Did she tell you the rest?"

"That was pretty well the end of the conversation. By the
time we got back to the house, smoke was leaking out around the
oven door."

We had a good laugh at this. "Roast coat-and-hat with gravy,"
said Sandy MacKay. "I notice you didn't hang around for supper."

"You've had a narrow escape," I said. "If you'd married her, she
might've served your saddle for dessert."

We hadn't learned much more about him after that. Archie
MacIntosh agreed to heat up his forge and do something about
shoeing that horse. By this time, Maude had taken Elizabeth and
the baby inside the Store so I crossed the old railroad grade to
fetch them. But Hueffner was close on my heels, talking about
some fool he'd known in Panama that chased a girl who didn't
want him and was stabbed by her brothers while having his siesta
beneath a eucalyptus. Then, once we were inside, he slipped without pausing into another of his adventures while digging the
Panama Canal. Only Mac's explosion was able to stop him.

He wasn't so talkative by the time we came back from
MacIntoshes'. Neither was anyone else, but we were reluctant to
go our separate ways just yet. I suppose this was why the stranger
decided he might as well introduce himself to the rest of us.
"John Wyatt Taylor, gentlemen." He said the "John" as if it were
only a title or an unimportant article before his real name, in the
manner of some Maritimers I've known. You knew he would use
the second name because the first was the same as thirty-seven
cousins. We shook his hand, but couldn't think of anything much
to say.

He sat on his heels to shake Elizabeth's hand as well, but when
he reached out to touch her curls, something in her face warned
him against it.

"You see," he said, showing his rejected hands and standing
again. "Even the young ones send me packing."

But someone said, "Poor ol' Mac," to remind us of the occasion. We looked across to the MacIntosh place. The barn was small, but the house had been built on the same pattern as most of our houses – a long box, gable-end forward, with a door between two windows in the front and an attic window over the front porch roof. The driveway was bordered by a row of young poplars Mac had called his "windbreak," as though he were still in Saskatchewan and hadn't noticed a million second-growth trees in every direction you looked. Archie would have his work cut out for him now, running that farm and the blacksmith shop at the same time. At eleven, Charlie wasn't old enough to be much help.

"You'll have to take your horse to town if you want it shod," Stokes said, shifting his shoulders around to entertain his boy, who was starting to fuss. "Archie could be tied up for a while."

"You're probably itching to get started for home," I said, "since your business here has come to a premature end."

From beneath his hat brim, Taylor watched Major Burgess's long black touring car drive past, off to deliver the roasts and cattle organs he'd stacked across the rear seat meant for royalty and mayors. "I don't suppose I'm in all that much of a hurry," he said. "But I don't see anything here that looks like a hotel."

"You don't see nothin' else much neither!" Sven Ahlberg said, grabbing his own thick nose as though to hold it in place. "You'd've seen even less if you'd come a year ago. Them houses and sheds are only a few months old."

"There's more out of sight in the bush," Charlie Sullivan explained. I suppose he didn't want this fellow to think we all lived crammed inside the three small houses he could see from where he stood.

"We built ourselves a school," Stokes said, "but no one's got time for hotels."

Taylor nodded, as though he'd expected to hear this, and watched Elizabeth climb into the Model T behind her mother.

"Then maybe one of you gentlemen has a shed where a fellow could curl up on a feed sack for the night? I'm not up to going anywhere today."

This brought on an awkward moment. Leena would take off Hueffner's remaining arm if he brought this fellow home. While Sven Ahlberg made a show of thinking about it, rubbing his whiskery chin, Howard Stokes lifted his boy down off his neck and led him by the hand towards his truck. Charlie Sullivan had plenty of room, but he had not been what you'd call sociable since his Violet went home to her widowed aunt in England.

"There's a hotel a few miles up the road," said MacKay. "Owned by some relative of your Macken tribe. But we can't send you there, he might have the same approach to hospitality as Nora!"

"And anyway," I said, "he's lost the place twice in poker games and so far only won it back the once." I cleared my throat and glanced at Maude, who was talking nonsense to Will in her arms. She would feed the world if you asked. "You're welcome to stop for a day or two with us," I said.

Sullivan turned to the side and spat. "That is, if you're up to helping Matt clear a couple of pastures before breakfast tomorrow. You'll work like a mule the rest of the day for your supper."

I knew what the others were thinking, once they'd got used to being glad that someone had let them off the hook. Trust Matt Pearson to jump at a chance of a free hired man. A skinny fellow, too, he would hardly put a decent dent in a meal.

"Once he's got my place whipped into shape I won't mind sharing him," I said, "so long as you send him back at night still strong enough to milk cows and shovel out my barn."

They smiled and shook their heads. They thought they knew me. Of course they could not have known that I'd pretty well made up my mind to leave.

Christina Ahlberg

When Johanna first saw that horseman, she thought this was how God had decided to make the impossible happen – a dark rider stained with the ravages of smoke! Not even her dreams had predicted this, she said. "It seemed that God's imagination was a good deal better than mine!" She stood up to watch him approach, but her legs weakened and she had to sit on the steps again while the man and his filthy mare trotted close enough for her to see that his face was not a face she had seen before.

She might have gone down to find out who he was and where he'd come from, but there was a good deal of laughter amongst the men. Johanna Seyerstad was certainly not afraid to speak up amongst men – heaven's, no! – but she imagined that this was the kind of talk that would come to a halt if she'd joined them. And there'd been the explosion across the road.

When she saw what had happened, her first thought was to get the boy away from there. As a teacher, Johanna was careful to have no favourites, of course. But she confessed to a soft spot for Charlie, who was a lively, eager, good-natured boy the rest of us had something of a soft spot for ourselves. Ellen was glad to have the teacher take him away, though he put up a fight against it. The poor lad wanted to stay with his father, naturally enough. Johanna flagged Carl Reimer down and asked him to take Charlie home to Mary and their boys.

Of course she had to go with them. Charlie would have jumped from the wagon if she hadn't been there to hold him, and Carl would not have cared much if he had, being Carl. An eleven-year-old boy was as strong as she was, but once they'd got up the road a ways he gave up his struggle and held himself rigid beside her, glaring at the trees they passed. That stretch of road up to Reimers' ridge was like the bottom of a narrow canyon, cutting through a dense stand of trees too lean to bother logging though they were more than a hundred feet tall. Since all their boughs were near the top, they made a sort of palisade of poles on either side. He shuddered a few times, but kept her from seeing his face. And as soon as they arrived, the Reimer boys dragged him off to join their games in the bush. "They were building a fortress in a tree."

"A fortress?" I said. What kind of fortress would it take to keep that child from harm? He had been his father's shadow.

She'd walked the hundred yards down to my tea room, once Carl had driven her back to the Store. "Spending time at the Reimers' is dangerous!" she said, throwing herself into a chair at the window table and flinging out her arms like someone shot in the head. "You could get yourself killed in the cross fire."

Coiled hair came tumbling undone. So did the blue, nearly transparent scarf she always wore. She pulled it free and let it drape to the floor, as limp as she was herself. Johanna's long pale throat was something every woman in the settlement envied.

"Coffee or tea?" I said, running to the kitchen for something to revive her.

"Too late!" she called. "Only a glass of Sven's cider could help me now. Put it in a teacup, though, I'm sure Leena's hot on my heels. Scared she's missing something."

My tea room was also our front room, as they call parlours and drawing rooms here, as well as Sven's office for his taxi-and-transportation business. Just three small tables were enough for me to look after, a place for neighbours to chat and for travellers to stop for refreshments. Coffee bread, or *kringla*, was the most popular item amongst the baking I offered, and *chokladmaranger*. Except for Lady Week in July, of course, when I set out ten or twelve items, starting with *nammnsdagskringla*, followed by jelly roll, four kinds of cookies and *tebrod*, and then *chokladmaranger*, *kinska pinnar*, custard tartlets, and finally a giant strawberry torte. Nearly every lady in the settlement indulged, with cries of gleeful protest, then spent the next week filled with guilt, I'm told, as though they'd taken part in some sinful orgy.

Johanna refused my offer of ginger cake, mainly because she had not been able to refuse Mary Reimer's tea. Mary was nervous of her. Not only was Johanna the schoolteacher, but she was taller than Mary and much slimmer – an intimidating figure, I suppose. Johanna was the tallest woman here, with something about her blonde hair and sharp-boned features that my Sven insisted belonged on a Viking warrior queen, if there was ever such a thing. She felt obliged to make sure that Mary did not imagine she was like some others in the settlement, who would snicker about the sort of filthy roots she'd dug up and boiled in her pot. Mary was a Comox Indian, who'd left her people to marry Reimer and help him start their sawmill. This was before most of us arrived.

Carl and Mary operated the sawmill together. They'd supplied the lumber for the shacks that we built to take the place of the tents we lived in first. Then they'd cut the lumber for the houses we built in front of our shacks, which were turned into chicken coops or storage sheds for the tools. You could recognize a Reimer board because its width was never the same at both ends. And you never expected straight lines. "Swiss and Indian should never work together," Sven said. "One's always in a rush, other don't care about time. Them boards don't know to go this way or that."

"Tell Ellen I'll keep an eye on her boy," Mary had said, though Charlie was already out of her sight. She'd poured tea at her kitchen table, which had been slapped together out of Reimer boards, rough-surfaced, odd-shaped, and tilted towards the wall. She only half-filled the teacups so they wouldn't spill. Not that a little spill would matter much in that kitchen. The floors and walls inside the house were as rough as the outside. The only real difference was that the outside was scabbed with shreds of bark while the inside was a porcupine's hide of slivers. They'd built their house from scraps.

The tea party did not last as long as it might have, however. Carl could not imagine a death important enough to keep his wife from her work. He'd stomped in to remind her that lumber orders waited while she sat jawing at the table. Sharp words flew. Carl thought nothing of calling her a dirty siwash in public, so he had no trouble calling her worse at home. She'd told him to stick his fat backside into a saw blade. "Me and this woman we got things to talk about here."

Then she had poured more tea. "First I want to know if Tommy's going to pass Grade Three for a change. That boy, he's nearly as stupid-slow as his old man there, but he's got my grandfather's hands when it comes to making things."

Just as Johanna had predicted, it wasn't long before Leena Hueffner came yoo-hooing up my front step, rattling the screened door with her knuckles. She couldn't bear to be left out of anything for long. "I can't stay," she called, just as she always did. "Hueffner will give away the stock if I leave him, that *hombre's* so lazy he don't even bother ringing up the till." She kicked off her rubber boots on the doorstep, and stepped inside, bringing with her the odours of cheese and onions that clung to the mustard-yellow smock she never took off. She tiptoed in across the braided rugs on my green-painted boards. Because she was used to oiled floors, whenever she came into my place she made a show of acting as though she were entering the heart of high society.

"You missed the gossip," she said, her face creased up like old leather with excitement. "What do you make of this – that fellow, he's after Nora Macken." She thumped herself into a chair across the table from Johanna, and barely nodded when I placed a cup of steaming coffee before her. Hanks of dark hair had come free from her kerchief. "Says she promised to marry him!"

Johanna had sat up and flipped her scarf around her throat again when Leena arrived, and listened with one free end across the lower half of her face – a wide-eyed Muslim. "She never mentioned any engagement to me," she said through the cloth. Nora had helped Johanna out in the school.

Nora had never mentioned an engagement to me, either, but then she had never set foot inside this house, nor offered me more than a nod in the Store.

You would know Leena's laugh from the far side of a field – a bark. She bent to slurp at the rim of her cup. Too hot. She put it down. "I bet she never mentioned it to Herbie Brewer neither." Her dark eyes widened in their fleshy pouches, and rolled up and over and down. "Maybe she's got a problem with her memory. She forgot she put this fellow's clothes in the oven too, to dry them out, and you seen what happened to them."

Johanna ran her fingers through her pale hair, and began to repair the chignon at her neck. Like the rest of us, she had to put up with dry skin and hair as brittle as kindling from the smoky air. I used up jars of hand cream, and rubbed lanolin into my scalp. It was too late to worry about Leena's skin – the Texas sun had turned it into boot leather long ago. Though Johanna was born just fifty or sixty miles down the road, her pale complexion and honey hair belonged in the mists of her granny's Norwegian fjords. She sometimes wore a broad-brimmed lacquered straw hat but had come without it today.

"Pearsons have got him now," Leena said. "Snatched him up and took him home. Are we surprised?"

We were not surprised. "Maude will feed him," I said. "It could have been worse. Matt will bend his ear."

"We don't have no graveyard here," Leena said, removing the pencil from her kerchief and using it to scratch down the back of her neck. "Mac's our first death, we never needed one before."

She eyed the plate of ginger cake but decided against helping herself to a slice.

"There's a cemetery in town," I said. There were two of them, in fact, just seven miles to the south of us.

Leena slipped the pencil beneath her kerchief and reached for a piece of ginger cake after all. "Should we go over there tonight, do you think? What are their ways?"

"There's no rule for this," Johanna said. "Not here, anyway. Everybody's from somewhere else. If it was Patrick Maguire that blew himself up, Bridget would be hiring people to keen. We have nothing in common here. Except three years of wrestling with those blessed stumps."

"And the War," Leena said.

Johanna looked at me out of disappointed eyes. Leena's mouth wasn't always connected to her brain. One of the better things about living here was that the War did not get mentioned often, especially in front of Johanna. She stood up, saying she had spelling tests to mark.

Leena jumped up and went with her. I watched them out the lane and up the road to the Store where Johanna climbed the clattering outside stairway to her rooms, her scarf over her head now and held tight under her chin – a peasant. No doubt she was wondering what to prepare for her dinner, and trying not to think about anything else.

She hated to see an equation worked out wrong. On Johanna's classroom slates, if you added one to one you had better come up with a two if you knew what was good for you. It upset her even more to see an equation left unfinished.

Tomas Seyerstad was still fighting his own war somewhere, she believed, trying to get home to the teacher at Portuguese Creek – which is what they called this place while they looked for a name they could agree upon. Six years had passed since he'd been reported missing. He was swimming channels somewhere now, or climbing mountains, or fighting bureaucrats. He was plotting against his jailers or crawling over deserts in order to get here, she was sure of it. Thinking of his Johanna's wide blue eyes, dreaming of his Johanna's breasts, her long white thighs. (She'd told me this in the quiet of my tea room after school.) Tomas Seyerstad, whose fingertips had left her tingling after six long years. My heavens! She'd made me blush.

Goodness knows she'd made herself easy enough to find. He had only to show up at his mother's house in town. "She's just up the road," his mother could tell him, "living above the General Store like a nun." Johanna visited her once a month for a cup of her weak coffee and a slice of buttered bread. Neither woman had received a word since the original "Missing in Action."

Even a stranger could have seen she was waiting for someone. Sitting on those stairs so much of the time, leaning forward with her knees sharp in her skirt, watching the road. Even at school in front of the children she found herself checking the road. No wonder she'd thought the man on the horse was a miracle trying to happen.

Matthew Pearson

It was impossible to know what the man was thinking. When we started down our lane, where there was nothing to see at first but small evergreens shooting up through a tangle of fallen trees, he must surely have compared this with his own straight driveway in Ontario, with its row of perfect elms and white board fence. His face had curiosity in it but you could see no hint of what he thought.

I don't know why I cared. That passive calm provoked me, I suppose. Of course I was anxious for this man to admire what I'd done with the place, but at the same time I wanted him to see

how impossible it was to make a decent farm of it. Perhaps I
needed a stranger to acknowledge that only a fool would stay.

He could see that we lived in a house much like the MacIntoshes'
– a long wooden structure with a door flanked by two windows
under the front verandah roof. Maude had painted ours cream,
with green trim, and planted the rows of wallflowers in the front
yard. Behind the house was a vegetable garden, a young orchard,
and a barn.

"I'd have expected a log cabin," he said, "if I'd thought of it."

"I imagine you expected Indians too," I said, "skulking behind
the trees. Maude would have my head if I'd built with logs. Even
this house is something of a comedown for her."

"Matthew!" Maude said, feigning amusement but mindful of
her reputation as the world's most reasonable woman.

Tanner leapt off the back porch where he'd been minding his
uncle, and rolled forward across the grass to throw himself into
a wrestling match with Buster, our border collie, who'd been
running in excited circles around the car. As we untied Taylor's
horse, I offered to show him around while Maude scared us up
some supper.

The barn was not the sort of barn I was used to, but it was the
sort that people built here – rather like an Indian longhouse, an
open structure of posts and poles and unpainted vertical planks.
Cattle stanchions divided the open mow from a lean-to that
stretched the length of one side. "Major Burgess built this for his
slaughterhouse before they convinced him to move his business
farther away. People didn't like to hear cattle waiting their turn."

There seemed to be a deep inner composure to the man that
took in the world the way a cow gazed at the horizon. It may have
been a kind of simplemindedness but I doubted it. He made you
want to show off.

At the bottom of the slope we came to the spongy ground by
the spring, where yellow cowslips bloomed around the crib I'd
built to keep out children and cattle. White clover and buttercup

had spread amongst clumps of sedge, where, in spite of the heat
and smoke, a cool dampness rose from the ground. "Most of the
others weren't so lucky. Mac had to dig thirty feet for his water."
My overflow spilled into a narrow creek that wandered out of the
woods and then straightened, with some help from my shovel,
to become a drainage ditch across the field. Nameless branches of
Portuguese Creek crossed nearly everyone's place like this, though
most of them had dried up this time of year.

"The well at the end of the world," Taylor said, as though to
himself.

He'd probably thought I wouldn't understand. "Do you think
anyone still reads that old book?"

"It does feel like the farthest corner of the earth here. I notice
you've built rail fences – no barbed wire."

Tanner stayed close to listen, but Elizabeth stepped into the
creek and splashed her feet, searching beneath the water for weeds
or bugs to draw in her notebooks. By now their bare soles would be
so toughened up they'd hardly feel the ground. "Here now," I said,
"your mother'll have your hide if you get mud on that frock."

They both laughed. Even panting Buster stood grinning at me.
Tanner joined his sister in the creek. "Stand in the water, Dad!"
he yelled. "Cool you off!"

"Get away with you."

Elizabeth came splashing up with a few drowned spike-rush
stems, and put her arms around my neck to whisper. "Please, Papa!"

"All right," I said, as she'd known I would, and sat on the grassy
bank to remove my boots.

No doubt Taylor could see I'd grown attached to the place.
But could he see why I'd made up my mind to leave it? With my
feet in the ditch and Elizabeth perched on one thigh, I drew his
attention to the work still ahead. In the acre of churned-up land
between the creek and the trees, for instance, I'd cleared away
the brush, but it was still just a dark expanse of disturbed soil and
rocks. Five remaining stumps were spaced out across the area, all

a dozen feet tall, blackened by loggers' slash fires, leaking white
pitch, and looking as though they would stay where they were for
ever. Two of them were only three or four feet across, but the
others were six or seven or maybe eight. "You wouldn't have to
wrestle with stumps that size in Owen Sound."

"Nor in Cape Breton," he said. "I didn't move to Grey County
until after the War."

"You must think you've fallen off the civilized world out here.
You'll be glad to go back to your tidy farm, after a little rest."

He smiled. "What I'm looking at don't promise too much *rest*,"
he said. "Didn't they tell me you wanted help?"

"Look here." I drew his attention to the pile of rocks in the
nearest corner of the field, the length and width of a kitchen, as
high as my chest. "Last year's crop." Some rocks were sharp-edged,
some round, large as bushel baskets and small as fists. "And there,"
I said. "The year before." In the far corner, the other pile was grown
over with a network of blackberries and morning glories. "Over in
that second field you can see where I started piling them up for
the walls of a house. If they tell you I'm even crazier than the
others around here it's because I started to build an Ontario farmhouse. Well, I've given up on that. You'd think the rocks would
give up too. If they keep coming up there'll be nothing left
beneath our feet to keep us from plunging to the flames of hell."

"Be grateful this isn't Australia," Taylor said. "From what I
hear, the natives would see their ancestors in these stones. You'd
have them creeping out of those woods to make sure you're taking
care of them."

Sometimes it seemed that a contest was going on between
myself and the earth, I told him. The fields would keep throwing
up stones and I would keep piling them out of the way. I saw
myself as an old man, hemmed in by rock piles high as trees,
amazed that the weakened earth had not caved in beneath me.
"Something is trying to tell me it doesn't want me here. Should
these children grow up in such a place?"

Taylor watched Tanner splashing in the creek, but said nothing. He'd no doubt decided I was lazy, or a complainer, or simply incompetent, like Hayden Evans and Hueffner.

But they'd promised us we could farm here. The Minister of Agriculture had got himself so excited that he sat up all night in his nightshirt writing out his Land Settlement Act. "So the Returned Soldiers can live as white people should," was his way of putting it. But the man who tested the soil was incompetent, or drunk, or a liar. Most of this was good for nothing but the timber already on it. There were so many stumps so close together that – as the joke goes – when you bought a cow you looked for one that was narrow between the horns, so it wouldn't get hung up between them.

We'd seen soon enough that since there was little chance we could make a living from it most of us would have to find work with the logging company, taking even worse risks in the woods than we did clearing land at home. Korsakov nearly lost a hand when a haulback cable broke, and Paddy Maguire would have been killed if a limb had fallen an inch closer. If this was supposed to be our country's thank-you, a man can only wonder if he's been made a fool of.

I could have been like the Swifts, I suppose, who'd drawn the sixty acres between us and the sea but hadn't done a thing with them. They'd never intended to. They'd put up a little English cottage, and planted roses, then scratched out a garden and cut trails through the bush so they could go on nature hikes. Lilly painted. Nigel read books. They lived on his war-invalid pension, because of his ruined lungs. Their skills were about as useful here as a pearl diver's from Japan.

But the Swifts had no children. The rest of us did what we had to do for the youngsters. Trying to make a safe and decent life for them here was about the only thing left worth working for, after making a mess of the world over there in France.

But there was little point in telling all this to Taylor. "I might

get all these stumps and rocks out of the way in time for Tanner
or Elizabeth to make a living off it."

"Ma's calling." Elizabeth jumped from my lap. "Supper's ready."
She took Taylor's hand to lead him. "Come and get it while it's hot!"

"There was someone sitting on the porch," Taylor said, while
we were coming up to the house.

"Maude's brother," I said. "He'll be back in his room by now.
You might want to hang your coat over that railing." Taylor
placed his hat on the porch railing and stooped to remove his
boots. Then he ran a hand back over the long black hair that had
fallen forward, and stepped in to the kitchen without removing
his coat. I imagined you would have to fight to get it off him.
Well, that was all right with me. So long as the smell didn't
sicken the rest of us, we might as well leave him alone.

As soon as we'd washed and taken our seats, Maude ladled food
onto our plates out of pots from the stove. "Plain as plain," she
said, "but we grew it ourselves." Peas, green beans, small round
white potatoes with the skins on, a pork chop drowned in gravy.
She smiled at me, the heat-flush in her cheeks giving a happy
glow to her eyes, and held my gaze while she ran her tongue along
her upper lip. Maude had a way of planting thoughts in your head
you had no business thinking in front of company.

I kept the grace short. "Our guest here must be starving," I said.
"I didn't hear him say Nora sat him down to a meal before she
booted him out." Maude's frown warned me off this sort of talk,
but the man had told the story before a crowd and he sat there
now with that smile on his face as though he welcomed this as
much as anything else that had happened to him today.

I said no more on the subject so long as the children were at the
table. Maude, who read every word of the newspapers her mother
sent from Montreal, tried to engage our visitor in political talk. A
flush had risen up her throat at the possibilities she saw in a visitor
from Ontario. She'd been a strong Tory like her father when we
married, but her disgust at the scandals during the War had made

her a Laurier Liberal by the time I came home, and lately she'd
been showing signs of shifting yet again. She wanted to know what
Taylor thought of Agnes Macphail, who'd been recently elected to
the House of Commons. "The first woman ever, no older than we
are, barely over thirty." She rested a hand on Taylor's arm. "She's
already organized the United Farmers!" Maude liked to touch you
when she spoke, as though she didn't trust her words alone.

But when Taylor seemed as unfamiliar as anyone else in these
parts with the accomplishments of Agnes Macphail, Maude hid
her disappointment and let the resentful glance she directed at
me shift into something more interesting. She adjusted a strap
inside her flowery cotton dress, which was a fairly shapeless thing
with its waistline down around her hips in the manner of house-
dresses meant for those with some notion of style.

At once I felt ashamed of the boasting and complaining I
had done outside, for here we were in this kitchen surrounded by
Maude's accomplishments and she had said nothing to draw
attention to them – the V-joint cupboards she had built on winter
evenings, the building paper she had pasted to the kitchen walls,
the mismatched chairs she had re-covered with a sturdy fabric
found in a shop in town. She disliked praise. "Plain as plain but
we grew it ourselves" was as close as she would ever get to a boast.

Because the children were restless, we spoke of school. Report-
card time and promotions were coming up. Tanner could not
promise compliments from Johanna Seyerstad so I put on a show
of indignation: "When we've sent that woman apples, headcheese, every sort of bribe we could think of!" Elizabeth only
grinned, knowing she would bring home a report card filled with
As, Grade One successfully behind her.

After the peach cobbler, the children excused themselves in
order to read to their uncle as they did every evening. Elizabeth
drew pictures for him, to illustrate her day. Drawings from other
evenings were tacked around the walls, tall flowers and leggy
insects and long-eared big-eyed deer. "We don't know how much

he understands," I explained to Taylor, "but he seems to like it."

"Passchendaele," Maude said, and shivered while she folded the serviette on her lap.

Over tea, Taylor wasted little time in bringing us around to his business here. "What can you tell me about this Brewer fellow?"

"A wild sort," I said. "No one could understand why he stayed here as long as he did, he wasn't a man to welcome hard work."

Maude said, "The truth is, Mr. Taylor – and I haven't heard that she told you this – the man has gone."

Wyatt Taylor listened to this as he'd listened to everything else, with an interest that betrayed nothing more than interest. He didn't even look surprised.

"They didn't have a wedding here," Maude said. "They went down-Island for that but she came back alone. If she knows where he went she hasn't told. He probably set off on a drunk and forgot where he started from."

"He'll be in Alberta by now," I said. "Forgotten he has a wife. Now, it's understandable that some war brides have deserted, and we've got men selling out and leaving for an easier life. But Brewer's the first to take off and leave his wife with the farm to look after on her own. That must be why she was up at her folks' place when you arrived – borrowing the old man's tools that Brewer didn't have brains enough to buy."

"Maybe she went for some help from the boys," Maude said.

Taylor made a doubting face. "Macken would never let her have one of the boys. He'd boot the backside of any that even tried to help her." His smile revealed a row of small white perfect teeth. "If she was foolish enough to ask, he'd say she should've thought of that before she run off. 'The boys're needed here.'"

"I hope you're not getting your hopes up," I cautioned him.

"Don't," said Maudie. "I'm sure she isn't the girl you knew back home."

I caught Maude's eye. We ought to have kept our mouths shut and let the man go home in ignorance. Nora Macken was out to prove something. Maybe she thought she'd do a man's work until Brewer came back, and make a farm in the bush, but she wouldn't be able to do it. Maude didn't like to hear me say this, since plenty of women had kept farms during the War. Of course she was right, but that was not the same as scratching out a living in a world of stumps.

"Maude," I said, "do I see pies on the windowsill?"

"Yes, well!" she said, pushing away from the table. "Blackberry." To Taylor she added, "The little trailing kind that grow where there's been a fire. I'll take them down to Ellen."

"You sure you'll be welcome there?" I said.

She pushed back a few stray hairs with her wrist and carried the pies to the table. "Heavens, Matthew! How could we not be welcome?" She stood over them, studying the golden pastry. Maude could not imagine herself unwelcome anywhere.

"I meant, is company wanted so soon?"

She moved the kettle over the firebox lid for dishwashing water. "You may stay at home if you wish but I shall go."

She would, too. You couldn't keep Maude from going where she believed it her duty to go if you rolled her up in chicken wire and tied her to the barn.

"In that case we'll all go," I said. "It will be a chance for Mr. Taylor here to meet some more of the settlement."

❧

Leena Hueffner

I never seen nothing like it. The Store was too small for all these stirred-up huffy females! You'd think they'd been insulted by the

Prince of Wales. As my poor ol' *mamacita* used to say, "Who put
the fox in the hen house now?" You only had to sniff to know how
bad things were. Heated-up perfumes mixed in with oiled floors
and cheese.

Anya Korsakov was in the icebox corner pouting. Arlette
Martin (Mar-*tann*, she insisted, Mar-*tann*) had wedged herself
behind the potatoes, her little eyes swollen and red. Maude
Pearson read the labels on the shelves behind the counter like
someone looking for the world's flaws. Dr. Chase's Nerve Food.
Van Camp's Tomato Soup, two cans for a quarter. Nell Richmond
took up the most space here, as she did everywhere. She'd set
herself before the front window, blocking out half the light, all
three of her chins a-tremble. That unicorn twist she always gave
her hair was a little tilted lighthouse on top of her head.

"It is their own grief, after all," Maude said, trying to make us sim-
mer down, I guess. "And what do we know about the MacIntoshes?
I suppose they have their way of doing things."

Maude would like to be everybody's sister. She was the one went
off to teach English ladies how to put up preserves, during the War.
We never heard if they were grateful. Of course she didn't stay. She
couldn't stand to be away from the son she left with her mother
in Montreal, she said. Counting back from young Elizabeth's age
I figure she must of stayed just long enough to meet with her husband once. During a leave, I guess. Not even Maude would have
the nerve to go looking him up in the trenches.

When Johanna Seyerstad come in she looked from one grim
face to the other and then raised her eyebrows at me. A screen
star ready to hear the worst.

"I don't know nothing about it," I said. I stayed behind the
counter and tried to unsnarl a knot in the spool of string. The
storekeeper don't take sides in a place like this, not if she's got
any sense.

Johanna was the teacher faced with students in a sulk. "Anyone
would think he'd taken the rest of your husbands with him."

"The MacIntoshes turned Arlette away," Maude said. "And Nell. We're a little taken aback."

Johanna didn't seem to think this was serious. "We'll be able to pay our respects at the funeral."

"But there will not be any funeral, dear!" Nell Richmond cried. She thumped her walking stick on the floor. "That is the terrible thing! Archie told us there will not be any funeral!"

"Would they get away with this in Scotland?" I said. "Or wherever it is they come from?"

Johanna closed her eyes and crossed her arms to place each long hand on the opposite shoulder while she thought. The MacIntoshes belonged to some sort of Society, she said. Archie told her long ago. "Maybe this was in Saskatchewan, I'm not sure. I suppose they don't believe in funerals."

"The question is whether there is a law," Nell Richmond said.

"The question is whether they care about that poor man's soul," said Madame Martin, drawing herself up to her four-foot-seven-and-a-half. She never breathed while she talked, she spit it all out in one breath and then stood gasping for air. You half expected her to drop at your feet. "Should 'e suffer torment because they 'ave decide to do without a funeral?"

Maude Pearson studied the picture she'd embroidered and more or less forced me to hang over the post office counter – a woman with the words "Peace – 1918 – Victory" at her feet. I knew that look. It usually meant that something political was coming. Maybe one of her Ottawa heroines had something to say about funerals. "If we were in Ferguson Falls we'd be getting together at Ellen's to exchange memories of poor Mac," was all. "But I suppose Ellen can't see that."

"In Ste-Agathe," said Arlette Mar-*tann*, "we would sit up all night with the body."

The others shuddered.

"Where've they got him?" I said.

"At the hospital in town, I imagine," Maude Pearson said. "Wouldn't there be a morgue? Until they take it away."

"Take it away for what, if there is no funeral?" Nell Richmond sneered. "Mary Reimer's out there with the men. What would her people do? Put it up in a tree, I suppose, for the birds." Then she turned on Arlette. "You scared them, madam. With your beads. Muttering Latin, I suppose. No wonder she was in hysterics, she was afraid you'd prop him up and throw a party."

Arlette turned red to the roots of her mousy hair. She opened her little mouth, but closed it. Something on the front of her dress needed picking at. She wouldn't fight but she'd never stomp out in a huff neither, in case she missed out on something.

"If this was Russia, my mother would make a sad dance," said Anya Korsakov's pitiful voice. We knew about her ballerina mother. Sometimes I could swear I seen every performance myself, all in front of the Czar. This prima donna was shot by the Bolsheviks just before Anya got out of the country with her valuables sewn into her clothes.

If this was Ste-Agathe, if this was Ferguson Falls, if this was Russia. Johanna just couldn't resist. She'd been listening with one long scarf-end flipped over her head – a Hindoo woman. "If this were India, Ellen could throw the body on one of their donkey-piles over there and set a match to it."

"But this isn't India!" they hollered.

Nell Richmond said, "We're not talking about India, dear, for heaven's sake. We're talking about *here*."

"And where is that?" Johanna said. She'd turned and leaned against my counter to address the room, teacher to the bone. "Have you found a stone tablet that says there's only one way for death to be handled in this place?"

Nell had no answer for that.

"There'll be other deaths," Johanna said. When it came to Nell Richmond, some things were irresistible. The Richmond brats had the same effect in the classroom. "Maybe the next one will belong to you, Nell, and you can set a standard for the rest of us to follow."

That struck us dumb in a hurry. Nell Richmond's mouth made a few tries at an answer. She even laughed, or made a sound like a laugh. Others murmured. Maude was shocked: "Johanna!"

Then Nell, who must of heard the falseness in her laugh, went for the door. "Where has Andy got to?" Her heavy body tilted and rolled a little with each step as she leaned on her stick, her unicorn spike rocking back and forth on her head like one of them buoys on the sea. She was wounded over there in France, nursing soldiers in a tent.

She pushed through the door to the world of men's voices.

"The men won't stand for it," I said. "They'll want a soldier's funeral, whatever the family says."

Johanna stepped behind the post office counter to help herself to her mail, which she knew was against the rules. All she got was one letter, from her mother-in-law in town.

"Well, I suppose we could turn the next death over to a committee," she said. She tore the envelope open. "If Nell decides to murder me, you have my permission. Come up with some patchwork thing that makes every last one of you satisfied."

I swear she wanted to see how far she could push before they turned on her. Nobody would. While she was waiting for that husband of hers they would forgive her anything. I never seen nothing like it. It wasn't even just that. You'd think they were sitting in the classroom looking at the woman who would give them their As and Cs. Maybe because she had some education. Maybe because she had a career. They were her age, some of them older, but they might of been girls who wanted to grow up and be like her, even though they knew she was waiting for her chance to be just like them.

❦

Matthew Pearson

When Maude told me what had been said in the Store, I wasn't surprised. I'd grown up amongst the farmers and small-town merchants of Ferguson Falls, many of us related, most of us going back a few generations, and all of us pretty much the same kind of people. There was a closeness amongst us, even when we squabbled. Here, on the other hand, there was only a sort of guarded friendliness, a willingness to help one another, but little intimacy. First you thought you weren't fitting in; then you saw that nobody else was either. The Maguires drove into town for Mass and visited with other Irish Catholics afterwards, the Prices kept to themselves, the Martins thought nothing of speaking French in public. You had no idea what went on inside the Aaltos's house. We helped each other with the bigger jobs because we could not have otherwise survived, but that was as far as it went.

Since there wasn't much point in getting riled up over a family's private business, I'd kept my opinions to myself outside the Store and chatted for a while with Hueffner at the foot of Johanna's staircase.

It wasn't hard to see why Johanna Seyerstad spent so much time on these steps. You were at the centre of things. You could see a good deal more than from anywhere else: Archie's machine shop across the way, MacIntoshes' farm across the highway, the stumpy pastures and fenced-in fields of the Ahlbergs' little place with the tea room at the front of their house, and down past the schoolyard as far as Richmonds' gate. You could also see any traffic coming north from the direction of town.

I sometimes joined her there, to argue for a while about books. They were living things to her, even those written centuries ago. But they had begun to seem like relics of a blurry past to me, with little to do with us here. She listened hard, with her blue eyes locked to mine, her head turned just a little to the side, and her long hands clamped to her shoulders. When she seized her turn to speak, which sometimes meant pushing in to keep me from going on as I will, she spoke with the strength and surety of someone who had done a good deal of thinking about the matter, yet tilted her head just a little, and bit at the edges of her scarf, to take any edge of belligerence from it. Sometimes I let her try to convince me there was still some sense in teaching youngsters the poems of Kipling, say, for the pleasure of imagining a life where I might still believe she was right.

Hayden Evans rode down the old logging grade and dismounted. His clothes were burnt through with holes from flying sparks, his whiskery face streaked with soot, his hair sweat-matted and thick with dirt. "I don't want to know what's going on," he said. "All I want is to collect the mail and get home. Just point me towards my bed, Matt. How's a man to sleep with an inferno roaring in his ears? One quick shift in wind and you're gone."

"You couldn't have worked hard enough, then," I said. "A man works hard enough he can sleep anywhere. I saw Dennis Price snoring on a fallen snag no thicker than my arm. Frenchie Martin sleeps on his feet. If there's a need to run he says he doesn't want to waste time getting up from the ground."

Evans scratched in his thinning hair. "Thing that got me was the way you'd go far enough from the fire to be safe for the night and then have to light a little bonfire to keep the chill off."

"Don't bother going in," Heuffner said. "Your mail won't tell you what's been going on today."

While I filled him in on the manner of Mac's death and the strange decisions of his family, Evans cocked his head and regarded me from one eye like a suspicious rooster, apparently unwilling to take this in all at once. "You don't even know the people you know," he said.

Al Hueffner screwed his weak eye shut. "I thought I was moving to a country where everybody's the same," he said. "I figured you'd all be English, but you're everything else *except*! Swifts are the only two. Where are the rest?"

"They only go where they can sit behind a desk and be the boss," I said. "And even at that they've got the Scots panting to do it for them."

"You had it wrong," Evans told him. "This is a country of Celts." The topic had sent hot Welsh blood to his dirty face. "Underdogs of every description, right across the landscape, people fed up with being kicked around somewhere else. Even Martins' folks in Quebec were from the poorest part of France."

Sandy MacKay came up behind Evans. His moustache was so large that giving it a home seemed to be almost the only purpose of his small red face. "That scorched fellow going to help you clear pasture?"

"Maybe," I said. "I showed him what there was to do and he didn't say he was heading home tomorrow."

MacKay approved of people who were willing to work. He was such a demon for work himself that the newspaper had sent a man out to do a story on him. In his first year he was supposed to have cleared twenty acres with nothing but stumping powder, his own wide shoulders, and his powerful arms. He had a body like a bull, they wrote – which was true, though his moustache was his dominant feature in the photo as it was in life. Leena Hueffner read the story aloud to everyone who came into the Store, including those who'd come in to buy the paper. He was presented as living proof that the agriculture minister's dream had not been squandered, but they didn't mention that Sandy had to work in the woods for wages like the rest of us.

"He can't head home tomorrow," he said. "He needs Archie to shoe that horse."

"He needs to take another look at Nora Macken too," I said. "He'll be around for a little while yet."

"Who we talking about?" Evans said.

"The only other man in the crowd that stinks as bad as you do," said MacKay. "See that burnt hat over there talking to Andy Richmond?"

"Fellow named Taylor," I said.

Evans shifted his head about to see the stranger through the shifting crowd. At that moment, the man turned abruptly away from Andy Richmond, snatching at my Tanner and the Reimer boys, who poked a stick at his coat as they ran past.

"That fellow's going to help you clear?" Evans had not done much of anything yet to his land.

"He'll be one more pair of hands," I said. "I don't suppose he's had experience. Those farms back east come already barbered and shampooed, you only have to comb them once a year. But we haven't scared him off."

Hayden Evans chuckled. "A good thing you didn't scare him off, you lucky bugger. He tell you who he is?"

"I know he's from Cape Breton by way of Owen Sound."

"Just a minute," Evans said. He pushed his way past Sandy MacKay for a better look. Now the man had Tanner's head in the crook of his arm, while Tanner kicked and laughed, trying to struggle free. "He didn't mention the War, did he now?" said Evans when he came back.

"All we had time for was a bite of grub before Maudie dragged us all back here. For nothing, as it turns out."

Evans was grinning now. "He didn't tell you he was in the mines in Cape Breton, then. Explosives expert. When he joined up they put him in the tunnels. The man was bloody famous over there."

"Jesus," MacKay said.

Evans stretched his neck to look again. "You say his name is Taylor?"

"Wyatt Taylor," I said.

"That's him," Evans said. "Skinny fellow. Pointed face. His men were coming out one time as we went up to the line. Blew four machine-gun posts all at once. I seen craters they left the size of your front pasture. He was one of the crew that put all them tunnels through the chalk up to Vimy Ridge. Miles of them, right back to the village – little offices and bedrooms inside. That man handles explosives the way you handle your cow's tits – second nature. Don't let him get away."

Sandy Mackay studied me for a minute out of those tiny suspicious eyes. "You don't need to think you'll keep him to yourself," he said. "If room and board is all he wants for his labour we'll shift him around. I guess the rest of us can toss a pile of gunnysacks in a corner as easy as you."

I was confused by the speed of this leap to the future. "And what if he wants to go home? He'll get sick of our stumps pretty fast once Nora's tossed him out a second time."

"We'll find a way to stop him," Sandy said. "Shoot his horse."

"And what if he asks for a decent wage?"

"We'll have to find a way to pay him then. We got plenty to keep him busy. He can keep the rest of us from ending up like Mac."

"Damn your hide anyway, Evans," I said, surprised at the way my blood had started to race. "If you'd kept your mouth shut I could've had a good thing all to myself."

"Not for long you wouldn't," said Sandy MacKay, a little too quickly, I thought. "Soon as you saw what a prize you had you'd be bragging all over the country. Like it or not, sooner or later you're going to have to share him."

Charlie MacIntosh

Here is something true about my dad. He could never hurt a thing. He couldn't swat the dog, even when it peed on the floor. If Mother told him to punish me he would take off his belt, "Y' know better than that, lad," but in the end he couldn't do it. He'd laugh. He would say, "Och, for heaven's sake, Ellen, do it y'rself if ye're so determined to beat the devil o' of him." This, too, would send him into whoops of laughter, and then Mother would be laughing, and after a while it would be safe for me to laugh too.

He wouldn't kick a cow if it stepped on his foot. He wouldn't shoot the bear that killed two of our sheep, he got Sandy MacKay to do it. He couldn't even butcher the animals he'd raised for us to eat. "How are we going to eat them, then?" Mother would say. "On the hoof? Charlie, go chop a leg off that steer." My mother was willing to chop the heads off chickens but she'd have nothing to do with cattle or hogs.

"I guess we'll have to eat fish," I said.

We laughed at that, too, remembering our first November here when Tanner Pearson and I caught three big fish with our hands, out of the creek. They were nearly the size of ourselves but we dragged them home across the pastures. "Lovely!" said Mother, washing off the dirt and grass and putting them into the oven. "This truly is the land of plenty." But as they baked they filled the house with a stench that turned our stomachs. When we opened the door for a look, they'd melted into a heap of pea-green mush. Rotten! We didn't know why this had happened until the teacher explained about spawning.

"I wasna' meant for a butcher," Dad said. "Maybe if we raised more vegetables we could trade them for someone's beef."

It was different once Uncle Archie came to live with us. It didn't bother Uncle Archie to kill things. "That's what they were put here for," he said. But before he'd come, Dad announced at breakfast one day that the five wee pigs were ready. "Will ye do it for me, Ellen?" he asked, just in case.

"I will not," my mother said. "But it must be done. We need one of them for ourselves, and we need to sell the others so I can buy a sewing machine at last."

"Aye, well, I tried to talk them into suicide," Dad said. "I coaxed them to the well and invited them to jump in, but they went squealing back to the barn."

"Get one of the men to help," Mother said. "Goodness knows you give them enough of your time."

"No use asking Mr. Hueffner," I said, just to see my dad react.

He slapped his ears. "Mention 'work' to Heuffner and he'll start to sweat and shake. He'll come down with his Panama Canal disease till ye're finished the job y'rself."

Hueffner was always telling about the illness he'd caught from mosquitoes while he was digging in Panama. *Naked and sweating, hot as the flames of hell, working like a nigger in the jungle.* This was before a crocodile took off his arm.

"Mr. Stokes is said to be good at it," Mother said. "Didn't you help him dig that drainage ditch?"

Dad's eyes bulged. "When they see the size o' Stokes they'll die o' fright."

Mr. Stokes was bigger than anyone else, and stronger too. He'd tossed a dog up into the branches of a tree when he didn't like the way it looked at him. He'd punched his own horse in a fit of temper, and killed him.

"Sometimes I don't know which of you two is the child," my mother said.

Mr. Stokes agreed to kill my dad's pigs but he didn't want to chase them. Dad penned them into one section of the barn and started the water boiling outside, in a drum hanging from a tripod of poles. When Mr. Stokes drove in and took out his hammer and knives, I went around to the milking door and climbed up to the loft where I could watch through the ladder hole.

"You get on back to the house," Dad said.

"I'm all right up here," I said.

"You want me to take the boots to ye?"

"I won't look," I said. I pulled back my legs and stood up so that I could see without being too noticeable.

"Let him stay," said Mr. Stokes. His voice was so deep you could feel it rumble in your chest. There was hair growing along the top of his nose, tufts of hair in his ears. "Maybe he'll learn something if he watches. Next year he can do this himself and save us both the trouble."

The pigs knew something was up. They rushed past the two men, and then rushed back again, squealing, and whirled at the corners of the room to go racing off again along the wall in search of a way out. They skidded on their own muck and slammed into one another. They slipped and fell on their haunches and ran on the spot while they tried to get going again.

"You'll have to hold them still for me, Mr. MacIntosh," said Mr. Stokes. He and my dad were always a little formal with one another. To show what he meant, he grabbed a leg as it passed. "Grab both hind legs and hold him."

My dad stooped and made several passes at the terrified pigs, who went squealing past in one direction and then turned and rushed past in the other. In and out of the dusty shafts of sunlight that streamed from between the upright planks in the wall. When he managed to get hold of one back ankle the squealing was cranked up to screams. "Here we are!" Quickly he grabbed up the other hind leg as well, and lifted the back end of the pig like a wheelbarrow. It screeched and twisted and tried to kick itself free but my dad dug in his heels and gritted his teeth and held on.

"Now hold him still." Mr. Stokes had to shout to be heard above the racket. The other pigs were turning in mad circles. I thought they might climb the wall.

Mr. Stokes set his legs apart and raised the hammer again, ready to bring it down on the pig's long forehead. "Steady, steady." But the pig was not interested in standing steady, he ran forward on his two front feet, pulling my dad behind him. "Hold there! Hold!" Dad cried, without letting go of the dainty pair of ankles.

As the squealing pig shot between Mr. Stokes's legs, my dad's forehead smacked against Mr. Stokes's forehead with a noise like empty crockery bowls together. Mr. Stokes staggered back and sat on the pig, whose fear was strong enough to keep him moving, with Mr. Stokes riding backwards across the room and my dad running against him still holding onto the two hind legs. The three of them did not fall apart until the pig risked everything on the chance of a miracle, tried to pass through lumber, and slammed into the door of the barn.

"Goddammit," said Mr. Stokes. The pig was away from them now. He had joined the others backed against the wall at the far end of the pen, all of them screaming for help. Now they knew what these two men were capable of they weren't about to go near them. "Goddammit, Mr. MacIntosh, I told you to hold that animal *still*."

"Dammit y'rself, Mr. Stokes," Dad said. "For a minute there I thought ye'd bring your hammer down on *me*."

"It isn't too late for that yet," said Mr. Stokes. "I would keep my distance for a while if I were you."

"I will have no trouble doing that," said my dad. "I didna' like the look in your eye while ye were getting ready to destroy an innocent animal's life."

They got to their feet, then, brushing hay and seeds and smears of pig manure from their clothes. "I think these animals have had enough excitement for one day," Dad said.

Mr. Stokes agreed. "I wouldn't want to eat them now anyway, not while they've got themselves worked up. They taste better if you surprise them." He gathered up his tools.

"I'll sell them alive," Dad said. "Would ye be interested, Mr. Stokes?"

Mr. Stokes shook his head. "Talk to me when they've regained the weight they lost today from the exercise."

"They taste better when death surprises them," said my dad, when Mr. Stokes had gone and I'd come down from the loft. The pigs were outside again in their pen. "Isn't that something to know, Charlie? The pigs were not the only ones that got a surprise today." He kicked apart the blocks of alder burning beneath the barrel. "What'll we feed the poor wee things tonight?" he said. "We'll ask your mother for something to settle their nerves."

Later, he sold the pigs to Mr. Stokes, who butchered them and sold two sides of pork to us. Dad didn't want to eat it at first, still feeling bad for the little one that took him and Mr. Stokes for a ride.

My dad never hurt a thing. Not even in the War, where he delivered letters to the soldiers at the front and then took the letters they'd written back to be mailed. He never fired a shot.

That's why he hadn't really left us, Mother said. Goodness was something that couldn't be killed. Dad's goodness was still around if you looked for it. That's what she told me to say when people fussed: "Poor little fellow, orphaned so young."

I wasn't an orphan, I said. I was Charlie Mackinaw. You can't kill goodness with a stupid old stack of stumping powder. It would take a whole lot more than that to kill my dad.

Matthew Pearson

We didn't know yet that the fire in the hills would soon make everything else unimportant. The smoky air and the dark boiling sky made sure we never forgot what was going on a dozen miles away, but we had got used to it, almost, and anyway could not have imagined the extent of the damage it would eventually do. For the time being, we were interested only in seeing if this Wyatt Taylor could make a difference to our lives. To be frank, I was as excited as a child.

When he came into the kitchen the next morning he was wearing his scorched and shredded coat again. Or maybe it was still. I could believe the man had slept in it, though he must have taken it off to replace his filthy shirt with the plaid shirt Maude had given him from my bureau drawer. The three of us had stood by the stove the night before while he dropped his shirt and socks into the firebox, before he went out to the toolshed at the back of the house to sleep. His hat still hung on a nail inside the door.

"He's wearing his courting clothes again," I said to Maude, who was dishing fried eggs and bacon and crisp potatoes onto our plates. "I hope he doesn't plan to chase after women when we've an appointment with my stumps."

Maude replaced the frying pan on the stove and poured thick coffee from the enamel pot into Taylor's cup. "You certain this isn't bad timing? So soon after Mac."

"I'm not letting him get away," I said. "'This boy lends mettle to us all,' as I think our Mr. Shakespeare said."

"A man who reads," Taylor said, loading his fork with a little of everything off his plate.

"Boxes of books came with us," Maude said. She stood behind me and placed her hands on my shoulders. "Most are still waiting to be unpacked." Maude had grown up in a house full of books and claimed she would never feel settled until ours were out on shelves.

"I was a teacher before the War," I said.

Maude's hands squeezed, the sort of quick secret message that could tighten my throat with gratitude. "'Of high ideals and virtue was his speech;/ And gladly would he learn, and gladly teach.'"

She took her own place at the table and smiled at me. "Chaucer," she added. "But it was Mr. Browning you used to quote at us. And Kipling. Sometimes that gloomy old Hardy. I don't suppose I've heard a word of Mr. Hardy since the War."

"Now Maudie reads the paper and tells me what to think, I haven't the time to read," I said to Taylor. "Sullivan's in the yard."

Charlie Sullivan and Howard Stokes did not refuse Maude's offer of leftover spuds. "While we still have some," she said. "I've discovered that Matt's been up to his old tricks again – gave away half the contents of our root cellar to Hayden Evans."

She was exaggerating, of course. The others knew it. "Poor Evans's gravel pit won't grow vegetables worth a darn," I said.

"Especially when he forgets to plant them," Maude said, pouring water from the kettle into the empty pan.

Stokes, who seemed too large for any human chair, sat at arm's length from the table, brushing his fingertips across the pale green paint of its surface as though he were trying to think what such smoothness reminded him of. He had a habit of curling his upper lip back when he was preoccupied, airing his teeth. Sullivan viewed Taylor aslant, as if he were looking at a creature who needed to be studied surreptitiously for signs of danger. Though both men had come to give me a hand, I knew they wanted to look this fellow over again, this time in action.

Sullivan placed his tweed cap on his knee, tipped his chair back against the wall, and, still looking at Taylor, confessed that the MacIntosh business had kept him awake for much of the night.

"He was a good man," Stokes said. "You were there when he saved Archie McGraw? *Canal du Nord*."

"I wasn't there," I said. We sometimes forgot that most of us had never set eyes on one another before we came here. I'd known Charlie Sullivan as a boy in the Ottawa Valley and had seen something of him during the War, but the rest of them were strangers.

"Well, he dragged McGraw back to safety is what he did," Stokes said, shifting his gaze to the flypapers that hung from the ceiling. We were not accustomed to this sort of talk. "This is what I heard, anyway. Brother Boche's machine guns strafing the earth all around him. He deserves a soldier's funeral at least."

While she refilled our coffee cups Maude took advantage of our silence to say what she'd been keeping to herself. "We must respect the family's wishes."

That put an end to the business for now, since a woman's opinion could not be contradicted in her kitchen.

Wyatt Taylor had listened with an expression that suggested the same deep composure that both pleased and puzzled me, as though he were interested in and amused by and at the same time quite distanced from the business of our conversation. I suspected that his facility with explosives – if Evans had got it right – might yet turn out to be the least of it. If you watched him long enough you half-expected him to blink, like someone coming out of a dream, and announce that he'd finally glimpsed, calculated, discovered, and fully proved the purpose of human life.

By the time we were ready for work we had been joined by Armus Aalto, who had brought his Kirsten stump-puller in his wagon. He'd brought the pair of long, thin, nearly identical Winton brothers as well, who waited out in the yard. You never saw them inside a house. They even avoided their mother's kitchen, choosing to eat on the verandah or out on the well-cover instead. "They heard that houses were women's territory," I explained to Taylor. "They're scared of stepping under a roof in case something in a dress grabs hold of them and turns them into idiots."

"Which is more or less what happened to their old man," Stokes said.

"You boys be careful," Maude said, when we'd started for the door. "I don't want to find out for myself what Ellen feels today."

"I hope it doesn't make you nervous having an audience," I said to Taylor as we were going down the back steps. Tanner had pushed Donald out onto the porch in his wheeled chair. We couldn't know if he would make any sense of what he saw, but activity could at least distract him. From a distance you wouldn't know that everything in the lower half of his face was removable, fashioned in some laboratory in Montreal.

Taylor pushed back his long hair before fitting his hat to his head. "We'll see how long you feel like audience. I don't intend to do my own digging. I won't pull them out of the ground after-wards, either, even with that fellow's machine."

I followed a few steps behind while Taylor walked over the torn-up clearing, the others coming along in a cluster behind me. Armus Aalto trailed, carefully picking his way around the holes and unpicked rocks and lumps of sod.

This was one of my favourite smells, raw earth exposed to morning air. You had only to kick aside the dusty surface to expose fresh soil. There was a mixture of sand and gravel and yellow clay only inches below the surface here, but little loam. This would not be a very good field but I would make something of it. If nothing else, it would supply pasture grass for the cattle while hay and oats were growing in the others.

Taylor visited each of the five big stumps, taking its measure, and kicked at the dirt around the surface roots of each. Dry and loose.

"Matt's got the small ones out already," Charlie Sullivan said. He stood with his hands deep in his pockets, testing the stretch in his elastic suspenders. We didn't want this fellow to think we were amateurs. Taylor would have to be pretty good to be better than we were, after all our practice. It was the *safety* of his exper-tise we needed.

Taylor put a hand against the rough charred bark of the nearest stump. "They won't rot if you leave them?"

"Too much pitch," I said. "They'll be standing where they are for our grandchildren if we don't get rid of them now."

Crows set up a ruckus amongst the dusty alders on the far side of the clearing. A bald-headed eagle launched out from its perch high in a skeletal snag, and set off to the south with strokes so slow and deliberate you could hear them. We all looked up to watch – a sight we'd never got used to here. The crows went after it, scolding.

Taylor examined a sixth stump, bigger than the rest, back against the edge of the woods. This one was taller than the others, and twisted, with jagged spikes thrust up from the top – a tree that had probably fallen when cut only halfway through. Some poor logger may have been killed by the kick. Its giant roots were half-exposed, curled around boulders as though refusing to budge, like a wisdom tooth wrapped around your jawbone. We would leave Old Wisdom Tooth for later, I told Taylor. "You have to stop somewhere. Every time you take out one of these things you can see a dozen more behind it."

I led him to a small shed against the backside of the barn, where I'd stacked boxes of stumping powder on a shelf. Several cartons of blasting caps sat beside them, and a three-thousand-foot spool of fuse – burning speed 120 seconds per yard. I had stacked it neatly. I had kept it dry.

"This for the whole settlement?" Taylor said.

"No sir, it is not," I said. "I'll use every one of those sticks myself and need more. Those boxes cost me six dollars each, minus the two-dollar rebate the government gives me for every box I use."

"I hope you've got shovels," Taylor said.

I fetched my two long-handled shovels from the shed, and handed them to Stokes and Sullivan, both of whom still looked as though they'd been invited to a charlatan's performance. Armus

Aalto brought two shovels from his wagon. Then Taylor instructed them to dig out the dirt from one side of each stump so that he could get down under the centre.

I let the others dig so that I could watch the expert at work. Together we carried the boxes of stumping powder outside and set one not far from each of the smaller stumps, two each by the larger ones. Then, as soon as the first of the holes had been dug, Taylor got down into it and cleared out a little more space and began stacking the eight-inch sticks of powder into the opening between the roots, beneath the centre of the stump.

"What's your way of deciding how many to use?"

Taylor answered while he stacked the paper cylinders into the cave. He estimated the circumference of the root system, he said. He estimated the weight of the stump, he could imagine the angle and breadth of the conical mass from the centre up and outward. "Now there, that's how many she'll need." He looked at the stack for a moment, then climbed out of the hole.

When he had stacked powder under each of the stumps, we followed him back to the shed, where he hung the spool of fuse over one shoulder, slipped my awl and hand crimper into a pocket, and then took a handful of caps from a carton of #6 and put them in the other pocket of his trousers. Then we followed him again across the dirt to the farthest stump, and stood back at a safe distance while he climbed down into the hole where the sticks of stumping powder were stacked like firewood drying in an open oven.

He cut an inch off the fuse, to make sure of a clean cut. Then he inserted the fuse end into a cap, and used the hand tool to crimp the cap end tight.

"Dennis Price crimps with his teeth," I said.

"Wore them down to little stubs," said Stokes.

Taylor punched a hole in the end of a powder stick with the awl, and drove the point a good three inches in. "I could crimp these with my teeth if you want me to put on a circus for you," he said.

"I could juggle five or six sticks of powder too." Then, keeping the fuse taut in his other hand, he inserted the cap into the hole in the powder stick. "I could dance for a while on these caps."

"We're not telling you how to do your job," I said. "We're just exercising our jaws. You keep your mind on your work."

Taylor climbed out of the hole, feeding the fuse off the spool, and then fed out more fuse for three, four, five backwards steps across the dirt. His hat brim was pulled so low that his face was mostly in shadow, but I could see his concentration in the set of his jaw.

"How far above sea level are we?" He looked towards the line of second growth as though he imagined he might see the Strait through the underbrush, though it was nearly two miles away.

"Hardly at all," I said. "Thirty feet?" I winked at Charlie Sullivan. Stokes was baring his upper teeth again, and frowning. "Don't worry, the tide won't come in this far."

Taylor nodded. "How long's this fuse been in that shed?"

"Maybe a month," I said.

"And the weather's been mostly dry."

The smoke boiling above the mountain range told him that. Taylor then stepped off another two yards and fished in his pocket again for the crimper and used it to cut off the fuse. Then he laid the end of the fuse on a granite boulder the size of a man's head and started for the next stump.

"You fellows can pack the dirt back in against them sticks," he said over his shoulder. "Be careful not to kick the fuse."

Stokes and Sullivan and Aalto used the shovels to pack in some of the dirt they'd dug out. The Winton brothers stood to watch, their long bony jaws grinding regularly at a wad of Copenhagen, spitting juice from the corner of a stained bottom lip. I set off after Taylor, who repeated the whole procedure at the second stump, and then at the others. For each of them, he left a longer fuse than for the one before, according to some interior calculation he didn't explain. When he had set them all, he called the Winton brothers over and directed them to fetch a few buckets of water. "We'll wet down some dirt and pack it in tight. We want them gases to do their work in there before they escape. We don't want rocks and roots breaking windows all over the country either."

"So that's what it means to be an expert," Tom Winton said as he set off past me towards the spring. "He's the fellow lets the others do the work." He cupped his own elbows in his palms, as though to keep them in place.

"That's exactly what it means," I said. "You boys supply the muscles so he can keep his energy for his brain. It's something to remember."

"Sure," said the other Winton, John, combing his fingers up through his beard from beneath. "And the fellow that does the least work of all is the one that owns the stumps. We'll remember that one too."

When we had gathered again below the barn, where the sod hump of the root-cellar roof would provide protection, I saw what Taylor was up to. "You're planning to do them all at once."

Taylor smiled. "I may not be a circus but I didn't say I wouldn't make it interesting. You sit here and relax while I put on my little show. Mrs. Pearson isn't going to come out and get in the way now, is she? Or your daughter?"

He was looking at Tanner, who'd come out to sit on his heels with the men, his eyes open wide with anticipation. I'd given him, and Elizabeth too, permission to stay home from school to watch this.

"They'll stay inside," I said. "The dog, too. I warned them."

"Then go warn them again," Taylor said to the boy. "Take your uncle inside. I'll wait until you get back."

We waited in silence for Tanner to return. I could see in all their eyes an excitement equal to his. The same excitement was there every time stumps were blown, but there was an added intensity today. Armus Aalto seemed to anticipate some kind of mysterious joke. Charlie Sullivan had forgotten his suspicions and was exercising his suspenders again, while his right knee vibrated like someone eager to dance. Howard Stokes – big enough and strong enough, you'd think, to wrench those stumps out of the ground by hand if you got him riled up enough – hunched down and squinted hard at Taylor, like a student trying to make sure he understood the lesson.

Their excitement could not be compared with what I felt myself. It was all I could do to keep from laughing. Tanner and I would be telling one another about this when he was himself a father and I a shrivelled old man with nothing to do but remember.

Taylor cut himself a length of fuse off the spool and then removed a jackknife from his pocket and cut a notch into it.

"This is something new," I said.

After cutting the first notch, he looked out at the stumps to remind himself of something. Then he cut four more notches into the length of fuse, a few inches apart.

"Maybe we're going to get a circus after all," I said, when Tanner had returned to sit beside me on the grass. "They watching from the window?"

The boy nodded, his gaze glued to Taylor's working hands. I put an arm around his shoulders and pulled him close. Nothing in life would have been as interesting without him.

As soon as Taylor had started across the dirt towards the farthest stump, I could tell he was aware of how he looked to the rest of us. There was no rush, but he'd added a sense of urgency to his movements. He was an actor out on the stage there all on his own. When he came to the fuse from the farthest stump, he took a match from his pocket and lit it with his thumbnail and held it to an end of the loose fuse in his hand.

"By God, so that's it!" I said, getting to my feet in order to see better.

When Tanner stood up beside me I pushed him down but did not squat again myself. I needed to see this, though the man was so far away I had to imagine most of what was happening. The powder in the length of fuse must have caught and sizzled – a thin line of smoke wriggled up. Taylor crouched and waited now – I suppose it was until the sizzle was approaching the first notch – then held that notch with its fire to the end of the fuse on the ground. As soon as that one caught, he set out in long half-running strides for the next one, so that when he got there the fire had reached the second notch just in time to set the second fuse going. And so, it must have been with a sense of joyful exuberance that he saw himself from our vantage point, a man running from fuse to fuse across this torn-up ground, his burnt coat flaring out behind him, setting fire to one after another fuse from the single sizzling length, and then running without real hurry back up the slope to join us.

"By Jupiter," I said.

"Get down," Taylor said. He got down himself, and sat with his back to the grassy roof of the root cellar. "Five, four –" He counted down to zero, and had hardly said the word when there was a muffled underground burp from the farthest stump, a *whoompf!*, a violent hiccough that lifted the stump itself and cracked it into four sections down the middle and flipped the sections out onto their backs on the dirt, opening up a hole in the centre. At the same moment a fine spray of dirt fountained out from beneath it. It hadn't even quite settled when the next stump was elevated and opened out like a four-petal flower with a second *whoompf!*

The men made noises in their throats like children at a fire-works display. I put a hand on Tanner's shoulder.

Whoompf! In the same way, the third was shaken up and split open and laid out.

And the fourth. *Whoompf!* Some burrowing creature might have been tunnelling furiously across the clearing, giving one stump after another a shocking punch from below.

After the fourth there was silence. We waited, and turned puzzled gazes on Taylor, who lay back against the sloped roof grass saying nothing.

"Moisture in the cap," Tom Winton guessed.

Stokes hissed.

Whoompf!

The final stump lifted, split open like the others. Dirt sprayed. The four parts of the stump fell out onto their backs on the ground. We applauded.

"You had me worried there," I said. "That last one nearly ruined a perfect run."

"Don't be a fool," said Howard Stokes. "He planned that little pause in case we lost interest."

It seemed that Taylor himself had lost interest. He gave the dead length of notched fuse to Tanner and went back to the shed where he restored everything to its place. Then he moved the cartons of blasting caps to the end farthest from the powder boxes. "They shouldn't even be in the same room," he said.

Now Elizabeth, set free of the house, came racing across the grass towards us with Buster dancing around her feet. I crouched with my hands out, and she leapt into my arms and threw her own around my neck. "*Whoompf! Whoompf! Whoompf!*" she cried, and laughed. Buster barked up at her twice, and then ran off to be roughed-up by Tanner.

Taylor looked for the sun in that smoky sky. "Nearly noon." It had taken us most of the morning. "I've got to take my horse to be shod."

"How do we know you'll come back?" I said.

He looked at me a moment. Then he said, "You paid me yet?"

"No sir," I said, "unless you count breakfast and that piece of paper I gave you for Leena. I want to make sure you come back with your horse wearing new shoes and promise to stay for a while."

Taylor was already headed towards the far end of the barn, where his mare cropped grass around the fence posts. He tugged at the front of his hat. "Suits me. By then you'll have time to see how easy I made it for you to get those things out of the ground. You'll want to pay me double."

"Well, hold on there a minute," I said, setting Elizabeth on her feet. She ran off towards the house with Buster barking and leaping around her. "Maude will rustle up some dinner for us soon. I've got some cider that ought to taste good in the shade while we wait."

Taylor set about saddling his horse and didn't respond.

"His mind's on more than Archie's blacksmith shop," Charlie Sullivan said.

"He's got to do something while Archie's shoeing that horse," I said, "so he might as well give Nora Macken another chance to ruin his clothes before she shows him the road again. Maybe this time she'll leave him nothing to wear but some buttons."

Charlie's laugh was a quick dry snort. "If he had any sense he'd know juggling dynamite's safer." He spat on the ground and wiped a long hairy wrist across his mouth.

I said nothing to that. The topic of wives and women was something we had taken care not to speak of from the day that Maude and I arrived and found the Sullivans already here, a surprise for us all. I did not imagine he wanted to change that now.

Taylor led his horse over to us. "Mrs. Pearson was right, by the way. It isn't just the family. It was your friend's wish too, that there not be any fuss."

We must have looked stupid, Sullivan and I, gawking at him.

"Met him in France," Taylor said, stepping into the stirrup and swinging up into the saddle. "It's true he saved McGraw's life but McGraw'd put them both in danger. He was saving his own neck as well. A third fellow wasn't so lucky."

Sullivan's big ears had grown red while he listened to this, his serious frown becoming an offended scowl. "You knew Mac?"

"Didn't say I knew him but I was there when it happened. After the little graveside service for the poor bugger he *didn't* save, he sidled up to the chaplain and muttered something I couldn't hear. The chaplain told me later what it was. If he ever took a hit himself he didn't want them fussing over his corpse, he said.

Once they'd tossed it out of sight in a hole he'd rather they just behaved as though he'd ridden off on his bike. The chaplain, of course, was shocked."

Sullivan may have been as shocked as the chaplain. He watched without speaking until Taylor had gone out of sight up the lane. Even then, neither of us spoke. We started across the grass towards the Winton brothers and Armus Aalto, who had flaked out on the grass to rest. In the churned-up patch of earth beyond them the five large stumps that had been unsettled and broken were ready to be pulled from the ground and burned.

"Do you see what this means, Charlie?" I said. "It isn't just that he'll make life easier. Watching him work, a fellow starts to believe we might make something yet of this place."

Sullivan regarded me for a moment. Then he looked off up the empty lane and resettled his tweed cap. He smelled like onions, new sweat mixed with the old cold sweat heated up in his shirt. "Fellow's too showy for me."

"I think you're wrong," I said. "I'll do whatever I can to keep him happy. I'll even help him win Nora back if that will keep him here."

Of course I had more than blasting stumps in mind. There was something about the man that intrigued me. It wasn't just his skill. His ridiculous clothes and his humiliating status as a cast-off lover may have made him look like a clown, but that calm, amused confidence with which he approached everything, including the hazardous art of blowing things apart, made me think he'd brought something with him that we needed more than just his skill with explosives. I suspected it was the children, Tanner and Elizabeth and Willie and all the other youngsters in the settlement, who needed him more than we did, in some fashion I didn't yet see.

Nora Macken

I seen him sneaking up the lane, bent over from the sack on his shoulder. Sneak? Maybe he *thought* he was sneaking. He crashed through the brush like a clumsy half-blind mule. He must have thought I was deaf. Did he think I couldn't hear his horse whinny when he tethered her at the road? He might as well have ridden her right to the door.

I'd heard the Pearsons nabbed him. It didn't matter to me if he went or stayed, I had work to do. There were spuds to be hoed, and carrots to thin. Also turnips. There was a wasp nest to knock from the overhang by the back door, a leak to patch in the roof, and a sagging fence to be mended. And there was a root cellar to dig. Or stake out, at least, for fall. I didn't have the time to wonder if he'd stayed.

I thought the flour might be a farewell present. Lord knows I could do with it. But the flour was only the start. I watched him through a tear in the curtain. He come back with sugar this time. Leena Hueffner must have told him I was getting low. Sugar on one shoulder, potatoes on the other. Leena must have told him Brewer didn't grow a single thing last year, not an onion.

He was still wearing that hat and coat. The others must have thought he looked a fool. I let him put his things on the step beside the flour and go down the dirt ruts again. If he thought I was going to invite him in for a meal he was crazier than he looked.

Then he come down the lane a third time. Eggs. Onions. A bolt of red-checked calico. He kept his head down, his face mostly shadowed by that wide-brimmed hat. He might be humming to himself, I could see the hollow of his throat vibrating with a tune.

Next he came back up the lane with three live leghorns in each hand. They were hanging upside down like bouquets of feathers that burst out flapping now and then but mostly stayed still.

I opened the door. "Take them back," I said. "I haven't got a pen."

He looked surprised to find me standing in the doorway of my own house.

"I'll build you a pen," he said.

"You will not," I said.

"Won't take me an hour," he said. "I see plenty of poles around, and that roll of wire over there. Give me a hammer and a handful of nails and these hens'll soon be singing in their pen like you never heard."

The hens were already singing. They twisted their necks up so the blood wouldn't run to their heads but they looked like they were just trying to see what was going on. Their singing was a low, sad, half-hearted complaint. They looked like healthy layers.

"You'll take them back with all them other things," I told him.

"It's paid for," he said. "I can't."

"Last time I saw you you were poor as dirt. How'd you pay?"

"I put in a morning's work for Pearson," he said. "He signed his name to a line of credit at the Store. There's plenty work around here yet. You folks have got more stumps than Cape Breton has coal, and it looks as if I'm the man to get them out of the ground."

"The Hueffners can cancel your debt," I said. "If you don't owe them anything there'll be nothing to keep you here. Leave the stumps where they are. Let the others get them out themselves."

"And kill themselves doing it."

"They aren't all as clumsy as MacIntosh," I said. "Bring your horse. You can load up without walking back and forth the rest of the day."

He gave up then. He walked down the lane with his narrow shoulders slumped and came back leading the mare. He didn't say anything more until he'd tied the mare to the porch and started loading things on her back. First the sack of flour and the sugar.

"I didn't want to say nothing," he said, "but I can tell you got a dead calf or something needs to be buried. You want me to dig?"

"I'll do my own digging," I told him. "You must have some nose if you can smell Sammy above the stink of your coat."

He stopped what he was doing. "That old spaniel's dead, that come all the way across the country with you?"

"He was getting on."

"You'll want a new dog then. Deer'll eat your garden. Weasels'll get your chickens."

"Don't buy me a dog."

He went back to loading his horse. "You got a lot of work ahead of you here."

I knew what it looked like. My two-room tarpaper shack with its one small window and a slab door: it could have been a storage shed for tools. You wouldn't find anyone living like this around Owen Sound, except maybe someone's crazy old uncle that hides from people. A stack of nailed-together slab-wood for a step. Half a chimney. And all around, this tangled mess of slash and stumps and second-growth you couldn't chop a trail through in a month, except where my little garden patch of dirt was hacked out, the size of a one-hog pen.

"I'm not afraid of work," I said. "You know who raised me."

"I don't see him helping out. Your brothers either."

"I got a roof, I got space for a garden, I got hands for doing anything that needs doing."

"And you got Herbie Brewer, too, if he'd just come back to give you a hand."

He looked away when he said that. I didn't answer. "You should buy a coat and hat with your credit," I said. "You look like you had a run-in with Hansel and Gretel's witch."

He looked off into the bush with his chin raised. "I won't take these off until you have me the way you promised. Or they throw me into my grave, whichever's first."

"Get away with you," I said. "You'll be the loneliest man in creation, nobody will come near for the smell."

He untied his horse and started to lead her away.

"Tell Hueffners I'll be up later," I said. "I'll trade some firewood for that sack of flour, before anyone else gets their hands on it."

He should have stayed in Owen Sound. His house needed paint last time I looked. Emily Paterson would have him. She told me once she'd take him if he asked. A mousy little thing, scared of her shadow, but she knew how to work. He should have stayed where he was and looked after the things that are his.

I didn't watch him out of sight. I grabbed up the shovel from where it leaned against the house and went around the back to bury Sam.

Christina Ahlberg

I'm afraid I don't know why they even had the picnic. I'd rather expected them to skip it, with Dominion Day so close on the heels of a death. But Ellen MacIntosh didn't want it cancelled. She made her jellied meat loaves and baked her oatcakes the same as last year and the year before. According to Leena Hueffner, it was all because Ellen wanted her bonnie wee Charlie to win the sack race again.

"I suppose I ought to give up trying to understand," Johanna said. Sometimes she suspected we were all a little crazy in this place.

Well, she sometimes thought our children were crazy too. They did their lessons like youngsters anywhere, then went out past the schoolyard to play in brush. They came in with faces smeared with dirt and wood-ash, their clothing torn, their hands bloody from blackberry vines and thistles. What had they been doing? Clearing land. Carving little dairy farms out of the bush. Making beds and cooking meals inside the hollow stumps. She taught them hopscotch, she showed them how to play softball, she went out herself and got them skipping rope. But the minute she turned her back they ran off into the bush, taming the wild frontier like their parents.

It was the same at picnics. Relay races were forced on them by mothers like myself who were teachers before we married. Lacrosse games. They played, but they couldn't see much sense to it. It was like learning a language they wouldn't use. As soon as they could, they ran off to the woods or down the beach to play pioneers.

The government had given us a stretch of beach for a park, two miles downhill from the Store, a grassy clearing between the driftwood and a stand of unlogged Douglas fir. Some believed there had been an Indian village there until Indians got wind of the settlement and left. You could imagine a row of longhouses, with totem poles in front and cedar boats on the shore. Dogs fighting. Fish drying on sticks. Half-naked figures moving around inside with the smoke.

I don't know that anyone ever saw the Indian woman, who was supposed to be camped somewhere in the bush behind the park. Kicked out, they said, by her people farther north. We heard she'd married a white man sent to prison and was waiting here until he was free to come and get her. You could see where small cooking fires had burned but no one ever caught sight of the woman herself. Every picnic, boys set out to find her. Tanner Pearson, Timo Aalto, the Reimer boys, Charlie MacIntosh. They promised to bring her in at spear-point so we could see that she was real.

"Somebody ought to quiz MacKay about her," Leena said. She'd seen Sandy driving down towards the beach at night a few times, without lights. "That jailbird husband might get a big surprise, a litter of junior MacKays clinging to her skirt."

"All with moustaches big as their faces," Johanna said. "That'd be something to put in their paper."

Ever since the newspaper made him out to be the prize specimen of the settlement there'd been a swagger in Sandy's step that
didn't sit right with some. They'd made him out to be proof that
taxpayer money wasn't wasted on their Land Settlement scheme,
though "strong as a bull" was what they praised him for. Leena
said, "If that's their idea of success they could of turned the district over to a herd of Texas longhorns."

As soon as people got to the picnic they laid their blankets out
in the shade of trees, or under a bush of ocean spray or against a
driftwood log. Major and Mrs. Burgess parked their touring car
under a fir and lived behind the lace curtains of backseat windows
like a home-from-home, ignoring the smell of roasts and other raw
beef cuts that were usually piled on the leather seats for delivery.
The others set up chairs on their blankets, got out books and
magazines, pulled toys from a flour sack. They tossed down pillows.
It wasn't much different from home, with everyone living on
separate little patches of the earth.

Women did the setting up, though we had put on our best
crêpe dresses or jackets and skirts for the occasion, and wore our
wide-brimmed hats that sat dead-level right down on our brows.
Men in shirts and ties walked out to look at the sea. They listened
hard. Waves breaking and falling back was all they heard. And
gulls. They didn't talk very much. Some never talked at all. You
could see they didn't even know for certain why they'd come.

Some had still not got used to the place. I'd heard them talking
about this in my tea room, sometimes up at the Store. I suppose
they'd grown accustomed to their homes – stumps and half-
cleared fields and donkey-piles of burning roots out every window.
But coming down to the beach reminded them of how different
everything was from where they'd lived before – Alberta or New
Brunswick or the Ottawa Valley. The trees were bigger than
they'd ever dreamed, too broad and tall, draped with heavy limbs
so green they hurt your eyes. The Island mountains were a high

blue jagged wall all down one side of the world, with nothing beyond them but ocean and Japan. You thought you might know the name of something you saw – flower or bush, twice the size you were used to – and discovered that you didn't. And the sea – just looking out at the Strait put some of them into a trance. They'd go cold from their toes right up to their necks, they said, sensing how deep and cold and wide it was, moving like something alive.

"The truth of the matter is," Johanna once told me, "this place scares some of them half to death. They don't even know where they are."

Nell Richmond told me that when she looked at the mainland mountains across the Strait she felt she'd been cut adrift from the world. I imagine some of those men were thinking the same when they stood out there above the driftwood and stared. According to my Sven, living here in this underpopulated place, and remembering what the men had been forced to see before they came here, it was possible to believe that most of the world's population had been slaughtered, the whole of the mainland gone silent.

Food for the picnic was stored where it would stay cool – between tree roots, in buckets of water. Bottles and crocks were sunk in the gravel along the edge of the tide. All this was for later on, when families would get together on their blankets to eat whatever they'd brought.

You had to be nosy to know what everyone brought. Perhaps they forgave me because of the tea room, they knew my interest in food. The Aaltos brought pickled fish rolls and rye bread pies. Mary Reimer packed pork sausages and cheese for Carl, but she wouldn't eat them herself. For herself she brought what she called "Indian ice cream" – wild berries and sugar whipped into a froth. Her boys ate both. Maguires brought the same every year, mulligan stew – Bridget was no great shakes as a cook. Johanna baked her usual *sukkerbrod* and almond butter tarts. And the Korsakovs – I could never remember the name of what they brought, but it was unlike anything else in the place.

Nell Richmond puffed out her bosoms to sniff the chili beans that Leena had baked for Hueffner. "Those people must have cast-iron stomachs," she said to me later. Nell's food was pale and runny.

It wasn't much different from staying home, I suppose, except that it was like opening up a wall of their houses. If you kept an eye open you could see a good deal more than you expected. Ruby and Hayden Evans talked to their youngsters but they acted as if they didn't know each other was there. The Stokeses doted on their boy, but now you saw how nervous Sarah looked whenever her husband took hold of him. A man that big could crush the boy in his hands. Lillian Swift sat under a willow, painting at her easel, almost invisible inside her giant hat, while Nigel kept his nose in a book until it was time to eat. The Reimers set their blanket out a good distance from everyone else so they could snap and growl without upsetting their neighbours. And when Major and Mrs. Burgess did finally step out of their touring car, it was only for long enough to walk to the edge of the sea, take a few deep breaths, and walk back to the car again holding hands.

I suppose the others could say similar things about us. Heavens, I suppose they would notice I talked to my family in the same quiet manner I have in my tea room, always the soft-spoken proper lady when she was reading your tea leaves, predicting mysterious strangers and exciting travels that seldom meant anything more than a salesman knocking at the door, or a shopping trip to town.

The Pearsons drove in late but didn't waste time setting up. They heaped everything against a shore pine and made a beeline for the water. Maude stayed in the spindrift with the baby, but Matt ploughed in with Tanner and Elizabeth until they were all three hollering about the cold and shouting out a countdown to get ducked. Then they swam straight out towards the mainland. A race. There was no telling where the finish line would be. It could be the other side, thirty miles away. But it turned out to be

where Matt decided. The two youngsters complained when he
won. He put a hand on either head and pushed them under, but
not for long.

Sally Mitchell must have stayed with the brother so the children could come to the picnic. This was Maude's friend from up
over the ridge above Reimers'. Nobody else got near him. If you
saw him at all, it was at a distance – his head bobbing in the back
of their car going past. They kept him in his room when you
went to visit. Leena said she would crawl in his window at night
to catch him without his mask if getting caught would not be
bad for business.

When Tanner swam off to join the other boys, Matt and
Elizabeth breaststroked in to shore. They were worn-out shipwreck
survivors crawling out of waves to collapse on the rocks. When
the girl went back out to ride a bobbing log, Maude and Matthew
sat and held hands to watch.

It was something to see, the way those two admired their youngsters. They were strict – you wouldn't catch them being slaves to
their children like some. Matt was the kind of father who loved
his children by letting the pleasure they gave him show in everything he did, even when he had to say "No." You'd think they'd
given birth to creatures from another world, meant to do big
things for *this* world before they were through. Young Tanner
might have been the first boy-child to win a race, Willie the first
to burble sounds. And Elizabeth with her red curls and bright
wide eyes might have been a princess some foreign king had sent
them, her every move and word admired like a gift.

There was no doubt she was clever. She came into the tea
room with Maude one day when Arlette Martin was already there
with her girls, chattering away in French. All at once Elizabeth
was speaking it too. "She's always been quick to pick things up,"
Maude said. Of course she was smiling.

"That's faster than quick," I said. "You must be teaching her
at home."

"No, no," Maude said. "There was a hired man in Ferguson Falls that spoke it. It isn't far from Quebec."

Born to be another schoolteacher was what you thought if you watched that girl at the beach. She ran off to join the noisy girls in a driftwood shelter and dragged them out to look for shells. Soon she would have them drawing pictures of what they found, while she told some made-up story about the hermit crabs who used to live inside.

You couldn't blame her folks for thinking she was extraordinary, but she was just as human as the rest of them. I'd seen her squabbling with the other girls, walking home from school. I'd heard her tease the club-footed Evans boy. Leena said she'd seen her almost snitch a candy bar from a shelf, stopping only because someone came in, tinkling the bell above the door. There wouldn't be any point in telling her folks, they wouldn't believe it. And what did it mean, anyway? Only that she had a way to go before becoming a saint.

Maude and Matthew went behind a bush to dress and came up to join those of us who'd gathered at the horseshoe pitch, where talk had got stuck on the MacIntoshes again. Some just couldn't let it go, even though poor Ellen was sitting just across the grass with her sister's family. Poor Charlie too. It appeared she didn't want him out of her sight. She kept touching him, as if she were frightened he'd disappear. It seemed to me that disappearing was what he wanted to do. It was a relief when Tanner Pearson came by and Charlie took off at a run, his mother calling after him. No swimming! No wrestling! No getting out of her sight!

Voices were raised at the horseshoe pitch. Nothing we hadn't already heard. It still rankled some that Mac was having no funeral. Men were bothered most. Nell Richmond puffed and sighed a bit before working up the steam to place some blame. None of this would have happened, she said, if the men had built us a church. "There'd be no question of avoiding funerals then. If we had a little graveyard they would see it was only natural."

Sandy MacKay held onto the horseshoe he was about to toss. "We didn't build one, Nell, because we didn't want one." Then he let the horseshoe fly out and clang against the steel peg and fall around it. A ringer. A cheer went up. "There was no shortage of churches in France," he said. "Steeples everywhere you looked and believers mowed down right in their shadow. Much good it did them. The sight of a preacher on these roads would make me bring up my breakfast."

"Mind, there's that little church they stuck in the bush between here and town," said Hayden Evans. We knew the one he meant. It was three miles south of here, sitting amongst some farms where people were given to building narrow two-storey houses that looked nothing like our own. "Nobody ever goes. The Murdochs, maybe. It's wasted."

"What sort of church is it?" said Nancy Price. "I never thought to look."

"Church of England, dear," Nell Richmond said. She didn't need to add "Of course."

"It's not much bigger than my chicken coop," Matt Pearson said. "A team of horses could move it if you wanted it bad enough."

"Matthew Pearson!" Nell cried. "Maude would never allow you to steal!"

"Well, it would add something we don't have," Matt said. "We have the Store. We have the blacksmith shop. We have the school. We'll need more than that if we're not to be just a crossroads place for ever."

"We should leave the church where it is," said Lillian Swift, still jabbing at her easel. "Do we need some preacher telling us we're a lot of Adams and Eves condemned to till the soil?"

"But given dominion, dear," said Nell Richmond, correcting an error on Dominion Day.

"Is that how you explain it, then – what you're doing here, with your axes and stumping powder?" She always sounded pleasant, with her English accent, even when she was setting you straight in no uncertain terms. She stuck her tongue in one corner of her mouth and leaned close to peer at her picture. "My goodness, doesn't anyone know how to read? It wasn't to bits of breathing clay the Almighty gave dominion. It has nothing to do with all that Adam nonsense. It has nothing to do with destroying the natural world. Dominion was what He gave to those who identify themselves with Him, made in His image."

"So that's what you think, is it?" said Sandy MacKay, winking at the rest of us. "Would you say that describes Nigel's approach to life?"

Nigel Swift might not have heard. He turned a page.

Lilly Swift might not have heard him either. "I would say dominion has little to do with bullying the world into shape, and more to do with allowing the power of God to run our lives. Oh, pay no attention to me!" she said, waving her brush around and splashing blue paint on her long pale nose. "If I'd lived in another age they'd have burned me at the stake."

You flatter yourself, I almost said. If you lived in another age they would have locked you up with the lunatics. One look at her pictures would have convinced them. She was painting the Strait but she must have seen something the rest of us had never seen. A patchwork quilt of ugly colour blocks was shaping up on her canvas.

"There you are." Sandy MacKay dragged the side of his boot in the sand to level it out around the stake. "If you had your church that woman would want to share the pulpit with the preacher! Leave things as they are."

Lilly Swift was not the only woman in the world with ideas. With so many people in one place, Maude Pearson saw a chance to practise her politics. Since we were already talking about what the settlement needed, she thought we should talk about building a community hall. A place for meetings, somewhere bigger than a schoolroom for the whist-drive dances.

Matt was proud of his Maude and her opinions, of course. But instead of listening this time he sidled over to talk to Johanna, who looked as elegant at a picnic as she did in the classroom, wearing a loose belted jacket I'd never seen before over her white blouse and long black skirt. And of course that elegant scarf she was seldom without. Today she wore it around her neck and loosely over her head, like a Biblical woman protecting herself from the wind.

I would not be the only one glad to see that Matt Pearson hadn't gone for his guitar, which was probably in the Model T. He loved to sing. He especially loved to sing those old Ontario folk songs. But unfortunately, he didn't seem to realize that he had no voice, possibly because he knew the children loved to hear "Land of the Silver Birch" and "Ye Maidens of Ontario," a song about women deserted by men who've gone west. If no one ever told him to give it up, I think it was because there was something appealing in the way he so obviously and innocently enjoyed what he was doing – as though it had never entered his head that he had little talent for it.

He hadn't talked long with Johanna when Nora's Mr. Taylor came riding down out of the trees and into the picnic area. He tethered his horse and walked over to stand at the edge of our group at the horseshoes pitch, nodding greetings all around. He wore his coat and his hat the same as usual, and his boots. I suppose he didn't suffer from the heat.

Taylor was a good-looking man, even with that pointed face looking out from the shadow of his filthy hat. Well, I suppose there were times when they all looked handsome in their way. Except possibly Sandy MacKay and the emaciated Winton brothers with their skittish eyes. Panama had left Al Hueffner's face looking boiled, and his worn-down rotted teeth did not do much for his looks. Taylor was his own kind of handsome, as a fox is handsome in a way that's different from a border collie. You could tell what Nora had seen in him once. Sharp bones – he would still look good at forty.

Matt Pearson was taller than Taylor, with a little more muscle on him. From a distance, his sharp features might have been carved from speckled stone, but there was something softer about his dark eyes and long lashes, as though he might wink at you any minute – except when he was in one of his broody spells, his hair on end from trying to figure out how the universe was run.

It was no surprise to me that he used to teach school. Matthew Pearson would talk your ear off. I don't know why he took up farming. He never said. What surprised some of us was that, like myself, he was still here. He never admitted this to anyone but we knew he was ready to quit, to find something to do with his life that didn't feel like ramming head-first into stone. Maybe it wasn't anything more than curiosity that kept him here. Maybe he wanted to see if anything might change.

When it came to talking, Johanna could match him word for word. He usually listened, too. But this time she let him go on by himself while she hardly took her eyes off Nora's love-struck clown. A joke on herself, was how she saw him. She told me she went hot from remembering how he'd got her hopes up, riding down that grade. She'd been raised by a widower father down-Island who taught her that life was out to make a fool of you whenever it could.

At least this Taylor was a gentleman, she had decided while she'd watched him. He lifted his hat to everybody he greeted. Smiled and chatted a bit, before moving on. "Of course this wasn't much to judge by, but I started to wonder why Nora would choose a Herbie Brewer over a man like this."

If he was looking for Nora, he wouldn't find her. No Mackens showed up this year. He talked with this person and that for a while but Johanna had decided by the way his eyes kept coming back to her that he was waiting for her to be free. She stood up and brushed at her skirt, and told Matt Pearson she would go for a walk.

Taylor didn't waste time catching up to her. "I wonder if I may have a word," he said, shy and polite. He took off his hat and held it in his hand. His hair was the colour of soot, the same as his eyes. "You're the schoolteacher."

She bristled at that, she told me. "I gave him my scowl that said 'Settle down, class,' and demanded to know why he thought he could tell!"

"No, no," he said. She didn't mind seeing him flustered. "Someone pointed you out. You're a friend of Nora's, I think."

"And you?" she said. As though she'd never heard of him before. She removed the scarf in a few brief movements of her hand, and tried it around her wrist.

Now he was even more flustered. He'd probably had trouble with teachers as a boy. "I'm sorry. The name's Taylor. I come here from –"

"Ah yes," she interrupted, leading the way down onto the rocky beach, "the heartbroken lover, all the way from the East!" She turned, smiling, and waited until he held out a hand to help her from one log to another. "You're lucky we have no poets here, you'd have found yourself in a song."

Of course, as soon as she saw his embarrassment she turned him into one of her ten-year-old students and hated herself for being cruel. "I'm sorry," she said. "You didn't seek me out so that I could mock you. Sit here, out of the wind."

They settled on a driftwood log that was lower than the others heaped around it. Wild vetch was in flower around their feet. When she came back later she was holding some in her hand. A mix of dark purple and pink.

She told me later what he'd said. "I've lost hope of winning her back, but I'd still like to make her life a little easier." He placed his hat on his knee and drove his fingers back through his hair. "You've been in love – well, of course you must have been. You'll understand I'd tear out my heart and put it into her hands if I thought that would make her happy."

She would bake it in the oven like your clothes, Johanna almost said. How had Nora earned this kind of devotion?

Here was what he wanted: Would she take his gifts to Nora and pretend they weren't from him?

She had laughed. "She'd know. She'd only make me take them back."

He looked destroyed by this, she said. "He glared out at the waves like someone planning to drown."

"They told me there was a stench from your coat that would make a person gag," she said, "but I'm hardly aware of it here. When the temperature goes above eighty will you still not take it off?"

"I've made a vow."

"Then you'll have to go naked under it," she said. "Or learn to swim with it on. On a hot August day you'll find us all in the water cooling off, splashing around like seals."

He stood up. "I'm sorry. I thought, since she was your friend –"

"You aren't interested in the picnic?" she said. "Some of them will put their boats in the water, to fish."

He shook his head, and started away. "I've never been good at play."

She called after him then. "I'll think of something."

He turned back, and tilted his head.

"Well, I suppose I must," she told me later. "To avoid seeing him torture himself. And we don't want him drowning from the weight of that stupid coat."

───❧───

Nora Macken

First thing in the morning I made the sign and nailed it to a tree out at the road. Four words. I meant them too. For him and for all

of them. I didn't want anyone interfering. It was because a knock
at my door woke me up out of a sound sleep. Three o'clock in the
morning! It was pitch dark out there, not even a sliver of moon.
There was no other sound but that knocking. Brewer would have
pounded harder than that, or yelled. I grabbed the shotgun down
from the wall and went to the door.

It was Wyatt Taylor. Half-whispering my name. Apologetic but
urgent too. He wanted me awake, but I could tell he didn't want
to be the one to wake me. Fool.

It wouldn't be like him to get drunk and hammer on your door
in the night. But who knows what happened since he'd fallen in
with these people? MacKay made his own brew. Armus Aalto
had whiskey. Charlie Sullivan was next thing to a drunk. Maude
Pearson would have port in her cupboard.

I didn't open the door. "What do you want?"

"So that you won't be frightened, Nora," he says. "I've put in
a few hours' work out here tonight. I wouldn't even tell you now
except I don't want you scared. You'll want your hands over your
ears in a minute. Sit on the floor against the wall. Keep away from
the windows."

I told him I would not sit on the floor. I would stand in my
windows if I wanted, or dance on the roof.

Then I heard him going along the wall and around the corner
of the building. "Best of all would be if you went back to bed."

And then there was this great thump and rumble that made
the floorboards leap. By the time I was under the covers there was
a second, and soon after it a third, and a fourth.

I knew what he'd done. In the dark! A fifth and sixth and
seventh *whoompf!* thumped in the ground. They went right around
the house, circled the house, and then they went around the
house a second time a little farther away, and then they went
around the house a third time farther away still, one after the
other. *Whoompf, whoompf, whoompf!* Drawing circles around me.

Once they stopped, I waited for him to speak. Not a sound. If he'd been hit by flying rocks it served him right.

I got up and opened the door and felt my way along that tar-paper wall as far as the corner. Darkness with darker shadows. "Mr. Taylor?" I said. He wasn't there. Only that sharp smell of blasting-powder smoke.

All around in the dark the stumps would be settling. Shook loose from the ground and split into sections and ready to be hauled out and burned. Out in the fallen snags and new-growth alder and tangled blackberry vines and stands of young hemlock. How had he got to them? His arms and face must be scratched and bloody, crawling through that jungle.

Now everyone would come traipsing down to see what he done. Thinking their thoughts. "She didn't do it herself," they'd tell Brewer one day. "She had help. That fellow she was supposed to marry. Decided a woman couldn't do it on her own."

So I made the sign and nailed it to a tree out by the road. I didn't have to think hard about what to put:

TRESPASSERS WILL BE SHOT.

<hr />

Christina Ahlberg

Johanna would sometimes cross the road to my tea room after school, before going back to her quarters above the Store. There would seldom be anyone else, since most women were home preparing their family's supper at that time of day. She always took the corner table, where she could gaze out through the window in the direction of town. She seldom ate anything with her tea, which may have been why she stayed so slim. If I could spare the time, I usually sat with her myself, with a cup of coffee and a slice of cake, while we talked.

They'd known each other for quite a while by this time, Johanna and Nora. When that brood of Mackens arrived from back east, Johanna had just begun to teach here, the rule against married women having been set aside for her, with her husband not back from the War. Nora helped Johanna out in the school-room, mostly I think because her father wanted her to keep an eye on her brothers, who would do just about anything to keep others from their work. But she stayed distant and mysterious, a little resentful, as though she believed she would make the better teacher if only she had Johanna's training, an opportunity she couldn't dream of for herself. They talked in the lunch hour, when they weren't busy chasing Maguire boys out of the branches of the tree behind the privy, or solving the problem of the window that wouldn't open.

Even after she'd stopped helping, Nora would drop in to the school after hours and sit at the front desk with a cup of tea in her hand. She quizzed Johanna: how each of her brothers was doing, down the long list of that tribe. Johanna sometimes couldn't remember half the brothers' names.

She'd seldom mentioned Herbert Brewer, though Johanna was aware of her interest in him. For a few weeks she'd even stopped coming, but then showed up again one day when Johanna and the rest of us had already heard about the elopement and her solo return. She sat at the same desk, wearing the same faded blue drop-waist dress that her mother had probably worn, and drank Johanna's tea from the same cracked cup, and stared at the carved-up desk top for a while before she said anything. Then she said, "You think there'll ever be enough students to need a second teacher?"

"There's babies hanging off every hip in the district," Johanna told her. "With a little luck they'll probably live to school age. Are you thinking of going to Normal?"

Nora shook her head and went silent again. Then she said, "I don't suppose you'd know how to fix a warped door."

She waited a few more days before she told Johanna what had happened. There was a wedding, she said. Maybe she knew there was some doubt about that amongst the neighbours. The rest she asked Johanna to keep to herself, which Johanna did except for telling me and swearing me to secrecy. There had been a wedding but there hadn't been what you might call a wedding night. While she was waiting for him to come up to their Nanaimo hotel room, Brewer was involved in a beer parlour fight. Both men ended up in hospital. When the damage to the other fellow was seen to be quite extensive, it looked as though Brewer could be spending time behind bars. If they caught him, that is. But they weren't likely to catch him. He was on the CPR boat to Vancouver and maybe even off it on the other side before anybody thought of making sure he'd stayed around. But he didn't leave until after he'd slipped a note under her door explaining this.

Nora never really needed to think of something to talk about when she stopped in at the school. She was always angry about something. And she didn't even need to have something, Johanna said, to get off her chest. She was a single woman like Johanna, one more bride without a husband. They were surrounded by women whose husbands were never out of their sight for longer than it took to put in a day's work in the woods. Two married spinsters having tea, was the way Johanna put it to me when she came across to have a second cup in my tea room.

Not that Johanna understood Nora. She said she could never guess what was going on inside that long narrow head, but she felt she had earned the right to an opinion. When she saw the sign that Nora nailed to the tree she picked up a rock, bashed the back of the board to loosen it, then tore it off the tree and carried it to the door of Nora's shack.

"A spelling error?" Nora said. "You want me to write it out fifty times?"

"An error in judgement," Johanna said. "But it will still make pretty good kindling." She looked for an axe, but of course Nora would keep an axe around the back.

"It'll make a pretty good sign, too," Nora said, "once it's back where I put it. You think I'm one of your Grade Two pupils?"

Nora did not respond well to interference, even from the only person she could safely call a friend. She told Johanna to march right back and put that sign where she'd found it. Johanna said she would put it in Nora's ear, but tossed it past her onto the kitchen floor.

Nora slammed the door in Johanna's face. A small pane of window glass shivered in its frame. Dust drifted down from the eave. Then she opened it again, her own face showing something like surprise, as though she thought Johanna was the one who had slammed the door. Or maybe she was surprised she'd failed to knock Johanna backwards into the dirt.

"I didn't come to visit," Johanna said, standing firm. "I came to deliver the sign before anyone saw it."

"Well, you did that," Nora said. "But you're still on my step."

"Someone will break a neck on this step," Johanna said, making the stack of slab-wood wobble beneath her. "It will probably be you, since your husband doesn't seem interested in getting himself this far."

She half-expected the door to slam a second time in her face. It was something that had never been spoken between them – that they had this thing in common.

Nora waited. Eyes dull, glaring at the intruder on her doorstep. Perhaps she thought Johanna would apologize. This far in, Johanna thought she might as well step further. "Your friend in the oven-baked coat would be happy to fix it," she said, and stepped back down onto the dirt to examine the makeshift step. "He'd decorate it with diamonds if you'd let him, and paint your whole blessed shack with gold. Do you think you deserve him?"

Nora let all the anger drain from her shoulders. "What should I do?" She waved a hand in the direction of the brush surrounding her shack. "You heard what he did? They'll all be coming around to have a look."

"I'll put your sign back," Johanna said. "But first I think you should change the way you spell 'shot.' Try 'prosecuted' instead. They may come for a look but that doesn't mean they should die."

Nora picked up the piece of board and placed it on her kitchen table. Then she went to a cupboard and came out with a can of paint and a jam jar of turpentine with a paintbrush in it. "I'd just as soon he left me alone," she said.

Johanna watched while she used crimson paint to cover the offending word and painted the new word beneath. "He won't," she said. "You might as well give in. I told him he could buy flour and sugar for *me* but he only laughed. He's scared you'll starve!"

"I'm a married woman," she said.

"Are you?"

She walked with Johanna back to the road, carrying the sign and a claw hammer and glancing here and there into the surrounding bush with something like nervous suspicion. "You think you'll see him?" she said.

"He gets in a person's way."

"Tell him no sneaking around at night."

She nailed the new sign on the same old leaning alder as before. "I don't need flour," she said, "but I'll need chickens if I'm going to have any eggs."

From up at the blacksmith shop they could hear the *clang clang clang* of the blacksmith's hammer. Archie MacIntosh had already started his day.

"Apparently my old Granny Hansen was a matchmaker in Trondheim," Johanna told me later, "and a busybody if there ever was one. She would be proud of me today, God love her."

But almost immediately she confessed that she was wondering what she had accomplished. Her granny had always known exactly what she'd done: banns would be read, mothers would be laughing through tears, girls blushing, bridegrooms contemplating emigration. Had Nora agreed to allow him only to lay gifts at her feet, or might he court her again as he did in Owen Sound? It would not be long before Taylor understood what everyone else had figured out – that her marriage wasn't a marriage, that there had been no wedding night and no sign of a bridegroom since.

There was still no sign of Tomas Seyerstad either. It was more than six years since he'd left, but Johanna hadn't given up. She refused to have any part in the war memorial cairn they built on the outskirts of town. People from all over the district were asked to bring stones from their fields. They came together on a certain day with their wagons and stoneboats and trucks, to drop off their contribution for a memorial to the men killed or lost in the War. Matt Pearson said he'd give them enough to build a hundred cairns if they let him – anybody in this settlement could do the same – but they only wanted hand-picked stones, one or two from each family, so the memorial would represent the entire valley. But Johanna would have no part in the business. She wouldn't give them so much as a pebble, she said, and she would not let them put Tomas's name on the plaque, though he was a local boy who signed up with the 102nd like many of the others whose names were listed there.

She knew that some people thought she could be made to forget him. "Do they think I haven't noticed?" she said. "Words I have to pretend I haven't heard. Men declaring their willingness to scratch the teacher's itch, as they put it. I'm careful to carry myself with the grace and satisfaction of a happy mother of three, but they can see something. I don't know what it is."

Apparently Archie MacIntosh was not like the others. He might have been as virginal as little Elizabeth Pearson, unless there was someone in town satisfied with quick visits on the occasional

Saturday afternoon. He never looked at Johanna. Archie sweated, half-naked, in the heat from his forge, pounding metal into the shapes of machine parts and wiping streaks of black across his face. He had the same muscles as Tomas Seyerstad, she knew, and in all the same places. She had no trouble remembering the sight of her Tomas at the foot of the bed walking naked to the water jug by the window.

"She is our own Penelope," Matthew Pearson said to me once. Matt tended to romanticize her a little, as though she belonged in one of those old books he didn't read any more. "You can't imagine her showing interest in another man. If he doesn't come home she'll be waiting when she's eighty-five. It's the kind of devotion you don't see in the modern world."

Still, you had to wonder if her Tomas Seyerstad deserved this sort of fidelity – a man who didn't care enough to write her a letter saying, "Wait longer, I am on my way," or even to break her heart with "Forgive me, I'm in a Belgian prison on a murder charge." Not even a note to his mother saying, "I am the father of five little Frenchies in Bordeaux."

So possibly Pearson was right and she would still be waiting on those steps when she was an old woman. Or maybe not. Perhaps she would be one of those women who wander the battlefields in search of identity tags or even bits of wool that were once part of a familiar pair of socks – eventually an old crone knocking on village doors and asking if anyone remembers a Tomas Seyerstad, did anyone fight beside Tomas Seyerstad, did anyone see him killed or captured or running for safety. She would haunt the hallways of the military, asking to see the documents once again, asking permission to cross-examine the so-called witnesses, demanding more than anyone is willing to tell.

She foresaw all this with a twisted smile. "There are more ways to be faithful than you might imagine, Christina," she said, shaking out her scarf and arranging it over her shoulders like an old woman's shawl. "On my eighty-fifth birthday I'll come back and get them to put up a statue of Tomas Seyerstad in front of Hueffners' Store, and dedicate it to all who failed to show up here for this crazy experiment in making something out of nothing."

Matthew Pearson

In the evening we sat over a pot of tea at the kitchen table, watching the light fade in the farthest corners of the fields while Wyatt Taylor talked wistfully about his farm in Grey County. The children were asleep. Maude had moved into the front room to work at her quilting frame. He went on to speak of the Cape Breton coal mines where he'd learned about explosives as a lad. Then, after a few moments of silence, he recalled a boy he'd known in the tunnels in France, whose face had been badly mutilated but patched up by doctors in a way that would have to do.

"He told me we should be digging right through to the far side of the Germans so we could surprise them from behind. He didn't look up, he kept writing in his little book. 'Or maybe you've already tunnelled through to another world,' he said, 'so you can leave this one for the rest of us to rot in. One morning you'll be gone, playing with the unicorns in some green mountain valley.'"

"Unicorns?" I said.

"He shouldn't have been there," Taylor said. "His notebooks were all that kept him from going completely mad. I suppose they were his own way of tunnelling through to that valley he imagined." He turned his attention to the world outside the window.

"It's your farm that makes me think of him. His valley would look like this, I guess. Grassy fields, standing fences, orchard trees in perfect rows, your little 'well at the end of the world' down there that Prince Ralf was looking in all the wrong places for. No burnt-out houses or tortured barns, no moans or screams or thunder of artillery trying to turn you into a corpse. You've built a little Eden here, well away from the world."

The fading light had erased the trees first, and then the fields and fences, and now was working on the nearer buildings. I reminded him that most of the settlement still looked a good deal like the world that boy was so eager to leave. The new clearing we'd worked in that morning, for example. A visitor from France would think battles were still being waged.

"Don't you ever talk about it here?" he said, his gentle smile as benign as ever. Taylor's face, shorn of whiskers and free of the shade from his hat, was as open and clear-eyed as any satisfied child's.

"Do they talk about it anywhere? Most of us are trying to forget it. And, anyway, the others wouldn't know what we were talking about. My mother was horrified to hear that I'd slept in barns."

He was silent for a minute, looking off across the fields. "But there must be times – up in the woods, say – when two old soldiers will remember something."

"When you suspect you've been taken for a fool you don't talk about it much," I said. "We're still trying to figure out what we're supposed to have accomplished."

"Back east they're saying we were being trained." He sat back and folded his arms and grinned. "Turning us into the puppets they wanted so they could have their way with us for all time afterwards. So we wouldn't take anything seriously again, especially ourselves and our little lives."

"Well, I came here because I didn't like the sound of the world they said we'd come back to," I said. "I came here to make sure it wouldn't be true for us."

Taylor put one hand on the top of his head and widened his eyes. "By trying to stay in the nineteenth century?"

I stood up and brought down the coal-oil lamp and set it on the table between us, but didn't light it yet.

"Maybe Owen Sound's too close to Europe," I said, "if they've got you believing the twentieth century's only what they tell you it is. Or has to be everywhere the same."

Taylor turned up his innocent palms. "I just meant that you've put yourself at a good distance from all those factories turning out things they want you to buy." He leaned forward with his folded arms on the table and studied my face. We were both of us, I imagine, beginning to disappear. "You might even be almost far enough from the men trying to get you to buy them, using the skills they learned writing lies for the War. But I don't know how long you'll be safe." He paused for a moment, gazing again into the shadows of the yard. "I wonder what your Donald must think of this."

I should have lit the lamp. In the dark it was too easy to bring up things that would not have been mentioned between us in daylight.

"We don't know if he thinks at all. If he even knows where he is."

Taylor had seen enough to know this himself. Donald slept most of the time, or sometimes sat in his wheeled chair with his head lolling on a neck that seemed unequal to its task. Taylor had seen him agitated, making unintelligible noises through the lips of his mask. He'd seen how Maude took the trouble to dress him every morning in a white shirt and black wool trousers and shiny boots. He must have noticed Tanner carrying his nightsoil pot to the privy. But he'd never asked what had happened.

"What happened to Donald is this," I said. "He was born at the start of the century is what happened. He could hardly wait to be old enough to fight – that's what happened to him too. He made the mistake of admiring his brother-in-law, of wanting to join me overseas. And of course there were the parades and the bands and the speeches promising adventure and heroism. He tried any number of times when he was too young, he and his chum, and they finally took him. Then, his first day at the front, a mortar shell blew away half his face and embedded shreds of metal in his brain. Eventually they built him that mask and sent him home to his mother in Montreal, who couldn't bear the strain of caring for him. So we brought him here. The children love him, though we have no idea what he thinks of them. Or us, or anything."

"And there was Hugh, as well," Maude said, joining us at the table. "Sitting in the dark! Now you must also tell about Hugh."

"Yes, well," I said, intending to put an end to the conversation before it went any further. Sometimes Maude was far too brave for the rest of us. She could look anything square in the eye without flinching. I reached for the box of matches on the windowsill, in order to light the lamp, but she stopped me with a gentle hand on my wrist.

"Hugh Corbett and my brother were childhood friends," she said to Taylor. "They signed up together. They went into their first battle side by side."

She was not about to let me avoid this. "If Hugh Corbett was alive today he'd be looking after Donald, I've no doubt of that," I said. "If they'd both come through the War unharmed they'd be one of those bachelor pairs you see growing old together in the same house."

"Not necessarily," Maude said. "I can see them marrying sisters and buying adjoining properties. Donald would be grooming himself for public office. Matt saw Hugh a little later, didn't you Matt? When he was transferred. His story is nearly as short as Donald's. And as terrible, I'm afraid."

"If you find it painful –" Taylor said.

"That's all right," I said. "She's pushed me this far now. We'll just pretend I'm talking to myself. In my sleep. By the time young Corbett came to us he'd been one of the few survivors of two different wiped-out platoons. God only knows what he'd come through untouched by the time we got him, though he'd been in France only a couple of months."

"Good instincts," Maude said. "He was a lively, quick-footed lad." Her wedding ring clicked against the teapot. "Cold. Shall I make more?" She had not removed her right hand from my wrist.

"Not for me," Taylor said.

"I'd known him in the classroom, you see," I said. "He'd been a student of mine. Maude's family used to spend the summers in our area – up from Montreal. This was how we met – Maude and I. This was how Donald and Hugh became friends. Hugh was an intelligent boy, and a good athlete. Sensitive, I suppose. In the old days he would have become a hardware clerk, or a farmhand like most of the boys in the class, but he was equipped to do much more than that with his life."

But as I tried to talk about him I knew it wasn't all right to do this after all. I didn't know where to start. What happened to Corbett later was all mixed up with the night he came to us with a number of other new recruits and transfers. I could not go straight to what Maude wanted of me. Her indignation rested upon a single fact. Mine had a thousand roots to feed it.

When he arrived at our unit he was gaunt and stumbling and exhausted, and didn't look to me like the lively, quick-footed soldier who could survive even where everyone else was wiped out. You could see right away that losing Donald had knocked the stuffing out of him, though he seemed to perk up a little when he saw he would be in my platoon. I suppose he would have tried to make a second Donald of me. But even if there had been time for that, it would not have worked. I was older by just that few too many years. Of course I would keep an eye on him, but I could not be another Donald.

There was some of the usual shelling that night, isolated explosions here and there. The eastern horizon flashed and winked with bursts of gunfire. The occasional whine. Whizzbangs. A few bursts of machine-gun fire. But there seemed to be little real enthusiasm for it. Both sides might have been waging a half-hearted battle with invisible men somewhere in the territory between us. Our troops were more interested in getting ready for an early morning attack.

But an hour or so after I'd sent young Corbett and the others off with Corporal Stewart, a distant moan that quickly became a whistle announced a Jack Johnson shrieking down on us. The explosion was close enough to rock the ground and shake dirt loose from the walls. A second, even closer explosion hit before I'd got out of my dugout into the trench and hurried down to see what had happened.

Someone was screaming where a trench wall had given way and spilled dirt and sandbags onto the sleeping men. There seemed to be only the one man screaming but the others around him were all talking excitedly at once.

The screams were young Carter's. His foot had been blown off above the ankle. Naylor stood ten feet away, holding a bloody boot in his hands. The torn flesh of Carter's leg poured blood through the shreds of his uniform. Corporal Stewart was down on his knees in his shirtsleeves trying to wrap his tunic around the leg to stop the blood.

"Stretchers!" I shouted, and could hear shouting go down the line. It wasn't necessary, of course. They would have been on the way the second they heard the hit.

"Carter," I said. "Hold on now. We'll soon have you in proper hands."

"Yes, sir," he said. His face was slick with mud. His hand repeatedly tried to get at the violated leg, and Stewart kept pushing it away, while using a rag to mop Carter's brow. This was a boy, somebody's son. There was more than fear and pain in Carter's eyes. There was wonder, too. He could not believe this was happening to him.

"It's Sergeant Fox too, sir," Corporal Grenville said.

"Where?"

"Here, sir."

I went down the trench to where young Hugh Corbett was bent double, gagging. He spat a string of saliva into the mud and wiped the side of his hand down over his face.

There were others down in the mud around Fox. I assumed it was Fox because that was the name Grenville had used, but there was no face left to tell me this. Much of his head had been blown away, along with the left shoulder. Fox's heart was pumping blood out onto the duckboards and into the dirt from the collapsed wall.

I put a hand on Hughie Corbett's shoulder. "You all right?" He would not have imagined any of this in Ferguson Falls.

"Yes sir."

"You were close when it happened?"

"Too close, sir. I've been trying to –"

He gagged once more, and wiped the side of his hand again down his face.

As soon as Carter and Fox had been taken away, and Lieutenant O'Connor had stepped in to restore order, Grenville tilted his head in the direction of Corbett and said quietly, "He was sprayed, sir. There's bits of Fox all over him."

There were grey and pink bits of blood and flesh on Corbett's forehead and in his hair. His helmet must have been knocked off by the explosion. Strings and flecks of flesh and bone clung to the lapel of his tunic as well. As I led him away by his arm, I would just as soon not have looked at him, but he would have noticed this.

"He was talking about –" he said.

"Who?"

"Sergeant Fox, sir. We was talking – he saw that I couldn't sleep. He started telling me about his sister, he started to tell about her hair – but he never finished."

He stopped and bent over to retch again, and spat between his boots. Again his hand swept down across his face.

We went in behind the sacking to the privacy of my dugout. The boy trembled all over, as though we'd stepped into an icebox. "Get hold of yourself, lad. You've been through worse than this."

"I'm sorry, sir," he said. "I can't stop shaking. I don't know what's the matter with me."

I unbuttoned his tunic and stripped it off him. As soon as Masters came in with water I started to wash the boy's stricken face. There were blackheads in the pores of his nose, I remember. His eyelids twitched. His teeth chattered. His breath was foul. He had looked this serious, I recalled, standing at the back of the classroom to recite "Ulysses."

> Come, my friends,
> 'Tis not too late to seek a newer world.

The eldest son of an uneducated farmer, with a superior intelligence and sensitivity. He wrote poems in imitation of Keats. I concentrated on his serious homely face as a way to avoid thinking at all about Fox.

"D'you think you'll be all right now, Private?"

"Yes sir," he said. "Thank you, sir."

"Would you like to stay in here for a few minutes, to get hold of yourself? You know we're moving up in a few hours."

Tears came to his eyes. You'd think I'd offered him a ticket home to his mother. "I'll be all right," he said, with too much gratitude. He might have been five years old. Clearly he felt safer believing his life was in my hands. A man from home. Did he think he'd tucked himself beneath the shadow of my wing?

They all did, the youngest ones. The boys. When things were bad. It was as if I had taken a school class out on an adventure hike and could be counted on to keep them safe from harm. They'd seen enough to know that no one else could be counted on to do it.

"I'm sorry," Maude said. "I should not have mentioned poor Hugh. It's just that I thought –"

They had been waiting for me. I don't know how long. "That's all right," I said. "The next morning after young Corbett arrived to join us, we were part of the second wave of an attack on Hill 70. You may have been there yourself. We were to jump up and go racing across open torn-up ground, keeping formation, while dodging machine-gun bullets. When Corbett wasn't amongst us after the enemy had turned us back, we assumed he'd been shot or wounded out there, though no one had seen him. One man reported that he'd been complaining of headaches and pains all through his body in the hour before we'd attacked, but the boy hadn't reported this to me. It wasn't until the next day that we learned he'd wandered off in the wrong direction and ended up, a few hours later, at the nearest field hospital complaining of his aching head. And not at all sure how he'd got there."

"The doctor examined him and said he was perfectly fit," Maude said. "Nothing wrong with him." In the dark you could hear what you couldn't see: her mouth tight with indignation.

Corbett thought he was joking, but the doctor was not a man who made jests. The next thing we heard, the boy had been court-martialled. Confined to a farmhouse on the edge of the village behind us while he waited.

"Some of the boys laid bets. We expected acquittal. At worst we expected a fine, or a long detention, or even field punishment #1 for a couple of weeks. After all, he'd taken part in a number of battles, he'd never gone missing before, there'd been the incident with Fox just hours before, and he'd been absent for only eight or nine hours."

Young Corbett himself was sure we'd all be laughing about it one day. "That doctor only wanted to give me a scare," he said, when I was permitted to visit. "Don't you think?" I knew better than to believe it was all a joke, but even at that my worst expectation was the humiliation of a wagonwheel crucifixion, for two or three weeks at most.

"Then two weeks later we were called out on parade to hear the sentence. Nobody won any bets. He was to be shot the next morning, by some of our own, for desertion. They didn't explain themselves, they didn't have to, but it was rumoured later that they viewed the lad's history of survival with suspicion. He would be shot by us for not being shot by the Germans.

"They kept him under close arrest that night. I was given permission to go in and speak with him, in case he had something he wanted me to tell his mother. But they had already started pouring drink down his throat, he was in no condition to think clearly, I wasn't even sure he knew what I was talking about. He babbled about Fox's sister. He called out for Donald, sobbing like a child.

"Nobody slept, you can be sure of that. Before dawn the next morning we were paraded again, this time behind the farmhouse, where a post had been erected against the muddy brick wall of the local abattoir.

"They had to carry him out, they'd got him too drunk to walk. They'd put his gas helmet on with the eyes to the back, so he couldn't see the familiar faces of the poor devils in the firing squad. It's unlikely he could have recognized anyone if they hadn't, he was nearly unconscious. His body sagged like some creature without a skeleton, even after they'd tied him to the post.

"My God, it was a terrible thing to watch! When he started to gag and retch, they loosened the gas helmet long enough for him to heave the contents of his stomach onto the ground. Then they yanked it back down and got out of the way of the guns.

"They didn't even do a proper job of it. The medical officer said he wasn't dead, so the Colonel they'd sent from H.Q. to make sure everything went according to regulations walked over in his shiny boots and fired a bullet into his head. The assistant provost-marshal looked at his watch and recorded the time of death."

"My God," Taylor said.

"Some of the boys were sick afterwards, though they tried to hide it. You heard vomiting. You heard muttered curses. 'Get a headache in this army and they blow your bloody brains out to cure you.'"

We ought to have mutinied, was the common opinion. We should have refused to let them do it. We should all have marched off in protest. "Why didn't we think of this before it was too late?" I let them say it. There was no harm in it now. But eventually I had to remind them that the army would only have planted a few more posts against the slaughterhouse wall and done the same to the rest.

Private Berry, who had a way of knowing peculiar facts unknown by the rest of us, announced that Hugh Corbett was the twentieth Canadian shot for desertion since the start of the War. "Not a single Australian. If you're inclined to headaches or confusion you should have emigrated down under while you had the chance," he said. "The Aussie government refuses to let them do it. Not ours. Not Borden and his generals kissing London arse. Anything for bloody old King George!"

"You think they'd have dismissed you if you'd asked?" Taylor said. "If you explained."

"They might have," I said. "I suppose I was a damn fool. I had some notion that I was meant to be his witness. So that I could tell them at home that the boy had died with dignity. Dignity! I must have swallowed the hogwash I'd assigned in my classroom. 'Gunga Din' and all that! God knows I've lain awake at night trying to go through every poem or novel I forced them to read, looking for that moment when I might have been responsible for causing boys like Donald MacCormack and Hugh Corbett to sign up willingly for the slaughter."

Maude's hand had never left my wrist through all of this. Now she squeezed, just lightly. "You mustn't," she said. "If even good men start doing that we'll all be hermits hiding away in the bush, for fear of doing harm."

Taylor smiled – I could see his teeth. I suppose he thought that hiding in the bush was precisely what we were doing.

"And listen to me!" I said. "Trained as a teacher but 'C minus for composition'! I haven't been able to tell you even this one small episode without leaning on the passive voice and that faceless 'they' for support. And you wonder why you don't hear me telling tales of my 'war experiences'? I am ashamed of the words I would have to use. We should all of us be like poor Donald in there, hiding behind a mask."

I should have lit the lamp and cut off conversation earlier. The little farm he'd flattered with the name of Eden faded into the red-tinged dark and only the battlefield remained. Later, with my head on a pillow slip that Maude had embroidered with a wreath of wild roses, I thought of the towering donkey-piles in all the district's churned-up fields, the giant pyramids of logs and roots dragged up to lean on their spar trees, glowing from living embers, beacons in a different sort of war. My shoulder wound ached, as it did whenever I let myself get agitated. I thought of young Corbett, who'd been far less drunk than I'd made him out to be. He'd begged me to do something to put a stop to the nightmare, to ride through the night until I found someone who would help. Then, when he was convinced that no one could commute his sentence except the Commander-in-Chief himself and that I could do nothing for him but speak to his mother afterwards, and take care of Donald, he begged me to shoot him immediately and save him the humiliation of the morning.

Sullivan had warned me that having Taylor around could be unsettling.

Rather than disturb Maude with my turning, I got up to check on the children in their rooms. Face down in his cradle, Willie snuffed and snorted, working hard at his sleep. Tanner rolled over from facing the wall and opened his eyes, squinting up at my candle as though he expected some message that displeased him. I touched his hot ear and told him to go back to sleep, though he was already turning away from me with his eyes closed again. In her own small room next door, Elizabeth lay sprawled on her back with arms flung wide, ready to give herself up to whoever might come along to admire her. She smiled, confident even in her sleep that she could trust the world to guard her, certain that she could inspire nothing short of awe.

I drew on my clothes and went out to saddle Orion. Though I took down the lantern from its hook I didn't light it, since a slim moon was sending down just enough light through the smoky sky to give some shape to things. Then I rode through that world of glowing root piles up to Reimers' place, where all was quiet, and down to Maguires' little farm where lamps were out and the dog lay asleep on the doorstep. Similarly, the MacIntosh house was in darkness, and the Ahlbergs' as well. At the Store, I turned onto the old railroad grade and followed it west towards the mountains – past the Macken road, and the Winton and Korsakov places. A faint light shone in one window of the Martins' little cabin made from squared-off logs. A sick child, maybe, though I heard no sound when I rode as close as I dared to the door. No weeping. No voices at all.

If any of the others had known they would think me strange, no doubt, and wonder if I was looking for something more than just the comfort of seeing neighbours secure in their beds. Perhaps I was. A discovery, maybe, that would tell me this place had more to offer than we'd so far been shown in daylight. Just as I would have liked to believe in an old Indian village down at the beach, as some of the others did, I suppose I'd have been happy to stumble upon the rock carvings of some ancient cave dwellers along the bank of a stream, or even a rusted compass dropped by a forgotten explorer passing through. Whenever I rode for the first time up a new trail in the woods I imagined the excitement of coming upon

a ruined statue, say, or a collapsed temple in the forest, some proof
that others had lived here before us. It was a mystery even to
myself, the comfort I imagined getting from even the slightest hint
of history in this unlikely place.

But none had shown itself so far, in daylight or at night, since
I was not willing to see the abandoned sawmill in this way. Often
my wanderings brought me to a stand of alders by the dark river,
and amongst the alders a roofless sawmill with young trees growing
out of the cracks in its floor. The building was open to the sky,
of course, its rough concrete walls rising to a sharp peak at each
gable end, a row of empty barred windows high along each side.
Before the first returning soldiers arrived to draw lots for these
parcels of land, a logging company had built it to fulfil the require-
ments for a timber licence. But as soon as the government papers
were signed, the owners dismantled the machinery and shipped
raw timber to mainland sawmills as they'd intended to do all
along. It was a ruin without ever having been anything else, a
thing of the past in a place that had no past, nearly the only thing
besides giant fir stumps and a few pioneer shacks that predated
ourselves, the Indians having had enough sense to avoid the place
except to pass through on hunting expeditions.

> *Here! creep,*
> *Wretch, under a comfort serves in a whirlwind.*

Something Johanna Seyerstad had pressed upon me. An
English priest, long dead but just recently published, complaining
so catchingly that you wanted to complain along with him, even
though others would think you blessed. But I had come to that
false ruin for another purpose this night. While Orion snuffled
and pawed outside, I prowled and touched and eventually squatted in one corner to look up at the sharp gable against the sky.
This building brought to mind a shelled and ransacked village

church in France, a rubbled space of stone block walls that stood amongst abandoned houses behind a part of the line where I'd fought at two different stages of the War.

This was long before Corbett. This was near the beginning. My eyes hadn't yet grown used to destroyed villages, let alone churches. This church stood where a narrow road from across the valley entered the village, most of its roof collapsed under shelling and the rest a network of lathes and rafters where tiles had slid to the ground. The lower half of the steeple had survived, and most of the stone walls, but fleeing villagers had stripped the building of statues and other ornaments and taken them to safety. The pews, I suppose, may have fed some earlier army's fires. Stained glass from the windows lay in coloured fragments on the rubbled ground.

For several weeks of that wet fall we'd been dug in just below the village, which had been abandoned by its farmers and shelled by Fritz till most of its buildings were heaps of plaster and stone. The enemy trenches were across a muddy valley, close enough for us to see the movement of individual helmets and sometimes over-hear their muttered conversations. Nights were embroidered with bursts of machine-gun fire, the whine and explosion of shells. On dark nights men crawled out with wire-cutters in hopes of leaping upon the surprised enemy and seizing prisoners or, even better, grabbing souvenirs: tin helmets, decorations, Jerry-made boots.

This had been a countryside of farms, of rolling fields and winding roads with here and there a little patch of woods. Every slight rise had its own crown of roofs and a single steeple, but every farm building had been shelled to a crumbling heap, and the fields ploughed up and pitted by bullets and exploding shells and under-ground mines. The only crop those fields produced was a harvest of arms and blown-off feet and lost buttons and helmets and the surfacing rotted corpses of the dead. The villages were uninhab-ited, of course, their citizens having fled to safety. Even the rats had deserted the buildings for the richer feasts in the trenches.

There were tunnels dug into the knoll behind us, some of them running right beneath the village and beyond it, surfacing into communication trenches that led to safer, distant ground. We'd dug still more, establishing a network of burrows connecting a number of dugouts beneath the village.

I'd walked above ground in the village on quiet nights when the cloud cover was so low that no movement could be spotted. Still, I stayed close to damaged buildings, in the shadow they might throw when flares lit up the sky. No more than a hundred people could have lived there. I counted twenty houses on the central street, which was intersected by a short second street of only a few more houses. One of the main-street buildings had been a barn, another a blacksmith shop. Any tools left behind we had already taken. The rest of the buildings were small one-storey homes that men before us had ransacked of any wine or food there might have been hidden beneath the floors. Even ceiling beams and wall partitions had been wrenched off, presumably for fuel.

The sounds of guns were muffled somewhat within the stone walls of the church. I came there in the hope of finding some small voice that could make a little sense of things. Maude's voice perhaps. Or my mother's. It was a place to think my way through the Lord's Prayer in private, and to empty my head of everything but a desire to listen, in case God took a notion to enlighten me. Maybe everyone had this need, in the midst of madness. Maybe others had found places of their own for this. I wished to hold off thought, find comfort, even look for joy again, though only God could know how this was to be done.

For weeks there had been little action along this part of the line. Once in a while one side or the other would scatter gunfire across the distance between us for a few hours, just to remind the enemy he was not alone, and to make sure that Stand To was never entirely free of dawn and dusk anxiety. We buried the disintegrating dead we'd dragged back from no-man's-land at night, and buried those of our own who'd been shot in the night while bringing in the dead. We fortified our trenches with sandbags and

wooden beams taken from the remaining village houses behind
us, digging out funk holes for sleeping along the sides, trying not
to gag on the sweet rotting smell of blood and cordite and sweat
and disinfectant and decaying bodies. We shot the hairy rats that
chewed on our legs as we slept or swarmed on the shallower graves.
We tried to rid our uniforms of cooties by running candle flame
along the seams. We sat for haircuts. Feet were inspected daily.
We argued over the booty from the night-time raids. We discussed the declarations of politicians as reported or invented by
the *Daily Mail*, and imagined aloud what lunacy the staff were
cooking up for us in their mansions safely distant from the lines.

Over time, we replaced old direction signs to suit ourselves. An
earlier battalion had named this whole network of trenches after
major streets of cities all over the world – front line, support and
reserve trenches, and the communication trenches connecting
them, as well as the saps that had been thrust out into no-man's-
land for observation posts and machine-gun positions. "Champs
Elysées." "Oxford Street." "MacQuarrie Street." You had to treat
this bizarre underworld as if it were a parody of a real city or you
wouldn't know where you were. But to my batman Private Banks,
even to think of it as a wry parody of a city was to grant it more
sense of normality than it deserved. Travelling up and down these
trenches, he said, was like scurrying about the corridors of an
asylum. He suggested new names. "Lunatic Ward." "Madman's
Retreat." "Shell-shock Alley."

That was all it took. Street signs came down. Pieces of lumber
and slabs of corrugated iron were painted over with new desig-
nations and re-erected at corners. "This Way to Isolation Ward."
"To Padded Cells." "Dangerous Offenders Only." Young Grenville
from Halifax nailed up "Delusions of Grandeur Wing" above the
sacking doorway to our dugout.

One of the men set up a large slab of corrugated iron against
the sandbag wall of the reserve trench, and painted RULES FOR
INMATES OF THIS INSTITUTION across the top. He printed only

the one rule himself: *Pretend you are sane*. And left it to others to add whatever inspired them.

   2. When advancing, don't turn back for lost marbles.
   3. If you are beside yourself with fear, let the other one take the hit.
   4. Leave lost limbs where you find them, but report lost minds to
     Matron.

"Matron," of course, was Major Mason, who quickly ordered these signs taken down. Only after listening to a submission from myself and Lieutenant Carson did he agree to allow the signs to stay, so long as they were accompanied by the original names of familiar streets. We complied.

Rule number 18, *Try not to lose your head, you'll never find it again in this muck*, was added by Lieutenant Charles Sullivan, joining our company after a convalescence in Blighty. I'd gone to Gentelles that day to meet a group of replacement troops and escort them up to the lines, but they hadn't yet arrived. Headquarters reported that they'd been delayed and would not show up until morning, so I sent Banks off with the car on a few errands in town, with instructions to meet me in an hour at Madame Dubois' *estaminet*.

Sullivan was alone at a small square corner table, beneath a picture of Marshal Foch, and staring into a nearly empty glass. When he saw me, he stood up. I suppose I looked as pleased as he did. "Harya, lad!" he said, exaggerating the Ottawa Valley accent as we sometimes did for one another.

"G'day, g'day! They sent y' back already, did they?" I sat on the wired-together chair across from him.

We hadn't known one another well at home but my family had done business with his, and that was enough to make us friends when we trained at Lansdowne Park. Like myself, he'd been promoted to Lieutenant after a few months of fighting but he'd insisted we were just shit-wallahs like the men who emptied the latrine buckets and dug the privies. Those fellows weren't the only ones trafficking in waste. "When I look at Ernie McGoogle with his shovel, his face don't look so different from my own."

He signalled Madame to bring a dark *bière* for me, and a second for him. He was leaner than I remembered. His long bony face seemed to have shadowy bruises beneath the skin. I knew he'd been wounded at the Somme offensive and had barely got out with his life. He was a bit shaky, I thought, possibly fighting pain. "You sure you're in good enough shape to be back?"

He shrugged. "I can carry a gun, can't I? I can stand. As far as they're concerned that's good enough." He tilted his chair back against the pile of his kit and studied the ceiling for a minute. When he looked at me again, he was grinning. "I've met a girl, Matt. A 'lady.' Money in the family – widowed aunt. She visited the wounded boys with magazines and bits of news, working her way down the terrace. But after the first few days she never got past my chair."

"You put her on a leash?"

He looked flushed and pleased with himself. "I made sure she didn't want to leave. The rest of the boys could go to the devil, I wanted her for myself."

"That means you bored her stiff with tales of how you got your wounds. Made a great hero of yourself."

"Not a word about it, lad. Not a word. Nor could I. How would she understand? She would think I was making it up. They all would, if I'd found the words for it. The papers over there are telling them about our glory and courage. While over here they're already calling it The Great Fuck-Up. Even in a war of bloody disasters this was one you'll be glad you didn't see."

Madame Dubois placed two beers on our table without interrupting her good-natured banter with a group of French soldiers at a table near the door. It seemed they were impatient for her daughter to come out of hiding, while she was insisting, flirtatiously, that she wanted all the handsome young men to herself and had no intention of sharing them with that young *péronnelle*. I was pleased to notice that my French was much improved.

The room had an air of impermanence about it, not just because it had been a bake shop before the War, with *Boulangerie* spelled out in faded letters across the flowery paper of the back wall, but because the furniture looked as though it had been gathered up from all over town, nothing quite matching with anything else. You could imagine coming back tomorrow and finding all of it gone and Madame Dubois behind the counter selling *des pistolets* and *des miches*.

"Well, I'm sorry you can't find the words," I said. "This means I'll never know what happened. I'll never be sure you didn't turn your weapon on yourself, just for a rest in Blighty and a chance to meet a girl."

"Hell," he said. "At least you've seen enough to know when I'm telling the truth."

He told me then that they'd been promised a huge barrage from the artillery when they made the attack, going over the top to rush across the quarter mile of scrubland to the first German trench. Their orders, of course, were to capture it, if they got through the wire. "But there wasn't a peep out of the damned artillery. Bullets whined around us, you could hear them, see them tearing up the dirt at our feet. Men went down on every side. It was a massacre, Matt. Blood everywhere. Men almost cut in half. Torn-open throats. Screams that tore your eardrums and vibrated in your bones long afterwards. The few of us who weren't killed or wounded pushed on until we somehow got through a gap in the wire and reached the first line and took it and then fought on to take the second line. Somehow, a handful of us even got as far as the third German line."

"Sounds like a victory," I said, though I'd already heard the end of this tale from others.

"It felt like a damned victory too," Sullivan said. The muscles in his forehead were tight, and constantly shifting. "But now we were out there on our own. *We didn't know the bloody attack had been cancelled!* The Colonel's order had reached the artillery in time, and it even reached the troops who were supposed to become the second wave behind us, but it hadn't reached our colonel until too late. We'd already gone. So – did they decide to follow us and take advantage of what we'd accomplished? Hell, no. They sent runners out to tell those of us who were still alive that we were to give up what we'd won and go back to where we'd come from. Son of a bitch! Back through a hail of Jerry bullets coming from three directions, running, or crawling, with our bloody backs exposed. Some fell. Marsden. Kristoferson. Then the same bloody artillery that had stood by without firing a shell to support us on the way out saw us heading their way and thought we must be Germans attacking! Not a word of a lie, Matt. They shelled us. And that made the rest of our own lines think we were attacking, so they opened up with machine-gun fire as well! Our own guys mowed us down. By the end only a few of us were able to drag ourselves back to the line. We left most of our men dead or dying behind us, or waiting in shell holes for help that would never come. I took a bullet in the leg just as I was sliding over the parapet into somebody's arms in the trench. You can imagine how happy I am to be back in this fray. I was hoping you'd get this thing wrapped up before I healed."

We still believed in "wrapping it up" then. We could still see ourselves as soldiers going home. We imagined the privileges and honours of being a returned soldier – the admiring glances of pretty girls, the words of thanks from strangers, the offers of jobs by impressed employers.

But apparently Charlie had changed. When Banks had come back with the car and we'd set off down the road out of town, he admitted he no longer believed there'd be any of us left to see what life would be like afterwards. "Someone's invented a way of clearing the earth of young males. If there's any 'afterwards,' only people we can barely remember will see it."

These were people Charlie Sullivan had already started to hate.

He'd seen them in London, he said. Women laughing at street corners. Well-dressed office workers. People living normal lives, without the foggiest idea of what we were going through over here. Or why. "Can you remember what you're fighting for, Pearson?"

"They sent you back too soon," I laughed. "You've a right to be cranky but for God's sake, we have to win this or the world will not be worth living in."

He snorted as he might at a naive schoolboy's belief in St. Nicholas, and shifted in his seat to look away.

We bounced and swayed along a narrow muddy road that appeared and disappeared and reappeared ahead of us as it passed over low hills and around knolls crowned with the snaggy ruins of villages and directly down between two rows of shelled and blasted plane trees, columns of writhing figures that appeared to have died while trying to free themselves from the ground. Along the far horizon line, heavy clouds had raised their lower edges just high enough to allow a thin line of light to leak onto the earth. Bursts of machine-gun fire at this distance sounded like an army of wood-peckers hammering away at dead trees.

Though I still had faith in an "afterwards" I had begun to find it harder to believe in a "before the war." Letters came from another life, from beyond a barrier that seemed to have only one-way doors. Maude had become, God help me, only the idea of Maude. It had become harder and harder to remember the touch of her hand, or the shape of her smile, though of course I said just the opposite in my letters. Home, too, was only an idea without any real embodiment in this world – an imagined house in an imagined farm in an imagined Ottawa Valley. The person who'd repaired that roof and milked the cows in that field was someone who might have lived only in my head.

It would be healthier, Sullivan said, to behave as though there were no "before" or "after" – nothing beyond the trenches and the countryside we could see from the fire step whenever we wanted to have our heads blown off. He wanted to marry the girl he had met in London but he could not believe he would ever do it. He was not even sure she existed, he said, aside from a delusion in a sweaty hospital bed. The undamaged countryside he'd seen from the window of the train that brought him back to France had looked like something out of a fairy tale book. He could not have been in it himself.

"There's so many of us living in this muck so close together we might as well be flies swarming on a shit pile. Rats at a corpse. We're all the same – mindless vermin. Operating on orders from some distant brain that sure as hell ain't ours."

"You think we've lost our minds, Charlie?"

"You're not blind. You must have seen this for yourself back there in town. Two hundred men lined up outside the *maison de tolérance* waiting their turn. I heard of one place where there were only three women. They last two weeks and have to retire. It's pretty hard to think of those two hundred men as anything more than 'two hundred men lined up for a call of nature.' No separate consciences at work there – you couldn't stand to think that."

I made a feeble sort of protest, not wanting to admit that I knew what he meant.

"We've given away everything we brought with us except our animal bodies and some of us have lost even parts of those. Snakes in a snake pit, flies on a manure pile. I know you'd just as soon not believe me, Matt, but it's hard work trying to believe what you believe."

We were both silent now as we passed by columns of men on the march and then a wagonload of heavy shells being transported to the front. The Salvation Army canteen and a Red Cross ambulance truck were parked in a soggy field, near the thick base of a tree whose upper trunk and branches lay out across the grass. Ration parties unloaded sacks of supplies off the company quartermasters' wagons – heaps of sandbags filled with meat and vegetables, canned food, mail, and bread.

Before he reported to Major Mason, I gave him a tour of the

reserve trenches with our new street signs, and showed him the RULES FOR INMATES OF THIS INSTITUTION painted on the slab of corrugated iron. He was pleased. "Well, there y'are. The lads are a jump ahead of you."

Once he'd added his rule 18, I walked with him up the tunnel as far as the entrance to Major Mason's dugout beneath the village church. It was clear that some disturbance was in the air. Naylor was talking excitedly on the telephone. The Major appeared to be grumbling to himself. When he looked up from the table he used for a desk he stood up, ignoring Sullivan. "Aha! Pearson. Take a look at this woman, willya, and tell me if she looks like someone who can make herself invisible."

A young woman, a girl, sat on a chair to his left, her gaze on the loose floorboards at her feet.

"Probably not, Major."

"Probably not. Yet somehow she got all the way in to the village above us without anyone stopping her."

Of course it was possible she had been brought in by some of the men for their own purposes. I thought of the two hundred men in Charlie's queue.

If this girl were a whore she was not a prosperous one. Her blouse and long skirt were torn. Her feet were bare. Her face, though pretty enough with fine features, was streaked with dirt. Her nails were bitten or broken right down to the flesh.

"You speak French, Lieutenant?"

"A little, sir."

"You, Lieutenant? Whatzzyername?"

"Sullivan, sir. Not a word, sir. I've resisted the language all my life."

"She says she lives here. *Chez moi*. In this village. We found her in one of the houses above us. Nearly shot her, too. I don't know how the hell she got so close without anyone stopping her."

The girl clasped her hands together in her lap and looked up at me as though she expected something.

"She could be a spy," Mason said. "Do you think she's a spy? I've half a mind to send her up to the front, make her wish she stayed at home. You think that's a good idea, Pearson?"

"Not for her, sir. I don't imagine that's what she came here for."

"How the hell would you know what she came here for?" he shouted. Then he shouted at the girl. "*Qu'est-ce que vous cherchez ici?*"

She didn't know what she wanted to find, she said. She had got lonely for her home. She had wanted to see how much damage had been done. She wanted to see if there were any of her childhood playthings left unharmed. They had had to leave in such a hurry.

"Why come looking for them now?"

She had no answer to that. She had been looking at me the whole time, as though she had decided I was the one man in the room who might think such a question needed no answer. It was a gaze that made me uneasy, challenged me in some way, imagined it knew me. Her eyes were long-lashed, her eyebrows dark and sharply defined. The fingers of one hand touched her lips for a moment, then rose to the tangled mess of burnished hair, and scratched behind her ear. Except for the eyes, her neutral expression did not change.

"Maybe she's sorry. Maybe she wants to leave," I suggested.

"*Où habitez-vous?*"

"*Ici.*"

"*Non! Je veux dire maintenant. Où habitez-vous maintenant?*"

"*Gentelles.*"

"Pearson, take a couple of men and make sure she's sent well up the road towards Gentelles," the Major commanded. "Make sure she understands she's not to come back here. I won't answer for what will happen to her if she does."

"You want me to take her right to the town?"

"Take her far enough. Make sure she doesn't follow you back."

Of course she was more careful after the first time, and was never caught again. That is, so far as I know, she wasn't caught by anyone but me. I found her two nights later in what was left of the church, directly above the dugout where she had been shouted at by the Major.

"Are you crazy?" I said.

She smiled but did not answer. She held out a wooden abacus whose beads had been worn or weathered of their paint. She had found it beneath her grandparents' house, she said. She insisted that I hold it in my hand, while she pushed the beads to one side, counting. Her laughter was soft, like a child's. *Un. Deux. Trois.*

She'd missed more than her home, she said. I was able to understand most of it. She missed the whole village. We had kept it too long. She missed the children playing at the cross, where they gathered to collect pails of water. She missed the women calling from door to door. She missed the bawling of the cattle in the barnyards, and the sound of her grandfather talking to his horse. It was all here in the church, she said. Everything of the past and future was gathered, invisible, here in the church, which was the heart and soul of the village. "*Écoutez,*" she said, taking my hand. If I was still and listened hard enough to the quiet, I would hear the voices of all the centuries here.

When she directed me to look up, I saw that the walls and partial roof framing the sky made even the clouds appear so distant as to be isolated from everything but peace.

Only once were we discovered in all the times we met there, and that was by Charlie Sullivan, who was on another of his mysterious visits to Major Mason. He stood in the doorway long enough for his eyes to adjust to the interior dark, and then said, "Sorry," and left. By the time we saw one another again and might have talked about this, two more years had passed and just about everything in my world had drastically changed.

And of course the matter was never raised between us after we'd discovered one another living in this place.

When sleepless nights sent me to the abandoned sawmill it may have been because I hoped that the ruin would offer something of what the girl had claimed for her shelled church – the past, the future, the heart and soul of the village. I may have come there for the same reason I would have liked to believe there'd once been an Indian village along our grassy stretch of seaside park, though no one had found any sign of it – not a post, not a pot, not a single skull. Mary Reimer was sure they wouldn't. She doubted this had been where Haidas from the north camped on their raiding parties for slaves, either, as some had suggested. It was where the Cape Mudge people rested, she said, when they came down to tend their potato patches and visit relatives in the Comox and Puntledge tribes. This was before the road was built. Now they used the road like everyone else, she said, though nobody ever saw them.

No one had settled here before us. There was no human history abiding in this place, unless you counted the mysterious figure they referred to as The Portuguese, whose cave and cooking utensils were discovered in the bank of the creek named after him, long after he had gone. Indian tribes had passed through. Loggers had worked here and moved on. No one had stayed. No one, so far as we knew, had ever been left to live or to die. In Ferguson Falls my father's parents lay beneath stones behind a church not two miles from the farm, and his grandparents beside them. No doubt the same could be said of Patrick Maguire's parents in Skibereen, and of Leena Hueffner's somewhere in Texas. Friends and colleagues had been left in the soil of France. But here, no ghosts inhabited the trees. No ancestors were buried beneath them. There were no ancestors here. Only a peculiar silence.

At only ten years old, this sawmill was hardly a substitute for history, though the fact that it had been built, abandoned, pillaged, ruined, and invaded by reclaiming trees might have suggested otherwise. Touch these concrete walls and I suppose you touched something someone else unknown to you had touched.

Lay a hand on one of the long low concrete slabs that must have been machinery footings and you could imagine you were touching the sarcophagus of a stranger. Some secret priest might have served communion from the altar where the trim saw once was mounted. When you looked up at the naked gables you could imagine someone had cared enough to do battle for this place.

But this was all imagination. The building had never been, and was not now, a cathedral or even a church, unless you thought of it as erected cynically for gods of convenience and greed, and quickly abandoned out of contempt for both the place and its future. We had a Store, we had Archie MacIntosh's smithy and machine shop, we had Johanna Seyerstad's school, we had Ahlbergs' Tea Room and Taxi Service, we had Carl and Mary Reimer's sawmill. But we had no church, no plot of ground reserved for a graveyard, no steeple rising above the roofs and second-growth trees, no building in which we could meet to worship, or on this occasion hold a farewell service for poor Mac, or – though it was hard to imagine this when everything was so new – on future occasions hold services for those whose weddings and deaths were yet to come.

No church was wanted here, or needed. So they had said, and perhaps they were right to think so. What sort of church would it have to be to satisfy the variety of faiths and non-faiths that had been brought to this place? This was not France. This wasn't even Ontario. Whatever beliefs had survived the years of conflict and the move west had survived in private. Religious matters were never discussed amongst us, though such topics were probably debated at length in towns and older communities elsewhere. As for myself, I was waiting. A blow had been dealt that required recovery. I knew what the sceptics meant. Yet a man as blessed as I was with life and family and a piece of this earth to live on could not help being filled with gratitude.

Sometimes it was better not to think of such things at all, and to contemplate, rather, the silence. Here at the ruined sawmill there was only the silence of the woods, except for the occasional rustle of deer moving past, or the hooting of an owl in the trees. The river's babble seemed to protect rather than disturb the quiet. Here too, from within this structure as within that ruin in France, the sky above had been sliced and framed in a distant isolation that knew nothing at all about anything other than peace.

Charlie MacIntosh

Tanner promised me a close look at his Uncle Donald's mask. I didn't want to see behind it, I didn't even want to think about what was behind it, but I would not turn down a chance to see how the mask was attached to the bottom half of his face.

One afternoon when we came back from exploring down an old logging grade he was out on the porch, nodding and muttering while Elizabeth read a picture book aloud. Pieces of Tanner's Meccano set were scattered on the floorboards. Tanner didn't mind this so long as she was making buildings to place along the tracks of his Dominion Flyer train.

But I knew I wasn't going to get close to the uncle after all because Tanner's father was out there too, sitting on the top step cleaning his rifle. There was an open box of shells on the step by his feet. "You come across anything that looked tasty enough to eat?" he said.

"You taking us hunting?" Tanner said.

His father shook his head. "Just thought you might have run into a kangaroo we could chew on."

"There's no kangaroos out there," Tanner said.

"How do you know? There could be anything out there. We didn't know about cougars till we saw one, did we, twitching his tail and wondering how we'd taste. This place could have a few surprises up its sleeve for us yet. Like that raccoon that stood up to Charlie's terrier."

Poor old Macduff was who he meant. The first time Duffy spotted a raccoon he took after it, thinking it was just a big cat. But it didn't run, it reared up and started a terrible fight, right on the edge of the creek behind our barn. If Duffy saw his mistake he couldn't do anything about it, the 'coon pulled him over the bank and held his head under the water until he drowned. I was too scared to do anything but yell. A good thing too, Dad said, since that raccoon could have torn my face to pieces as easy as not. I still felt bad about letting poor Duffy down.

I thought Tanner would mention the bear that wandered into the school while Mrs. Seyerstad was marking papers at her desk. The two froze for a few minutes, each staring at the other. Nobody was surprised the bear knew that he'd met his match and backed away, head swinging, to turn and go loping out the door and into the bush.

Maybe thinking of Macduff made Tanner remember that we'd seen a golden collie playing with Buster down by the barn. "What's Mr. Sullivan's dog doing here?"

"You walked right past his cattle too." Mr. Pearson's face was sad. "I brought them home. Sullivan seems to have gone."

He'd ridden over to Sullivan's place two days in a row, he said. No sign of the man either time. His dog came out from under the step to greet him but his owner wasn't there. No answer when he called. "I went inside that house he never finished, scared to think what I'd find. Everything was tidy. Sullivan was as neat as a woman. His bed was even made."

The cows were bawling from the pain in their swollen bags. Mr. Pearson walked all over the place, expecting to come upon Sullivan somewhere behind a tree. Someone with a gun might have shot him for a deer, like the third Winton brother soon after they'd moved here. But Sullivan wasn't anywhere.

Mr. Pearson milked his cows out onto the ground the first time, as Sullivan would have expected him to do. When he sat on Sullivan's step to think about this, the dog pushed his nose between his knees and gazed into his eyes while he stroked the top of his head. The second day the same. "So I brought them home. The cats can take care of themselves."

"Maybe he went to London to find his wife," Tanner said.

I knew about the wife. An English bride as pale and pretty as some delicate garden flower, my mother said. She hadn't lasted long.

"Or maybe Toronto," Mr. Pearson said, "to talk with those relatives who didn't come through with a job after the War. Or maybe back to the Ottawa Valley. He has hundreds of cousins there, as I have. He missed his father, I think."

He looked off towards the barn for a while. "That's something you never hear about," he said. "Your mothers go on about missing their mothers – advice their mothers aren't here to give, habits their mothers passed on, recipes their mothers copied out. I don't suppose it would occur to Mrs. Pearson that I might brood about my parents now and then. You never hear men saying they wish the old man were here to give advice. It was something that came to me while I sat on Sullivan's step wondering if he'd gone home."

I'd never heard anyone talk like this. Maybe this was meant for Tanner. It might have been meant for me.

There were times when thoughts of his folks were so painful that he had to put them out of his head, he said. They would grow old without setting eyes on their grandchildren again. "Sometimes when I look over this little place and admire those orchard trees, or my sturdy barn, I imagine my father removing his pipe from his mouth to give that little quick twist of the head – his mute approval. When I scratch my head over a piece of broken-down machinery, I know Walter Pearson would probably have the solution at his fingertips. If he didn't, he would come up with an answer quicker than I could.

"This must sound pretty strange to fellows your age, but a man could just quit and go home to his dad."

Tanner scooped up a handful of shells from the box. "*K'pow!*" he said. Grabbing his stomach, he folded down and fell to the grass.

"Put them back," his father said. "You know better than that."

Tanner held the shells to his nose first, and smelled, before putting them back in their box.

Mr. Pearson placed his rifle on the porch boards and picked up one of the bullets between the thumb and index finger of his right hand. Then he held it out in front of us. It was about two inches long, slim, a brass casing with a long pointed tip of lead. There was a slim rim of dirt under his nails, the kind that stays no matter how much you scrub. The thumbnail was cracked, and split open part way down the middle. "These things look pretty small," he said, "but they aren't something to fool around with."

"How d'they work?" I said. My dad hadn't owned a gun. This was the first time I'd seen a bullet.

"Pretty much the same as blasting powder," he said. He narrowed his eyes as though he could see inside the shell. "The firing pin in the gun sets off the first detonator inside here." He tapped the butt end of the shell with a finger from his other hand. "That ignites the explosives. Fire, heat, gas! The gas expands, trapped in there, until it's got no choice but to push the cartridge out through the barrel. *Wham!*"

"And right through the head of a deer," Tanner said.

"*Something* is not the same as it was before," his father said. "That's what fire and heat and explosions do, they change things!"

He put a hand on my shoulder then. "What happened to your father could've happened to any of us," Mr. Pearson said. "These explosives are dangerous. Look at Neil Mitchell, he knew all there was to know about this stuff and still he blew off a foot."

"Mother called him silly," I said. "Being a big kid got him killed."

Mr. Pearson smiled at that. "The reason your father acted like a big kid was because he *was* a big kid. We all were. We might seem pretty old to you but we're hardly used to being grown-ups yet. Sometimes your dad was more of a grown-up than the rest of us." He thought for a minute, looking off towards the bush. "Well, let me tell you – if it wasn't for him being a big kid a whole lot of us might've drowned, year before last, not long after we first got here. You remember that?"

Tanner looked as though he didn't believe it.

"Drowned in our own misery if not in water," his father said. "We would've called him a hero if he'd have stood for it."

Elizabeth left her uncle and came over to push herself against her father. Mr. Pearson put his arm around her and held her close, and smelled her hair before pretending to mess it up. You could smell their supper cooking inside – lamb. You could hear Mrs. Pearson slapping dishes onto the table. I should have been heading home.

Mr. Pearson said, "This was when we were all still living in tents, down below the Store. You remember that? Tanner might remember. I don't know about Elizabeth. The roots of all that curly hair take a lot of nourishment from her brain, they might not have left her much to work with."

Elizabeth slapped his thigh.

"That's right," he said. "I forgot. Elizabeth remembers everything. She even remembers the look of horror on my face the first time I saw her."

He put his hand over hers. She leaned her head against his shoulder and gave me a look that said: He's mine, go get your own.

"We'd had our fill of tents long before we came here," he said. "But we didn't have much choice, we had to live in them until we'd helped the government clear the first ten acres of our place."

If the men were sick of tents, he said, you could imagine how the women felt. Charlie Sullivan's wife had been raised by a wealthy aunt in London, with paintings on the wall and servants to wait on her. Mrs. Price was a doctor's daughter in Manitoba, and had lived her life in a fine house with a front verandah on the main street of town. And Mrs. Pearson had never slept a night of her life without a proper roof over her head, they'd had a sturdy little house in Ferguson Falls before they'd come here, and she'd lived in a kind of a stone mansion in Montreal before they were married. When they saw the tents for the first time, they let out such a great moan that – this was how they would tell it – one of the tents collapsed in a fluttery heap. The Martins'. "Poor ol' Frenchie was never able to get it to stay upright after that."

Of course they didn't cook in the tents. They had to cook over a fire in a pile of rocks, traipsing through the dirt. Raising dust when the weather was dry, and sinking to their ankles when it rained. A Mrs. Kuziak sat in the road and told her husband to take her out of here or she was going to set a match to every tent. "Next morning the Kuziaks were gone, no one knows where they went."

Most of the women set their jaws in the way that Mrs. Pearson's jaw was sometimes set even now, he said, and went about making a home out of that little triangle under the canvas roof. Sweeping the floor fifty times a day. Making meals you could cook in a single pot. Hanging their washes back in the bush away from the dust, but not too close to the pines with their blisters of pitch, or the stumps with their scorched coats or too close to anyone else's washing where they could see how threadbare your sheets and underpants were when they went out to bring in their own.

"Oh, they were brave and strong and patient. But at night you could hear a murmur of weeping all down the row, from the Store right down to what is now Richmonds' gate. You might have mistaken it for a creek trickling over rocks if you didn't know better. Deer came right up to the tents, wondering what they could do to help, I'm sure of it. We men were too tired to chase them away – worn out from the long day of working in the woods before coming home to clear land or build a tarpaper shack or start the backbreaking task of digging a well. It was the women that had to start out every day pushing thoughts of their mothers out of their heads and reminding themselves that they were putting up with this so that their children could have a better life than they would have had if they'd stayed home. Any one of them might have turned on us. If we'd stayed where we were they could be drinking tea from their mother's teacups, if they hadn't married they could be sleeping under their father's roof!"

The uncle had started to make gurgling noises, like someone wanting to get out from behind that mask. Tanner moved along the step until he was close enough to take the uncle's hand in his. He could still listen.

"And your mother was as brave as any of them," Mr. Pearson said to me. "I never heard her complain, though you and your folks were just three tents from us. You'll remember some of this yourself. But what I'm going to tell you about was something that happened while you youngsters were sound asleep."

This was November, he said. Rain had fallen for seventeen days without let-up. You couldn't even call it mud any more, you needed to invent a new name. You laid down planks to walk across to your tent without sinking up to your thighs and for two or three days it worked, but by the fourth day the planks would have disappeared into the muck and you had to lay down more.

Then my dad got fed up. Fed up with working in the rain all day in the woods where he was setting chokers for the Company. Fed up with walking home in the rain from the Store where the crummy let the men off. Fed up with seeing his family peer out from that triangle of tent like rabbits hiding beneath a bush. Fed up with listening to the steady drumming of rain on the canvas all night and the dripping of rain on the floor beneath a small tear in the tent and, who knows, the muffled sounds of his wife trying not to let anyone hear that she was crying from exhaustion and frustration and regret, not to mention despair. "I'll be damned if I'll put up with it," he said, and got out of bed and walked stark naked into the night where he sang the whole first verse of "Do Ye Ken John Peel" at the top of his voice.

"My dad?" I said.

"Yes, your dad. By the time he'd started into the second verse he'd been joined by a naked Charlie Sullivan and a naked Hayden Evans. 'Sullen Charlievan' and 'Heating Ovens' he'd renamed them, the same as he'd renamed us all, whether we liked it or not.

Both of them sang hard beside him, and not much later they were joined by five or six more, and by the time they'd got to the end of the song there were two dozen of us out there making fools of ourselves in the dark. Then he says, 'While I have your attention, lads, do we have a commonality of opinion on this rrrrrain?'

"'We do,' we shouted. 'We've had enough of it!'

"'Do we agrrrree, lads, that if this mud and gravel we call home didna' soak up the rain like a sponge, we'd be living now in flood conditions of Biblical proportions?'

"We agreed. If someone from town had driven out they would have taken us for mad. And so we were, thanks to Mac. And happy in the rain for the first time since it started. 'And do we also not agree,' he says, 'that it's about time we shut the damned thing off?'

"We agreed to that, heartily. For a moment we wondered if your dad might know how to do it. There were faces looking out from all the tents. Wives who hadn't been weeping before were weeping now. Rain had driven their husbands out of their wits. If I heard a voice calling 'Matthew!' I ignored it. I looked to your dad to lead us into some sense. Instead, he led us through the verses of 'Loch Lomond.' Then he made a speech. 'Lads,' he said. 'We've had enough o' life in the mud, we've had enough o' flood, the time has come to fix bayonets and go over the top and seize the buggers by the throat.'

"Hayden Evans hollered, 'If you got a plan will you spit it out for God's sake, man, we're freezing our arses off here!'"

"Matthew," Mrs. Pearson said through the screened door. Tanner grinned at me.

"So Mac smiles and looks from one of us to the other, sleek drowned rats standing ankle-deep in mud, and says, and I won't try to imitate his accent, 'If they brought us here and left us living in the middle of a real flood what would we do? We might build an ark if we had the energy. We might hoist all these tents up into the trees and build bridges from one to the other and hope our babies don't fall and break their necks. Or we might head into town where the government officials sleep in their nice dry beds, and move in with them. It was government invited us here. It was government set up this lottery. It was government promised to clear the first ten acres and lend us money for the cows and give us credit for seed at the Store. It only makes sense that people as thoughtful as that would not want us drowning while they're snoring away in their beds. The only question left is do we go right now or wait till morning to do it.'"

Mr. Pearson still had one arm around Elizabeth, but now he put his other hand on my shoulder. "The night was pretty far advanced by now, so we decided to wait until dawn to make our move.

"It was a little crowded in those houses in town. The government men didn't like it much, but their wives took to our wives right away and wouldn't let them move us to a hotel. When the rain let up there was some that didn't want to see us go. But we came back. It wasn't much longer we had to live in the tents, but we had a few good laughs that winter when we thought about your dad's solution to our misery. I don't believe he knew himself what he would say when he went out into the rain. I think he just wanted to register his outrage. Or maybe, being still mostly a boy as your mother never tired of saying, he just couldn't resist stripping down and singing out there in that downpour. When we finally took down the tents some thought we ought to leave one standing, with a sign out front and a picture of Mac in the rain singing 'John Peel' at the top of his lungs. You can bet he was just a boy. So were we all. What would we have done if we hadn't been?"

Mrs. Pearson had been at the door for a while now, clearing her throat. Now she said, "It's after five, Charlie." She knew she was to tell me so I wouldn't give Mother something new to worry about.

"You have to go?" Mr. Pearson said, his dark speckled eyes shining.

"I have to feed the chickens if I want my supper," I said.

"If you feed our chickens we'll give you supper too," he said. "You can have Tanner's share."

Tanner laughed.

"Matthew," Mrs. Pearson said, from inside the kitchen.

"You can have my share as well if you milk the cows," he said. "I don't know what you'd have to do for Elizabeth's. Tidy her bedroom for her, I imagine."

"Matt," Mrs. Pearson said.

Elizabeth's freckles looked as if they would leap from her face. "He's not touching my room."

Mr. Pearson squeezed my shoulder, almost too hard. "I guess that means you might as well go, since nobody here will feed you. Say hello to your mother for us. But don't forget, there's a seat on this step whenever you want to hear about your dad."

He coughed and stood up. "Now go over and say good-bye to Tanner's uncle. We don't know how much he understands but he might be sitting there hoping to shake hands with a hero's son."

So I went over, holding my breath, and took hold of the hand that hung down the side of the chair. My face burned, the rest of me was cold. If they hadn't been watching I would not have done it. He might have been trying to get a good look at me but his head jerked this way and that so fast that I don't think he saw very much.

"This is Charlie," Mr. Pearson said. "Charlie Mackinaw, he insists on being called now. He just wants to say good-bye before he goes home."

I said it, but had to say it a second time for even myself to hear it.

Everything below the eyes was made of something that wasn't flesh or skin, too smooth for a man. No pores. A nose, a moustache hiding the mouth, a jaw to one side right up to the ear. Only Mrs. Pearson was allowed to take it off, in order to wash whatever was behind it. Nobody else ever saw. That was what Tanner said. I wondered if my father had been allowed to look this close. If he had, he'd never mentioned it. It was something else I would tell him about after supper, when I went up to the attic for my cigarette.

___

Leena Hueffner

Now I warned Taylor about this. I said, "Don't let her go bustin' your heart again." Even if she let him buy groceries and dig her fence-post holes and build her chicken shed and wait on her hand and foot, she was still married to the crazy *hombre* that owns her place. She could send him down the road like that!

I could see her doing it, too. She come from that big family of laughing pranksters but she had her old man's grim rough edges. I don't know what she expected out of life.

"Let me take a good look at you," I said to Taylor once when he come in the Store. "I can't tell if you're some kind of saint or a fool."

He grinned and yanked on his burnt hat and took a turn around the room. "Are those my only choices?" He lowered the sack of potatoes off his shoulder and rested it on the floor between his feet.

"Well, she sure as shootin' ain't no raving beauty," I said.

People count on me to say what I think. Taylor wasn't surprised. He wasn't even surprised when I said, "She's got a tongue in her head like a whetted scythe and don't care who she hurts with it, neither." Then I said, "In Texas I knew some mules that weren't as stubborn." He just pursed his lips, thinking it over. He scratched beneath his hat. Too polite to just walk off. "She led you on a wild goose chase across the country. You think that's the end of it?

Any man crazy enough to hitch his life to hers is asking for a load of misery. That's my opinion and I won't charge you a nickel for it, neither."

His grin spread out so wide it must of hurt. "Well," he said. "If you'll excuse me, I want to deliver these spuds for her supper."

"You going to peel them for her too?"

Hueffner figured Taylor was a simpleton. "Pearson thinks that look on his face is a sign of wisdom. I think somebody dropped him on his head."

He never stayed long in one spot. There was always something else he had to do. It was a full-time job catering to Nora Macken, but it was also a full-time job helping people get rid of their stumps. He had to do both. As far as I could see it was taking every cent he earned or expected to earn to pay for the supplies he bought for Herbie Brewer's wife. She went all the way from doing the work of three strong men herself to telling him where he should put his gifts. I hoped she took a minute now and then to thank him.

You'd think old Macken would of put a stop to it. We knew he didn't like what was going on. Since she married one man against his advice she didn't have no business taking favours from another. She hadn't suffered enough for ignoring him yet. He never said much about it, that I heard. He never usually said much of nothing, just grunted into his grizzly beard the words for whatever he wanted to buy, and then grunted his thanks and hoisted his trousers up his skinny hips and left. He wasn't the sort you wanted to keep around. It was like he had to look as sour as he could to help Nora balance out all those high-spirited sons that thought blowing up the school privy was high-class entertainment.

I never knew nothing about his wife. She looked pleasant enough through the window, I guess, a small dark round-eyed woman sitting in the Overland. They said there was a little Blackfoot in her. He met her in the Dakotas somewhere. Those who'd got to know her said she was kind, though not so spirited as her boys. She looked to me like she couldn't believe where her life had brought her to, or what she'd gone and set loose in the world.

You'd think Johanna would of stayed right out of it, once she'd talked Nora into letting Taylor help. She must of done it out of sympathy for Taylor. She would know how he felt, since she'd fallen for her husband in a way that didn't leave no room for another man. If he never come back she'd be a teacher down in that school for ever.

There was plenty of other things she might of done with her summer. She could of moved in with that mother-in-law in town, where there'd be motion pictures and a library and other teachers to talk to. She could start up a summer school right here. She wouldn't have no trouble finding pupils. Little girls all spent their summer holidays pretending they were her.

Maybe it was because she wanted things tidy. They say that when Johanna Seyerstad picked up a piece of chalk, equations had better work out or else. Maybe she was scared it wouldn't happen to her. Any husband that took so long might never find his way home. Or maybe she was just worried Nora might bust his heart again and she wanted to be there in case she could help. What did she think she could do?

She didn't say. She walked to Nora's every day but didn't always hang around for long. "She doesn't make it easy for him," she told me. One morning she found them in a fight. Taylor sat on the roof of the squatty chicken coop he'd built and Nora stormed around in the yard, kicking up dust and slapping a stick against the shed to start the chickens squawking behind the wire.

"Ask her to put the ladder back," he said. "How much use will I be if I jump and break my leg?"

Nora glared at Johanna like a playground bully. But Johanna was used to bullies, she glared back.

"Ladder's right where she threw it," Taylor said. "In the huckle-berries there."

"I don't know what they'd been fighting about," Johanna said. "I waded into the bush – look at the scratches – and set the ladder against the henhouse. I told him some girl in Owen Sound might be glad to hold the ladder while he built her a shed."

"She might not be so much fun," he said. "Nora may drive me mad but she's a challenge."

"A cougar cub would be a challenge too," I told Johanna. "Why don't he try courting a wounded bear?"

We don't know what the three of them were thinking. But I know that when she come home Johanna always sat out on that staircase to read a book until Taylor rode up and almost went past. Then he would come back and get down off his horse and climb the steps to sit. I've never been a natural-born eavesdropper but they usually sat near the window. I could hear what they said even if I didn't want to, even with Archie MacIntosh throwing machine parts around across the way.

Nora was driving him loco. I figured that out fast enough. Sometimes she made him think he'd finally made her see what a prize she'd thrown away. Once she even let him hold her for a minute in his arms. I had my doubts about this, but it was after he raised her wash-line pole so I guess this softened her up. Then the next thing he knew she was raising Cain for treating her like a woman that couldn't do without him.

So he backed off. Who wouldn't? For two whole days he didn't go nowhere near her. He didn't stop to talk with Johanna neither. We figured he'd decided to stick with blowing stumps, or maybe even go home.

Then it looked like he wanted Nora to see he was more than just a workhorse. When he wasn't breaking his neck for her he was breaking his neck for somebody else. Aili Aalto. Nancy Price. It wasn't just Nora he was courting, it was every woman in the settlement. It was the settlement itself.

"Now we know he has rocks in his head," Hueffner said, "if he thinks being a working fool will get him a harem."

For a change I bit my tongue. It'd take a darnsight more than a harem to make Hueffner a working fool.

Here's what he done. After helping Armus Aalto with a few stumps, Taylor stayed to connect the water pipes under Aili's sink. "In Finland even my grandmother had running water," Aili told me, "but here, that Armus he expect me to carry pails from the well until he find-it time to finish the job!" Thanks to Taylor, life here had caught up to rural Finland.

Korsakovs had only the one big stump that needed blowing right away but Taylor didn't leave until he'd built a firebox under the kettles in Anya's washhouse, exactly like the one her mother's servants had in St. Petersburg. At Prices' he turned a bunch of broken machine parts into a steam press for Nancy to iron her sheets. "Just like my mother's in Dublin," she crowed. I thought she was going to do a little dance right here in the Store to show how pleased she was.

Arlette Mar-*tann* rose up on her little toes, her blue eyes nearly exploding out of her head. *Naturellement*, after M'sieur Taylor had spent the morning outside with the men, she says, she wouldn't let him to leave without a dinner. *Rouleau de boeuf.* She dropped back on her heels and bugged her eyes at Nell Richmond, who was waiting for me to wrap her order.

Hueffner ducked into the storeroom whenever Arlette Mar-*tann* come in. Her gush of words always left him gasping, he was afraid he might pass out.

"After they finish, Fortunat and the others they went out to the field again and I apologize to M'sieur Taylor. 'It was not so very superb dinner, I am sorry.' Of course he was the gentleman. It was delicious, madame, he say. *Delicieux!* He say it *en français.* He especially like my *rouleau de boeuf.*"

Up on her toes, down on her heels. She wrung her little hands beneath her little chin.

"My goodness," Nell Richmond said, rolling her eyes to show me what she thought of the French. Excitable!

"'It is so difficult to make the superior meals in such a kitchen,' I tell him. '*Ma mère*, her kitchen was as big as this house! *Grande* table in the middle. Room for seven *enfants* to play on the floor.'

"So he ask about the house of *ma mère*. Stone walls, I tell him. Grand fireplace in three rooms. Dried dill and onions hanging from the ceiling. A wall of copper pots. Braided rugs on the floor, one on top of the other, warm and cosy. 'Such cooking utensils I have,' I tell him. 'That cookstove – *là!* – a piece of junk. You should have seen the cookstove of *ma mère*, it was a royal queen's compare to this. With a reservoir on the side, so she did not 'ave to boil the water to bathe *les enfants*.' By the time he left I was feeling so sorry for myself! I will pack my clothes and take the children home, I think. Of course I know I will not.

"Then only a few hours later – two, three hours, I don' know – he comes again to my door. 'Madame Mar-*tann*,' he say. 'I have brought you something 'ere.'

"At first I do not know what it is. A metal box, with pipes.

"'A reservoir,' he say.

"What did he do? He 'as borrow Archie MacIntosh's forge. So he come into my kitchen and down on the floor with his tools and connects that reservoir to my stove. Hot water! 'Like your *Mama*'s!' he say. 'The cookstove of a royal queen.' Then he say: 'Is it not amazing what 'eat and force and a little thinking can do?'"

"Ain't it amazing what a small French lady with big blue eyes can do?" Hueffner said, once she'd cleared out of the Store and it was safe to come out of hiding.

"It's wearing him out," Johanna told me. She looked worn out herself, leaning against the door. She spoke to the ceiling. "Now everybody has something they want him to do. Blowing stumps is not the half of it. I told him he should learn to say 'No.'"

I knew this already. The window again. "I can't help myself," he said. "Mrs. Mar-*tann* works so hard, and I saw right away how I could make life easier for her – a simple matter. It doesn't take long but these small things can make a difference."

"And what will you do when you see it's impossible to turn this crossroads into a modern city by yourself? They'll kill you with their demands. I've seen what miracles they expect of the teacher, they'll expect even more from you."

He sighed. "But you," he said. "You haven't asked me for a thing."

"What could I want?" she said.

"I don't know," he said, "but when you think of something I won't refuse. Because so far you've asked nothing except the chance to help me melt that girl's stubborn heart. You're a better friend to Nora than she will ever know."

"She's acting like she's had a spell put on her," Hueffner said. "It ain't healthy. She don't think of nothing else."

Matt Pearson wasn't surprised to hear about Taylor but he wasn't so sure we ought to be pleased about it. Pearson was a kind and likeable man but took himself too seriously. No, he took the *rest* of us too seriously. You'd think we were all his children, or his students. You'd think he'd been elected to public office.

I was sorting mail when he come in, tossing letters and newspapers into the pigeon holes across the back wall. He leaned down with his elbows on the counter and peered through the opening with his hands cupped up either side of his jaw.

"Nothing so far," I said.

"That's all right. It gives me a chance to see how our taxpayer money is spent." Sometimes I forgot how young he was. Ten years younger than me and Hueffner at least. So were most of them here.

When I told him about Arlette, he nodded inside his cradled hands. He wasn't surprised. He seen Taylor on his way to the Martins' that morning, he said. He straightened up to fish his tobacco out of his pocket. He'd just been over to Sullivan's place again to see if Sullivan had come back. He hadn't. Said this put him into a cranky mood. Through the pass-through I could see him stuff a pinch of tobacco into his pipe and then return the package to his pocket. He bent to put his face in the wicket again. While he was sitting on Sullivan's step, he said, Wyatt Taylor had ridden down the lane.

"I'd been sitting there thinking about how Sullivan was so proud of all the ditching he did. A mile and a half of drainage ditches is a good bit of work to turn your back on. I was trying to figure out why I haven't done the same myself when Taylor rode in. 'Taking a shortcut through to Martins',' he said. 'There's cow trails back through there that cut off a couple miles.'"

Pearson knew every shortcut in the district, I guess, from his night-time wanderings that he didn't think the rest of us knew about, but he said he didn't like Taylor using Charlie's place as a pass-through. The man was acting like Sullivan's farm was some sort of dead space belonging to nobody, free for all to use.

"I know Sullivan wouldn't mind," Pearson said. "The man was heading off to give help, for heaven's sake. At least he wasn't wasting his time on Nora. But it rankled anyway, the way he'd made this place his own so fast."

"Now this is a turnaround," I said. "I figured you liked the man."

"I do," he said. "There's something in him I like. Can't help it."

I finished sorting the mail and went out to straighten a few of the cans on the shelves. Pearson turned and leaned against the post office counter to watch, one hand kneading his bad shoulder. He was still talking like someone thinking out loud. He hadn't lit his pipe, which was fine with me. "Missing Charlie brought it on, I guess."

It was a funny thing to say. Anybody could see there was always a stiffness between them two. I used to wonder if there wasn't a feud that was never mentioned. Maybe Sullivan wanted to marry Maude before Pearson won her. Maybe their grandfathers voted different back in Ontario. They were never as easy with each other as you'd think long-time friends'd be.

"So he's decided to shower benefits on the ladies," he said. He tossed this over his shoulder as he opened the door to go out, with a half-joking tone to his voice. "Not satisfied with clearing fields, he's got himself inside their kitchens as well." He laughed, like he recognized an old trick. "Maybe we should remember how he learned his trade – tunnelling under people to blow them up."

"What's that supposed to mean?" I said.

He looked shocked himself, and closed the door without going out. All them faded freckles took on a hefty blush. "Nothing," he said. "I don't know where it came from, Leena. Forget it. I like the man. I even like whatever it is that gives him the energy to earn a living off us and court that woman and do favours for everyone else in the world at the same time!"

"Pearson thinks he owns people," Hueffner said later. "Nobody asked him to be the mayor of this place."

Taylor didn't ignore Nora while he was courting the others. But he started to worry that building, digging, blasting, clearing, and hauling wasn't enough. A brother could of done that much, he told Johanna. Building and digging and all the rest of it were nothing more than doing favours for someone in need. No more romance in them than there was in handing a woman a broom to sweep her kitchen floor. Nora wasn't no happier now than when he started.

"Of course she ain't," I said, when Johanna told me this. "Why would she let him think she's satisfied? He might slack off a bit."

"He asked about the whist-drive dance on Saturday," she said.

He knew there wasn't no orchestra for these things. After we put away the cards and pushed back the tables and chairs, Johanna usually hammered at the school piano while we danced. Sven Ahlberg fiddled, to give her a rest. Sometimes Lillian Swift squeezed her box accordion for a while. He offered to add his humble talent to this.

"I thought your talent was explosives," she said. "Will you blow up the school?"

So now we learned that our Wyatt Taylor, on top of everything else, was a singer – or thought he was. Oh Lord, another Matt Pearson! Did he think he'd win Nora by singing songs she wouldn't step outside her shack to hear? Maybe he planned to sing outside her window. Did he think we lived in Spain?

"Hueffner thinks the man is simple."

"Is that so?" Johanna said. "Did Hueffner study brainiology while he was digging in Panama?" She never liked Hueffner much. He wasn't exactly crazy about her neither.

"What is he then? He ain't no genius, not if he hasn't figured out that life with Nora would be just as tough as catching her's been."

I don't know what Johanna was thinking. Maybe Hueffner was right and she was under some spell. She helped Taylor decorate the inside of the school: bouquets of dog roses, wild spiraea, honey-suckle, twisted lengths of coloured paper. They stacked the rows of desks along one wall. They borrowed tables and chairs from people's kitchens. The rest of us brought box lunches, the same as usual, and lowered crockery jugs and bottles into the well.

Nora wouldn't come. What did they think? A few of the Macken boys showed up to see what trouble they could cause but the parents didn't. Most of the rest of us turned out. Rumours had spread. Nosiness had got into our blood. It wasn't easy to keep your eyes on your cards and the door at the same time.

Mary Reimer won the Store-donated sack of flour the same as she always did. She was so good at cards they should of banned her from playing. Only second prize mattered and bloody Carl won that: so-many crooked-board feet of donated Reimer lumber! The fat son-of-a-coyote kept it, too. He didn't see no reason to pass it on. He would donate it again for the next whist drive, he said, unless somebody made him an offer to take it off his hands. Nobody did. People wanted to eat.

Usually, before we started to auction off the box lunches we could count on Sandy MacKay for a surprise. He didn't play whist, so he usually waited until the prizes had been given out before he showed up in some crazy outfit to give us a laugh – a kilt, or a short-pants suit of blue velvet with a curly wig on his head and a blue ribbon stuck to his moustache. This time he wasn't dressed up at all. He come in the door looking pleased as Punch and drag-ging a logging chain behind him.

"I caught 'im!" he hollered.

Of course we all stopped what we were doing and looked. "Caught who?" someone says.

"The Portuguese," he says. Nobody ever seen The Portuguese they named the creeks around here after. Some ol' prospector that didn't stay long, before we got here. But in comes Sandy with this logging chain dragging on the floor and at the other end of the chain is this giant creature wrapped in a bear skin off somebody's floor. Barefooted. Hunched forward like a caveman with his hair all standing on end thick with soot from under a stove lid! "Found his hiding place," Sandy says. "Opened up his cave by mistake when I blasted that stump behind my barn. Now we've got him, what'll we do with him?"

"Chain him to the piano," someone said. "Make him play."

Even with his teeth blacked out and scars painted onto his face we recognized Howard Stokes from his size. Stokes would never play for dancing, his taste was more for the fancy classics sort of stuff. So while we ate he dragged his chains up to the piano and gave us a taste of Schubert or one of them Europeans. It was so strange to hear them high-class notes coming from that hairy beast that we sat and watched with our mouths hanging open, feeling kind of cold and nervous, as if The Portuguese really had come up out of his stump hole to pay us a visit.

Once Stokes got finished, others had to take a turn at showing off. Fortunat Mar-*tann* sawed on his daddy's fiddle, then Lilly Swift pumped her button accordion in and out across her hollow chest. Bridget Maguire tortured our eardrums with her little tin whistle, and Sven Ahlberg blew into his flute. Anybody who could make a noise filed up to do it. Hayden Evans even thumped for a while on a washtub. No more than one song each, usually the same one they played the last whist-drive dance, and the one before. Matt had left his guitar at home, so we were spared another bout of "Land of the Silver Birch."

Once we'd eaten and started pushing back the tables for dancing, Taylor sent one of the brothers off to talk to Nora. "Just to watch, if she'd like," he said.

But the brother come back and showed his empty hands. "There!" I nearly said it out loud. "You should of known!" I didn't say it, though, because Taylor looked like he couldn't believe it. He stood up there by Johanna's piano during "All by Myself" scratching up under his hat and looking this way and that like a boy that couldn't believe his puppy ran away.

They didn't say nothing to each other, him and Johanna. I was watching. But as soon as Johanna hammered the last chord of "I'm Always Chasing Rainbows" she stood up and crossed the room and went out into the night without a word. She'd gone to town for a new haircut the day before – short as a boy. She also wore a dress I never seen before, pine-green, a bodice skirt with boxed pleats and one of them jacquettes.

Hueffner watched her go. He saw this the way he saw everything – plain as the nose on your face. "Schoolteacher's gone for the truant," he said. "An arithmetic problem don't have its answer yet."

Well, she came. Johanna stepped in through the door with her hand on Nora's elbow. Nora's head was high, as you'd expect, like someone who wasn't about to notice there was others in the room. She might of stood where she was if Johanna hadn't raised an eyebrow to make me give Nora my chair. Then she went to the piano again without even looking at Taylor and hammered another chord. Maude Pearson dragged The Portuguese onto the floor for a waltz.

Maybe Nora was just as nosy as the rest of us. Maybe Johanna had threatened her with something. Or maybe Nora was just plain ready for something interesting to happen to her outside the boundaries of Herbie Brewer's property. Anyway, she'd come. She'd even put on what must of been her best dress, a pale yellow crêpe de Chine straight-line. She was almost pretty. Well, she *could* be sort of good-looking in a narrow, gawky way. She even smiled at Ruby Evans and Mary Reimer, one on either side.

She made as though the dancers were all that interested her here, even when Taylor stood by the piano and launched into a song that nobody in that schoolroom had ever heard. Her expression never changed, even when it was plain the song was made-up, praising the strength and hard work of some unnamed woman who'd have his heart in his hands the whole rest of his life. If Taylor was a simpleton, he was still smart enough not to mention her name. He wasn't fool enough to praise her beauty neither, or make a public plea for affection. This would of only sent her away.

Frankly, I figured she wouldn't stay to the end of the song. But she stayed and applauded like everybody else, still acting like the song had nothing to do with her. She even got up and danced with two of her brothers, one after the other, and then with Matthew Pearson after Maude had prodded him into it. It didn't seem to cause her too much pain.

When Taylor crossed the room to ask for her hand in a waltz, she took her own sweet time before she stood up. A look of pain passed across her face so fast he likely didn't notice it. Her eyes darted around the room. Who was she looking for? Her father? Herbie Brewer? The coast was clear. At any rate, she raised her hands and stepped into Taylor's arms. She leaned back, kind of stiff, and let him steer her around that floor.

They danced that dance and the one after it and the one after that one too, but I never seen them speak. Not a word. She didn't speak with The Portuguese neither, when he tapped Taylor on his shoulder and whirled Nora just the once around the room. Still, there was a kind of general sense in the schoolroom that she had given in.

She was still there at the end. She even stayed to help put the school back in order, after Hueffner and me went home, and was even sitting beside him on the school steps when Johanna left.

Taylor looked scared it was only a dream, Johanna told me. "His face as red as the words on that Rogers Golden Syrup can."

She didn't hear what was said between them. She had to wait for Taylor to report whatever he was willing to report the next day. And then she passed it on to me in the Store.

She thanked him for the song, she even wept a little. Nora Macken bawling! Who would of thought it?

Now he was going to have to stop, she said. All of it. Everything. The songs and the building and the fencing and all the rest. He'd gone too far. They couldn't pretend no more that he was just an old friend helping her through a rough spot while her husband was away. He had to go. And he had to forget about her. She couldn't in a million years be who he wanted her to be. She wasn't the woman Wyatt Taylor needed and wanted and thought she could be for him.

"So he's going," I said.

"That wasn't the end of the conversation," Johanna said. "If she really wanted to get rid of him it was a big mistake to admit she wished they could turn back the clock."

"I shouldn't listen to this," I said. "Sometimes I talk too much. I think I'm going to keep something to myself but my mouth don't always get the message in time. And anyway, what sort of gentleman would tell a thing like that to you?"

"He didn't mean to tell me any of it. I had to work hard."

"How long did it take her to say it, did he tell?"

"Most of the rest of the night." She looked out the window for a while. "I couldn't sleep, so just before dawn I got up and walked down to the school – just to make sure we'd locked it. They were still there. They didn't see me." She still looked out the window, thinking something she didn't say. Then she said, "I don't think Wyatt Taylor will be going east for a while."

Matthew Pearson

Someone must have said something to Taylor. Maybe Hayden Evans or one of the Wintons drew his attention to that fire still burning in the mountains, reminding him that the settlement was still in danger and that every man in the place had taken a turn at trying to put it out. I suppose Taylor saw this in the only way he knew how: it was time he did his part. He decided to go up for a couple of days and do what he could, since so long as that fire was burning Nora was in as much danger as everyone else. If he'd kept his mouth shut the day he arrived, when everyone assumed that he'd just come down from there, he wouldn't have had to do this.

"Who told men that women want them to be heroes?" Maude said. "Not their mothers."

Maude had never seen for herself how the fire was fought, of course. They wouldn't let women go up, though she and a few of the other wives had offered to fight alongside their husbands. When the Company refused, the women were incensed. "It doesn't matter if you men scorch off your eyebrows and come home with blisters all over your stubborn hides," Maude said, "but you don't want us spoiling our lovely complexions! Or our delicate hands. I don't know what you think is happening to our hands while we scrub floors and wash dishes and boil the sheets in lye. Some of those men have probably never looked at their wives' hands for so long they think they are still as soft as they were when they laid eyes on them first."

Maude's hands were a little rougher than they used to be, but she took care of them the best she could, just as she clothed herself as smartly as made any sense in this place, with dresses she made from patterns inspired by pictures in catalogues. Maude's beauty came as much from her appearance of merely "making the best of it" as from her long limbs, or the green eyes and prominent

cheek bones she'd inherited from her splendidly handsome
mother, a woman who would be appalled to see what rough living
I'd brought her daughter to here.

By this time I was beginning to understand that it wasn't just
that Taylor wanted Nora Macken badly enough to work his fingers
to the bone and stay up all hours inventing ways to make her fall
in love with him again, he was incapable of withholding any effort
that might make *anyone* happy. "I don't know how they did it," he
explained, "but my folks convinced me that the worst crime a
person could commit is disappointing people. That's probably why
I work with explosives. You can usually think up ways for heat and
expanding gas to please someone. It'll probably put me in an early
grave, but there doesn't seem to be anything I can do about it."

"You could give it up," I said. "You could admit you're never
going to satisfy everyone no matter how hard you try. You could
move on."

"I'd only be doing the same in some other place."

Some other place was where I was beginning to think he
should be, but this might have been because of Charlie Sullivan.
Some other place was where Sullivan was by now, but I had no
idea where that might be, or why he had gone there. There wasn't
much satisfaction in a letter with no address inside. It was stamped
in Vancouver, but he'd probably just been passing through. He
thanked me for doing what he knew I would be doing without
having to think about it much – looking after his cattle, feeding
his dog, visiting his farm now and then. He didn't say where he
was going. He didn't say he'd return. He did not name plans of any
sort. He didn't even give a reason for leaving.

So now Taylor discovered one more thing about life in this
place the rest of us could have told him: that there was more than
just a lot of churning smoke up there in the hills. There was heat
and noise too, and wind, and flying sparks, and heavy burning
limbs that tumbled through the air. Wind snapped and flapped
the flames around, alive and greedy, racing across the crowns of

trees to strip every bough of needles and twigs and leaving tongues of flames behind to lap away at the trunks and lower bushes and go down amongst the networks of roots if there was oxygen enough to keep them alive.

It was mostly a matter of carrying a can of water on your back and a spray nozzle in your hand, squirting water on every telltale wisp of rising smoke, putting out embers, walking around in the burned-over parts making sure there wasn't anything left that could blaze up again. The worst of it was that you could be walking across solid burned-over ground and all of a sudden fall through to an underground furnace, setting a whole new inferno free to lay waste to whatever was left of the world.

The other thing you might be asked to do was use a shovel or axe, making a fire break, so that if the wind turned, the gap without trees would be too wide for the fire to jump. So far, no one had been able to cut down enough trees or turn over enough soil to make a dead space wide enough to keep this one contained.

We didn't know until afterwards what happened to Taylor up there, of course. And I wasn't told until long after everyone else had heard, since disasters of my own would mean I was not in any condition to care about anyone else.

When the fire had started a few weeks earlier, the logging company brought some of their equipment down out of the hills, but there were still steam donkeys and a lot of other machinery up one ravine at the head of one railway spur line. Company men were swarming all over the place, giving orders, estimating the damage, sending back reports to the office in town. They were the generals running the war. It was the evening of Taylor's second day up there that one of the Company bosses decided the fire was getting too close to their equipment. It had to be taken out. He sent the train up to get what they could, and the fire-fighters helped them load it.

I don't know why the straw boss chose to ask Taylor if he'd ever worked on a steam locomotive. Maybe for the same reason that everyone else seemed to think he could do anything you asked him.

"Rode one once," was all he shouted back, but it was good enough for the straw boss.

"You go with Corky," he said.

So Taylor's job was fireman shovelling coal on Corky Desmond's locomotive, hauling flatcars of expensive logging equipment to safety. Engines. Winches. Cables. Block and tackle. He didn't mind, he told me later. It was dark by the time they got going, and there was a fine strange feeling to it as they moved downhill through the night, with their lamp lighting up the tracks ahead, making everything on either side seem darker than a person could imagine. Animal eyes shone back in the light: deer, an elk, maybe a bear. For a while he thought it was worth crossing the continent on horseback just to ride on that throbbing monster down through the pitch-black timber, with all of nature watching him go by in the night.

That was before they saw what mischief was up ahead. The fire had come down a sidehill and started to eat up the wide timbered canyon they were entering. The wind had turned. Corky swore, "Goddammit," and pulled levers to slow them down. They couldn't tell yet if the flames were close to the tracks. The trouble with a train is that you can't make a detour when you don't like what you see ahead. So they snaked uneasily downhill through the trees, the fire coming into sight for a while and then disappearing behind a curve of stone outcropping, then coming into sight again.

The tracks followed the twists and turns of the river, with the canyon getting narrower as they descended, so they didn't know the fire had crossed the tracks until it was less than a few hundred feet ahead of them. Almost immediately they were engulfed in smoke, coughing and choking and holding rags to their mouths. Corky brought the locomotive to a stop, cursing both the Company and the fire.

They didn't have too many choices. They could leave the train where it was, jump in the river, and try to stay underwater long enough for the current to take them beneath the fire and beyond it – where they would have to walk for miles to a road, with that fire still on their tails. They could reverse, and try to push those cars uphill – and sooner or later have to abandon it anyway where it could be swallowed by flames, maybe all the way back where they'd started. Or they could work up a full head of steam and take a run at it, and hope to get through to the other side of the fire before the smoke killed them or the locomotive exploded and blew them all over the mountain.

"Goddamn sonofabitching fire," was all that Corky had to contribute to the discussion. "Stupid fucking Company."

Corky Desmond was an experienced engineer but he was not someone who kept a cool head in an emergency. He panicked. He jumped. Taylor thought he must have rolled down the slope and plunged into the river but he couldn't see for sure. He couldn't even hear the river for the roar of the fire.

Taylor's choices were fewer than Corky's. He couldn't swim. He didn't even think he could float. And he wasn't going to hold his breath under water while he was dragged through rapids and skeletons of fallen trees and got his head bashed against rocks. He'd watched Corky close enough to know how to get this clumsy parade of machinery moving. First he soaked the rags in more water and wrapped them around his hands and head, leaving his eyes uncovered. Then he got the engine moving about as fast as it could go down that slope, and plunged right into the flames with several tons of steel behind him, hoping there'd be a far side not too distant down the tracks.

It didn't last too long but it lasted long enough. He couldn't stand still, he had to keep turning – he'd rather roast on a spit than burn to a crisp standing still. He turned like that right through the fire and out into dark again without the engine blowing up or stalling. He was alive. He hoped Corky was alive too, but there wasn't much he could do about that in the dark. He thought about stopping, maybe going down to search along the river bank. But now he saw that the wooden steps on both sides of the locomotive were burning. Instead of stopping, he pulled the throttle up full and the train went rocketing through the night, while he crawled back to try beating out the flames.

The flames spilled off the moving engine onto the timber they passed. Fir and hemlock flared up on either side like torches dipped in pitch. A lengthening trail of scattered flames stretched out behind him. When he looked back he saw he'd turned the railway grade into a sizzling fuse that was bringing the fire down out of the hills as fast as any reel of Black Clover cord could have done.

He knew he didn't want to bring it all the way to the settlement. Instead of outracing the flames, he could see he was dragging an inferno along behind him, so he pulled more levers and brought the whole parade to a screeching halt. The locomotive had to be left where it was while he set out running down the tracks. He thought he was doomed. That fire could travel faster than he could run. I'm sure he thought he was offering himself as a sacrifice – by stopping the train where he did, he was giving himself up in order to keep the fire from following him right to our doorsteps.

In a way, he'd already brought it too close. He'd got as far as Howard Stokes's place before he stopped the train. He was surprised to see a light. Someone had come out with a lantern onto the porch of a house he hadn't known was there, to see what was going on. This was Howard Stokes, who, like everyone else, had been sleeping with one eye open and had got up to find out why a logging train was roaring down from the hills in the middle of the night.

Mary Reimer

I knew that fire was going to come for him. When he was up in the hills there fighting that thing I prayed hard it wouldn't hurt him too bad, and it never touched him. But now it was going to come down and get him at home. I tried real hard to pray again but I couldn't think. My brain was going in circles. It was coming for him but it was going to hurt the boys too. "We got to get out of here," I said. But he says, "Not yet." I said, "We got to get the boys out of here." But he says, "Not yet, Mary, god-dammit, stop nagging."

"Stupid contrary bullheaded Sweitzer!" I told him I'd knock him out with a two-by-four and take the boys. I'd let him burn. I never should've left the Reserve. "To hell with your piece of stupid marriage paper," I said.

He didn't listen. He'd been down in that hole behind the house all week. At first it was just a hole that he never filled in, left by a pulled-out stump. "One of these days, the boys," I told him a hundred times. In my head I seen it filling up with water the first good rain and both boys drowning right behind their own house. "Yeah, yeah," he said. He didn't like it neither.

Then he went down with his shovel and started to make it wider. Every night he went down there with his shovel and dug a little more. When he come in he was too tired to sleep. "What you doing this for?" He wouldn't say. He slept a little and then he got up early and started digging again. The hole got wider. And then he started making it deeper too.

Then I seen that he knew the fire was coming for him. One night he come into the house and said, "Give me a hand, willya Mary?" He carried out two kitchen chairs and took them down into the hole, backing down this ladder he made. You could put the whole of our house down in there if you wanted.

"We got to send the boys out," I told him. But he wouldn't answer. "We got to send them as far as MacIntoshes' anyway," I said. "If they're closer to the Store there'll be someone to take them out."

"Get the bedding," he said. "Get the dishes. Holler when you get to the heavy things."

He went out to the sawmill and started taking it apart. Piece by piece he took it down the ladder into the hole. That fat man is crazy, I thought. I carried the towels and sheets and pillows down into the hole and stacked them in one corner where he put gunnysacks against the dirt. Back and forth in the dark, up and down that ladder. I carried the clothing out of the chest of drawers. "We ain't gonna let some goddamn fire come down and wipe us out," he said.

Maybe he wasn't so stupid after all. Something in the air-smell told me it would be coming for us by morning.

Matthew Pearson

At first I thought I was feeling the usual flush of dread that would be pushed aside once I remembered where I was. I'd been waking at 4:20 every morning for years. But then I noticed there was something different in the air – a different sound, a different smell, a different colour in the light outside the window.

From the porch I saw that the sky was boiling with brown smoke, one great rolling thundercloud out of which bits of leaves and twigs and bark were smacking down onto the ground and bouncing like hail. Across the tops of the timber I could see the fire had come down off the mountain. There was a roar – I couldn't be sure if I was hearing it with my ears or if it was coming up from my feet through the nerves of my legs. Milk cans blew across the yard.

So I roused the others – Maude, Elizabeth, Tanner, Willie curled like a snail beneath his blankets. Donald.

"But where will we go?" Maude said. "Are you certain this is necessary?" She went from one room to the other, looking at things. I knew what she was thinking. What could she bear to leave?

"Take a change of clothing for the children."

"And food?"

"There'll be someone to find you food if you need it."

She whirled in a doorway. "But where will we go?"

"Maudie!" I said. "There'll be people in town ready for you. Everyone else will be there."

It was enough. She took hold of herself. Maude did not easily fall apart. "Elizabeth," she said. "Fill your pillow slip with clothing. Tanner's too."

I sent Tanner out to start the Ford and bring it up to the house. Then I helped Elizabeth make decisions. "A book, Papa. I must have a book. Two books. What if we don't get home today?"

"Take two books then and hurry."

"What if there's nothing left?" The thought had only now crossed her mind. "I can't leave everything."

"You'll not stay here," I said. "You'll get out and save your freckled hide." I assured her the fire would probably die out before it got to our place, or change directions. We were playing it safe.

Everything would probably be just where she'd left it, she could be home again by night.

Then I went down behind the barn and filled the water troughs. There was water in the ditch as well. I opened the gates but there wasn't much more I could do for the cattle. I turned the chickens free to look after themselves. Then as soon as I saw that the others were ready to get into the Ford and head for town I saddled Orion and rode off to see if anyone needed help.

Tom Winton

It's a wonder we didn't burn in our beds while we slept. If I blamed anybody it would be Ma. She was always the first one up, crack of dawn, hollerin' across the ladder. "Up and at-em!" By the time we come in from the garage she'd have our bowls of porridge on the table and the coffee boiling.

But she wasn't feeling so hot for the last while. Complaining all day long. We stayed away from the house as much as we could. Stomach cramps. Headache. There wasn't nothing she couldn't find to gripe about. Backache too. Even her feet were giving her trouble.

She slept in the house. Me and John, we slept above the garage. We didn't have no windows to see out of, night and day was all the same to us. So her shout was the first we heard of it. When I came down the ladder she was in the doorway looking out. Eyes bulging from her head.

Burning twigs were falling out of the sky. Smoking leaves and flaming sticks. Maybe it was the roar that woke her, like fifty locomotives all at once. It was starting on the timber out the front of our place. Right across our road. Three hundred yards away and coming fast. I could see we wouldn't get out.

Hayden Evans

What I thought when I saw that bastard coming was "To hell with it." I'd had enough. That bloody piece of land had been nothing but a backbreaker from the first. What did I have to show for it? A two-room tarpaper shack. A bit of garden I didn't have the energy to work in when I got home from the bloody job in the woods. And a wife that was always reminding me she never expected to live in a place like this. So when I saw that fire coming our way I laughed. "You want 'er, you can have 'er!" Then I told Ruby to pack her things and say good-bye to the stump ranch, we was heading somewhere else. I harnessed the horses and whistled up the spaniel Clemenceau, and couldn't stop chuckling till we were a couple miles down the road. Ruby started crying because she'd forgotten her mother's ring, so I told her if she wanted the ring she could damn-well walk back for it because I was going nowhere near that place for the rest of my life.

Leena Hueffner

Nell Richmond was the first, rattling my door at five in the morning. "If you let me put my housecoat on I'll make us some coffee," I said. She thumps into the Store with her walking stick and turns around a few times and then limps out again. Then, a minute later, she's back. "Haven't they talked about this, dear? Isn't there some procedure?"

By this time I seen for myself what'd got her out of bed to lace her corsets and twist her hair up into that unicorn spike and nag her husband into driving them up the road. I guess I'd been waiting for it.

"They've talked about it," I says. "You're doing the right thing. Word will come here first."

As soon as I got the coffee on, I started gathering the mail out of the pigeon holes and tossing it into the middle of a tablecloth I never liked. Then I tied the four corners together and dragged the bundle out to the door. Sven Ahlberg could take it to town the first time he went in with his taxi.

"My mother was planning to visit from Winnipeg," she says. "I was already wondering what she'd think about what I have to put up with here. Can you imagine what she'd say about *this*?"

❦

Lillian Swift

Mr. Swift would have had us flee to safety, but I got up at dawn, as I frequently did, and went down through the woods towards the beach with my sketching pad, in search of wildflowers I might draw for my letters Home. Larkspur grew in the grassy areas then, a rich dark purple flower on stalks as tall as my waist. Wild spiraea hung from its bushes like heavy clusters of seed pearls, just beginning to turn from the cream of spring to the toasted hue of summer. Red and yellow columbines nodded delicate heads along the trail – each bloom the shape of five tiny doves in a ring, as its name implies. "Culverwort," my grandmother told me it had been called in olden times. The pigeon plant.

Into the woods I went, away from the footpath, in search of the calypso fairyslipper, those purple orchids so deliciously perfumed I could sometimes smell them before my eyes had detected them in the shadows. Beneath a mighty cedar I found where I might sit and study a perfect specimen.

Would the Almighty bring us to this place and then abandon us? I was certain we would be safe without fleeing. I sketched with my back to the fire, to show my disregard, and kept my thoughts focused on the perfection implied by that splendid flower.

Matthew Pearson

I rode to Charlie Sullivan's place and went inside to see if there was anything valuable he might want me to save, but nothing looked more important than anything else. For all its tidiness, the whole house had the sad empty look of a building whose mistress had deserted it and whose owner was interested in only getting by.

When I stopped in on the Reimers to make sure they were ready to get out of there, Carl turned his thick pock-marked face away and said that they weren't going anywhere. They had too much to lose, they would stay and fight it if they had to. They had a good well, he said. They had plenty of gunnysacks they could soak and put on the roof if sparks began to land. "Well, you'd better send the boys out anyway," I said. But he shook his head. He would send the boys up onto the roof if he needed to, to stamp out flying sparks.

"Where's Mary?" I said, since I was sure that Mary would have more sense.

So he took me round behind his house to where Mary was step-ping up out of a great hole as wide as the house, brushing dirt from her hands. The boys came up behind her on a ladder of unpeeled poles, as crooked as everything else that Carl Reimer ever made or even thought of. "You got it wrong if that's a reservoir you're building," I said. "It's not a rainstorm that's coming. The only thing it will fill with is ashes and burning limbs."

Then I saw they had moved their entire household down there, or nearly all of it. Tables, chairs, beds, chests of drawers, dishes. Machine parts too. And circular saw blades. Tools. "We're about to fill her in," Carl says. "You're just in time to give us a hand. First I got to go down and lay some boards over top of it all." He had a whole lot of warped and crooked and pitch-bleeding Reimer sawmill boards lying against the mountainside of dug-out dirt. Slab-wood too.

"I think you'd better just get in your vehicle and follow the rest of us to town."

Mary didn't even blink. She'd been living with that lunatic too long. "You could help us get the kitchen stove down there before you go, eh," she said. "We couldn't lift it ourselves."

I turned around and rode back to the Store. By this time there were wagons and cars and trucks and every sort of transportation parked in front, and people standing around and talking. What they were doing there I don't know. If they thought they had the time to stand gossiping they should have stayed longer at home gathering things to take, or putting their best belongings down the well.

They were waiting for permission. The Maguires, Sandy MacKay, the Richmonds. They didn't want to be the first to leave, they didn't want to stay too long and perish. If you stayed home you didn't know what anyone else was doing, you could be the only one left behind. If you came to the Store, you could find out what was going on. Leena Hueffner would sell drinks out of her icebox until she was choking on smoke.

Hayden and Ruby Evans came out the old railroad grade as if the fire was licking their heels. They didn't so much as slow down to wave good-bye, they swung out onto the road and headed for town, their dog yapping behind them.

"The Martins?" I said.

Hueffner shrugged. "Damned if I know," he said. Sometimes he behaved just a little too much like an outside observer for my taste. Today the Texan was watching the natives go about saving their necks as if it had nothing to do with him. His bearing suggested that a man with only one arm had already faced much worse.

Nobody had heard from the Martins so I rode up the logging grade and veered off down their narrow lane. Pandemonium. They were trying to get everything they owned out of their little house of squared-off logs and onto the back of their truck. By this time there were burning twigs falling from the sky, with fires starting up wherever they fell. There were small fires licking at their roof. Their little boy ran across the yard with a cushion, then yelped and dropped the cushion, slapping at his head. His hair was alight. I grabbed him and wrapped his shirt up over his head, then rushed him over to the well and pumped water onto his scorched and stinking hair.

"You damn fool, Frenchie," I said. "You want to see these youngsters burned? Get that outfit on the road!"

He went back inside for one more load so I ran to his truck and told his wife to get in. "You drive?" She was too shy to look at me but shook her head, so I told her to slide over behind the wheel. "Advance the throttle," I said, and showed her how. "Now, retard the spark. Pull out the choke. That's it, now turn the key." I went to the front and cranked the engine and ran back, as soon as it started, to advance the spark. The children climbed in. "There's nothing to it once you've started moving."

As soon as he saw his truck taking off without him, Martin came hollering across the yard and jumped behind the wheel himself. "*Calisse!* Get outa my way," he hollered, as if I were the one who'd been holding him up.

When I got back to the Store, Hueffner came out again and held my horse's bit and frowned up at me with that weak left eye of his closed. "What about your own people?" he said, and looked away, to suggest it didn't matter much to him one way or the other. "They planning to sit where they are?"

"Hell, no," I said. "I made sure they were packed and ready before I left myself."

"That's what I figured," Hueffner said. "But Leena, she could tell you every wagon, horse, or truck that's gone down that road this morning, and she says she didn't see no other Pearsons today but you. Maybe you better go have a look."

Christina Ahlberg

My husband spent most of that day on the road. As the taxi owner he was expected to ferry people to safety. Sometimes it was other people's children, when the parents were not quite ready to leave themselves. "The Pied Piper," he joked, when he stopped to fill a water jug. Back and forth he drove, up and down every road and lane where he knew he might be needed, collecting people who lived closer to the fire than we did. The McLaughlin-Buick was overloaded every time it went past our house. He squeezed the horn so that Monica and Gunnar would wave.

"Will you be all right, Christina?"

I assured him that I would be fine, of course, having the horse and buggy if we needed to escape in a hurry.

"You will keep your eye on the children?"

I was confident I would know when it was time. He was worried, I suppose, because once a horse had come close to running down our Gunnar, who had dashed out onto the road when he was meant to be holding my hand. "Children must be watched every moment," he said, as though I didn't know better than he did how quick and unpredictable small children can be. Before our marriage I was the teacher back in Fort Vermilion, Alberta, presiding over every grade from one to eight – nine children in all. I hadn't completed high school myself, though I had always been a reader. No child had suffered disaster while in my care.

Naturally I did not expect any business in the tea room. That was not my reason for remaining at home for as long as I did. Even on a normal day there was only a little business, except for people stopping to arrange matters with Sven – to deliver their children to cousins in Willow Point, or to bring out a new chair they had ordered from town. Often they felt obliged to stay for a cup of tea or coffee and a slice of my *Norska linser*, and since the tea room was also our parlour, this was always a comfortable situation for a restful chat.

I could see the traffic passing by on the road and I doubt that anyone even looked our way, so intent were they upon getting to safety. I concentrated on my tasks – this was a day for scrubbing floors. It would seem ridiculous afterwards, getting down on my knees to scrub floorboards while neighbours were fleeing from floors they might never see again. I suppose that is what I have always been like. Something will not allow me to act like the others. Something will not permit me to feel alarm, even when there is good reason for it. However, I knew enough to check the sky every so often, so that I would know when the fire was getting too close, and I knew enough to make sure I was aware of the children's whereabouts, and the horse.

When I looked up to find Johanna Seyerstad standing in the doorway, I thought at first that she was perhaps a passenger in the McLaughlin-Buick and had volunteered to replenish Sven's water supply. But I saw immediately that something was wrong. She looked about the room like someone seeing it for the first time, wondering how she had got here. "Oh, Christina," she said. Perhaps she hadn't noticed me at first, down on the painted green floor.

I stood up immediately. "Come in," I said. "Sit down. I'll have coffee for you in a few minutes." I hurried back to the kitchen. "The *tebrod* is yesterday's, though."

"No," she said, having followed me as far as the kitchen door. "I hoped you might help. Nora refuses to leave."

Charlie MacIntosh

I could smell it even in my sleep. I was riding my bike up the road from the beach, in a hurry to get home in the dark. The bush was black and silent. The uphill road away from the beach was getting steeper, so that I had to stand on the pedals, working hard, wobbling this way and that. I had to get home before Mother noticed. The black woods on either side was inhabited by animals with eyes that could see me even though I could not see them. Owls. Deer. Raccoons. Bear. Cougars. Maybe even wolves. The sound of my tires on dirt could be sending out signals that would bring a pack of wild dogs to snap at my heels.

Both tires had gone flat. Loose rubber and metal wheel rims creaked and squealed against stones. Some of the sprockets had snapped off; the chain buckled and slid; the pedals slipped through part of every turn without doing me any good. The crest of the hill was still a mile away.

Cougars lay along the lowest branch of every overhanging tree. Their tails hung down, twitching. When they dropped onto my shoulders, their claws tore my shirt and dug long, painful bloody gouges down the flesh of my back as they fell to the ground and became part of the snarling crowd of cats at my heels. One of them would eventually get his teeth into the back of my neck and bring me down. This was what they did to deer.

My dad appeared at the crest of the hill with a light. "Harder, Charlie! Push harder! They havena' got ye yet, laddie. Keep pumping!" But he didn't come down the hill to fight off the mountain lions himself. "I'm waiting on ye, laddie," he called. He had no legs, he had blown off both his legs. He had to stay in the buggy, fighting with the reins, trying to keep the terrified horses from fleeing.

Then the largest cougar leaned down in front of me, putting its vicious face between me and my dad so that I couldn't see him any more, placing its claws on my shoulders, saying, "Come on. Let's go. Don't make a fuss now. Don't upset your poor mother."

Uncle Archie scooped me up and was carrying me through the house. "It's all right. Don't panic. We'll soon have you in the buggy and safely out of here."

"Where's Dad?" I said. "I want to go with my dad."

John Winton

We didn't have no choice. We had to get into the swamp. Tom said it looked like a stupid idea to him, the water only come up to our knees. But it was better than trying to fight our way out.

We'd took too long trying to talk Ma into leaving. She thought she'd be safer under the bed. By the time we dragged her out the door the flames were less than a hundred yards away. We were lucky there was still some water in the swamp, even if it wasn't much. Frog slime and mud. It stunk.

Ma put up a fight.

Well, she never liked to get her feet wet, and here we were telling her to wade in and sit. All the time she's screaming. It was that or fry, I told her! I put my hands on her shoulders and pushed her down. She thought I was gonna drown her.

Mary Reimer

My brothers Floyd and Jack, they never set foot on our place before. Nobody in my family ever came. I was dead to them. They never spoke one word or come near since I married Reimer.

But it was them, riding that old truck over the rocks and holes, raising dust.

"What you doing here?"

"Chief Sam and the old ones sent us," Floyd says. He gets down off the truck. Floyd is as broad as a horse across the chest and stomach but narrow as a fox below that. Jack is not so big. He stays behind the wheel with the motor running.

"Chief Sam never sent you," I says. "Chief Sam wiped the air clean of me long ago."

"Our mother told us to bring you home," Floyd says.

"Our mother told me I was closing a door that would never open," I tell them. "Has she found a second mouth to speak from now, or has the door fallen off its hinges?"

"What're they doin' here?" says Reimer, coming around the house with a shovel. He wouldn't speak to them. He wouldn't even look at them. He leaned on his shovel handle and looked at me. "Why're they standing there jabbering? Tell them to give us a hand, we got to get this done."

Floyd says, "You give me that shovel I'll bury you with the rest of the shit."

"Tell them to git," says Carl. Then he says, "Mary?" Meaning, You tell them two fat Indians to bugger off so you can get back to work with that shovel.

I closed my eyes a minute and prayed.

"They come to carry the stove," I tell him. "Come on," I says to Jack. "Git down here and give us a hand, eh."

Carl come up and we run planks under the stove, and each of us lifted one end of a plank. The boys come down off the roof and helped a little bit too. We carried the woodstove out and around to the back and put it down. Carl rigged up the ropes and the six of us lowered it into the hole.

"What good is burying all this if you're only going to be burned to ashes yourself?" says Jack. "Who you saving it for?"

"Tell him we won't be burned," Carl says to me. "We're going down there ourselves."

Both my brothers look into the hole. Then they look at me. Floyd says, "You better come."

"Start using that shovel," Carl says to me. He's got boards laid across the top of the stove, right across the hole.

"How you gonna breathe down there while fire's burning your house?" says Floyd.

"You never mind," Carl says. "We'll have our own air, don't you worry. I've rigged it so we'll be sealed off with our own little room. That fire won't take so long to go over. If we wait till the last minute and close it off behind us, there'll be enough down there to breathe until it's passed."

He's saying this to me as much as them.

"You better come with us," Floyd says again. "This *mesachie*-man is dangerous."

"Your sister don't want nothing to do with you," Reimer says.

"You better go," I tell them.

Floyd took hold of my arm and tried to drag me to the truck. But Reimer come after him with his shovel raised. Floyd let go and run at Carl and drove his head into Carl's stomach. Jack grabbed the shovel and tossed it to the side. The three men rolled on the ground, grunting and punching and throwing each other around. The boys tried to get in on it, too, but I shoved them away.

"Here, you," I yell. I grab up that long-handled shovel and bring it down on Floyd's back. "Git offa him." I swing it at Jack, too, but miss. They fall apart but go after each other again. Carl gets his hands around Floyd's throat so I swing the shovel again and again, not caring who I hit. All over them, all three. Arms, legs, heads, whatever gets in the way. So the men fall apart, cursing and holding the places the shovel hit.

"Git out of here," I tell them.

Floyd gets up first, and looks ready to yank that shovel out of my hands and beat me with it. I glare into his eyes, daring him to try. Jack gets into the truck and sits behind the wheel.

"Take the boys," I tell them.

"Don't you even try," Carl hollers, springing to his feet.

"Take them where?" Jack says. "To our mother's house?"

"It don't matter," I tell him, though our mother's house is small and filled with dogs. "Just get them outa here."

"Try it, I'll wring your necks," Carl says.

I'm still holding the shovel. "Shut up, you *kalakalahma!*" Then I get the boys into the truck. "This here's Floyd," I tell them. "This here's Jack." They never seen my brothers before. They never even heard of them I guess. "You can jump out at the Store if there's anybody there. Or you can keep on going to town. Pray hard, but keep your eyes and ears wide open. If your father don't get us killed I'll want to hear about every lie my crazy mother tells you. Don't fight with her stupid dogs."

John Winton

No chance it would change directions now. It was coming right for the swamp. Ma screaming and trying to get out and me holding on. She would've fried if I let her have her way. She couldn't outrun that thing if she had wings on her feet.

She went crazy. Maybe we would've gone crazy ourselves if we weren't so busy trying to keep her from running out of that swamp. She cursed us both. I figured if we ever got out alive we couldn't expect her to cook another meal for us. I saw the look in her eye and I knew she would slit my throat if she could. She just wanted out of there. But we had to duck under the water best we could, what there was of it.

I put my hand on Ma's head and hollered for her to take a big breath but she wouldn't stop screaming and thrashing around so I had to just push. It was her only chance. I had to push her head into the water and hold it there and hold my own head down under the water too and hope she wouldn't drown before it went past. Even under the muddy water I could hear the hot wind roaring over, even with Ma thrashing her arms around.

❧

Tanner Pearson

I tried. I told them to hurry. But Mother didn't believe the fire would reach us. She said the wind was bound to change direction. As soon as Dad was out of sight she said so long as we were ready to flee it was all right, she didn't see any reason to leave our house before we had to. Elizabeth kept thinking of things she wanted to take with her. Another book. A doll. Then she had to find her cat that had gone into hiding. Every time she went back to the house Mother went in as well to bring her back but she always came out with something else of her own that she wanted to save. Foolish things: her sewing basket, her bread tins, a pair of shoes.

I got Uncle Donald into the Ford and kept it running, ready to go, but then it shuddered and stalled. I started it again but after a while it died a second time. Then it wouldn't start at all. I cranked, but nothing happened, it didn't catch. I ran for the horses and got them hitched up to the wagon as fast as I could, and brought them up to the Ford so we could load the things we were taking.

The horses were nervous, so I had to stay on the wagon to hold them still. Uncle Donald was nervous too. He groaned and flung his arms around, he knew something bad was happening. Burning limbs were rolling across the fields now, bouncing and leaping and turning and dropping all around us. Sparks were landing. Small flames ignited on the chicken coop. An apple tree hissed and exploded into furry grey smoke. The wind was so loud you couldn't tell if you were hearing it or not. It was nearly as dark as night. Every fence post was on fire, like candles marking out the borders of the fields. The cows were bawling, running back and forth not knowing where to go, tails high with runny manure flying behind them, trampling Mother's garden into a chopped-up terrible mess. We were all coughing now, holding cloths to our mouths.

I had to watch the fire coming, I couldn't turn my back on it. It was like walking up the lane in the dark and getting the idea a bear or cougar was stalking you, you'd rather turn and walk backwards the rest of the way so you could see it coming. Otherwise you'd have that feeling low in your spine. Only this was worse than cougars, this was the end of the world roaring up towards us. The horses rolled their eyes, snorting and neighing and stomping their feet, scared and ready to flee, so I grabbed up two of my shirts and told Elizabeth to soak them under the pump and put them over their faces while I called on Mother to hurry. If the horses went off without us we'd be trapped.

That's when my father came down the lane. He jumped down off his horse already yelling, "What's the matter with you? I told you to get them out of here! Why aren't you in the Ford?"

He ran inside, breathing through a sleeve held up to his face.

Then the horses got their heads free and started running towards the chicken pen. I stood up and held back on the reins but they paid no attention. I pulled hard to one side, trying to work them around towards the house again, but the reins might as well have been made of paper. They turned at the fence and ran towards the barn and past the barn and into the pasture. There was no sense to it, they had gone mad, not even trying to find a way out but just running for that sense of escape that running gives. Uncle Donald was making terrible sounds in his throat. Not a word from Elizabeth behind me. When I looked back she was sitting bolt upright, holding her pillowcase, staring ahead at the horses out of eyes too scared to see.

Dad burst out of the house hollering, "Jump! Jump!" Running down towards us and waving his arms. I let go of the reins and ran to the back of the wagon, rolled Uncle Donald off the back and leapt off after him, hollering "Jump!" rolling across the grass until I came up against one of the stone half-walls of his "Ontario house." The wagon went bouncing on across the newly cleared field behind the horses with Elizabeth still in it. Dad ran after it hollering "Jump! Jump! Get out of there! Jump!" but Elizabeth didn't jump, she turned back to us with her mouth open, no sound that I could hear above the fire's roar, her arms still tight around that pillowcase. She was looking back at us when the horses and wagon went rattling and bouncing down the lane and into the flames.

Lillian Swift

"Is that what God has told you to do, paint pictures of flowers while your neighbours' lives are in danger?" It might have been Mr. Swift who said that or it might have been a voice in my head, but it brought me to my senses. I had been mesmerized by my own piety. Of course I was right to remind myself that God was not behind this horror, but that was no excuse for doing nothing to help.

We drove out to the road end with the idea of inviting them in. Our house was down near the beach, so if the flames got too close we could always go into the water. There was our rowboat, and a little raft that Mr. Swift had made of logs, chained to the shore so that it wouldn't float away.

They were moving down the road by now, families in wagons, some in cars with their lights on. Even the Hueffners – the Store had been abandoned. Some cattle came by too, unattended. And horses. Refugees. Mr. Swift said that it brought to mind Belgian peasants leaving their villages. You could see the same combination of reluctance and urgency in their eyes, he said. Frightened children, determined women with their gaze fixed ahead, slope-shouldered men bowed with defeat and wondering if they had given up and taken flight too soon.

They were bent on getting all the way to town, as though a forest fire could not wipe out a town as fast as a farm! All those wooden buildings. "The ocean!" I called. "The ocean will turn back the flames!" But they plodded by. "Leave!" they called out. "Get out of here yourselves, you'll perish!"

The fire wouldn't touch the ocean, I told them, we lived with the sea at our feet.

And there were Shadrach, Meshach, and Abednigo to inspire us. Oh I was tempted to remind them of those three gentlemen, tossed into the flames but able to walk out later without even the smell of the fire on their clothing. But they would only have laughed, if I had urged them to keep in mind the protection there was in such powerful faith. No, it wasn't mere faith. Those three men *knew*! But my early training, you see. There were things one didn't say. My mother's voice. Even in the face of this disaster I was restrained. And I could see that the road was all they could think of now, and town.

Only the Prices took up our invitation. Their smallest child had been burned on the arm by a flying brand. Mr. Swift stayed out at the road end to watch for others while I took the Prices in to the house and attended to that burn. Afterwards we had a little picnic down on the logs with our feet in the water. The smoke was frightful. At times we could barely breathe. But the fire did not trespass onto our property and we did not have to set sail on logs to escape it. We felt wholly protected precisely where we were. And we knew, too, that it could not last for ever. The fire would have to pass right by or change direction soon, or die out altogether. There was only so much for it to burn.

Christina Ahlberg

Frankly, I could see little point in trying. If a woman as stubborn as Nora Macken had decided to stay where she was, there wasn't much chance she could be persuaded otherwise. Certainly I was not willing to risk my children's lives on the slim hope that she would listen to reason. Still, since I could see that Johanna was not about to abandon the attempt, I called Gunnar and Monica and attached the horse to our buggy. If I must pay a visit to Nora Macken the children would have to come with me.

There was good reason to flee, I saw, when we had set out for Nora's. Why had I left it so late? I had heard of women who'd been stunned by lightning and wandered unconcerned inside a house that burned down around them. Down on the floor with a pail and scrubbing brush I had been almost oblivious. The sky had lowered its dark roiling belly to just above the treetops, blocking out all but the most unnatural sort of gauzy daylight. Hot red brands shot past like glowing bees. A bit of burning twig caught in the folds of Johanna's skirt and sent up an immediate curl of smoke. She stood up in the buggy to brush it away but others landed and had to be brushed away as well.

"Nora will have rags to tie over our hair," I said.

Nora had decided to burn, I think. Perhaps she saw herself in an heroic light of some kind. You could even imagine her getting pleasure from dying if she thought others would be sorry. She had barred the door from the inside, to make a funeral pyre of her shack.

Johanna was quick to act. A piece of slab-wood from the step was enough to break in the glass of the little window. But this only brought Nora to the window to abuse us.

"Hurry," Johanna said, "or you'll have Christina and her children on your conscience, as well as myself."

Since Gunnar and Monica were already close to tears, this was enough for them to set up a wail. But Johanna's was not the sort of appeal that had any hope of success, since Nora had never cared for me. She had decided I was one of those who thought themselves above her, though of course I had never thought any such thing. In a place like this there was no question of being "above" anyone else, since we were all scrambling for a living in difficult circumstances. But she was not someone to change her opinion in the face of logic. If I thought myself so much above her, why would I risk my own and my children's necks to get her to safety?

She shouted at us through the broken window. "Go away!"

Johanna found a large stone and stepped up to the door, ready to bash that open too. "We won't let you perish here."

But Nora surprised us by opening the door before the stone made contact with the boards. "I'm not a fool," she said, once Johanna had recovered her balance and tossed the stone aside. "I'll leave when I'm ready to leave."

"How?" Johanna said, a challenge. She meant that Nora did not own a horse, or any sort of vehicle.

"On shank's mare if I have to," Nora said.

Since Mr. Taylor had been up in the mountains for two or three days, she could only mean that she was waiting for her father. This fire had given him an opportunity to overlook her headstrong break from the family. She was giving him the chance to recall that she was still his daughter, and that he still cared what happened to her. She was – and I imagined this to be a brilliant insight – a girl who was waiting for Daddy to forgive her.

But Johanna knew this woman better than I did. "Taylor is probably trapped behind the fire. He'll expect you to have the good sense to wait in town where it's safe."

"Johanna, the children," I pleaded. Monica had climbed down from the buggy to pull on my skirts, her face streaked with sooty tears.

"Go," Nora said.

"Well then, you're a fool, Nora!" Johanna said, pushed beyond the limits of her patience. "To throw away your life on the chance some man will come to the rescue."

The sound of rapid footsteps from behind us drew our attention. Someone was running up the lane, coattails snapping at his heels. Perhaps Nora was not such a fool after all.

"Mr. Taylor," I said.

Johanna said, "Ahhh. . . ."

Nora smiled a terrible smile, like the schoolyard girl who is pleased to see you have torn your skirt and will be whipped for it. There was pleasure in it, and of course relief, but it was as though she had just been given permission to show her dislike for us openly.

Tanner Pearson

I tried. I got my father's horse hitched up to the milk cart as fast as I could but he wouldn't get in. Mother wouldn't get in either, she was hollering about Elizabeth. But he pushed her up into the cart with Willie in her arms and then lifted Uncle Donald up and told us to *Git*. I told him to get in too but he didn't seem to hear. "Go! Go!" he hollered. He slapped the horse's rump to get her moving. Then he ran down across the new field towards the lane the wagon had gone down. It looked as if he were going to run right after it into the flames but I didn't stop, I got that horse moving as fast as it could with the weight it wasn't used to dragging behind it.

I couldn't bear to hear Mother. Trying to comfort poor little screaming Will but sobbing at the same time herself, and saying Elizabeth's name. "He'll find her," I said. "Maybe she wasn't hurt." I kept the horse going as fast as it would go. Out to the road and then down the road past Mr. Sullivan's road and the Store. Mr. Hueffner was out on the road waving us on, his face black and his clothing in tatters. Soon everyone would look like Wyatt Taylor. "Keep going!" he shouted. "Don't stop now. Right into town."

We passed right by the Korsakovs, who had stopped to pick up something that had fallen off their truck. Mrs. Korsakov waved cheerily at us, as though this were a great adventure. "Oh my God, your father will perish too," Mother said. "I know him. He'd rather die than lose Elizabeth. Tanner, we have to go back!"

I pretended not to hear.

"Someone has to go back," Mother said. "We can't leave both of them in the fire." She wiped a handkerchief over her face and blew her nose. Then she tried to stand up. The Barclays were pulling out of their gate in their truck, the back of it loaded with daughters. "Stop!" she said, grabbing at the reins.

We pulled up beside the truck where Mother could speak to Mr. Barclay through his window. "You must turn back," she said. "Matthew has gone looking for Elizabeth. You must fetch him, you have to help them both."

Mr. Barclay looked alarmed, maybe because he had never seen Mother like this. "I haven't the room, Maude," he said. "I have to get these girls to safety first. Then I'll come back."

When the Barclays had pulled ahead of us she said, "You'll have to go back when we get to town. No, I won't have you lost as well. Someone else will go."

She said nothing for a while after that. The baby had stopped crying now as well. "I don't know how I allowed myself to fall apart like that," she said. "Nothing good ever comes of losing control. He'll be fine. He has to be fine. They both do. What do we know about fires? For all we know you could break through to the far side in a matter of seconds, with nothing but a few small burns."

We both knew more about forest fires than that. Those flames could be burning back there for miles, and even beyond that there would be trees crashing down and fiery limbs thrashing their way through the air. Fires gone underground. But I wasn't about to say this. I shut my mouth and kept us going as fast as we could to town.

Matthew Pearson

I knew better than to run straight into that fire, though I ran far enough to singe my hair and burn my eyebrows off and dry my face to hot paper before I came to my senses. I could not save Elizabeth if I were dead myself. I retreated before that wall of flames as far as the spring, Taylor's "well at the end of the world," and climbed inside the open box to sink to my chin.

When the fire ignored the well, I ran up to the house and found gloves, and changed into my thickest boots, and grabbed up burlap sacks to wrap around my arms or even my head if I should need to. Then I took my 30:30 down off the wall and loaded it, and put more shells in my pocket before slinging it across my back. All this at a run. I hurried back to the spring to soak the burlap. I'd seen enough of fire to know what I might expect.

By this time I could see it had turned. By whatever reason or unreason that governed these things, it had licked along the wall of the barn and then decided to veer to the west and miss our buildings altogether, at least for now. So when I ran back down the lane in the direction the horses had gone with Elizabeth I was not running into a wall of fire but into a blackened world of drifting smoke and burning snags. I was still hollering, of course.

Smoke rolled out to greet me and even surround me. Inside its grey shifting clouds I ran down the wheel ruts past the abandoned walls of my dreamed stone house into what was half-cleared pasture (now burning stumps and crackling bushes) and deeper into the second-growth timber. Coughing. The ruts would lead me to an alder firewood lot and the natural clearing of a shallow swamp. Daisy and Joe might have risked the fire for the safety of the water.

If this was punishment, it was already more than enough. I tripped and fell to my knees, my gloved hands in smouldering twigs. And rose, to stumble on, beating out the smoking gloves against my thighs.

The taller firs and cedars were dark smoking poles stripped to hairy twigs in their upper boughs. Alder and willow still burned. The fire had gone through so fast that the smaller bushes had been bent by the force of the wind and stripped, scorched, eaten up on only the upper sides, leaving the undersides green. Bowing in the direction of the departed flames.

A limb dropped to the ground ahead of me and flared up. Small fires were burning all around. Flames licked up the trunks of the larger second-growth timber, blazed and roared in the pitchy stumps, shot like a lighted fuse down the length of low evergreen limbs that had somehow escaped the first assault. Everywhere smoke drifted. It was impossible to see more than a few feet ahead. My eyes watered and stung. It was painful to keep them open.

It was like searching for someone in the poisonous clouds of a
gas attack. I couldn't breathe without choking. Wrapping one of
the damp gunnysacks around my neck and across the lower half
of my face, I shouted from within it. There was uproar all around,
of crashing limbs and crackling fires. There were howls in the distance, too, I believe, of pain.

The earth had been layered with ash, with half-burnt fallen
limbs, with drifted boughs and bushes. And the dead. A cow,
maybe one of my own or one of Charlie Sullivan's herd, lay on
its side. There was little that was cowlike to it now, except its
shape. Burnt, broiled, roasted, melted, a crisp bovine hump in the
blasted earth. It must have been one of my own, since Charlie
sawed the horns off cattle as soon as he'd bought them.

A pheasant looked as though it had crashed headlong out of
flight into a burning bush. A second cow had died with a heavy
limb, still burning, across her back.

The voice was not my own. *C'est là qu'il faut chercher.* Somewhere in the drifting smoke, ahead of me.

But it was not her in the drifting smoke, it was a slender tree,
stirred by the moving air. Behind it was the wagon. Daisy stood,
though sagging. Joe was down on his side, his thick belly heaving
mightily. They had dragged the wagon into this weedy swamp as
I thought they might, a natural clearing with little to burn. No
doubt there'd been some water in it when they got here. Damp
mud at least. It would have boiled around their fetlocks. Now it
was as scorched and dry and smoky-ashed as everything else.

The horses breathed, but with pain. They coughed. Groaned.
Joe heaved, as though to bring up his internal organs. There was
a gash of bleeding flesh on his back where I suppose a limb had
fallen. And black blisters where his haunches had been cooked.
Daisy's eyes had been scorched of vision.

There was little point in unhitching the wagon. There was
not much wagon left – only iron wheels, iron axles, iron bolts in
the scorched wooden tongue. Neither I nor the horses could

wait. The gunshots, I thought, might bring her back. If she heard.

If she'd leapt free of the wagon, she might have run on ahead to where the world had begun to cool.

If that was the case, she had not got far. She sat beside a green elderberry bush at the edge of the swamp. The bush had not been burnt, nor had Elizabeth any sign of fire or smoke upon her. Her curls were untouched. Her dress. Her freckled skin had not a smudge of soot. She sat as though she'd been lowered from the sky onto this tiny green island long after the fire had passed through. Nothing else in all this blasted world had been left so perfectly untouched.

Her hand, even on the floor of this dying furnace, was chilled.

There is no remembering the next few minutes of my life. I may have knelt and lifted her immediately in my arms, or I may have howled like an animal and beaten my head against the charred trees before lifting her in my arms and beginning to walk. I do not return to the house, for some reason I may never know, but carry her farther into the woods and across the back line of my property into the nearest of Patrick Maguire's smoking fields. The Maguire cottage has collapsed, joists and rafters and studs have fallen gracefully, folding into a tidy smouldering pile. The paint has been scoured from boards, or blistered. Only the Connemara fences they have built from the stones of their fields are left standing, though they too are black and smoking from fallen limbs. The Maguires are not here. Patrick will weep until his potato nose is red, and will blame God until the priests rebuke him for it.

I wander west from Maguires' and up the dirt road (why? why?) and cross the highway and carry her now (hands bare so that I won't smudge her with the filthy gloves) up the devastated slope of the opposite ridge, and come out of the stripped and blackened pines into a clearing where there is a smouldering heap of collapsed tangled lumber, it is the remains of a sawmill, and a house, though there is little left that you could call a house, only blackened uprights, collapsed roof, walls fallen outward onto the ground where they are being eaten now by small, mean spirals of smoke.

A woman's head appears from beneath the earth, like a curious marmot. Then a broad torso. Then a full soft woman standing beside the hole. Is there a doorway leading from hell? She has come up from beneath the earth but, like Elizabeth, has not been touched by the flames. "Here, let me take her, here."

She means the child in my arms.

"Poor child. Oh, Mr. Pearson, how did this happen? Poor little child."

She takes the perfect child from me, and carries her towards the smouldering ruins as though the house were still intact, but turns with a cry of surprise and heads for the doorway to the underground.

A voice from my throat makes noises.

"Don't take her away!"

I am trying hard to say it.

"Reimer!" she cries. "Here you, Carl Reimer! Bring me up a sheet, you. And a blanket!"

A second figure appears at the door in the ground, and stands in earth to his waist looking at me.

"Matt?"

"The girl," the woman says. "Get down and bring up a sheet I can wrap her in."

The fat man disappears. Then he appears again with a white folded cloth that he hands to his wife. In the other hand he holds a milk pail. "Water," he says. He puts the pail on the black powdery earth and scoops out an overflowing cup, spilling water on his boots, and offers it to me.

But my hands are empty. "Elizabeth?" There is a world of smoking snags out there to search through yet.

The man pulls at my arm.

"Stay here," the woman says. "I'll find something for them burns."

But I stumble past the heap of sawmill timbers and into the stripped black woods, running, or trying to run, with the voices behind me weaker.

There is no Elizabeth here. There is a dead four-spike deer. There is a willow grouse stripped of feathers. There is the shape of someone's cow on its side, a black bubbled hide, eyeballs pale and huge. There are tiny birds attached to limbs, small dark roasted figures fused to perches. Other birds lie about on the dark, papery, evil-smelling ground. Robins, sparrows, meadowlarks, cowbirds, it's impossible to tell.

The stench is thick, this is like breathing a thick rotten soup. When I am tripped by roots again and fall to my knees it is to vomit sour liquid onto the earth. But my burning knees and hands drive me to my feet. There are fallen limbs here that glow red within a coat of white ash, this is a dying campfire I am stumbling through.

Charlie Sullivan's house has escaped the end of the world, though it stands not far from a giant willow that has been stripped and baked, a twisted figure out of wrought iron. When Sullivan doesn't open the door I stagger down his steps and across his yard. "Charlie, you tried to warn me."

Beyond there is only devastation. Black earth, black stumps, black snags, everything smoking, everything licked by flames. A tree falls, and there is a hiss. A staggering blinded cow groans hideously out of a featureless face. I remove the rifle from my shoulder and put an end to it. I would put an end to all of this if I could. I plod on. Looking for – I forget what I'm looking for. Is there a way out of this? A hole in the ground, perhaps. A sunken road that leads to a door in the earth that leads to some tunnel and safety, another world. But I have lost that too, that door, and the woman who came out of the earth and the man with the water pail.

No doors open in the earth of Wintons' back pasture. Though they are a good distance from me, the smoke here has cleared enough for me to see the two figures up by the house, and for

them to see me. "Pearson?" They holler me up, but I mustn't stop,
they'll only want to talk, those two. But they come down the
slope, two long, loose, skinny bony-jawed men who look as though
they've been rolling in pig wallow. Even their hair is plastered to
their skulls with mud.

"What're you doin' here?" says John.

"We come through it all right," says Tom, excited as a boy. "We
hid in the swamp."

"We could've been boiled alive," says Tom, "but it turned away
in time."

"Look here," says John, getting serious when he sees I am about
to leave. "You can't go walking in that! Lookit, your boots are
smoking!"

And Tom. "Git up to the house and we'll see what Ma can do
for them clothes. She ain't mad at you, she's only mad at us."

But I cannot stop for Mrs. Winton to dress me. I leave them
behind and head west again, and cross another road, and walk
through the smoking remains of Hayden Evans's place. The house
is still standing but it won't be standing for long. Smoke leaks
everywhere. "This is a terrible joke the bloody government has
played on us," Evans once said. "Why didn't they throw us into a
hard-labour prison camp somewhere instead?"

He should not have built a house, no one should have built a
house in this place. Here you can be killed by either side. I have
been left behind to find my own way out through the kingdom
of the dead past young hemlock and white pine and alder as
naked and pitiful as the bones of the dying who cry out for help.
I am stumbling.

Through another dried-up, licked-up, sucked-up swamp, and
over a smouldering ridge. Here is Armus and Aili Aalto's little box
home, painted white and green like a house in Finland. *Suomi.* It
is untouched by flames. The barn is untouched as well. And the
chicken shed. And the orchard trees. And the little cedar-shake

brow of roof over the doorway to the root cellar, which has been dug into the side of the hill. Aalto and then his wife and their boy and finally a dog come up out of the root cellar like silent gnomes to watch me pass by. There is no point in stopping, since I can see that no one I am looking for is amongst them.

I am straining now to see with eyes that are watery and sore and swollen almost closed. It is like looking out through a slit in a barn door. But I can see that I have brought myself to a steam-bath house by a river, where a fringe of trees is still green, and where others are here before me. Mallard ducks bob near the weedy bank. A small black bear stands to its belly in the current, nervous and uncertain about me, shifting its head, ready to charge me or run. Farther on, three Holsteins stand facing upstream as though waiting for word from that direction that it's safe to go back to dry land. Aalto's sorrel mare is tied to a tree, swaybacked and placid, a few feet out from the bank. A second horse has freed himself, and drags his rope downstream as though he knows the river will eventually take him all the way to town.

I let myself be led by moving water further from the smoking battlefield and deeper into green, still unassailed by fire or shells. Here are trees only lightly scorched, and brittle but living grass, and wild rosebushes with a few pale flowers left clinging to the stems. And then, half-hidden behind the narrow trunks and sagging leaves, there appear the roofless walls and empty windows of the ruin. There are no villagers. None of the village houses are here. Alders have grown up where houses once stood. Everything but the shelled and crumbling church has been reclaimed and consumed by the earth. But this, I know, is what I have been travelling towards all along.

I fall to my knees in the gaping doorway. I am alone here. The killing has become a distant roar. A familiar alder grows from a crack in the floor and reaches beyond the empty windows to match the height of the concrete gable ends.

Here! creep,
Wretch, under a comfort serves in a whirlwind.

I have come to this little French church to ask something of God. What is it? Not comfort, not consolation. I must be inconsolable. It is too late for anything else. If God will not reverse what has happened, then I am too late for anything. Because my sore eyes are too swollen now to see more than indistinct shapes, it might be only a bracken fern that moves in the passing air before me, or it might be her.

My throat is too parched for words so I do not know if it is my own voice, or hers, or some voice from the uncurled fern that brings Hebrews down to echo within those ruined walls. *Cast not away therefore your confidence, which hath great recompense of reward. For ye have need of patience, that, after ye have done the will of God, ye might receive the promise.*

And what is the will of God but to love Him, and to love one another, and to refrain from acts that bring hurt and grief and death to the innocent? But I cannot turn back the clock, I cannot revive the dead, I cannot undo the damage I've done, I cannot even protect my family from harm. Dear God, I cannot do a single thing alone!

Charlie MacIntosh

My dad would have laughed if he'd been there. "By heavens, Charlie, they've gone and dragged out the same damn tents again!"

Maybe they were the same tents. Somebody had set them up in neat rows in the park at the edge of town, where the river turns a sharp corner and goes under the main-street bridge. Rows of them on the field. Men were setting up more tents down by the maples. Dad would have gone poking at the first one, then the next. "Which d'ye think was ours, lad? Aye, where's that stain where ye couldna' wait to pee? Not this one. Not this. I want the very same one. Nothing else will do." He would have gone down the rows looking, grinning at the people who sat in doorways, shaking his head and winking at the strangers from town. "Right back where we bloody started!"

Of course Mother would have hushed him. There wasn't anything funny about this, she'd say. She would tell him to grow up. This was an emergency. A disaster had taken place.

But as it was, Mother did not say much. She let strangers help her down from the buggy and then followed them to the Red Cross tent, where two women in the uniforms of nurses asked her questions. No injuries to the MacIntoshes, we hadn't been touched. No, we hadn't brought any of our things with us. No bedding. No food. No extra clothing.

"The first families have been taken into homes," said one of the women, who had hairs growing from a dark spot on her cheek, "but we're waiting for more offers. In the meantime we can give you shelter here." She led Mother to a tent where a stout woman in an apron backed out and smiled at us. "I've just laid out some blankets, dear. There'll be food beneath them trees."

Then I saw that Uncle Archie had returned to the buggy.

"You could help here," Mother said. "I'm sure these people could do with another pair of hands."

"Town people can do it," Uncle Archie said, and flicked the reins.

When Mother saw Sally Mitchell hurrying towards us she started to cry. "You don't want a tent of your own, love," Mrs.

Mitchell said, holding Mother against her. "Move your things to ours. I've got a nice pot of tea ready. Be a good lad, Charles, and carry those blankets for your mother."

"You seen anything of the Reimers?" someone said from the doorway to a tent. Mrs. Korsakov. Half a dozen weak-eyed Korsakovs looked out from behind her.

"They've taken Mr. MacKay to the hospital," Mrs. Mitchell said. "A few mild burns to be looked at. The Maguires went straight to friends in town. Some people were put up in the hotel. The Stokeses, of course." She said this as though the Stokeses thought themselves too good to live in tents. At the two-storey hotel directly across the road from the park, people were gathered on the second-floor verandah. Some leaned on the railing to look this way, others were talking in groups.

"Look. The Richmonds."

The Richmonds' car had overheated. As it approached the gate to the park, steam rose and engulfed the driver and passengers in a pale cloud. Mrs. Richmond stood up and leaned out, waving her walking stick and shouting orders. "Left! Left! You'll hit the gate post. Now you're free. Turn right. Andy, you must let us out, I'm afraid this thing will explode."

When Mrs. Richmond had got out of the car and stood turning this way and that, Mrs. Desmond stepped out of a crowd to greet her. "Who has let this happen?" Mrs. Richmond demanded. Her eyes flashed about as though looking amongst the tents for culprits.

"They will be made to pay for this," Mrs. Mitchell said to Mother, without explaining who "they" might be. "We've been told the premier will come for a look. We will be interviewed."

An unfamiliar man dressed in the white shirt and tie of a town store clerk passed by, raising his voice to someone I couldn't see. "He says he hasn't heard anything of the Mackens."

A second man came into sight from around the side of a tent. He wasn't anyone I knew, either, but his clothing was smudged and burnt like someone who'd been closer to the fire than the man in the white shirt. "I tried to get up their road but the fire had cut it off. It looked to me like the place was surrounded."

"Jesus," the first man said. "And none of them out?"

"I've just brought in a truckload of wives and kiddies from the beach road," the other said. "I'll head back out and give 'er another try."

Pearsons' milk delivery cart was pulling in just as we got to the Mitchells' tent so I tossed the blankets inside and ran over to meet them. Tanner was driving the horse. Mrs. Pearson held the baby in the crook of one arm but she had her free hand to her mouth. She looked at me as though she might never have seen me before.

"Where's your dad?" I asked Tanner. I figured he must be coming just behind with Elizabeth, in the car.

"Shut up," Tanner said. He reined in the horse and got down and then helped his mother down. Mrs. Hueffner came out of a tent and put an arm around her. The two of them helped the uncle down and guided him towards the women in uniform. "What do I do with Orion?" Tanner said.

Most of the horses were tethered at the far end of the grassy field, so I walked in that direction beside him. "Elizabeth went into the fire," he said. "My dad went after her. We won't see them again."

He might as well have punched me in the stomach.

"That's not true," I said.

"Bugger you," he said. "I saw it."

He kept his face turned away.

Mr. Pearson had promised me that place on his step any time I needed it. He'd invited me to shake Uncle Donald's hand. He'd treated me the same as he treated Tanner. Better than Uncle Archie. Better even than Mother, who had herself to think of, as Uncle Archie liked to say. I felt a furious thumping inside my chest, a panicked need to stop something from being true.

"He's smart," I said. "He'll know what to do to save her."

"Sure," he said. He slapped the horse's rump with the reins. "Git up, you lazy son of a bitch, you think we're out for a stroll?"

When we'd unhitched the cart and tethered the horse, we followed the curve of the riverbank, walking along the top of the dike they'd built to protect the park from flooding. There wasn't much chance of that now. The river had sunk so low that gravel sandbars and patches of reeds had surfaced, high and dry.

The sky here was nearly as dark as what we'd left behind. Smoke clouds rolled over us, dropping soot and ashes. Across the river, the town buildings were dull in the smoky air. It was hard to believe that people were buying and selling long johns over there, and sacks of chicken feed, and perfumed face powder. You could hardly imagine them sitting behind their desks, adding up columns of figures, or writing letters to complain about the last shipment of Five Roses Flour.

"We could go over to town," I said. The main-street stores were just across the bridge. The pool hall was up the slope. We could hope for a fight to spill out of the beer parlour of the Riverside Hotel. "Maybe the Maple Leaf'll show a matinee."

"It ain't Saturday."

"Maybe they'll do it anyway, for refugees." I liked the word. "We could stop by the Creamery. They might feel sorry enough to give us free ice cream."

"Ice cream," he said, as though ice cream was disgusting. "I'm not staying." He stopped in his tracks. I could see this was something he'd just thought of.

"Where you going?"

I guess I'd pushed it away, but now it came back cold as river water in my veins. Tanner's father. How could I have thought of matinees?

Before he'd got far, I heard his mother calling. She stood outside a tent still holding the baby, waving us over.

"You stay away from that river," she said when we were close enough.

"Yes ma'am," Tanner said.

"I'll not have you drown. You stay where I can see you. We must stay close together until your father arrives." She caught her breath. "With Elizabeth."

"What are we supposed to do?" Tanner said. "Sit in that stupid tent and play with our toes?"

"Mind how you speak," she warned. "You can go over and fetch us a pail of water. And see if they've got anything to eat. I'm sure Charlie's mother is wondering where he is."

We hadn't got as far as the canteen when the Ahlbergs pulled in through the gate in their taxi. Mrs. Seyerstad was with them. She jumped down onto the grass even before the taxi had come to a full stop. She didn't look as pretty as she did at school. She didn't look pretty at all, she looked as though someone had taken a fork to her hair and stirred it up into a haystack. Her eyes were strange, too. She noticed us, "Oh, hello Charlie, hello Tanner," but she didn't really look at us. She was looking out at the little tent city like someone who had been captured and brought to the wrong place. China.

"Oh, we can't stay here," she said. "We should have gone into town. To my mother-in-law's."

"That's all right," Mr. Ahlberg said. "If you can wait until I get my family settled here I'll drive you."

"No," Mrs. Seyerstad said. "I don't want to have her clucking over me. If I'm trapped in town I'll never know what's happening to anyone else. I'll go across to the hotel. Tanner, Charlie – you'll go over and see if they've room?"

"We were just leaving," Tanner said. He started away in the direction of the horses.

I set out after him. "I'm coming with you then."

"We might have to ride right into the flames. You'll be scared."

"I'm not staying here."

"Your ma won't let you go. You got a horse?"

I shook my head.

"We can ride double on Orion," Tanner said. "Or you can take someone else's."

"Whose is that little pinto?" The pinto was cropping grass near the wheels of a democrat.

"Korsakovs'."

That's what I thought. "I'll take it," I said. "I guess Korsakov can't get too mad at a kid that's father has died."

It was the first time I'd said such a thing. It left me gasping for breath.

"Shoot," Tanner said. "We could both of us end up the same."

Christina Ahlberg

The gentleman behind the hotel counter was a small man with a tiny moustache over his thin hard lip. One of the Stantons from up the Lake Trail Road. When Johanna complained that there should be a list of names so you could know who had got out safely, he said he knew quite a few people from out our way. "And there are those who keep me informed. There are Barclays registered with us at the moment, for instance. Are you interested in anyone in particular?"

She wasn't sure what to say to the man. The only name she could think of was Stokes. "Has anyone seen them?" she said.

"Came in an hour ago," he said, looking pleased with himself. The tiny mouth was capable of only a tiny smile but it was proud. "The wife and little boy, anyway. I don't know if Mr. Stokes is with them."

His eyebrows asked: Anyone else? He must have guessed that she wasn't very interested in the Stokes family.

"The Mackens?" she said.

"We heard they were trapped." He paused, in case he would have the pleasure of seeing that she hadn't heard this. When he saw that she had, he went on. "But the fire must have passed by now. Others can go in and see what damage has been done."

"And Nora? I don't suppose there's a Mrs. Brewer here?"

"Not here, ma'am." He didn't even have to look at his book. "You may ask the volunteers across the road. There is someone over there recording names, I believe."

She was not going back to the tents, she announced to me. From across the road it looked too much like a newspaper photo of training camp.

Once we'd climbed the carpeted staircase to our rooms, Johanna went right out onto the verandah. When the children had settled, I went out as well. There were others at the far end, most of them people whose faces we knew but not their names. We nodded to Mrs. Stokes. Lanterns had been lit across the road, some of them moving amongst the tents and others glowing from within the canvas. With so much smoke between us and the sun, one would almost think it was night.

On an ordinary day, without this smoke in the air, we would have been able to look up the road, across the bridge, and straight up the main street of town to the glacier that sat across the top of a broad blue mountain. A white whale, the Indians called it, left stranded by the receding waters of the Big Flood. When this smoke lifted, you wouldn't be surprised if their whale had had the good sense to leave.

She stood at the railing. She paced the length of the building. She brought out a chair and sat beside me. She stood up and paced again. There was a peculiar restlessness in her, she said, as though her body knew of something she ought to be doing. Something was wrong, something besides the fire. She found a cigarette in her bag and lit it. In the circumstances, why should she care if she shocked a few of the others?

An hour later, perhaps, there was a timid knock on the door of the room. She went in past the bed and opened the door. "You were inquiring about a Mrs. Brewer." I recognized the voice of the little man from behind the desk. "There was someone below just now who asked me to tell you this. She has gone to the hospital, he says, where her mother has been taken."

"Who is below?" she said. "Who asked you to tell me this?"

"A gentleman, ma'am. In a hurry. He asked me to tell you that he would return with further reports. He insisted I make it clear the lady you both consider a friend is herself unharmed. But her mother was overcome by the smoke and is being looked to."

"Is he below?"

"Gone, I'm afraid."

"A man in a burnt hat and a coat filled with holes?"

"Every man that sets foot in this hotel tonight is dressed in burnt clothing filled with holes," he said. Pleased with his cleverness. "It has become the local costume."

"When he returns, tell him I'm waiting."

"You should get some sleep, Mrs. Seyerstad. Tomorrow you'll be grateful for the rest."

Of course she didn't sleep. She came out onto the verandah again with her cigarettes, and sat with a blanket over her lap. The road to the hospital branched to the left along the river and then followed the shoreline of the bay.

It was dark – true night now, with only two or three lanterns still burning across the road – when we heard him ride up and dismount. She went to the end of the verandah and down the outside stairs to meet him. I went to the railing to look down. He was wearing the same hat and coat and boots he'd been wearing since he arrived, and Matthew Pearson's shirt and trousers, but the shirt and trousers looked as though they'd been dragged through a fire and beaten with burning boughs, and the coat and hat and boots looked less strange than they had. Things were beginning to match.

His face, she would tell me the next day, was darkened by sun and blistered by heat and smeared over with fingers of soot and grit. His eyes were red-rimmed and swollen like everyone else's, including her own.

"Nora's mother?" she said.

He shook his head and looked away.

She led him up the stairs to the verandah where he sat in the second chair and leaned back with his legs stretched out across the floor, crossed at the ankles. A motorcar ticked by below. "Nora has asked me to leave."

I excused myself and went inside to be with the sleeping children, though because of the heat I could not close the door. At any rate, from the bed I could see their two figures in silhouette through the window, and in all likelihood would have been able to hear much of what they said even if the door had been shut.

She waited through a long silence while he looked across the tent city to the shadowy woods beyond the river and the dark rolling sky.

"It's turned inland," he said. "I suppose you knew that. There isn't much of it left now, and what there is can be put out by the men who've been sent to do that. It came close to the Store, but didn't harm it. It left MacIntoshes' place untouched, and Richmonds'. Maybe it will lose its willpower now, or whatever has been driving it, and people will have the chance to take back their lives."

"If they want them," she said.

Again there was a long silence. Then he made a noise that was close to a groan.

"I was just starting to believe that she could remember why she loved me once."

After a while he told her that they'd come out onto the road from Nora's lane, riding his mare that he must have left tethered

behind her shack when he went to fight fire. And then along
came my Sven in the McLaughlin-Buick, heading south with a
load of Desmonds from up on the ridge behind Reimers' sawmill.
He stopped and told them to leave the horse and hop in with
him. They refused. Then Sven drove ahead a bit and stopped
again. "Your folks get out?" he said to Nora.

"What do you mean?" Nora said. "Surely he'd take them all out
at the first sign of danger."

"Not so far as we know," Sven said. "In fact, we were told they
were trapped. Nobody can get out at the moment, nobody can
get in to help. We're just waiting to see if they manage to pull
through."

"We have to go back," she said. "We've got to help."

"If they can't get out we can't get in," Taylor told her. But she
insisted that they turn around and try. Sven left them to it.

Taylor didn't know how he was going to do this but he knew he
had no choice. He would have to go into the fire and rescue at least
some of her family members if he was to have any hope of getting
her to town. They rode back to her shack first, where he got her to
pour buckets of water over him. Then he poured well water over a
blanket off her bed, and wrapped it around himself, and poured
water over a threadbare flour-sack curtain off her window, and tied
it across the bottom half of his face. Then he filled two water pails
and hoisted one of them onto Nora's lap on the horse and then
climbed up behind her with the second pail and a shovel across his
lap, and asked the horse to move as quickly as it could without
causing the water to spill. They rode up the old logging grade and
then up the narrow lane onto Macken property. The fire was still
burning here. The horse would not go close. Whole sizzling boughs
went rolling through the air in front of them. Even in his soaked
clothing he could not advance closer on foot.

"I couldn't turn back now, not with Nora frantic. I asked her to
pour the other two buckets over me and I set out at a dead run."

He didn't pretend to understand what happened next. A miracle, perhaps. A coincidence. An example of love intimidating nature. At any rate, though he expected to be flung back by the force of impossible heat or drawn in by some ugly vacuum and gobbled up like the huckleberry bushes, he was able to run right up that lane and into what had been an inferno only seconds before. It peeled back, he said. The wind must have shifted direction. It was as though the flames cringed back and swung away from him and turned fleeing in another direction, so that he was able to keep right on going up that lane with fire falling back to one side like turned pages or waves of the Red Sea. Right to the Macken doorstep, with Nora not far behind.

It had fallen back from all around by this time, and set off towards the mountains. But not without first burning the barn to the ground, and the sheds, and every living plant or bush or tree on the place, and probably every animal as well. Fence posts still flared up. Stumps crackled and roared. Black snags discharged shredded spirals of dark grey smoke. The black blistered corpse of a pig lay with its fat still bubbling not twenty feet from the house.

But the house was more or less unharmed.

"It was typical of old Macken that he checked the site of his barns and looked over his fields and stood cursing over the black carcasses of his cows and even searched out his horses until he found them in the creek before it occurred to him to wonder where his wife had got to."

Taylor hadn't thought to wonder himself. There were so many humans there and so much for the mind to take in that the absence of one small woman wasn't noticeable. "And even then it wasn't Macken who wondered first, it was Nora." Nora had gone about rounding up the youngest ones, checking their wounds, looking into their red swollen eyes, giving them comfort. She was too busy being a mother to the boys to wonder where their real mother had got to.

They all tried at once to tell what had happened. Or some of them did. A couple of the older boys went off to beat out fence post flames. The quiet blond one got up onto the seat of the Overland, as though he believed there was nothing left to do now but leave.

They'd thought they were doomed, they told their sister. That fire had come right up and breathed down their necks and they thought it would kill them all. But the old man had kept them busy. Down the well on a ladder for dippers of water, which were taken up another ladder to the roof. Soaked gunnysacks were used to beat out the sparks that landed. The cattle panicked, they said, trampling the garden. When they ran off, you could hear their bells for a while and then their terrible cries. Reg had got a burn to his leg. Morris had fallen off the roof but had broken nothing. Faces were blistered. Hair had been singed. Everyone was bruised and scraped. Clothing was riddled with black-edged holes. The dogs hid under the kitchen table, panting, they said, and wouldn't let anyone near them even now.

Macken came back up from the barn leading the horses, pleased to find that not all his livestock had gone to the flames. He bragged of their intelligence. "It proves that horses are smarter than cows," he said. "If there was any doubt."

"Where's Mother?" Nora said.

For a moment nobody said a thing.

"It was her job to stay in the attic," one of the boys said, "to beat out sparks that got in."

"Annie!" their father yelled. "Come down now, there's Nora here in the yard."

"Mother?" Nora ran to the house and called again from the step, and when there was no answer she went inside still calling. Taylor went after her.

"There was a rough homemade ladder up the wall of the kitchen to a hole in the ceiling," Taylor said. "Nora's skirts swished out of sight just as I started up behind her. Just as she cried out, I put my head and shoulders through the hole. Through a thick smoke haze I could see her kneeling beside her mother, who was lying across the loose boards that had been placed across the joists."

She was unconscious but she was still alive. "The smoke!" Nora cried. They were both coughing – Nora and Taylor. But Taylor crawled up into the attic and helped bring the mother to the trapdoor, and then went first down the ladder to help bring her down – with a half-dozen burnt and soot-smudged boys gathered around the foot with their hands outstretched in case they needed to break someone's fall.

It was clear to Taylor that they had to get her to help quickly, though Macken tried his usual remedy first. He shouted. "Annie! It's gone! We're saved! Get a-hold of yourself! Come around now, look who's here!"

Fortunately the quiet brother in the Overland had better sense. He got out and cranked the engine. Then he drove it up close to the door and helped carry their mother out to lay her across the seat.

"They all came. Those that couldn't find room in the Overland with their mother came in the wagon. They probably thought this was just a sort of postscript to the disaster, something added to the adventure they'd already turned into the tale they'd been telling us. We drove as fast as we could down that lane through the smouldering devastation and then down the highway towards town and the hospital. Where we couldn't do anything but wait."

"But they didn't save her," Johanna said.

"We didn't have to wait long. I rode back to leave you word with the man below, since I knew you'd be worried about Nora. By the time I got back to the hospital she'd gone. She may have died while we were taking her there, I don't know. A doctor came out and took Macken aside to tell him. Then Macken took Nora aside and told her. And then Nora told the boys."

The boys were unbelieving, Taylor said. "After coming through that fire alive I guess they couldn't understand how she could die in a hospital bed of nothing more serious than smoke in her lungs. They were filled with smoke themselves. They took turns at fits of coughing. She'd changed the ending of their adventure tale."

"And Nora took it hard."

"She didn't want to let it show in front of the boys so she went off by herself for a while. When she came back she asked me to leave."

"She's been telling you that since the day you got here but it hasn't made much difference. She's started to like having you around."

"She wouldn't admit it. Anyway, things have changed. She's decided she has to go home."

"Of course," Johanna said. "That will be so that she can step into her mother's shoes for a while, until some arrangement can be made. Cooking. Cleaning. Can you imagine cooking for that tribe? She will want to be there for the younger boys, too, who will be upset."

"She says she means to stay," he said. "For good."

"And when her husband shows up?"

"He won't. We talked for a long time, Johanna. There was a ceremony but, well, nothing else. When she came home she was just as she'd left. She is nobody's bride."

"Of course," she said. "I knew this." She pushed the blanket to her ankles – too hot. "His property could be sold from under her."

"But that's not why she'll go home. I offered to sell my farm in Ontario and buy something here for the two of us."

"You proposed," Johanna said.

"I should never have left," Nora had told him. "If I'd been there, Father would not have been so stubborn, he'd have sent us out. I was the only one he was ever soft on, he would never have risked *my* life to save the house. If I'd been there he would have sent me out and I would have refused to go without Mother, and Mother would have refused to go without the boys. He would have been forced to give in. Mother would still be alive."

"You can help them without living with them," he had reasoned. "You could visit them every day. We could buy a place near by and build our own house. You could be within shouting distance if they needed you. The boys could take turns staying overnight."

"Mother was all they had to soften their life with him. I can't abandon them now."

For a few moments Taylor said nothing more to Johanna. There was no traffic on the road below them now. There was only one lantern burning outside a tent in the park.

"I told her I'd wait," he said. His voice was barely audible, as though he'd lacked the courage or energy to say the words distinctly.

"The youngest boy hasn't reached school age yet," Johanna said. "You could wait for fifteen years."

He got up and walked to the farthest corner of the front verandah and stayed there for a while, leaning against the railing. Then he came back and sat in his chair again and leaned forward with his elbows on his knees and the lower half of his face in his hands. He might have been crying, though Johanna thought he was simply staring into the night and trying to absorb the blow. The only face she knew to be wet was her own.

The Fields of France

1918 — 1919

Paris, May 6, 1919

Dear Maude,

Even before I opened your latest letter I was certain you would wish me success in this mission that neither of us could have imagined just a few years ago. My mother would likely prefer that I'd discreetly disappeared in the final battles! Another wife might wish I'd been one of those fellows who were killed during the mutiny in Wales, sparing both of us the challenges ahead. The challenge you have given *me* is to honour the generosity of your extraordinary heart.

Not even the delays in Rhyl or the confusion in London could provoke half the frustration routinely produced by the paper-work authorities of the French Republic. Granted, the French have more important matters than my petition to deal with, but I have endured my share of wasted time, and need to put my own life back together just as they must mend their country.

The dark stone face of the building I visit most often seems to scowl whenever I approach its heavy doors. Not so Monsieur Lafleur, the man I seek amongst the clattering typewriters. He sits behind his desk and smiles apologetically when he sees me. "Nossing today, M'sieur Pee-song," he says, throwing wide his hands. He tries to look as distressed as he imagines I feel, but eventually he breaks into a smile, anticipating the pleasure of our predictable exchange. "*Rien. Rien. Je regrette de ne pas avoir de bonnes nouvelles. Demain, peut-être.*" He assures me that my petition is proceeding as it should, and that I must be as patient as everyone else has learned to be in these confusing days. What is one small child when thousands of *enfants français* have not yet recovered their disrupted lives?

On your advice I paid another visit to the office of the *Commissaire général* and to your mother's acquaintance, the congenial Monsieur Dion, but have yet to see that either his sympathy or his efforts have been of any real assistance. He smiles, and encourages me not to abandon hope, and wonders to himself why his inferiors have not got rid of me long ago. Perhaps your mother has written him of your shocking conversion to Whigdom during the profiteering scandals, and your tireless letter-writing campaign against every move of Sir Robert's government since!

I wish I could spend more time with the child, but what sort of life would it be for a three-year-old to traipse from office to office up and down these cold, wet, crowded streets? I go up to the country when I can, to her great-grandparents' village in that landscape of shattered trees and human limbs and abandoned machinery, and twice I have brought her back to the city with me for a few days so that we can become better acquainted.

We've poked about together in the streets surrounding my *meuble* in Madame Tournier's house, shadowy cobbled lanes shooting off in every direction, windows shuttered, streets too narrow to be thought of as canyons even. Chasms rather, or trenches. They seem to lean in, pinching the heart, though this child of a country village marvels at such wonders – faces appearing in doorways, old men walking dogs on bits of rope, women gossiping at intersections, pairs of laughing soldiers suddenly appearing from around the corner.

We have wandered through the markets, touching washed carrots and potatoes, and stopped to breathe in the coffee smells from cafés and the scent of violets from the flower stands. We visited the *Jardin des Plantes* so that she might see the sugar maples brought back from Nouvelle France and admire the stuffed beaver and polar bears inside the Natural History Museum. But she showed more interest in the African animals arranged in a long "parade" beneath the high glass roof, especially the large tusked elephant that leads the column of rhinoceroses, zebras, antelopes, giraffes, and dozens of other exotic beasts. Gazing up at the elephant's trunk, she was disappointed to hear that there are none of these creatures where I will be taking her to live.

We have gazed in awe upon the tall magnificent windows of the Sainte Chapelle, where the entire Bible is illustrated in panel after panel of towering glass. How I wish you could see this! It is as though we looked on stories from *inside* them, and saw a thousand different versions of ourselves embedded in the walls. The war may not have destroyed everything after all.

Madame Tournier stands at the bottom of the stairs each morning with arms thrown wide to welcome us into her day. "*Ahhhh – ma petite Elise! Comment allez-vous aujourd'hui, mon petit lapin?*" She stuffs us both with her coffee and bread and powerful-smelling cheese before allowing us out onto the streets. Sometimes she walks as far as the market with us. She takes the child to the nearby Luxembourg Gardens while I visit Monsieur Lafleur, and remains with us as long as she can once I've returned. This small child has cast a spell upon our *concierge* as she will I am sure upon you. Mothers watching out for their own children gaze on her instead, and eventually shake their heads to throw off the charm. Old women gossiping on the benches beneath the plane trees try to entice her closer with offers of food or trinkets, whatever they find at the bottom of their bags, unsatisfied until they have touched her red curls.

Monsieur Lafleur has seen so much of me that he has begun to think of me as a friend. Yesterday he joined us for our visit to the Gardens, which are not far from his bachelor rooms on *rue de Medicis*. Like the others, he may also have been charmed by the girl. She, on the other hand, has fallen in love with a long-haired, sleepy-eyed Shetland pony, and insists every time that she ride

no other but him. He has been waiting for her, she insists, he has
been sad without her. Monsieur Lafleur and I walk beside her,
down the sandy avenue between the rows of leafy trees whose
name I do not know. He is a small man with narrow forward-
leaning shoulders, who walks with his delicate hands clasped
together high against his chest, his thin lips pressed in a tight line
while he listens, you suspect, for something you might be trying
not to say.

You would think Monsieur Lafleur were considering emigration himself, he asks such eager questions about our life in
Ferguson Falls. My responses are interrupted constantly by "*Papa,
régarde!*" and "*Régardez-moi, Monsieur Lafleur.*" Parental voices are
heard crying out on every side – "*Julia, viens ici!*" and "*Laurent,
dépêche-toi!*"

The faces of the pony-riding children display a variety of emotions, from terror to outright joy. The parents are not so easy to
read but seem (to me) to express a similar range, though somehow
all at the same time. It is probably the aftermath of a war that
may not have reached their streets but certainly made a horror of
their lives. It is too soon for the constant expectation of terror to
have faded altogether, and too late for the joyous relief to have
remained unquestioned. Those aristocratic women of Paris who
pull their hair back in the fashion of ballerinas display foreheads
engraved with worry lines. Fathers (I may only imagine this) keep
an eye open for the Mills bomb that would blow off their children's limbs.

Monsieur Lafleur is not a father, and might never have had a
worry in his life. I've begun to think that it is not friendship that
drives him to seek our company, but a desire to investigate my
character. After Elizabeth had grown bored with the sand pit in
the "*aire de jeux des tout-petits*" he insisted on buying us lunch in
the restaurant he regularly patronizes, a great cavernous room with
towering mirrors, clusters of globe lights, and rows of hat racks
between the tables. Cadaverous waiters in black vests and white

shirts lavished good-natured affection on M. Lafleur but quickly adopted our Elizabeth as well, while barely noticing my presence.

"Tell me again about your son," said M. Lafleur. "You have given him your mother's – how do you say? – maiden name?"

"Your life as a university student in Ottawa," he said, "it must have been very stimulating, *n'est-ce pas?*"

Elizabeth said, "*Papa, régarde. Je mange.*" And got most of the thin soup from the spoon to her mouth.

Madame Tournier later complained that I had worn the child out. "*Tu es fatiguée.*" She must lie down immediately for a nap. "No more outings today."

But as soon as she awoke, we walked to the river. That is, I walked, while she rode my shoulders with the same sort of energetic delight she had displayed on the pony's back. We browsed amongst the old prints and books at the *bouquinistes'* stalls along the quay. (I'd hoped for a copy of a Balzac in English.) Elise – our Elizabeth – showed more interest in the barges gliding past. She insists that when we leave on our grand adventure it must be on one of those graceful conveyances. A yellow one, she hopes, down the river to the sea and across the Atlantic Ocean to her new home. I don't know how much she understands of this.

She is a surprisingly happy child, eager to take in everything she sees and pleased to play language games with me. Her English is weak, naturally, but she learns quickly. I hope to have her speaking like an Ottawa Valley native by the time we disembark in Halifax or Montreal. If you come down to meet us as you've suggested, there will be time for everyone to become acquainted before we get back to the farm.

May 9, 1919

I do go on, but the evenings are sometimes long, and I wish to keep you informed of as much of this as possible.

Between the lines of your letters I sense concern that the mother may turn up to complicate matters. Of course she has no parents, and the grandparents who raised her claim to have had no knowledge of her whereabouts for nearly a year. And Monsieur Lafleur has reassured me she has probably forgotten the child by now, and found a new family somewhere – if she is still alive. If she suddenly reappears and demands that my claim be rejected, he believes the wheels of bureaucracy have already ground on so far that they would be incapable of reversing themselves. If the paper-work says that she has disappeared, deserting the child, and is almost certainly dead, leaving no relatives in this country capable of caring for the girl, then her reappearance would not be a serious challenge to the "facts." They wouldn't believe her even if she claimed I were not the father after all, since they have themselves remarked the similarities between us. I have made sure they've seen us together. I've told you, I think, that though she has her own mother's eyes she has *my* mother's nose and brow and pale scrubbed-rust skin (mine and Tanner's as well). Both Monsieur Lafleur and Mr. Brock are in possession of papers asserting my acknowledged paternity, the mother's proven abandonment, and my willingness to sponsor her immigration.

When I explain to Elizabeth about the brother she has yet to meet, I tell her he is strong and kind and wise, and, because he is older, will protect her if she needs protecting.

"From what?" she says. In French, of course. "From guns?" Her *arrière-grands-parents* speak of little else but the guns that drove them from their home.

"There are no guns," I assure her. At least there will be no guns directed at her.

"Tigers?" she asks. She wants to know if there are tigers where we will go, or lions. I have bought a few children's books and sent them home for her great-grandmother to read. But as it turns out, the old woman doesn't know how to read and it is left to me. When I was in London for Charlie Sullivan's wedding I bought her books in English as well. She studies the pictures when she's alone, and while I am reading she softly mimics my words.

Before leaving for England Charlie tried once more to convince me to abandon this business. Because he has no experience with women like you, he imagines difficulties I know you've already overcome. He can't forget his own astonishment in August, for instance, when he learned that I'd agreed to meet with the grandparents who appeared from nowhere with the child, nor his alarm on hearing that I had, in my regret and confusion and guilt (and stupidity, he insisted), confessed everything to you in a letter. He called me a babe in the woods for informing on myself, where thousands like me would go to their graves in silence. "How did they let such an innocent into the army?" Nor has he forgotten how amazed he was that you'd forgiven me, though of course he wasn't aware of the hurt and anger in your first letters, nor of the demands and conditions and extracted promises that followed. Even so, he was alarmed that I plan to make the girl a part of the family. "If you want to take a souvenir home, why not one of those mines under Messines that haven't exploded yet?" I hope his bride will give him the chance to discover, as I have, how large a woman's capacity for love can be.

May 11, 1919

I had forgotten that you asked for a report of the wedding. Most of it can wait until I can tell you in person. I crossed the Channel three days before the event to fulfil my duties as groomsman but wished that you could have been there as well. You and I would certainly have found the time to visit the British Museum and, though you might not have been given permission to address the House of Commons in order to set them straight on a thing or two, we could at least have taken an excursion barge up the Thames. As it was, I spent most of the time following Charlie from haberdashery to haberdashery, and playing checkers to keep his mind off the wedding. I took him walking as well, and he was so preoccupied with the looming nuptials that he didn't even ask why I'd brought him to Gough Square. I wanted to see the house where Dr. Johnson wrote his dictionary and to imagine the new words he would add if he were here today. What would he make of "lousy," I wonder, or "frigiped?" We'd even walked as far as Wentworth House before he woke from his trance and wanted to know where the devil I'd brought him. "A poet lived there, Charlie," I said. "In the left half of the building. Living in the right half was the girl he loved. Even while he was writing love-notes to her from his sick-bed he knew he would never live to be the lucky man you'll be tomorrow."

Turning away from Keats's house, I felt a strange nostalgic sadness for the man – as though he were someone I had known and then abandoned. As of course I had. His poems have been no part of my life for years. Like his house and his lady-love and his unhappy life, his lines of verse belong to a world I can hardly believe I once inhabited.

Sullivan would have protested more rigorously still if I had somehow led him all the way out to Windsor. Being in that town had done more than raise the ghosts of poets, it had conjured up images of students in Ferguson Falls reciting lines that must have made little sense to them. I would have visited Windsor for young Hughie Corbett's sake, since I remember the day he commandeered the boys of the class into reciting, in pairs, the whole of George Peele's *Polyhymnia*, which was first performed for Queen Elizabeth beneath her gallery window in the tilt-yard there. I'll never forget the lad's face, when the others had read their parts, as he stepped to the fore and without warning raised his voice in song for the sonnet that closes the jousters' performance. Of course I don't remember all of the words but there are phrases that have come back to me now that I've left poor Corbett on the

battlefield. "Beauty, strength, youth, are flowers but fading seen;
Duty, faith, love, are roots, and ever green." What do you suppose
the words meant to him then? This question has sent me to a
library for the words that follow:

> *His helmet now shall make a hive for bees,*
> *And, lovers' sonnets turn'd to holy psalms,*
> *A man-at-arms must now serve on his knees,*
> *And feed on prayers, which are age his arms:*
> *But though from court to cottage he depart,*
> *His saint is sure of his unspotted heart.*

(When you asked for details of the wedding you meant the
fabric of the bridal gown, and I give you London's forgotten
poetry!)

Poor Sullivan was beside himself with nerves. He was anxious
that I meet his girl immediately and yet delayed our meeting with
lame excuses. Eventually I insisted on being taken to her aunt's
residence so that I might make the girl's acquaintance.

The aunt, a spice importer's widow, lives alone except for a few
servants (and, before the wedding, her niece) in a fine old house.
The girl is obviously much in love, and Sullivan worships the
ground (and imported carpets) beneath her feet. Tiny feet, I
noticed. She has small hands as well, and very large damp eyes,
a pale dainty flower of a girl as her name suggests – though you
would be better able than I to judge whether she is really a simple
"Violet" or some robuster flower.

The aunt has forgiven Charles for being a colonial, possibly
because he has told her of a successful family business in Toronto,
something he'd never mentioned to me. He was vague when I
questioned him later. Apparently the family connection is more
distant than he'd led the aunt to believe, but he is confident of
being given a position of responsibility when he returns. His

wound, his uniform, and his decorations ought to count for something. The girl seems ambitious, eager to become a member of an
important New World family.

The day of the wedding was cold and grey, like the days leading
up to it, with a rain so fine that it seemed incapable of falling to
the ground, remaining suspended in the air like a mist. The ceremony was simple, attended by only a few of the girl's cousins
and some of Sullivan's friends who had also stayed behind to
marry their sweethearts and make arrangements to take them
across the Atlantic.

When they saw me off at Victoria Station, everything in me
longed to be going with them when they leave for home, taking
myself as fast as possible to the Valley, which seems farther away
from me now than ever before. In France I noticed that English
soldiers spoke of being at the end of the world, though many were
only one hundred miles from their own doorsteps! Their relatives
in Kent could hear the rumble of artillery along the line. They
were no farther from home than you are from your mother in
Montreal! They could barely comprehend what real distance
means. To see the Sullivans holding hands at the station made me
sad to think that I may never see my friend again, for it has come
back to me how vast a country we live in, and how unlikely it is
that those of us who fought together will ever again cross paths.

You will already have guessed from earlier letters that I've little
interest in returning to the classroom. At the moment it seems
inconceivable that I might stand and read Tennyson to boys who
would remind me daily of the lads I saw killed so recently – some
of them while in my care. And to girls who would remind me of
sweethearts left to spinsterhood. I cannot imagine taking a
classroom full of youths through "Tintern Abbey" again. Even
Archibald Lampman won't do! To milk peaceable cows and culti-
vate rows of dull potatoes seems the more honourable life. I have
been responsible for harm enough already.

I do not think of working beside my father as I did at weekends before the War. Something new has come up. While I was in London, Sullivan told me about the plans of the Dominion and some provincial governments to grant parcels of land to returned soldiers interested in opening up new territory in the West. Apparently they will supply the land, the surveyors, the first stage of clearing for farms, and even a loan for materials to build a house and for buying one cow. Each soldier will be sold several acres, at a low price to be paid over twenty years, the locations drawn from a hat. In return he's expected to clear more fields himself and culti-vate a profitable farm. I think we might consider this. A home in a new location may be preferable to remaining in Ferguson Falls.

This move would have the additional advantage of removing you a distance from Parliament Hill, to somewhere you may be less likely to make enemies by declaiming your new enthusiasm for Laurier and his men! The battle to hold onto the vote for women may be carried on in even the remotest parts of the country, while local issues will also require your attention.

How proud your mother would be if she knew everything I know! If it weren't for the necessity for discretion I would be tempted to tell the world of your splendid generosity of spirit. As it is, I can only pray that I prove worthy of your forbearance and charity, and demonstrate that what you have brought about is a kind of renewal, though a renewal that will probably require a continuous remaking. Your letters of the past few months will give me strength for the task, as will the resumption of your daily companionship,

which is eagerly anticipated by

your loving husband,
Matthew

From Matthew Pearson's Notebooks, 1923

1918: August 7-8, Eve of the Battle of Amiens

We left Amiens under cover of night, riding in buses and boxcars through a congestion of tanks, guns, motor vehicles, and supply wagons moving in the same direction, and then walked the last miles to Gentelles and settled in a dark wide plain behind a patch of woods to await orders. It was almost, in a certain sense, like coming home. I could imagine the Moreuil Woods not far to the east, the River Luce, the Paris railroad, and the little familiar ruined village ahead. For a moment of confusion I half-believed the entire war had been rearranged in order to force me back to face the scene of my transgressions.

Fires were not allowed, nor any noise above low conversation. Obviously we were about to take part in some kind of surprise, but it had been arranged with such secrecy that it would be as much of a surprise for us as for the enemy. We could not tell what numbers were gathering around us in the dark, or guess how far we were spread out across the fields and into the woods. We were aware of teams of horses hauling heavy field guns past, machine guns passing by in their little motorized wagons, and truck after truck full of ammunition. Red Cross trucks threaded their way up along columns of silent troops. Tanks rolled past like giant crustaceans creeping inland from the sea, the wooden dummies indistinguishable from the real.

"Something big's in the wind, boy," someone hoarsely whispered. "Let's hope they don't put the lunatics in charge again." A voice from the Maritimes.

"The lunatics have *always* been in charge," said another. "Why should we be surprised?"

"Fellow claims he seen Currie. You think he'll tell us what the hell's goin' on?"

KEEP YOUR MOUTH SHUT had been attached to our pay books, but nobody had told us exactly what we should keep our mouths shut about. The men were used to being left in the dark, but officers and NCOs began to suspect a plot that everyone had been told about but ourselves. In the past few days we'd been sent all over the countryside. Somebody in charge was confused, or determined to confuse someone else.

First they'd sent our battalion north to Arras, where we were put on a train that hauled us through the night and let us off somewhere in the country at five o'clock in the morning, there to set out on a two-hour march to a village where we then spent three days in routine activities that seemed to have little point to them. Clothing was brushed and picked nearly free of lice, buttons were polished. Without explanation, we were awakened just after midnight and sent off on another march to another village where another train waited. There was barely time to grab a cup of tea and a biscuit at the YMCA counter before we boarded. At eight in the evening the train pulled out without a man of us knowing where we were going, or why.

This train took us to the coast, where we disembarked and marched to a nearby field for a period of rest. Three hours later we set out on a march that lasted until four in the morning when we reached a village and settled into billets. The following day they allowed us time, in the rain, to wash and shave and get cleaned up for whatever they had in mind for us next. We would have believed anything – England, Russia, a suicide mission in the south.

We were herded onto a fleet of buses and arrived some time around 1:30 in the morning at the city of Amiens, whose streets were teeming with movement. Here it was obvious that something important was afoot. The roads were clogged with troops,

tanks, motor trucks, and guns. Rumours sprang up and ran their
course, but still no one knew what the generals had in mind. By
the time we reached Gentelles I'd already begun to realize that I
would find myself back in the same section of the line I'd occupied twice before.

And now that we'd settled in that dark wide plain beyond town
– the First Assembly Point – Colonel Calhoun gathered the
officers together and filled us in on what had been learned when
the sealed orders were opened. Then he took the men aside, one
company at a time, to explain what they could expect. There
had been nothing like it before. All four Canadian divisions were
being assembled along these fourteen miles of the line for a
massive attack, which would take place in the morning, with the
Australians to our left and the French to our right. There were over
one hundred thousand of us here, with more than four hundred
tanks, seventeen brigades of field artillery, and nine brigades of
heavy artillery. All that chasing about had been to confuse the
enemy, who had long ago figured out that wherever the Canucks
were sent in large numbers, a major attack would soon take place.
So we had been taken north in daylight to suggest an assault near
the Belgian border, then secretly brought south again in the dark.

The attack would begin before dawn – 4:20. The first sound
would be a tremendous counter-battery barrage of two thousand
guns. Then we would be off behind the tanks and hope the enemy
would be as surprised as we'd been promised. This would be a new
kind of battle, as we'd begun to suspect from the sort of training
they'd put us through in early summer. We'd been forced through
thirty-mile marches in the heat of midday carrying a hundred
pounds on our backs. We'd spent long hours on the rifle ranges,
we'd practised various methods of attack, mostly on the run.
(General Currie had become an admirer of Stonewall Jackson, we
were told, and was determined to make us the equals of the fierce
Confederates. No one raised the awkward issue of the rebel army's

fate.) Everyone was in better shape than ever before. We were certainly ready for something different. No short raids just to grab an enemy trench, apparently. We would be up and moving across the landscape for long periods of time.

Our immediate objective was to free the railroad connecting Amiens with Paris, but the plan was to drive the Germans back (eight miles was the goal) and begin the process of finally sending them all the way to Berlin.

"Our turn to loot and rape," Fraser fiercely muttered. "Give them some of their own."

While we waited for the order to move up and into positions, I left Eaton in charge of my men and crossed the field to the temporary Orderly Room set up in the kitchen of a farmhouse near the edge of town. Inside, Henderson and Cox at a corner table had fallen again into their old predictable argument about the Americans, who had waited so long to join us. To Henderson they were heroes who would change the course of the War. To Cox they were johnny-come-latelies who had stayed out long enough to make themselves rich. By taking advantage of corruption in the Canadian government they'd made disgusting profits out of munitions fraud. By lending money to Britain and France they would have both those countries at their mercy after the war.

"What 'after the war'?" said Belliveau. "It don't matter if the Yanks are in, this war will last for ever."

So much effort had been put into creating confidence in our mission of the next day that this statement shocked the other two men into silence. Belliveau lowered his voice, not to be overheard. "No matter what we do tomorrow, this bloody war will go on to the end of time. Sooner or later everybody in the world will be fighting it. Living in trenches, going over the top, crawling across that muck-heap of rotting bodies, and getting hung up on barbed wire. Don't you know we're in on something new here? In a hundred years they won't remember that the world was any other way."

We laughed. Though we had all at one time or another suspected the war might never end, we had never considered that it might become something normal.

Belliveau said, "Us, we'll be the pioneers of a whole new civilization, eh? We'll have to teach the newcomers how to survive."

"If there are any of us left," Cox said.

"To tell the truth," Henderson said, "I'm not so sure I'd remember how to live in the normal world."

"I won't have any trouble," Cox said. "I'll go home, kiss Margaret, and take up making saddles where I left off. This whole thing will be a nightmare that happened somewhere else."

He looked as though he'd intended more but broke off and stood to attention and saluted. The others did the same. I turned, to discover another captain had come up behind me. Grinning Charlie Sullivan, who paid no attention to the others.

"Captain Pearson, by God!" He laughed. "Have you spent the whole damned war in this place?"

"*Captain* Sullivan now?" I said, though not without some irony in my smile. "Since when?"

"Two weeks." His big ears flushed red and he shifted his gaze away, frowning. "You must've heard that Martins was killed."

Sullivan was, like me, repeating history. He'd been wounded a second time, this time in a shoulder, and had convalesced again in England. This was why I hadn't seen him at the Dominion Day celebrations in Tincque, where I'd expected to find him winning prizes in the boxing ring or making cynical remarks about the visiting Prime Minister's speech. He had returned to France just in time to take part in this push, wearing a new waxed handlebar moustache and a second decoration.

He growled when I asked him what he had done to earn the DSO. "Nothing that any other damn fool wouldn't have done."

"Your girl impressed?"

He shrugged. "She hasn't thrown me over yet."

Outside, he fell into step beside me. "Dark night," he said. "You got any sort of feeling about tomorrow?"

"They haven't managed to get me too excited about it yet," I said. "Coming back to the same place we were fighting three years ago only shows you that nothing's been gained. What the hell's it been for?"

"Well – has Matt Pearson joined the rest of us at last? Most of us started asking that after the first few months."

He put a hand on my arm, indicating that I was to follow, and stepped off the road where it passed close to a barn. In the deeper shadows just inside the open door, he produced a flask and offered me a drink. It was good whisky. "One of the privileges of promotion?" I said, once I'd had my pull at it.

He didn't respond to that. "I heard some of what they were saying in there. That man Cox is a damn fool if he thinks he'll go back to the way things were before."

"Things can't have changed all that much in four years," I said. "Not at home, anyway – so far from all this."

This was one thing I had tried not to let go of, especially in the worst moments of this madness, a picture of life at home where things could go on pretty much as they had before. Maude and family and farm and work and community. Milk pails. Cattle auctions. School concerts. If you hadn't that sort of stability to hold to, your brain would fly apart.

He studied my face for a moment as though he were gauging whether I had meant what I'd said. "Nothing will be the same afterwards."

He looked so fiercely at me that even in the barn-wall dark I could sense his impatience. "This has been more than just a bloody interruption in things, for God's sake. Do you think everybody'll forget what they learned? It'll be more than wristwatches, paper banknotes, and cigarette-smoking women. Imagine a world where everyone has found out just how much lying they can get away with. Rewarded for! Is there a reason to think they'll stop? Newspapers. Politicians. My God, what will happen when the men who got so good at writing the lies for this bloody war start selling their skills to others?"

He paused, and sucked on his cigarette, and shuddered.

"We'll have to make sure you aren't wounded again," I said, hoping to lighten his mood. "Every visit to England sends you back crankier than the last one. When they made you a captain, they didn't force you to renounce these opinions?"

He mightn't have heard. "Think about it. It'll be a world run by people who've found out what you and me and the rest of us here found out a couple of years ago – that we're no more important or noble than the swarms of rats out there eating the guts of the slaughtered horses."

I could think of no answer to his bitter speech. Had something terrible happened to him, or had he been listening to bitter speeches himself in London? He growled into his own shoulder and flung his cigarette into the muck.

What he foresaw could not be taken seriously at a time like this, before a battle. Otherwise, how could a man stand up and do his job? The world Sullivan had described was a world I would resist, if I managed to survive. And if I could not resist it I would have to find a way to avoid it. Surely the years of fighting over this one small torn-up patch of earth could not have the same effect upon all corners of the world. There had to be places where its ugliness had not yet reached, and never would.

"The reason I stopped you here," he said. "Someone was asking for you in town."

"Me?"

"Isn't your name Pee-*song*?" He laughed. "A pair of rickety old peasants, so bent and shaky they could barely stand."

"Well, they're mistaken. They want someone else."

"I don't think so." Captain Sullivan sucked air through his teeth. "The old fellow was carrying a child."

When I made no response, he added, "I chased them off. Told them they'd be shot if they were caught again. But maybe everyone in that family can make themselves invisible when they decide to go where it's impossible to go. They knew you'd be here. Peasants know things the rest of us don't know until we open a sealed envelope. They're probably skulking around the far side of town right now, if you're fool enough to go looking for them." He consulted his watch. "We should be moving into position within the hour."

We moved up in the dark past stripe after stripe of white tape laid out across the ground – marked jumping-off places for those still coming behind us – and at 1:30 a.m. reached our own position in the reserve trench below the village. I don't suppose anyone settled into sleep, though most tried to get some rest. Some scribbled into notebooks or onto pieces of paper what could become their last-will-and-testaments, good-byes to the folks at home. When I'd completed letters to Maude and Tanner and my folks, and went out of the dugout to check down the line, the smells and sounds were more familiar to me now than any I could recall from my father's farm. Sour earth, sweat, rotting flesh. Sergeant Sommers reported that his men were ready, though that was yet to be seen. What he meant was that each man had his gear: rifle and bayonet, 120 rounds of ammunition, first-aid packet, filled water-bottle, steel helmet, gas mask, two Mills bombs, and a ground flare. Who in civilian life would accept a job that required so much weight on his back?

Out there in the black night was a stretch of land I knew well from weeks of staring at it in daylight and months of seeing it in memory. It wasn't likely to have changed very much. The river was out there, and the railroad. What was left of Moreuil was on the knoll across the valley. The Germans' barbed wire was still where it was, and probably more dense than before, the blasted

trees a little more shattered from shrapnel, the enemy's trenches
more strongly fortified. There would be bodies out there that no
one had yet been able to bring in. Maybe whatever was left of
young Calvin Dawson, who never came back from a night souvenir raid. New pieces of old bodies must have surfaced. New
craters would have blurred the edges of old ones.

This was the sort of night where it was possible to believe the
sounds from out there were not wild dogs snarling over corpses.
You remembered talk of the hordes of crazed deserters from both
sides who had been living together in underground caves and
tunnels but came up at night to rob the dead and dying of food
and drink, squabbling and even killing one another for what
there was to be had.

You began to think too, on a night of waiting like this, of what
there might be beneath you – Fritz, maybe, tunnelling under the
space between us to lay mines they planned to explode the second
they got wind of an attack. I believed I could hear them with my
bones if not my ears – the thump and scrape of pickaxes and
shovels below. Of course this could have been our own men somewhere, or it could have been that I was hearing sounds carried
from some distance. Yet it provoked an uneasy suspicion that the
solid world was being undermined beneath one's feet. It was not
an unfamiliar sensation by this stage of the war.

Though there was a sense this time that we might be about to
enter into a battle that would bring about a serious change to
things, no one was so foolish as to think there would be no casu-
alties. We were aware of the first-aid dugouts, the field hospital
set up behind us, the stretcher-bearers ready to jump and run, the
clearing station prepared. Trucks were parked where they could
rush the wounded away. By now there must have been in the
memory of every man some moment when a friend had cried out
and fallen in an explosion of blood where he hadn't been able to
help. And every man knew that even if this attack were a glori-
ous success, in the chilly morning there would still be the terror

of going over the top, and the strafe of machine-gun bullets setting the broken ground to dancing. Men would scream, and roll forward, and fall where we would have to step over them while they grabbed at our legs and begged for help. We would trip over abandoned wagon wheels, and fall into craters where the decomposing corpses of horses and men would stare at us from eye sockets cleaned out by rats. Tanks would break down, or tilt into German trenches and get stuck, or the men inside would suffocate from the motor fumes. And there was always the possibility of gas.

None of this was spoken of. By now such knowledge had become as certain and inevitable and unconscious as the knowledge of the existence of our own limbs.

We had become unconscious of the limbs of others as well. I'd got all the way back to the dugout entrance before realizing I had passed between walls where coat hooks, hat racks, gun rests, and book shelves had been improvised out of hands and feet and fragments of leg protruding from between sandbags or out of raw dirt. Some had deteriorated to naked bone. Others, presumably still fleshed, were wrapped in rags. They projected into our underworld like the unearthed roots of trees.

Our signs for the corridors of a lunatic asylum had been removed by men who had made this place their home since we'd left it. Sober men, apparently, and not the men who had put the protruding limbs to use. "Madman's Retreat" had not survived. Nor had "Shell-shock Alley." But against the wall of our dugout Henderson discovered a sheet of corrugated iron which still had our RULES FOR INMATES OF THIS INSTITUTION on the back. He turned it out to face us. *Pretend you are sane* was still the first rule. We would wait for 4:20 in what had once been the Dangerous Offenders Ward.

I determined not to think of the village above us, or the tunnels that ran into the hill and under its buildings, or the dugout beneath the church. I had seen a world of villages and churches

destroyed since I'd been here last, heaps of rubble like smashed
crockery on every knoll. Spires rising above a mess of collapsed
roofs. Stone walls disintegrated into mounds of dusty debris.
Brick walls fallen apart like mangled jigsaw puzzles and roofs
without tiles become sagging lattices. Anything upright was
only a grotesque suggestion of what had been there before. Every
march between billets and trenches had passed by one after
another of these abandoned piles, nothing left of their former
selves but a sign announcing a name. You forgot that people had
lived there once.

　　You forgot the people who had died defending them, too. Boys
and men whose names stretched out behind me so far by now that
some of them were already beyond recall. Friends, some of them.
Rivals. The wise and the foolish. The eager and the frightened.
Grateful boys who were half in love with you and sneering men
who watched for your mistakes. Faithful batmen blown to pieces.
Former students, like Corbett, shot by his own countrymen. Men
you knew you would have nothing to say to at home, and men you
believed might have become chums if they'd lived. Greg Horton
and Billy Morris and Jake Devries. Reynolds, Hollingsworth,
Young, Landers, Goldman, Richards, Hansen, Fitzgerald, Blake,
Davies, Lavin, Saunders, Massett, Sillence, Munro, Piercy,
Macleod, Wassileff, Bond, Arnold, Holmes.

　　I refused to think of the names any longer, or of Sullivan's
vision of the future. Sullivan must have been driven a little mad.
I would think no further of the village above us either, or the
destroyed church, or the gentle girl who had found her childhood
abacus in the ruins, or the ancient couple I had gone out to meet
with, against Sullivan's advice, in Gentelles. And I would not
think of the morning, when I no longer knew if I cared what happened to me. While Henderson slept in a chair, and Fraser lay on
the chicken wire of my bed to stare at the ceiling beams, I laid
claim to the books left behind by some soldier who had gone
where he did not, presumably, think he would need them: *Pilgrim's*

Progress, Hardy's *Far from the Madding Crowd*, and Bridges' *Spirit of Man* anthology, all stacked neatly on a makeshift shelf wedged into the sandbags. "Man is a spiritual being," Bridges' introduction claimed, "and the proper work of his mind is to interpret the world according to his higher nature." What would Sullivan say to that? I turned pages – Milton: "A thousand fantasies / Begin to throng into my memory." Wordsworth admitted that,

> *To her fair works did Nature link*
> *The human soul that through me ran;*
> *And much grieved my heart to think*
> *What man has made of man.*

Fragments swam up, and almost made sense, and floated away. These were voices speaking out of a life that had receded too far for me to hear, in a language I could barely follow. When Sullivan pushed in through the sacking and sat on a chair with his hands clasped together between his knees, I ignored him. I studied pages as though I were trying to memorize sentences I could barely see.

"You better tell me what they wanted," he quietly said.

"What are you doing here?"

"Official business further along. Tell me what they wanted, in case you take a hit tomorrow. There might be something you want me to do about those old folks afterwards."

I turned a page, stared hard at words.

"I'd forget them," he said. "These people have had plenty of practice surviving. Centuries of other people's soldiers passing through."

"This may sound foolish," I said. "It *does* sound foolish now. But there was a day when I hoped to remain unspotted by the world, as James instructed the twelve scattered tribes. I imagine I was even a bit of a prig about it. I'm sorry."

"We are killing people," he said. Patiently, I thought. "That's why we're here. You cannot remain unspotted by the bloody world when you *are* the world! Pearson, we're the world the others would like to remain unspotted by."

"Anyway, I made pretty fast work of that, didn't I? And I can't even remember why. Distance, confusion, loneliness, fear – none of it will do as an excuse. When I look back on it, it seems that we were two frightened children clinging to one another while the adults destroyed the world."

He could be right about the peasants, I thought. What did I know of French farmers? There could be a history of such arrangements down through their centuries of wars. Perhaps the race had developed an instinct for knowing when the end of fighting was near and had learned how to make certain that those who would try to leave them to their own devices were encouraged to stay on, or otherwise be of service.

III

A Helmet for the Bees

1996

(i)

Elizabeth's funeral was held in the little Anglican church on the northern edge of town, beside the graveyard filled with valley pioneers and across the road from the War cenotaph made of stones from farmers' fields. I remember thinking that nearly everyone had come. Well, everyone came that could, I suppose. The Maguires, Richmonds, Swifts, Hueffners, and Martins, all in black: wool suits, crêpe dresses, and veiled hats. Macken with two of his boys. The Korsakovs, who had already moved to town. The Evanses and the Mitchells had gone from the district altogether, leaving their farms to be later taken over by a new batch of dreamers once the green had begun to grow up through the ash.

Even Carl and Mary Reimer came, shutting down their sawmill for the afternoon. Carl had his blades and belts and greenchains back together before the world had stopped smoking, and was already sawing boards out of trees with surface burns. Because there would soon be a big demand for their lumber, they'd probably fought a loud and violent argument in their underground shelter before Carl agreed to shut down long enough to attend.

I remember we got there early – Mother and Uncle Archie and I. There wasn't any question of not going, Mother said. Not wanting to do this sort of thing ourselves was no reason to show disrespect for the choices of others. It was a matter of simple courtesy. She would not sit in the back row, as I'd hoped. She was determined to let them see we had come.

The Pearsons sat in the front pew. Mrs. Pearson was at the aisle, with her face barely visible behind the black veil, her gloved hands folded in her lap. Beside her, Tanner looked hot and furious and red, twisting to scowl at others coming in. Matthew Pearson sat between Tanner and old Dr. Moon, who must have wanted to keep an eye on his patient, both of them glaring at some spot high in the corner where the side wall met the front. Pearson's hands were wrapped in white bandages. A good portion of his face was hidden by bandages too, making me think of Mrs. Pearson's brother. Would Matthew Pearson also have to wear a mask for the rest of his life?

I ducked my head and hoped this wouldn't last long. I didn't want to think of my dad. I didn't want to imagine what it must be like for the Pearsons. I was so overtired from not sleeping that, as my mother put it, you only had to look at me sideways to have me in tears.

I hadn't slept since the night we found him. I knew that if I slept I would wake up screaming from dreams of Elizabeth, or finding Tanner's father in the doorway of the abandoned sawmill, his clothing burnt, his hands and arms scarred with black blisters, his hair scorched back to little more than you get on a chicken after you've plucked it. He'd been lying on his belly across the threshold, his smoking boots splayed in the dirt and his blistered hands reaching out across the concrete floor of that abandoned building. One more father dead, was what I thought.

By the time we found him it was night. You could see nothing but the orange-red light of things still burning in the distance, and the little bonfires licking at bushes here and there, and at stumps. Donkey-piles had flared up everywhere you looked. And the whole dark ground was alive with millions of small red glowing lights, like Uncle Archie's forge when the coals were hot, a bed of still-living embers.

Tanner got down and shook his father, hollering into his ear, but Matt Pearson didn't respond. "He's breathing," Tanner said.

He had his ear down close enough to hear. My chest hurt. I realized I'd stopped breathing.

I thought we were going to have to throw him over one of the horses to get him to town, but Tanner sent me off through the woods to get help from Armus Aalto.

While we lifted Mr. Pearson onto the back of the Aaltos' truck, Tanner acted as if it had been someone else's sister lost, and somebody else's father we'd found. He was always able to set his mind to a job and not think much about himself until afterwards. I was trying hard to do the same but a panic had taken hold of me. This wasn't just a job.

Once Tanner had climbed onto the back with his dad and the truck had set off, I followed on the pinto, leading Tanner's horse all the way in to the hospital, where a pair of nuns would not allow me past the front desk. I tied Tanner's horse to a post near the door and rode the pinto back to the tents.

The Red Cross women had given out parcels while I was away. Used shirts and pants with worn-thin knees. Canned tomatoes and bags of Lake of the Woods flour and tins of Braid's Best Tea. Black-bottomed cooking pots with copper rivets plugging the holes. Books. There was a book of Elizabeth Barrett Browning poems in our box, and a weather-swollen copy of *Tales of Unrest* by Joseph Conrad. My mother said she would give the Browning to Mrs. Seyerstad, who was the only person we knew who read poems. I don't know who she thought would read *Tales of Unrest*.

Lying awake through the rest of the night, I heard the coming and going of people outside. More families moved in who had stayed to fight the fire but lost in the end, or at least had lost more than they wanted to face before morning. Men came back to report on things, and some of them slept a bit before going back. There were small fires to be put out yet, in case the wind came up again and everything started over. And there were people still needing help.

In the dark, I held the damaged book and tried to imagine what the stories might be about if there were light in the tent to read by. But my thoughts kept slipping off the imagined page and into that fire. Charred and smouldering Matthew Pearson at the abandoned sawmill. Elizabeth. What it must have felt like when she went into the flames. What Tanner had told me while we were looking for his dad: "She wasn't my sister, really."

"Don't be stupid," I said.

He turned on me, narrowing his red-rimmed eyes. "If you tell anyone else I'll kill you. She was adopted."

"You're lying," I said. "You're being stupid."

"She was a war orphan. They told me not to tell anyone, not even her. They wanted her to think she was part of the family." He turned away from me with a fierce jerk, possibly to hide the ugly distortions in his long freckled face. He'd had little practice with anger. The corners of his mouth pulled down as if yanked by cords he could not control.

I was afraid to sleep. I began to shake. Even wrapped in the donated blankets I was cold. *See what you done*, I said to my dad. *Mother was right. It was your own stupidity that you blew yourself up. You were supposed to be a father, not just another kid.* If Elizabeth wasn't safe with a father like Matthew Pearson to look after her, how safe was I without any father at all?

By noon of the following day, everyone knew that Nora had shown Wyatt Taylor the road, this time for good. It wasn't long before Taylor himself stopped in at the little tent city and talked for a while with the Hueffners and Sandy MacKay, whose arm was wrapped in bandages. Taylor mostly watched the toes of his own warped and charred and tied-together boots, and nodded now and then.

I could tell they were trying to talk him into staying. That fire had gone through too fast to do the stumps much damage. They'd been gutted a little, and charred, and some would still be burning where there was plenty of pitch, but they were still standing where they'd been standing before – in the *way*. For those who would decide to go back and try again, they would still have to be blown and pulled out, and dragged into piles to burn.

"Gentlemen," he said, "on my little farm outside Owen Sound there isn't a stump in sight." He pushed back the brim of his hat that usually kept his face in shadow. Taylor was leaner now than when he arrived, his features more pointed, the whites of his eyes more noticeable in his soot-smudged face. And his burnt hat and coat were far more tattered and ugly than they'd been that day I'd first seen him. "There's not too many trees, either," he said, "and few rocks I couldn't lift with one hand.

"Besides," he added, looking away, "nobody's come right out and said it yet but sooner or later someone's going to blame this mess on me."

They scoffed at this. Hueffner said, "Sooner or later it would've happened anyway."

"Nobody's gonna blame *you!*" said Sandy MacKay, his face colouring up with anger. "It's the bloody government and the logging company we'll send the friggin' lawyers after, once we seen how much damage's been done."

Taylor noticed me then. "Tanner at the hospital? I should go down and look in on Matt."

"I'll go with you," I said.

"Son, your mother already told you to stay away from there," Hueffner said, laying his hand on my head. "That ain't no place for kids."

I ducked out from under his heavy hand. This was a terrible thing the adults were doing to me. I needed to see for myself that Matthew Pearson would recover. It was important that I somehow put myself where he could see that I was all right, too. But they'd taken him behind the wall of secrecy that surrounded families in trouble. I didn't belong with them.

"Matt will need your help worse than ever now," said Sandy MacKay to Taylor. His giant moustache had been singed and curled by fire and partly burned away so that you could see that it had been hiding a crooked scar.

Taylor shook his head. "Too many people wondering if I've got over Nora yet." He said this off in the direction of the town across the river with a private sort of smile. "And your daughters are all too young to be serious distractions. I'm sorry, gentlemen, but you'll have to set your trap for the next poor bugger who stumbles in from the world. Or train these young fellows like Charlie here to take on some of the work."

As he turned away to his horse, making a kind of *tchh*-ing sound from the side of his mouth, he winked at me. "I'll tell him you said 'hello,'" he said. "I'll let you know how he is."

Neither Tanner nor Wyatt Taylor had returned from the hospital when I noticed Mrs. Seyerstad sitting on a chair she'd brought out to the edge of the road before the hotel. She looked like someone waiting to collect tickets from cars driving by, or the only person who'd shown up for a parade. I crossed over to find out why.

"Waiting for someone," she said. "Do you have any objections, Charlie?"

She was smoking a cigarette. I tried not to stare when she raised it to her lips. I don't believe she'd even thought I'd be surprised. Her scarf, which was riddled with burnt-edged holes, was over her hair and tied at the base of her neck, its long ends hanging down her back.

I could see no reason why I shouldn't go up the outside staircase to look in through the windows of the hotel's second storey. I did, but I didn't see much. Messy beds. Flowered wallpaper. There was more to be seen by looking out on the world from the second-floor verandah. The town, the river bridge, the tent city in the park across the road, the fringe of trees along the curve of the river and the low, thick smoky haze above them. From up there, too, I could see Wyatt Taylor riding back from the direction of the hospital.

It must have been Taylor she'd been waiting for, but before he spoke to her he got down off his horse and pushed back his hat in order to look up at me. "He's got some bad burns, but they figure they can fix him up. He wasn't in any shape to talk." Then he squatted on his heels beside Mrs. Seyerstad. "Of course he's torn up about the girl."

I sat on the verandah floor against the wall with my head on my knees.

"Poor Elizabeth," Mrs. Seyerstad said. "And Maude?" Then, before he could tell her anything about Mrs. Pearson, she said, "Were you planning to say good-bye, or were you going to sneak off like a thief?"

I could see Wyatt Taylor down through the gaps in the floor-boards. He raised his hands and dropped them, to slap against his coat. "I would have looked you up even if you hadn't become a Customs officer checking passports here."

"I heard you were heading east." She put a new cigarette to her lips and lit it with a match. Her cheekbones made a sharp curve when she sucked on it.

"Where all I have to do is farm, and don't have to take on all the forces in the world to do it."

"I'm about ready to leave myself," she said.

She waited through a long silence after that. Then she raised her voice. "Charlie. Cover your ears."

I pulled my knees up higher and buried my face.

"How far you going?" he said.

"Do they have schools in Owen Sound?"

"I guess they do," he said.

"I was right the first time," she said. "God's imagination is better than mine. I should have known when I saw you ride down from the mountains —"

"I wasn't coming from the mountains," he said.

"I should have known you were a sign that I ought to give up. But I guess I needed this time to find out there wasn't anything left to give up except the habit."

"And now you've given it up?"

"Brace yourself," she said. She waited a minute then, I suppose to make sure he was ready. "I was sitting on my staircase one day, looking down the road with the same old feeling of hope, and for a terrible moment I couldn't remember what I was hoping for. There was just this awful absence I could put no word or face to. I spent the rest of the day on my bed staring at the ceiling. The next day, or maybe it was the day after that, I realized I couldn't remember his face without looking at the photograph on my dresser. And even staring at it, I couldn't recall his voice, I couldn't force a memory of his voice. I couldn't even imagine him talking or moving about or touching me with his hands. I scared myself half to death."

"Six years is a long time to wait."

"For someone you hadn't known for very long in the first place. Soon after this, while I was walking home from that whist-drive dance in the dark, I felt as if a thin cold veil had been dropped over me from the sky, touching my skin. I knew he was dead. There wasn't any question about it. He'd been dead all along. The night was filled with his absence – he wasn't just absent from here, as I'd believed, he was absent from everywhere."

"So you don't have to stay where he can find you. You can go anywhere you want."

"That isn't all of it," she said. "I didn't really need to discover that. With the worst timing in the world, what I saw was not only that he was dead but that he had been dead for a long time. You see, until then I'd been so busy trying to get Nora to fall in love with you that I hardly noticed what was happening to myself."

There was another long silence from both of them after that.

I think I'm getting this right. I remember leaning forward to see the look on Taylor's face. His mouth was open a little, though he wasn't saying a thing. He looked at Johanna Seyerstad as though he'd never seen her before, and at the same time he looked like a small boy trying to figure out what the devil had been going on in the world. He walked the full way around his horse and came back and said, "What?"

Her students knew she hated repeating herself. And she never answered to "What?"

He crossed the road and stared for a minute at the tents. When he came back, he put his fingers down inside the front of his belt and leaned forward and lowered his voice. "You mean what you said?"

She didn't answer this one either. Mrs. Seyerstad always meant what she said. He should have figured that one out by now.

"Well," he said, turning away and speaking more or less to his horse, "I guess I would have found it out for myself sooner or later." He ran a hand over the horse's face and up over its head and down its mane. Then he laid his hand flat against the rippling muscles of the shoulder. "I'd noticed it wasn't quite so interesting doing things for Nora when you weren't around to help." He turned away for a while, maybe to think about what he'd said.

Mrs. Seyerstad raised her voice again. "Charlie, don't you repeat a word."

I started to shake, I couldn't help myself. It was as though something chilled had taken hold of me and wanted to rattle me apart. I kept the crying as quiet as I could, with my face to my knees, but Mrs. Seyerstad heard. "Charlie? Are you all right?" Then she came up the stairs.

So at the funeral service I didn't want to look at her either. Or at Wyatt Taylor. Or at anyone else. When my neck ached from keeping my head down, I looked up at the windows. No one had cleaned the stained glass. Smoke or soot had left a dark film on the outside nearly thick enough to block off light from the sun. The little room was dark and hot, even with the door left open. People began to sweat as soon as they'd settled into the pews. Men removed their jackets. Women used the prayer books to make a breeze at their throats.

The preacher must have known there was something remarkable in the gathering. The entire settlement had turned out – or
all that was left of it now. Even in town the air was still thick with
the smell of smoke, and the earth was layered over with a carpet
of ashes that left grey powder on your boots and up your legs. If
the man had paid a visit just a few miles north of town he would
have seen a landscape of angular snags and dark skeletons leaking
smoke. He would have thought we were crazy to stay.

But he must have known that those who hadn't already left
were determined to try, because after saying all the things that
have to be said at funerals, he went on to hand out advice. He
knew about the fire and the destroyed homes. He knew about
Mrs. Macken, buried the day before from this same church. He
knew, or said he did, the sort of task that lay ahead of everyone if
the place was to be put back in order and land still turned into
homes. Ashes, he said, could be good for the soil.

He suffered as much as anyone from the heat. He wiped a white
handkerchief across his wet forehead and down around his heavy
jaw, but his discomfort didn't cause him to hurry. He leaned out
from his pulpit to address us with a passion that suggested he
knew he would never see most of us again, and had only this one
chance to make an impression.

To tell the truth, I'd never heard of Nehemiah. That may be
why I listened hard enough to remember. Nehemiah set out with
plenty of help, the preacher said, to rebuild the crumbled walls of
his city. But the whole time he was at work there were those who
tried to discourage him, tried to take his attention off the job,
tried to draw him away to other things. "Sanballat was the worst
of 'em," the preacher said, mopping his shiny jowls. "Sanballat
and Tobiah and Geshem the Arabian and a whole lot of others. It
doesn't matter what their names are because they find new names
every time they try their tricks on us.

"*Come, let us meet together in some one of the villages in the plain
of Ono*, they said. But Nehemiah knew what they were up to. *I am*

*doing a great work, he said. Why should the work cease, while I leave
it, and come down to you?*

"Oh, they tried everything – they still *do*," he said. "They sent
a letter to Nehemiah, making accusations. The whole idea was
to weaken the workers' resolve, to fill them with doubts, to make
them afraid. But Nehemiah prayed for the strength to finish his
task. He made sure every builder had his sword at his side, he knew
it wasn't enough just to build, they had to *watch*."

He paused, and looked from one face to the other as he mopped
his forehead again. Mrs. Pearson was still staring at her gloves, but
Matt Pearson was looking at him now. The preacher seemed to
have got his attention at last. "And so do we all, dear friends," he
said, "so do we all have to watch. It isn't enough just to work, we
have to work while clad in the armour of God. And what is the
armour of God?"

He went on to name that whole long list we've all heard at one
time or another: the breastplate of righteousness, the girdle of
truth, the shield of faith, the sword of the Spirit, the whole business, everything to protect us from the fires and tragedies and
anything else that would try to stop us from doing what we have
come here to do in the world.

That was how he got back to Elizabeth, by painting her death
as a temptation – an enticement to give up in despair, to walk
away and leave the job undone, to question the wisdom of relying
on God. And so on. "*Every man's work shall be made manifest; for
the day shall declare it, because it shall be revealed by fire; and the fire
shall try every man's work of what sort it is.* First Corinthians."

One of the hymns we stood up to sing was "Nearer, My God,
to Thee." I don't know what it meant to Matthew Pearson, or
anyone. The stones, maybe. "Out of my stony griefs / Bethel I'll
raise." Maybe while they were standing to sing they thought of
their own scorched fields with the habit of sending up a yearly
crop of rocks to the surface, cold and hard as grief. They still had
to go home to the backbreaking job of starting all over again at

something that didn't promise much more than a place to live –
not a fortune, not even a living, and certainly not an eventual rest
from labour. Just a place to try to set down their roots.

❦

(ii)

Even after all these years I have no trouble recalling the pain I
felt at the funeral and immediately afterwards. Especially afterwards. Not only *recalling* the pain, but still feeling it, a great
empty longing that seemed to have hollowed out everything
that wasn't bone. Something more had been taken from me. I'd
hoped to speak to Matthew Pearson afterwards, or at least to get
close enough to be noticed. I imagined him breaking into a grin,
insisting I be brought over so he could thank me for my part in
finding him. It wasn't the thanks I wanted, it was his attention.
He wasn't just Tanner's father any more, he wasn't even just the
man who invited me to sit on his porch and ask questions about
my dad. He was the man who had lost his daughter and gone
wandering through the smoking landscape after her, and nearly
died himself.

But he was taken back to the hospital right away. After the
service, a few families went to the Pearson house, but I was not
allowed to go anywhere except home. Uncle Archie guided me by
the upper arm. "You and me have got a fence to mend." Somehow
this catastrophe, though it was mine as well, had sealed Matthew
Pearson inside a world that didn't include me.

Those who visited him in the hospital brought back word that
he had begun to recover from his burns but was not recovering

from the loss of his daughter. Of course that wasn't something you'd expect him to recover from, but they were worried about the way he brooded. They said he stared fiercely into space. He broke off in the middle of sentences. He blamed himself, they said, as any of us might do. He was sure that the girl's death had been a punishment for something. But while others from the settlement talked about cleaning up their houses, fixing their fences, and buying cattle on the strength of promised government relief, he stared out the window without showing a flicker of interest. He showed no interest even when the premier of the province came up to look over the damage.

I couldn't stand this for long. On a Thursday afternoon while my mother thought I'd gone fishing with Tanner, I rode my bike in as far as the park that had been the site of the tent city and then along the river and the shoreline of the bay as far as the hospital. I arrived hot and tired and sweaty, and was not in any mood to argue with nuns. When the Sister looked up from behind her desk I told her I'd wait right where I was for my mother, who was visiting a friend. I opened the magazine she gave me, but when she turned away to find something in a cabinet I dashed as quietly as I could down the hallway and up the staircase to the second floor. Even if she came after me and dragged me away, I was determined at least to let him see that I'd come.

Strangers looked back from their beds – town people. The only nursing sisters I saw were busy talking into one old gentleman's face on a pillow. Matthew Pearson had the farthest room to himself, a harsh bare place where my footsteps echoed. He was sitting up in bed, looking out the window, and didn't notice me there until I put my hand on the iron railing at his feet.

His eyes took a moment to focus. Then there was just a hint of a smile, muscles twitching at the edges of his mouth. "Charlie," he said. It wasn't a greeting, only a label for what his eyes had noticed. But he tightened his lips and looked quickly towards the doorway, in case there were others behind me perhaps, and then again to the window. He looked out from that stark room onto the bay and the smoky mountains on the far side of it, and the Company's log booms and pylons and dumping wharf. Sunlight flashed and danced off the surface of moving water – the river through town being stirred and absorbed into outgoing tide.

The bandages had been removed from his face, though not his hands. At one temple and down along his jaw the flesh was the colour of raw meat, shining with a smear of grease. His lashes and eyebrows had been burned away.

"I snuck in," I said. Rather proudly, I suppose. "But I don't have anything people could catch."

"Neither have I." He blinked heavily and smiled. "Let us hope."

His movements were slow, as though every tiny muscle had to be operated separately, like the cranes and carousels we sometimes made with Tanner's Meccano set. His voice seemed to have pushed its way through a fog. "I could bring some books," I said. "I could read to you."

Read what? *Tales of Unrest?* Mrs. Seyerstad had told me I was a good reader for my age but I would stumble over the words of an adult book, embarrassing us both. And anyway, he could read for himself. So far as I knew his eyesight had not been harmed.

On the far side of the bay a logging train was stretched out along the Company wharf – tiny at this distance – its miniature logs being tilted off the gondola cars and into the water. Explosions fountained up. "Merv Gardner drove off the end of that once," he said. "He was drunk. He thought it was the bridge in town."

I didn't know who Merv Gardner was. And I couldn't tell from his thick slow voice if this was meant to be sad or amusing. "Did he drown?"

Another long pause. "Friends saved him, but they couldn't do much for his car."

"You mean it's still there?"

"If they'd got it out fast enough and rinsed off the salt, I suppose they might have saved it."

We waited in uncomfortable silence again. He might have forgotten I was there.

"I'll go," I said. "I just wanted to tell you I'm sorry."

He turned a helpless, disconsolate look upon me that I thought was also filled with pity, for me or for the two of us together. "Oh, Charlie," he said. His voice was heavy, weary, deeper than sad. What did he want to say? I couldn't imagine at the time, though now I suppose he was thinking that anything he might want to say should not be said to an eleven-year-old boy.

Another heavy blink and I wasn't there for him any more. His gaze went back to the window.

He did not look to me like someone who'd survived a disaster, he looked like someone who still needed rescue from something only he could see. What would it feel like to watch someone drive off a logging wharf and almost drown? In the weeks that followed, my poor skull ached from thinking of what to do.

I didn't know until many years later just how terrible were the demons he struggled with. By the time Maude got around to telling me what went on between her and her husband in that hospital room I was a young man, working for the weekly newspaper in town and living on the little hobby farm that the Prices carved for me off one corner of their property. I'd been coming around to Pearsons' fairly regularly by then, often staying for meals. It had broken her heart to see what had become of him, she told me. "Not just the physical wounds, Charlie. They were healing well enough, most of them. But the way he was blaming himself. He wouldn't look at Tanner. He wouldn't look at me. He was ashamed. He believed he'd been punished, you see. He'd always claimed not to believe in the old-time wrathful God of his mother's, but some traces of it must have stuck. He taught Sunday School in Ferguson Falls but argued sometimes for hours with Reverend Clarke, against the notion of divine vengeance. But it seemed he never managed to *feel* what he said he thought. He'd been waiting for something like this to happen."

We were in her cool parlour, just the two of us, one afternoon
after I'd returned a set of headcheese pans she'd lent me. She was
working on a piece of embroidery for some charity auction, and
had invited me to sit. This was obviously something she'd been
planning to tell. The curled and twisted shapes of verandah
honeysuckle vines shifted in the patch of autumn sunlight on the
painted floor. Her coloured embroidery threads were laid out in
rows across the large Bible on the table beside her.

She'd wondered if the hospital had something to do with it,
she said. Crucifixes hung on the walls, signs of torment everywhere
you looked. Nursing sisters in mediaeval habit swished in and out
of the rooms, bringing medication and sympathetic pats to the
wrist. "And righteous judgement, he probably thought," Maude
said, "though I saw nothing but compassion there myself."

She lost patience with him. "Do you really think that God
would destroy an innocent child in order to show His anger with
you? Good heavens, Matthew, *think*! I've never known you to be so
self-centred."

He'd made her feel excluded. By taking the blame, he was
keeping the grief to himself. She thought that drawing this to
his attention might allow him to see how he'd left her outside, as
though he thought she hadn't been affected too. He had always
been so mindful of her feelings.

"Of course, as soon as I'd spoken I felt even worse. After all, I
thought, it was selfish of *me* to demand comfort!"

She looked up at me, and then to the side, as though she had
heard something in the distance she wanted to identify. Her hand
froze for a moment, the needle poised at the end of a short scarlet
thread. Then she went on.

He hadn't responded at first, she said. When he spoke, it was as
though she had given him permission to say what had been floating all along just below his self-condemnation. What had been his
fault was suddenly hers. "You didn't listen to me, Maudie," he said.

He said it softly. Almost kindly. "If you'd got away when I told you, the girl would still be alive."

I found this hard to imagine. Even hearing it years later I didn't want to believe it. I had never witnessed Matt Pearson being cruel – to child, woman, man, or even his most cross-natured cow.

"Did he imagine I hadn't thought of this myself?" she said. She looked up again from her needle, directly into my eyes, as though she expected an answer. I believe she was pausing to make sure she had full control of her voice. "While he was lying there moaning about being punished for his sins, I had been fighting with my own guilt. I *had* taken too long to get away! I *hadn't* realized how urgent it was that we leave! I *had* got muddled and could not make up my mind what I should take with us and what I could bear to leave behind! But it was already terrible enough to bear the loss of the child, and to think of what she must have suffered, without forcing still more pain upon myself." She lost the struggle to keep a catch from her voice. She waited, looking towards the outside door, as though to remind me of his absence from this room. "It was possibly the greatest blow of my life, to find him capable of this."

This may or may not have been true. It would be a long time yet before we would learn about Elizabeth's origins and try to imagine Maude's shock upon receiving Pearson's first letter on the subject. This too, she would tell me in time, was possibly the greatest blow of her life. "I had to read the letter several times to understand what he was on about. My brain just would not take it in. I felt myself turning to ice, weakening to the point where it was necessary to go to bed. When neighbours summoned my mother from Montreal, she was convinced I'd got word of Matthew's death but couldn't bring myself to admit it. She cared for Tanner and allowed the grieving widow to adjust. Beneath the blankets, the 'grieving widow' let time go by while she gradually thawed out her senses with the heat from an increasing sense of betrayal and humiliation and anger. I expected to rise up in fury, spraying flames, but I did not put foot to floor until the day I awoke from a terrifying dream of gunfire and discovered I was flooded with gratitude that Matt was, so far as I knew, still alive. I decided that I would not let this or anything else defeat me by twisting me up with bitterness. I would find a way of letting my gratitude lead me to some place where forgiveness was possible. As I do when things need straightening out, I began a letter-writing campaign – a paper blizzard roaring across the Atlantic."

As for the hospital room accusation, she wished that someone else had been there to hear. The doctor, perhaps, so that he could have told her that her husband was out of his mind with grief, striking out at the nearest person when he couldn't bear to strike at himself any longer. She knew this but she would have liked to hear it from someone else, so that she could dismiss his words as she would if they'd been spoken by some lunatic stranger in an asylum. As it was, she carried the words alone, and could not imagine how he and she were to live the rest of their lives.

Once he'd been released and had rested for as long as he could bear to be shut up inside the house, he made some effort to get his damaged farm into good repair. He started to replace the charred planks along one wall of his barn, but he soon lost interest and began to replace a few of the fence posts. Then, when he had split fewer than half the cedar posts he would need, he decided he should fell some of the scorched trees at the back of his property in case they should fall on the new cattle he hadn't got around to buying yet. His heart was not in this.

His hair had begun to grow in. Burns on his face had started to heal. The scars on his hands had begun to fade to a less violent colour. He was a young man, he had every reason to think he would recover his health. But he knew that something was wrong.

We all knew something was wrong. He tried to treat Tanner the same as before but it was obvious that he was uncomfortable with his son around, attempting to help him with the chores. When Tanner saw this, his face closed off in anger. He turned on me and made it clear that my help wasn't welcome either. "You got no home of your own?" He went alone, then, fishing, or down to the sea for a swim. I stayed away like someone sent into exile.

No, that isn't true. I did not stay away. I stayed away from Tanner but not from his father. Whenever I saw him riding Orion past my attic window, I followed on my bike. Sometimes I lost him. Sometimes I guessed where he was going and got there soon after him.

He rode down to the beach and sat for a while on the driftwood logs, looking out at the Strait. I stayed behind some underbrush. Sometimes he walked the length of the park, along the gravel slope above the tide, watching the toes of his own boots, and then turned and walked back. I didn't intend him to see me, I didn't intend to speak, I just wanted to be close enough in case he needed someone, like Merv Gardner in his drowning car.

He rode back to the river, and went inside the abandoned sawmill for a while. Sometimes he sent Orion home on his own, and then walked across Aaltos' property and Evans's abandoned farm, following the route he had taken through the smouldering aftermath of the fire – but following it in reverse, as though he might unravel time and find Elizabeth alive after all at the swamp at the back of his place. I followed, making sure he didn't hear. After the first time I knew the route, so it didn't matter if I lost sight of him. Eventually I would find him at the swamp where the horses had stood in water that boiled around their ankles while flaming limbs fell on their backs, and where he had found Elizabeth. He sat on a log near the large tilted wheel-rims from his burnt wagon, and stared at his hands. Sometimes he put his hands over his face. Sometimes he kneaded his damaged shoulder. I crouched on my heels behind the charred trunk of a fallen tree.

He knew that I followed him, of course, though I wasn't aware of that until the third time in the swamp. "You'll never make a private investigator, Charlie," he called out. "You're too twitchy. A private investigator has to have patience and *stillness*. You might as well come out of there and walk back to the house with me."

I stepped out into the swampy clearing, face burning, and expected to be faced with embarrassing questions. But he looked at me as though he would like to figure out what I was made of without having to ask.

I tried to apologize and explain, but could only splutter.

"That's all right," he said. "I can imagine your father sneaking through the bush to make sure I didn't do something stupid. He wouldn't be able to explain himself either."

He stood up from his log and started up the wheel ruts in the direction of his farm buildings, holding out one arm in a gesture that invited me to get myself up there beside him.

"The thing is this, Charlie. You don't want to get near me. Right now I'm not fit company for humans."

By this time, people were helping one another with repairs and reconstruction, but Matt Pearson discouraged them from coming onto his farm. He even rejected offers of help from Wyatt Taylor, who'd moved into Sullivan's house while he and Johanna Seyerstad tried to make decisions about the future. Taylor had had his eye on Hayden Evans's abandoned place, but Evans decided the place he'd been so glad to leave behind was worth a fortune now that someone wanted it. There were other farms he might have had – the Mitchells had left the district, glad to see the end of that rock pile up on the ridge above Reimers' mill – but in the end he'd got permission, from those who knew Sullivan best, to move into Sullivan's place in order to keep it up. Until its owner returned.

It was a terrible-looking place – the whole settlement, all of it. Besides the tall snags left behind by an earlier fire, the standing timber and the man-high second growth had been flayed and beaten and stripped to skeletons too. Houses and barns not reduced to smoking heaps were charred and blistered and foul to the smell. Fences were dark tilted sticks outlining fields, where the black stumps and donkey-piles were the most substantial things remaining. The smoke was still so heavy in the air that sometimes it was late in the morning before you could see the barn from the kitchen window. It made the heart sink to imagine starting again.

And yet some people were doing it. They had to, most of them, those who had stayed. Most of those who had stayed were too poor to leave, but they tackled it with energy anyway, restoring buildings and tidying up their farms in the most desolate place you could ever imagine. As Patrick Maguire put it, he felt as if he'd settled amongst the singed hairs on the backside of some black gigantic beast.

Pearson tried for a while to assist those who were worse off than himself. He rode over to help the Maguires put up the frame of a new house, for instance, but he had only begun to toe-nail a row of wall studs when he found himself expecting Elizabeth to show up any minute, her curls bouncing, bringing him a jar of cold water and an apple. He hung his hammer on his belt and left.

He tried again. He rode up with a group of men who'd already started to help Howard Stokes rebuild his barn and this time managed to work for a day and a half splitting shakes for the roof before Elizabeth arrived. At first he heard her laughing with the children who played in the yard, entertaining the Stokeses' little boy. He shook himself free of that but he was unprepared for a cold shiver down his back, a certainty that she was right behind him, waiting for him to turn around. Like everything else in the world she smelled of smoke, but he knew that if he turned he would see that she'd been untouched by the fire, her eyes wide and shining with laughter while she waited for him to drop everything and lift her in his arms.

When Stokes asked why he was leaving, he blamed the boy. The child's loud racket had been getting on his nerves. Anger flared up for only a moment in Howard Stokes's eyes. There was a time that giant would have knocked him senseless for a comment like that, before the child had come along and made a softer man of him. Instead he walked Pearson to the gate. "Go home," he said. "I can't think of anything worse than what's happened to you."

Pearson had trouble understanding how the others had the heart to rebuild. When he stopped by Reimers', where Mary and Carl were converting their underground shelter into a permanent house, he sneered at what he called their giant root cellar. "You might save yourselves from the next fire but how much will that matter if you've already drowned in the rain?"

Carl went on hammering as though he hadn't noticed Pearson, but Mary removed the nails from between her teeth and turned on him, planting her fists on her wide hips. "You think this is any crazier than that big rock house you started down there once?" She grinned, determined not to be provoked. She would not have forgotten the sight of him stumbling towards her through the smoke with the child in his arms. "Why don't you go home and finish that thing? If you're running out of rocks we can ship some over."

Pearson could not help smiling back at this woman who, he knew, could just as easily have turned her sharp tongue against him. "No danger of that," he said, lowering himself to sit on a pile of slab-wood and fishing in his pocket for his tobacco. "I've run out of something else – steam. I can't get worked up to believe in it any more."

Mary squatted on her heels. Late afternoon sunlight laid long narrow shadows of skeletal trees across the ashy yard. "I don't think so." She tapped a finger against her left temple. "Up here in your head you see that Ontario house still waiting. It's a disease you brought with you from that other place, eh. Like them Maguires with their Irish fences and Mac's windbreak poplars." She scratched with the nails on the ground and sucked at a tooth while she thought over what she'd just said. "Maybe a good thing you stopped it. All it showed is you don't think much of this place the way God made it."

"I never got to see the way God made it," Matt Pearson said, lighting his pipe. "Those logging companies managed to make a mess of it before I got here."

She made a face that suggested doubt, and shook her head. "Makes no difference. If you got here before them loggers you would still figure it was a mess and go crazy putting your perfect corners on things."

He tilted his head and raised an eyebrow. "Not with Reimer lumber I wouldn't."

She laughed. "Maybe we do that thing on purpose."

"Well, at least we didn't steal the place from anyone, Mary. If we'd taken it from someone we'd be thinking now that we'd been punished for it."

He probably shouldn't have said this to Mary Reimer. "You think you didn't take it from nobody?" she said. There was a dangerous edge to her voice.

"That's right," Pearson said. "Your people never used it. They had more sense."

"Maybe they thought that was what it was here for," she said. "To be left alone so there'd be spaces between us, eh. Them Frenchmen over there, did you ask them if there's any places they'd just as soon not have the Germans build a town?"

"I'll take that with a grain of salt," he said, "because it was you that brought Reimer onto this place before the rest of us got here. If you really thought we shouldn't be trying to make something new out of this place you should've married a fisherman instead of Carl. You should have waited for Nigel Swift – there isn't much chance he'll make many changes to the landscape."

He hadn't realized what a deep well of anger he was able to draw from, he confessed to Maude. "I find myself saying things that I know are bound to hurt, and taking pleasure from this, even though I'm horrified at the same time."

He was saying unkind things to people he liked, people he respected and had never wished any harm, but saying them anyway because it seemed as though these things just had to be said.

"This isn't you!" he would tell himself, astonished and ashamed but still eager to discover what he might come up with next! But he was afraid at the same time that it might turn out to be him after all, and be him for the rest of his life. In the Ottawa Valley, Maude told me, he'd taught next door to a woman who had been disappointed several times and had developed a sharp tongue. She couldn't seem to keep from humiliating her students. She tried to bite off her words but failed. She despised herself even as she was doing it, but she couldn't stop. In other ways she was quite a good teacher but she ended up doing far more damage than good. "In the end she took her own life."

Leena Hueffner told him to *vamoose* for a while. "We know folks in Texas would put you to work on a ranch so big you wouldn't be able to *find* nobody to snarl at. Rattlesnakes will think you're one of their own."

He brooded while he worked, while he ate, even while he made an attempt to spend time with his family. Elizabeth was constantly showing up to interrupt whatever he tried to do. He thought of my father and began to wonder if he might blow himself up with stumping powder and make it look like an accident.

One evening while Maude was writing a letter to our elected Member in Victoria, demanding funds for better fire-fighting equipment, he sat across the kitchen table from her and said, "Do you think that you may have wanted – just a little – for it to happen?"

She thought she might collapse. She had held her tongue in the hospital but would she again? She looked out through the window onto the blackened fields. "Only a stranger could imagine such a –"

She cut off her own words, refusing to defend herself. She would not remind him of what he could not have forgotten.

Elizabeth's drawings were still tacked to the walls and the cupboard doors. Neither of them had been able to take them down, though an unintended glance would make their legs go weak with grief. Intricate seashells. Carefully drawn woodbugs. Wyatt Taylor in his foolish costume. A drawing of Uncle Donald on the porch was curling at the edges above the door to the pantry.

"Possibly you never loved her," he said. "You were brave, and forgiving, and worked hard to be the perfect wife and mother, but maybe you wished all along that she had never come into our life."

What had he hoped for from this? A confession that all her forgiveness and understanding had been merely play-acting? That she had seized pretence as a way of preserving her pride and a marriage he had otherwise ruined? I believe he wanted only to hurt, and the surest way to hurt Maude was to suggest that everything that had defined their life together had been false. He wanted to see someone else hurt as badly as himself.

Maude did not respond to this. Maybe she was steeling herself to answer, but she didn't have to say anything. Tanner spoke from the doorway to his bedroom. "Dad?" It was clear from his face that he'd overheard.

Pearson had thought his son was outside, that he and Maude were alone in the house, except for Will and, of course, Donald, sleeping in his room. The alarmed look on Tanner's pale face told him where he had brought himself with his hurt and anger and self-hatred: far from the boy, far from them both, and everyone. In front of his son and his wife he had brought himself to shame.

"Son," he said, when Tanner had stepped in to the kitchen for some explanation, "I think you should take your old man out in the bush and shoot him before he does more harm. I will thank you to do it fast."

Tanner began to cry.

Outside, Pearson strode across the scorched grass and down the slope through the orchard, past the chicken run and the barn and across the field to the open spring. Cows ought to be drinking from the creek that led away from it but of course he had no cattle. He ought to be doing something about the stumps that Taylor had blasted in the churned-up field between here and the

forest of naked trees. The big one he thought of as Old Wisdom
Tooth was still untouched behind them, its thick roots anchored
deep amongst rocks in the soil. Elizabeth was just as solidly rooted.
Nothing could proceed without her. She ought to be hanging onto
his trouser legs, begging him to chase her, catch her, throw her up
over his shoulder and run, with Buster and Sullivan's springer
spaniel barking at his heels. He rested his elbows on the top plank
of the crib wall and peered into the water. Only his own miserable face, spotted and patched with new skin, and behind him the
cloudless sky. Long-legged creatures moved across the surface as
though his reflection were on solid glass, or ice. And in fact the
air that rose off it was so cool and pure it might have come
directly from a slice of underground glacier.

He'd heard somewhere that drowning was a relatively painless death. He didn't believe it. Relative to what? A chest blown
apart? A skull crushed beneath a tank? He doubted there was such
a thing as a painless death, just as he doubted now that there
was such a thing as a painless life. Everything from before the fire,
including the War, seemed now to have been less painful than
he'd thought, just as everything ahead promised to be weighted
with more pain than a person could bear.

But, you didn't drown yourself within sight of your wife's
kitchen window, however tempting it might be to plunge into
the numbing cold. Though you might wish to sink lower than soil,
and roots, and the stones still working their way to the surface
of earth, and to dissolve eventually into a tributary of Portuguese
Creek, you did not subject your remaining children to that horror.

He didn't hear Taylor ride into the yard and walk down across
the grass towards him. He wasn't aware of Taylor at all until the
man was within a few yards. "You aren't taking it literally, are
you? Morris's well at the end of the world?" There was laughter in
Taylor's voice, or at least a readiness to laugh.

In the old novel, the sought-for well was supposed to be filled

with water that healed the wounds of battle. Taylor's was not a
voice he wanted to hear.

He'd tried not to think about Taylor at all, he would tell
Maude. He didn't want to deal with what he was bound to think,
that there was something dangerous about Taylor he couldn't put
his finger on. Sullivan knew it. "If Sullivan were here he'd be able
to tell us a thing or two about Taylor."

He didn't quite hit Taylor. He turned and struck out at him, but
Taylor caught hold of his fist and held it in his own. For a moment
their linked arms were rigid as iron, veins swollen, as they stared
into one another's eyes. Pearson, for all his hospital rest, was not
a weakened man.

Taylor tried to laugh at the absurdity of this. "Let me go, Matt.
This makes no sense." But didn't relax his own grip, nor pull away.

"I won't let you go."

By this time Tanner had exploded out onto the porch and
down the slope, shouting for them to stop.

"Not until you tell me who you are. Why are you here, anyway?
What did you want from me?"

Taylor grunted, breaking the hand grip, and stepped back. For
a long moment they regarded one another – Pearson belligerent,
alarmed, Taylor puzzled and almost amused. Tanner had come to
a halt a few feet away, and stood waiting, his wide eyes watching
his father.

"Look," Pearson said. He could barely see, everything had
blurred, the dark landscape trembled: buildings, fence posts, spiked
snags beyond the ashen fields. "Look at our 'little piece of Eden'
now, Taylor! Still smoking, some of it." He turned, and had to
grasp the rough planks of the well crib to restore his balance. "It's
as though we hadn't ever got away from that hell hole over there.
Worse, it's as if we'd torn our families away from their homes and
thrown them into the horror."

"There are no guns, Matt," Taylor said. "It'll grow back."

Pearson might not have heard. He lowered his brow and glared up at Taylor. "You mocked us when you first got here, for trying to escape the world. Well, I hope you're satisfied. The factories and their paid liars haven't caught up to us yet, but we've managed to land in an ugly new world without them." Again he turned away, and with his back to Taylor regarded the naked woods beyond the pasture. "My good Lord, I thought it was a mess when I first saw it but at least I believed I could tidy it up. By the time you got here I was ready to quit, but you convinced me to change my mind. Now this. Worse than when we started!" He completed the turn and looked at Tanner. "This time we'll go back to Ontario with our tails between our legs. At least we can say we tried."

Tanner had begun to shake his head even before Pearson finished. "I'm not going." Unafraid eyes were levelled at his father. "Neither will Mother and Will."

"He's right," Maude said, when they'd gone inside. "Mother is as stubborn as her son. We've made this ours. We've done too much here now. It's home."

"I'll tell you what," Taylor said. He studied Maude a moment, possibly having second thoughts about what he'd intended to say. Then he looked at Pearson. "I'll keep an eye on things around here if you like, while you go away for a time, if that's what you want. It looks as if I'm not exactly in a hurry to leave myself. Tanner and me and Maude'll look after the place. Tanner's old enough to hold the fort for a while."

Maude did not object. There was still something he had to come to understand for himself, she would tell me, something about that day he hadn't acknowledged. "I couldn't just tell him, it would only seem that I was refusing to share the blame. He would have to come to it on his own: that things might have been different if he had taken us out of there himself instead of thinking he was so important he had to check on everyone else. Who did he think he was – the mayor of some European village?"

Maybe he needed some distance to see what she had seen.

Over their after-supper tea she announced that she thought a time apart might be good for them both. Since their first separation had brought more trouble upon them than either could have dreamed, maybe a second could reverse the damage. Either that, or they might discover they were too much changed from the people they'd been to continue as man and wife.

(iii)

The film did not take us as far as Matt Pearson's return to France. I suppose they believed that Elizabeth's funeral was a natural place to stop, since it brought so much of the settlement together before everyone had to go home and face the rest of the damage done by the fire.

Because I was nearly the only one left who could remember back that far, I was pestered for information. How much had the Store been changed since then? Which road led to Pearsons'? They were probably trying to make an old man feel important. "Who all came to the funeral?" they said. "Where did they sit?" Frankly, I don't know why it mattered where people sat, after all these years. They shouted, of course, as though there were a glass wall between us, taking it for granted that ol' Charlie Mackinaw must be deaf. "Can you remember what families showed up?"

When they study movie-making I suppose they're taught what to use and what to leave out. I was disappointed to see how Matthew Pearson had been pushed to the background in the film, but it is well known around here (with amused tolerance) that I had made Pearson something of the main figure in my version of

things. Others see stories from their own particular angle. Someone must have decided that the tale of Johanna Seyerstad, Nora
Macken, and Wyatt Taylor would sell more tickets.

We knew the boy wasn't making a documentary, but some
wondered why he couldn't have stuck to the facts. The truth is,
young Macken could not have made his movie at all if he'd stayed
strictly with the facts, because then he would have had to treat
everyone the same, with no main characters at all. Everyone was
the main character in his own version. I can see that now. No
matter how many versions you considered, there would always be
another you hadn't thought of.

By the time he started working on his movie, most of the old-
timers who might have helped him had already gone. What he
started with was something a local fellow had written twenty years
before. This was a grandson of Corky Desmond, who interviewed
a lot of the survivors, including myself, some of us several times,
and then wrote it up the way he imagined we might have told it
if we had told it all at once quite soon after the fire. "Voices from
Portuguese Creek." He gave printed-up copies to those of us he'd
interviewed, but despite the theatre posters' claim that the movie
was "based upon the book" he never actually published it as a
book – probably because he saw it was impossible even to *finish* it.
There would always be another voice to hear from, or another
version, or something new just remembered, or an older memory
reconsidered. He could have spent the rest of his life trying to nail
down every wrinkle and still have failed. By this time I was editor
at the weekly newspaper in town and ran his "Voices" over several
weeks in a local history column called "Getting the Story Straight"
– all the publication it ever got. Later, he published a magazine
story called "The Perfect Daughter," where the Nora Macken
character is portrayed as a woman whose love for Taylor was as
powerful as any found in the legends but whose ties to her family
were so strong that she could not choose the man from Ontario
once her mother had deserted her by dying.

Only minutes into the movie we could tell the boy had not only read the story but had interviewed his Great-aunt Nora as well. Nora was in her nineties by then, but still alert enough to make life miserable for the nephew who'd taken her in. Her view of things was different from ours, naturally, and even more complex than the Philip Desmond version. To those of us who had watched her grow old she may have seemed a family-obsessed scold, but to the boy's way of thinking she had, as a young woman, sacrificed her happiness for the sake of her brothers. A model of fidelity in a world of a thousand betrayals.

Young Macken interviewed me at length, of course. I was even able to show him the copy of *Tales of Unrest* – still unread – that had been in our gift package to the tent city in town, but he showed little interest in it. He talked to people who remembered what their folks had told them, of course, and also questioned his own grandparents in the little house they'd moved to in town after selling their farm – a subdivision in the middle of what had once been some other farmer's field.

I don't know what he wanted the reviewers to say. Something we would never have noticed if the papers hadn't told us was how he was trying to make you think of the old Greek gods. Of course the characters were really a bunch of Returned Soldiers and their wives trying to get started where they could scratch out a living, but I remember that when the boy was planning his film he asked me how it felt to remember back to Creation. We both laughed at that, but he said that when he thinks about those old people that came here when my parents did (his great-grandparents too) they seem like the founders of Rome to him, or the thirty thousand deities squabbling on the slopes of Mount Olympus. Particular, of course, to this little nowhere place. I suppose I know what he meant. My father, who was killed when he and I were both too young, had got braver and stronger and funnier as the years went by. But I would have to see the movie a second time if I wanted to find out how the boy had got that notion onto the screen. If I'd thought to mention Herakles and the poisoned shirt, I wonder if he might have given Pearson a larger role.

He used any number of locations around the district. Some places hadn't changed. The back end of Wintons' property still has those ten-foot stumps the Wintons never got around to clearing – black and jagged-topped and hollow, big enough to live in. There's a donkey-pile in one corner of Barclays' back field even now, grown over with ivy and blackberry vines like a living pyramid. The old concrete sawmill hasn't gone anywhere. People drive out to snoop around it, they think even a modest ninety-minute movie leaves some magic in a place. The fellow who owns the property keeps a close eye on it now. No litter. No campouts. No souvenirs.

Of course he couldn't use Reimers' place. The boys had dismantled the sawmill and filled in the underground house years ago, when they converted the whole property to a seniors' retirement park. All the trees had been cleared away, in order to attract people from the prairies. A circle of faded trailers looked onto the muddy water of Reimers' swamp, most of them occupied by ex-farmers from Saskatchewan and Manitoba. Brochures had promised an escape from winter, a beautiful landscape, and quiet solitude free from the trouble of yard work. The retired farmers had bought into the place while it was still under construction, but could see in the large billboard painting that it would some day be everything that was promised. By the time they'd moved in, they could see that the view was mostly Reimers' mosquito swamp cleared of hardhack, the easy-care landscaping was a blanket of pea-gravel spread from one end of the property to the other, and the quiet solitude something that existed only at night when the highway truck traffic died down for an hour or two. They began to look into the reputations of local lawyers, but by the time they'd found out for themselves that an escape from winter did not mean freedom from rain and dark low skies, they had grown too old and disheartened to care about suing the

Reimers. At any rate, when the lawyers examined the brochures, they determined that the English language had been carefully used by experts in order to avoid anything you could prove to be outright lies.

"Nobody lies any more," one of the lawyers said. "They just change the meaning of the words."

We all went out to watch the filming whenever we could, but there was more waiting around than action. Actors hid in their trailers. Technicians stared into space while they waited for decisions to be made. We stood around and chatted about the TV news – fighting in Sarajevo, and the latest drive-by gang-war killings in Vancouver. We were anxious to see how he would shoot the fire, since we didn't want him starting something he couldn't stop, burning us out a second time. But it turned out he would add the flames in a studio somewhere, using computers. When actors ran through the woods impersonating terror, we had to imagine the fire.

It was a shock to see how young my parents' generation was at the time. What business did the country have, sending these youngsters out to take on the forces of nature? "Matt Pearson looks like a boy!" I nearly said out loud on the set. But of course, though he'd seemed a middle-aged man to me at the time, he'd been somewhere in his early thirties. I can remember that he was youthful in his restless energy, in his kidding around with his children, and in his earnest need to see everything in the universe make sense.

It was probably his need to see everything make sense that fed his decision to return to France. Except for himself and Maude, no one thought it a good idea. The men could not imagine wanting to visit French countryside again themselves, and didn't like to think of Matt Pearson over there on his own. "A man torn up with grief?" said Sandy MacKay to the others outside the blacksmith shop, where Uncle Archie had me hanging up his tools around the wall – bellows, sledgehammers, tongs. "That's

the last place he oughta go. A man in his state, he oughta stay
where folks can keep an eye on him."

Sven Ahlberg agreed. "Way he's been lately, he's liable to throw
himself into the North Atlantic."

When Matt Pearson strolled across from the Store to join them,
Al Hueffner was the one who warned him against going. His
younger brother had gone back to France, he said. He'd had so
much trouble sleeping after the War that he'd gone with the idea
of looking his terror in the face but returned to Texas a worse
wreck than before.

"You had a brother in the War?" Pearson said.

"Airman," Hueffner said. "I couldn't go myself with one arm
still in Panama but my kid brother signed up the minute it started
in '17."

The others waited politely with their eyes on their toes until
he had finished telling about his brother's airborne heroics, driving
the Germans single-handedly out of France. Then Sandy MacKay
said that it was too bad nobody told his brother the war had
started in 1914. "By the time he noticed there was something
going on we'd already lost a few men."

"Well, sure," he said. "We knew the French were having a rough
time of it over there. That's why he went."

"I don't think Sandy meant the French," Matt Pearson said. "I
think he was speaking of us. Howard's brother here was killed at
Vimy Ridge along with thousands of others. Sandy's cousin died
in the Somme offensive. They tell us more than eight thousand of
our own boys were killed at that one."

He knew better than to try to convince Hueffner that in
August of 1918 one hundred thousand Canadians stretched out
over fourteen miles had pushed a wedge into the enemy defences
that broke their morale and helped turn the tide of the war. Even
the Germans had referred to it as "a black day" for their army.
Hueffner already had the look of a man who thought they were

pulling his leg, who didn't want to upset them by challenging their version of things.

Of course Hueffner won that one eventually. We know that now. He only had to wait. While young Jeff Macken was planning his movie he asked me what I remembered of the War. "What *could* I remember?" I said. "I was born in 1911. I wasn't old enough to fight it."

"Oh yeah," he says. "That's right. It started when you were six."

"By the time I was six my father had been fighting for three of those years," I said, trying not to shout. "What kind of research have you done?"

"You sure?" he said. He hadn't started reading the right books yet for his background. He'd been watching movies instead. Videos. *Wings*! All those films where Hollywood took over and pushed us out of history. I think they sent Al Hueffner and others like him up here to get us ready for this.

Once Matt Pearson had gone, we didn't have to wait long before Maude began to get letters from him, and passed on his news at the Store. Leena Hueffner reported what she'd heard, in whatever manner she thought appropriate. She referred to Pearson as "The World Traveller."

"The World Traveller has arrived in London. I hope the King is pleased."

People laughed when she made her joke, but some of the men still worried aloud about him outside the blacksmith shed. "She'll be laughing on the other side of her face when he throws himself in the Thames."

Howard Stokes made a lot of noises in his throat and spit on the ground and made a few false starts before he found a way to say what was on his mind. "A distant relative of mine went back, I heard. We didn't know why till later. Turns out he wanted to finish what the War had failed to do. Tromped around the battlefields until a bomb blew him to Kingdom Come."

They were silent after that. When they noticed me standing still to listen instead of scraping clinkers out of the forge they found a new subject to talk about.

But I'd already begun to see that life had become a story of people leaving. Sullivan's wife was the first that I remembered, then Sullivan, and the Korsakovs, and the Evanses, and the Mitchells, and my dad. Now they were trying to add Matthew Pearson to the list.

I could not depend upon Tanner for news of his father. I saw little of Tanner, who spent his time with the Reimer boys now. And even when I did see him, at school or on the road, he wouldn't speak of his father. You'd think he was as fatherless as I was. Leena Hueffner filled me in, just as she did the adults who cared to ask.

He'd worked his passage on a freighter to Liverpool and then travelled down to London where he sought out the house of Sullivan's wealthy aunt-in-law. Sullivan's wife wasn't home, he wrote to Maude. Neither was the aunt. At least she wasn't home to him. A young woman servant told him, with obvious distaste, that the niece had found employment with the family importing firm and was presently at work. She insisted emphatically that the husband had not showed up at the house – had not displayed such poor judgement, was her way of putting it – and suggested that Pearson follow his example.

He hated to walk down the streets of that city, he wrote, for he could not travel a block in some parts of town without passing two or three or a dozen veterans who were crippled and bandaged, dressed in rags, holding up signs that begged for employment or displaying trays of trinkets they wanted to sell.

As shocking as everything else was the discovery that he might purchase an illustrated Michelin traveller's guide to the battle-fields. Already the trenches had joined the pyramids and Niagara Falls as curiosities. He dropped a copy back onto its bookshop table, but later returned and bought it to take with him to France.

"Now The World Traveller's in Paree," Leena Hueffner said, rolling her eyes and wiggling her hips as she handed out mail. She told Hueffner that if he ever got it into his stupid head to follow Pearson's example she would separate him from his remaining arm. Hueffner squinted down at his hand like someone wondering if he was willing to pay the price.

I was in the Store at the time, buying a newspaper for Mother. Nora Macken was at the counter. "I guess can-can girls are more attractive than a fence that needs repair," she said, when Leena had put a can of Magic Baking Powder and a box of Dominion Matches in front of her. She gave Leena a list of items to fetch from the storeroom, and waited until Leena had started putting everything into paper bags. Then she said, "Climbing the Eiffel Tower's more exciting than making sure your family is fed."

"His family's being fed," Leena said, brushing flour from the mustard-coloured smock. "Can you imagine Maude not making sure of that?"

"What do you think?" Hueffner said. "You think he's kicking up his heels on a grand tour?"

"I wouldn't call it touring," Nora said. "I'd call it desertion." She passed the bags of groceries to the three brothers she'd brought to carry them home.

Born to be a mother, Leena said, once she had gone. You'd think she'd given birth to those boys herself, and couldn't imagine a better way to spend her life than working herself to death for them. "You see that smile?"

Hueffner had seen the smile. "It wasn't there until you mentioned Pearson. I wouldn't want to ask her what it means."

Matthew Pearson visited the Luxembourg Gardens, where he sat on a bench to watch children ride on a shaggy-haired sleepy-eyed Shetland Pony. He ate lunch at Monsieur Lafleur's favourite restaurant, but made no effort to look up the curious bureaucrat who had taken such an interest in his case. After a day or so of wondering why he had even come to this city, he took the train

north to Amiens in order to visit the Michelin battlefields of
Picardy. Everywhere you looked, he wrote, crews of men were
busy reburying the war dead in tidy cemeteries. He'd met middle-
aged couples who had come from Canada to look for the graves of
their children. Some had found them, and applied to have the
bodies taken home, only to be refused. Soldiers had to stay in the
countries where they'd died. One bitter woman admitted that
she had hired a local farmer to dig up her son in the night, and
had almost got his body out of the country before she'd been
caught. Since hearing of a Toronto woman who'd succeeded, she
was determined to try again. "They can't do much about it once
you've got your sonny safely buried at home."

Eventually he returned to the village where he had been
wounded in the battle of August 8th, 1918. The astonishing thing
was that the churned-up, pulverized, burnt-out land had already
begun to recover, he wrote, in his letters, as well as in the notebooks Maude would turn over to me years later. Where there'd
been mud and broken trees and shell holes there were grass and
the tall stems and seed pods of last spring's flowers. Where a long
fence-line row of poplars had been sawed off at the ground, every
set of roots had sent up six or seven or more new shoots, already
ten feet high, aflutter with tremulous leaves. In some areas the
grass had grown over heaved-up ground that made you think of
the surface of a choppy sea, but there were places already where
farmers had ploughed and harrowed and levelled things out to
make proper fields again. He saw a shell crater that had become a
watering hole for a farmer's cattle, another where small children
sailed their wooden boats. The silence surprised him – there was
not a single echo here of the uproar that had sometimes filled his
head at home.

"The first villager I came upon was Emile, cleaning out his
barn." Of course this farmer was someone he'd got to know during
his visits to the village just after the War, though Maude did not
mention those earlier visits to Leena or anyone else at the time.

Emile wasn't even surprised to see him. "You keep coming back, you people, one way or the other," he said, laughing, and explained that just a month ago he had found a skeleton with a Canadian identity tag in the scrub bush behind his barn.

He was still turning up shell casings and parts of bodies in their fields, he said. Once, he'd ploughed up a bayonet – its sheath was already thick with rust, but its blade was as shiny as new. A neighbour had been killed by an explosion not twenty feet from his door. The war was still doing all the damage it could. Himself, a simple *poilu*, he had come right through the war unscathed, thanks to God, and then this stupid thing happened when he'd been home for almost a year. He pulled up one trouser leg to reveal a wooden stump not much thicker than a baseball bat, and rapped his fist where a knee ought to be. Blown off while bringing in the cows.

"I suppose I will be ploughing up bayonets and shells and human limbs every year for the rest of my life," he said. He seemed to find this amusing.

"More dangerous than my annual crop of stones!" Pearson said.

The farmer led Pearson to his house, which was next door to his cattle shed and not far from the village well. This was a white house, recently rebuilt and repainted, with tulips blooming in the front yard, the only two-storey building in town. The young man pointed out the small craters in the stone wall, on either side of the door. "The Hun's calling card," he said, and laughed.

Inside, the man's wife made them coffee. Emile brought out a bottle of his own wine and poured three glasses. Children peeked out from around the edge of a door, and ran giggling up the stairs. The wife shouted something sternly at them, then giggled herself. Her face was wide, her cheeks reddened, Pearson assumed, from working outside with her husband.

Emile groaned as he lowered himself to a chair, and used both hands to lift the wooden leg to a second chair. "At least I'm alive," he said. "My wife's brothers, all nine of them was killed by the Boche, most of them in the first two years of the War."

The wife, who sat across the table from the men, did not understand most of what was being said. When her brothers' deaths
were mentioned she smiled and nodded at Pearson, much as she'd
smiled and nodded at him earlier when he'd arrived.

Eventually Pearson asked about the old people next door. In
Maude's report to Leena Hueffner they were only "an old peasant
couple he'd got to know in the War." Since their small cottage
looked as though no one had made any repairs, he thought they
might both be dead. Its narrow windows were without glass, half
the roof was without tiles, and fallen beams and other debris had
not been cleared away from around the front door.

They were living in it still, though the young farmer said their
health was poor. The old man would potter away at repairs whenever he found the strength, but he hadn't made much progress,
nor had he yet made any attempt to start working his farm. They
ate what neighbours left on their doorstep, though the old woman
went out sometimes and came back with vegetables she'd robbed
from other people's gardens.

Of course I understand now that Emile or his wife must surely
have asked about Elizabeth, and that Pearson must have told them
what had happened. The young couple would then assume that
he had come to deliver the sad news to the old people in person.
Maybe they tried to persuade him not to. What was the point in
telling them now? They had given up their great-grandchild,
they had probably forgotten about her. Why bring upon them the
obligation to feel grief? Did Pearson wish to make them feel that
they were at fault, that if they had not given up the girl to this
foreigner she would be alive today, in an orphanage somewhere,
or in the home of some wealthy family in France?

When the old folks answered their door they seemed to think
for a moment that he was someone they ought to fear. A stranger.
An *anglais*? It was possible that they had deteriorated to a point
of losing memory. He didn't know how to remind them of who he
was. The patches of new skin on his face disguised him, perhaps.

Anxious to let them know he meant no harm, he told them he had come – and he thought of this only while he was standing outside their half-opened door – to help them rebuild their home.

"The Maguires will want to hear this," said Leena Hueffner, raising her eyebrows to a Saturday-morning cluster of women come in for supplies. "Mar-*taans* could do with some help too but I guess their brand of French don't sound exotic enough. Don't she ever ask him what he's *doing* over there?"

Wyatt Taylor laughed when he passed this on to me. "Matt's probably doing what he would like to be doing at home – except he don't have the rest of us watching him do it."

Of course Taylor saw nearly everything through the benign haze of his own new hope. It was true that Johanna Seyerstad had decided, despite falling more than halfway in love with Wyatt Taylor, that after all those years of allowing her life to be governed by a man – even an absent man – she didn't really need a male for her happiness. Still, she was willing to allow him to court her, in case she changed her mind. Not only that, but she was willing to let him court her without requiring an endless supply of expensive provisions and interminable hours of labour in the slim hope that he would be rewarded with a smile of gratitude. Johanna wanted nothing that Nora had required. She asked only that they behave in the most conventional manner, typical of the courtships of ordinary people and appropriate for a widowed schoolteacher who had waited as long as anyone could reasonably expect for her husband to come home from the War.

They attended moving pictures at The Maple Leaf Theatre in town. They danced in the pavilion above the bay where they were both surprised to discover that Taylor was a natural expert at the Charleston, every one of his joints double-hinged like a swinging door. They rode out on Sunday afternoons for picnics – sometimes down at the seaside park, sometimes back at the river by the abandoned sawmill, and sometimes at a quiet beach of endless white sand a few miles up the coast – and ate ordinary meals of potato salad and cold sliced meat with their bare feet in the water.

Of course she was expecting more than an ordinary courtship when she talked him into spending a few hours every week inside a classroom. Whenever he stood still long enough she had him instructing us in the manly arts of making cookstove reservoirs out of scrap metal and converting broken machinery into efficient wash tubs, complete with diagrams on the blackboard. The miracle of fire and imagination. She prodded him into answering our questions about the beauty and variety of the wide country he had crossed on his lazy horse in order to find the woman who overcooked his clothing in her oven once he got here. And she coaxed him into relating anecdotes to illustrate the causes and results of the Great War that had ended when most of us were still crawling on our mothers' floors.

Tell us about Matthew Pearson, I wanted to ask. Tell us what you know about the village he's in. But I could not ask this while Tanner was in the room. Tanner had refused to read any of his father's letters, even those addressed to him. He never mentioned his father. He had begun to "run with the Reimer boys," as the adults put it, speaking as though they were a pack of dogs that chased deer in the night. They raided orchards, opened gates to let cattle onto the road, defied Johanna Seyerstad when they didn't feel like doing the tasks she assigned. They stole anything that could be slipped into a pocket from the shelves at the Store, and pulled a few teeth from the Barclays' sway-backed horse.

"He's mad at his old man," Leena Hueffner said, after she'd caught him stealing cigarettes.

In the midst of a noon-hour game of scrub football I found a chance to knock him to the ground. I wasn't sure why. Once he was in the dirt I jumped on him and punched him in the nose again and again. Blood was flowing from both our noses before Mrs. Seyerstad came out to stop us.

I got the worst of the fight but the cuts and bruises distracted me from a deeper hurt I couldn't put a name to. Mrs. Seyerstad took us both inside and made us sit in opposite corners of the room. Then she brought her own chair out from behind her desk and talked to me, quietly, while sitting where she could force me to look in her eyes.

"Now what was that about?" she said.

"Nothing," I said.

"Tanner's having a rough time," she said. "You're smart enough to know that, so it must be something else."

She waited for an explanation, but I had none to give. When she went to talk to Tanner I put my head on my desk and turned my face to the side. Tanner had been my best friend once, the nearest thing to a brother. I felt inside the desk for my compass and pressed the point into the back of my hand until there was blood running off my fingers.

Taylor still wore the baked hat and coat on occasion, and sometimes even the decaying boots, but he had got into the habit of removing coat and hat in the classroom. It was a shock to see how skinny he was. We didn't know which of their faces was the more interesting to watch – his filled with excited animation as he explained or recalled or painted word pictures for us, or hers as she stood against the windowsill with her arms crossed and her blue eyes rivetted to him and her mouth smiling while the muscles of her face imitated the shifting muscles in his. With a corner of her new scarf pressed to her cheek, she didn't remove her gaze even when it was necessary to reach out and rap her knuckles on Tom Reimer's head to stop him from using the elastic band he had stretched behind Eddie Macken's ear.

Sometimes she sent Taylor into a corner with just a small group, for drill with English Grammar. He made us follow as he read aloud from the text. "*Observe the following.*" He repeated the word "observe" as though it tasted foreign.

"*I will go to town.*

"*You shall accompany me.*

"*He shall remain at home.*

"*These sentences express desire and resolve.*"

He read aloud hesitantly, as though this were something he hadn't done for years. You could tell that "desire" and "resolve" were not words he would have used himself.

He read: "*What have you to say about the following uses of shall and will?*

"*I shall be drowned; nobody will help me.*

"*I will be drowned; nobody shall help me.*"

We waited for him to make sense of this. You could see he had no more idea what was expected than we did. His eyes darted to Johanna Seyerstad and back to his book. Eventually his narrow face broke into a grin. "Well, I guess if you're drowning it don't matter so much if you get the grammar right so long as somebody's there with a rope."

He looked again at Mrs. Seyerstad, who looked up to smile from where she was bent over Lise Martin's desk. He raised his voice to read the next example: "*I will not remain another minute.* I guess there isn't much doubt what's meant by that."

"Oh, but you *shall* return, Mr. Taylor," said Mrs. Seyerstad. "Since you promised to help the youngsters build their tree house during lunch."

Older students sniggered about this at recess. "It's indecent," some of them said.

"No, it's romantic," said others.

"Why don't they just get married and behave like normal people?" This was a Richmond opinion.

It was probably the opinion of many of the adults as well, though Leena Hueffner seemed to think the couple were providing welcome entertainment at a time of hardship and endless work. "It serves Matt Pearson right that he's missing this. He thinks he's in the country of romance, the centre of the civilized world."

Pearson's letters suggested no such thing, at least as Maude reported them. For many of the following months he slept in a lean-to at the back of the old people's cottage and, with what he could find in the rubble around the village and the neighbouring villages, helped them restore the ruined building. He rebuilt the chimney, bricked up gaps in the walls, retiled the roof, helped them apply whitewash to the stones and bricks, inside and out. He helped the old man work his farm as well, which was a mile or so from the village. Together they ploughed the fields for the next spring's crops, milked the cow, and cleaned out the little barn.

Emile was a source of information when he needed it, and an extra pair of hands when he needed an extra pair of hands. He was also someone to chat with in front of the fire after the old people had gone to bed. They might have been brothers, Pearson wrote. Cousins, rather. "Two country souls raised in different languages, but sharing a weakness for putting our heads up against the puzzle of the universe. He is quick with the dismissive shrug. To Emile the world at large is a huge mysterious heartbreaking tragedy, though he will not take himself or the rest of us seriously."

In the evenings he wrote his letters to Maude and the boys, in which he tried to make it clear that no day went by that he didn't wonder if he was a fool to be where he was instead of with the family he loved. No amount of heavy labour and bone-aching weariness was able to erase the pain he still felt at the memory of his cruelties to those who were dearer to him than all the world. "In short," he wrote, "I am still here because I still believe that this is the greatest good I can do you. Selfishness would have me race home, but to do how much more damage than I've done?"

He also added pages to his notebooks, where he tried to work his way through the War – attempting to nail pieces of it down when he could figure them out, he said. Looking for fragments of himself that he may have left behind. He later gave the notebooks to Maude, who would long afterwards give them to me. I suppose this was because I had stayed to make my life right here while Tanner had moved away. Will had little interest in such things.

Something he did not write to Maude but recorded only in his notebooks was a suspicion that occurred about this time and wouldn't leave him alone: that he had been sent away from home so that a miracle could take place in his absence. This was completely unreasonable, he knew. Still, he began to suspect that Elizabeth – whom he remembered as completely untouched by the flames that had devastated both his property and his life – had not really died but had been taken by Mary Reimer to the hospital when she saw that the unmarked girl was still breathing. "The fire has sucked the soul right out of her," he imagined Mary saying, "but only for a while. It left her body still breathing." They had kept this from him, afraid of how he'd react. They wanted him out of the way while the doctors stood guard over the breathing child, waiting for some sign that her soul had returned to the world. As soon as her eyelids fluttered and the colour returned to her lips, he would receive a letter from Maude telling him it was time to come home.

"Nonsense, of course," he wrote to himself. "Still, there was a good deal of mystery surrounding her death, from the point of view of someone confined to a hospital bed. I was permitted to attend the funeral only because I insisted. I did not ask to see the child, knowing that I would not be able to bear it. The manner in which I spoke to Maude in those days would not have encouraged her to confide in me – only to make her want me out of the way."

He knew Maude would not have deceived him. Subsequent pages of his notes demonstrated that he tried, but failed, to let reason deal with the temptation to hope. Lying at night on his nest of rags, tired enough from his day's work to sleep for two or three nights but unable to doze off for even the one, he would think – a flashing image would invade his ringing skull – of the small pale child, her freckled skin unmarred by flames, her tangled red hair growing thicker, lying in a secret room of the hospital where nuns and doctors looked in on her, poured nourishment down her throat, spoke to her in the hope that she might hear and awake. Sleeping Beauty, hidden from him behind a bramble hedge of secrecy. He smiled, allowing himself to believe that it might be true.

(iv)

Now even Leena Hueffner thought the time had passed for making jokes about "The World Traveller." She wished Maude would stop sharing her letters. "One of these days it's gonna hit her, he's just another husband that didn't come home."

Nell Richmond puffed up her considerable weight and sighed. "If he stays much longer, dear, I wouldn't *have* him back." She scowled at me as though I already had plans one day to run off and desert someone.

So now that none of their earlier predictions had come true they'd given me something else to worry about. The possibility that Matt Pearson might never come home at all bothered me enough to risk bringing it up at the supper table.

"What goes on in the Pearson household is hardly our business," my mother said. Her ruddy face was always angry now, her eyes always swollen and red.

Uncle Archie agreed. "You want something to worry about, lad? Worry about keeping yon woodbox full for your mother. Time you spend poking your nose into folks' business could be better spent with me across the road."

Uncle Archie believed that if I was to be of any use to this world it was time I learned how to shoe a horse. This was something I

would have liked my father's opinion on. It was something I
would have liked to talk over with Matthew Pearson on his back
porch step.

But, from the tone of his letters home, it seemed to me that he
had been growing far too interested in things over there in France.
The village church, for instance. He mentioned that the villagers
had long ago taken down what was left of their destroyed *église*
and erected a new one upon the old foundations. "Some of the
materials were saved and reused, but most of the rubble was shovelled into the tunnels and dugouts underneath." Crucifixes, chal-
ices, altar cloths, and other paraphernalia had been brought home
by those who had taken it with them to safety. A statue of the
Virgin had been rescued at the last moment when it was learned
that one villager had sold it to an American who was about to ship
it to Philadelphia.

In his notebooks he recorded his astonishment at the confidence with which the villagers had apparently held onto their
old faith, after all they had witnessed. "I see the whole village
traipsing over there on Sundays," he said to Emile. "I see women
stopping in every morning of the week. Has no one turned their
back on God, for allowing the savagery to happen right here in
your fields?"

Emile puffed on his pipe for a moment, evidently thinking
about this.

"No one here can remember seeing God shoot anyone, or run
anyone through with a bayonet." When he smiled, deep creases
ran out from the corners of his eyes. "They saw only men killing
men." He sucked for a few more moments on his pipe before going
on. "Whatever was making us kill one another was not something, I think, from above."

"Yet prayers were sent up. Services were held. Men were blessed
by priests before battle. I remember seeing little crucifixes at every
crossroad. None of it did any good."

Emile shrugged and puffed and stared into the fire as though he hadn't heard. "Perhaps there was too much pleading and not enough listening. Everyone was busy telling God to get busy and do His work with miraculous bullets but" – another shrug – "maybe He doesn't work with bullets."

He spoke rapidly to his wife in French for a moment, and she responded with an even more rapid burst of excited sentences. Emile raised his eyebrows and turned again to Pearson. "She says the idea of God interfering is foolish. She says He does His work by speaking to the heart, suggesting a change in thought. Of course someone has to be listening."

He turned up his palms as though to say: I'm sorry but that is the best we can do.

Pearson laughed. "I wonder if your priest across the road would agree."

Emile returned the pipe to his mouth.

"Their little rebuilt church has nothing of the beauty you find in the great cathedrals," Pearson wrote. "In fact, it is a squat homely thing. Yet, there is a simple comeliness to it as well. And when the villagers are gathered inside you feel that all of community life has come together, present and past, in a sort of celebration, breathing praise for the giver of life."

At first, he refused invitations to attend services, but eventually began to sit in, very much aware of himself as an outsider. He perched at the back, close to the door like someone who might be called away at any moment, and slipped out when the others rose for communion. "All the same, I think I would have been tempted to leave some part of the church unfinished, so questions would still be asked."

Wyatt Taylor was so sure Matt Pearson would be back that he was prepared to act on it. He made his proposal after a midday dinner, as he and Howard Stokes and Sandy MacKay were going back out to blow a few more stumps on Stokes's property. The strain of restoring the farm had taken its toll on the Stokes family. In his impatience with having to build what he had already built once before, and with cutting fence posts for fences he had already worked hard to put up only three years earlier, Howard Stokes's famous temper had begun to show signs of returning. In her alarm, Mrs. Stokes had taken their little boy and moved in with the Swifts while she considered the possibility of returning to her parents' home in England. Stokes was beside himself with worry.

This was probably why Taylor had chosen to blow a few more stumps in his pasture. A distraction was needed. He also thought it was a good time to suggest his plan for welcoming Matt Pearson home. Taylor told me about this while I was helping with some Pearson chores that Tanner refused to do. "'He's hanging around that foreign church without even knowing why,' I told the men. 'It's because you don't have one of your own.'"

Like the rest of them, he and MacKay and Stokes had seen the great cathedrals of France, rising to the sky at the centre of even the smallest of towns. He'd spent time in Amiens. He'd been to Chartres, and to Rheims. Even little country villages could be spotted from miles away because of the spire that soared above the roofs. He'd also lived in Cape Breton, as well as Ontario like Pearson, and was used to seeing church towers and steeples above every cluster of buildings. "This settlement will never be any-thing but a crossroads so long as it don't have a church. People think that a place without a church is a place without a soul."

Sandy MacKay reminded him that the reason we didn't have a church was that nobody wanted one. "Leave it alone. If you think a church'll start Johanna Seyerstad planning a wedding, just drive her past them ones they got in town."

Taylor ignored this. "Even if you never set foot inside it, it would make this little nowhere place look like somewhere you mean to stay."

"So would a jail," said MacKay, "but we don't need one of them yet neither."

By this time Taylor was crimping blasting caps. "A courthouse with a statue would do as well, or a town hall with a clock, but you don't have the legal right to them. More important, you don't have a courthouse or a town hall that just happens to be down the road a few miles from here and hardly ever gets used."

The little cluster of scattered farmers three miles closer to town had a tiny Church of England building in the woods. "They probably wouldn't miss it," Taylor said. "You never see anyone going near the place."

He didn't have to explain. They knew what he meant. The only thing he had to add was this: "We should probably do it at night."

The others were silent for a moment, thinking this over.

"I'm an honest man," Stokes eventually said. He thought a little longer. "But I suppose the worst they could do is make us take it back."

"Don't be too sure of that," said MacKay. "They could throw us in jail for theft."

"Only if someone cares enough to charge us," Taylor said, though he was only guessing. "The Archbishop of Canterbury don't care if one of his buildings shifts itself three miles up the road. He's got more important things on his mind."

Sandy MacKay grinned, though his moustache hid most of it. "We'll say it was the Holy Spirit moved it."

"A miracle," Taylor said. "We could do it tonight."

But the other two men weren't ready yet. Taylor would have to bring the matter up a few more times before they'd get used to the idea and then begin to think it was inevitable.

With every letter that arrived I felt more keenly that something was wrong. His *absence* was wrong. So much of the world had changed since my dad ran down to check on his stumping powder that I couldn't stand a change that could be avoided.

For everyone else his reports had become the thread that stitched together their efforts to put things right at home. When he was spoken of, it was "Pearson will be surprised I've built my

new barn on the far side of the field," or "He's going to wonder why
we didn't use the same house plan as before." No one resented the
way he'd behaved before he left. Whether he came home or
stayed away for ever, they'd made it their goal to get the settlement into some sort of civilized order that would please him.

This wasn't easy. Though Mrs. Stokes eventually returned to her
husband, thanks to the calm advice and good example of Lillian
Swift, the hardships of putting life back together where fences,
buildings, and animals had been destroyed had taken its toll on
other marriages as well. Bridget Maguire made no secret of the fact
that she and Patrick had got into the habit of fighting over everything that came up between them – the children, the cost of nails,
the possibility that they'd made a mistake in staying to rebuild.

Strong men were faced with challenges they could not have
imagined. One morning Andy Richmond was out in a field, steer-
ing his plough behind his team of horses, when both scorched
handles broke off in his hands. He hadn't realized the burn had
gone in so deep. He sat down where he was in the shiny furrow and
sobbed into his folded arms. When he didn't come in for his hot
noon dinner, Nell set out with her walking stick to bring him in.
He was ashamed to be seen weeping like a child. "I can't stand this
any longer," he said when she found him. "No man should have
to put up with a life like this."

"He has begun to fear for his sanity," Nell confided to Mrs.
Barclay in the Barclay kitchen. "No doubt he's not the only man
in the settlement who's afraid of going mad from the little things
that plague him."

It helped that Taylor had stayed. Besides taking over the repairs
and farm work on the Pearsons' place, he'd continued to work for
others as well. Of course Taylor had stayed so that he and Johanna
would have some time to carry on a proper courtship. They didn't
want to be over-hasty. How would it look if they'd simply run off
together right after Nora had shown him the road? This way, they
could still change their minds.

After sitting for years on a staircase waiting for a husband that never showed up, Johanna Seyerstad was not about to take a passive role again. She wasn't going to make a fool of herself again, either, if she could help it. What she wanted was what she had: a career she was good at and a man who thought enough of her to show up when he was supposed to.

We expected more than that of a man who'd turned aside a fire like the Red Sea in order to make a route for Nora to get to her family. Taylor expected more of himself. One Friday in spring he showed up after school and took her riding with him, back along the old railway grade to the river, and across the plank bridge to the logging railroad where he'd arranged to have a little yellow Company "speeder" waiting on the tracks. He'd taken the school's gramophone as well, and a picnic basket he'd prepared himself in Sullivan's kitchen.

By this time he was wearing his roasted coat and hat only when he was blasting stumps. For this excursion he had put on a crisp white shirt and narrow trousers with a crease down the front. With his hair slicked back with water, and a new brimmed hat at an angle, he looked like someone from town.

"I don't see any guns, so you aren't taking me out to the bush to shoot me," she said. "I don't see any luggage either, so I guess we won't be staying."

He helped her up into the contraption and invited her to sit on the rear seat, which was intended for the behinds of visiting dignitaries and Company bosses in a hurry to check up on work in the woods. He placed the gramophone on the floor between his feet. Then he started the gasoline engine and set them sailing along above the bank of the river, slowly at first, its twelve-inch wheels glinting sunlight. *Putta-putta-putta*, the canopied gondola glided through the dark skeletal ashes-smelling woods and then curved further inland a little faster through the spiky devastation and more slowly up the long grade of the incinerated foothills of the mountains, the little one-cylinder motor working

hard. They travelled in silence up the same route Taylor had
brought the flaming locomotive down, and for a while followed
the river upstream that Corky Desmond had thrown himself
into and then crawled out of an hour later when both fire and
train had left him behind. After they'd veered off onto a spur
line leading away from the river, he wound up the gramophone
and lowered the needle onto the sound of Enrico Caruso singing
an aria from Verdi and then moved over to sit on the floor,
facing forward, beside her legs, with his face against the flesh at
her hip and a hand gently stroking her ankle as they moved into
a narrowing draw of destroyed timber and still deeper into the
canyon where spiky walls sloped steeply up either side. Then
they streamed on, without slowing, into a passageway so narrow
that they might have reached out and touched the stony cliffs
on either side.

"*Back to God's Country*," she said. "You must think we're star-
ring in a movie of our own."

They came out from the narrow canyon and looked down on a
valley of soaring green forest still untouched by fire or logger's axe.
Johanna leaned forward and requested that Caruso be silenced.
They sped downhill and skimmed across the mossy ground of a
spongy meadow, approaching and then entering the channel
that had been cut for the railroad through the thousand-year-
old trees. Trunks like dark pillars flashed by, their bark as thick
as the stitched-together furs of winter coats. Their lowest boughs
made an arched luminous ceiling high above them, that only a
pale green light shone through. Bracken ferns grew as high as the
speeder's roof. Sword ferns looked like trunkless palms. Rotting
windfall trees were blanketed with moss and inhabited by wide
white flares of fungus and rows of infant trees rooted in the decay.
Johanna thought of the imagined prehistoric forests in the school
books. Dinosaurs could be feeding somewhere close. She saw that
the forest floor was decorated with cones the size of squirrels and

populated by flowering plants she'd never seen before, or even imagined. For a while the trunks soared up from a grove of cow-parsnip grown tall as humans, their white flower heads as wide as parasols, a crowd.

Then: "Devil's Club," Taylor said, and pointed out the pyrami-dal flowers on floating islands of gigantic horizontal leaves.

"Now close your eyes," he said.

When he told her to open them again they had left the forest and were sailing again through a world destroyed by fire. "Look," he said. The naked trees went on for acres, perhaps for miles, like the charred upright skeletons of a million oversize herring, but they appeared not to be rooted in earth so much as anchored to the unseen floor of a sea of startling pink.

"Fireweed," he said, bringing the speeder to a stop.

Fifty, sixty acres of fireweed bloomed around them.

"And more beyond that rise."

She stepped down onto gravel between the railroad ties and waded in, clusters of pink petals flaming up on leafy stalks around her hips, some of them to her shoulders.

"All this was burned off two or three years ago," he said. He stood on one of the ties but did not come down to join her. "There's young alder growing out there, and trailing blackberries along the ground, and tiny evergreens started from seeds blown in from the timber."

"And bees!" she said. There were hundreds of them. She watched one insert itself into a blossom that lay against her arm, hover a moment, then back out and move on to another.

"Can you imagine setting hives out here?" he said.

She shaded her eyes with a hand in order to see him, a dark figure raised against the sun. "You're planning to stay?"

He removed his new hat and tossed it onto the floor of the speeder. "Someone will do it. It doesn't have to be me. What do you think?"

She brought a cluster of blooms to her mouth, and breathed in the scent. "Honey." She imagined a hundred, two hundred tall white hives set out amongst the flowers across the slope. She thought of herself and Taylor in veiled hats, removing combs.

"Sullivan's place is bound to come up for sale," he said.

She looked hard at him until he shook his head.

"But I don't intend to stay behind in it by myself," he added.

She came up out of the sea of flowers to where he sat on the step of the speeder, and walked into his welcome – his arms and legs spread wide, his mouth ready for hers. With one hand on the back of his head and the other on a bony shoulder, she drew him down so that she could show him her own hunger. All the air above them was alive with the bees.

After a while she turned inside his arms to look out again across the long pink slope. "All this is so strange," she said. "You think of the mountains as mountains, the timber as timber, it's real but only as part of the landscape. Yet here it is – alive – because we're in it! We could be on another continent."

"The men who work in the woods are in it every day," he said. Then he said, "Into the speeder, Johanna," standing to take her arm. "Bear."

From the raised platform she could see, once he had pointed it out, a heaving mound of black fur, pawing at the ground at the foot of a tree just a hundred yards away. "As far as he's concerned those bees are working for him," Taylor said. He lifted her hair and kissed the pale clear vulnerable skin at the back of her neck.

He'd known there would be a moon. By the time they'd moved on to a wooded ravine beyond the next ridge and had eaten his picnic supper by a pool at the base of a falls, the sun had gone behind the mountain peaks, draining the sky of all colour but the yellow light of a three-quarters moon. On their voyage home they sailed through what might have been vegetation drowned in a moonlit sea, with Enrico Caruso's sentences and Johanna's

pale scarf trailing like slender weeds along the shifting currents
of the night.

Of course I have had to imagine much of what went on during
that lovers' excursion into the mountains, with only the slimmest
of hints from Taylor to go on. But I had got to know them fairly
well by this time, and all the years since have given me both the
experience and the arrogance necessary for filling in the rest.
After a lifetime of "Getting the Story Straight," as my newspaper
column claimed to do, I can take advantage of an opportunity I
could never hope for as a newspaperman – to add to what I remember seeing and hearing myself, and to what I've been told by
others, the products of my own imagination. Old age has encouraged me to assume that I can know now what I did not know then
– that is, what other people were thinking or feeling even when
they kept it to themselves. Old age has brought distance, too, and
a little courage, and with distance and courage an expanded point
of view, and with an expanded point of view a willingness to play
a kind of local gossip-god. Knowing, after all, that mine is only
one more voice amongst many.

Even so, I would not presume to know what Nora thought of
Taylor's second courtship, if she heard of it – despite the fact that
she's one of the few still around that I might ask. No one asked
her then, either. No one saw very much of her, since it was a full-
time job looking after that crowd of brothers. She rode to town
with her father once a week for supplies, and sometimes sent one
of the boys to the Store for mail. Only occasionally did she drop
in herself for something she needed in a hurry. She exchanged
pleasantries with Leena, or with anyone else who was there,
answered harmless questions about members of her family, and
offered observations on the weather. She never mentioned Taylor
or Johanna Seyerstad. She never asked about Pearson either,

though Leena sometimes brought her up to date, just as she did for everyone else.

"Maude may overlook this," Nora said, "but don't he know what a chance he's taking? His boy may never forgive him."

Everyone knew what she meant. She didn't have to mention the fire in Pearsons' barn that Maude had discovered just in time to beat it out. She didn't need to mention Tanner's run-in with the police, when he and the Reimer boys had broken into the pool hall one Saturday night. And she probably didn't yet know that Tanner had twice been caught by my uncle stealing engine parts from the blacksmith shed.

"What is she, twenty-two?" Hueffner said, once she'd gone. "She looks forty-two to me. She even looks like she's glad to be forty-two. I don't like her smile. She looks smug."

"How do you want her to look?" Leena said. "She knows what the rest of us think. She knows about Taylor and Johanna. She's embarrassed."

"What she is, is damn *virtuous*!" Hueffner said. "She thinks we oughta be lining up to congratulate her."

Leena pushed him aside so that she could wrestle a sack of flour into position against the wall. "A woman makes a sacrifice, she has the right to be admired. Give me a hand with this."

"That's just it," Hueffner said, making no effort to help. "I don't think she made a sacrifice, I think she got what she wanted."

By this time, the settlers had made a good deal of progress. The Reimers had moved into their underground house, which was made on much the same principle as everyone else's cellar, with walls of slab-ends and rough lumber, covered over with a peaked roof of tar and hay-growing sod. A family of marmots, Mary Reimer said. "That tar it stinks, eh. And it's too damn dark, but when do I ever get inside in daylight? That fat Swiss, he keeps me working like a slave morning till night."

The Martins had been delighted to discover their cabin of squared-off logs had somehow survived the flames, but they had no sooner moved back before Arlette was making plans for improvements. The house would have to be much larger, since in their pleasure and gratitude at coming through the fire unharmed they had pledged to become the largest family in the settlement. The four children they already had were just a beginning. "My Fortunat, 'e promise to work 'ard to make sure we 'ave twenty before we are through!" She drew plans for converting the attic into a second storey and for adding several bedrooms out the back. She dropped in on everyone, even those she barely knew, in order to get ideas – or to make a list, as Leena Hueffner put it, "in case she has to resort to theft."

But the Reimers had the good fortune to be making money, or promises of money at least, out of everyone else's need for lumber. And the Martins, because of their pleasure in finding their little house unharmed, were unique in remaining unmoved by the hard work still needed on their farm. Others found progress more painful. Andy Richmond had been given the use of the Barclays' plough and any other farm machinery he wished to borrow, but his team of horses had been growing steadily weaker since the day of the fire. Dennis Price had made no progress at all, since he spent most of his time and energy planning or writing letters to the government, speaking to lawyers, urging neighbours to get involved in suing someone for damages. He was convinced that if the government would not be swayed the logging company could be found negligent, and was determined to see the whole settlement take one or the other to court. He sat up late over his figures, estimating that each farmer ought to be able to claim between $2,000 and $10,000 in damages. He didn't know who the enemy was but he was determined to find someone to fight. "God knows we've got enough witnesses to put them on the run." It was only after several months of this that the others agreed to come to his meetings.

The Winton brothers had lost heart altogether. Their mother's frightening attacks of hysteria meant they had to swallow their fear of being indoors in order to take turns with her in her kitchen, or more often her bedroom. The brother who remained outside wandered around the devastated farm halfheartedly making gestures that amounted to nothing – straightening a fence post that tilted and fell the minute he'd passed, turning up a small patch of garden that would never be planted. They didn't care enough to take advantage of government money for cattle. They didn't show any interest in Dennis Price's lawsuit. They alternated at a single job in the woods but came home to spend their evenings wandering around the property, content to leave its restoration to nature.

This was spring now. New grass had grown up to obscure the winter-browned. Bouquets of pussy willows had gone to seed on kitchen tables, and been replaced by jars of ocean spray. Once again Wyatt Taylor suggested to Stokes and MacKay that they steal the church. Because they'd had time to think about it, they didn't take long to agree to take part in the adventure that seventy-three years further down the century Nora Macken's great-nephew would borrow for his movie, ignoring the calendar and of course the motives in order to shift it to some time before the fire.

On a Friday evening, when they had already put in a long day's work in the woods and a few more hours on their farms, they gathered in the Store where Leena Hueffner had pots of her strong coffee ready. Sandy MacKay brought a bottle of whisky. Dennis Price brought his tractor. Howard Stokes showed up in his bear-rug costume of The Portuguese, as he did now for every public occasion requiring a sense of ritual, and stood in the doorway beating his chest to show he was ready to get this show on the road.

I'd known something was up. Instead of falling asleep that night I'd climbed up to the attic and kept a watch on the Store as they gathered. Taylor, then MacKay and Stokes, and Dennis Price. I waited awhile and then tiptoed outside, hurried across the road, and ran straight into Taylor coming out the door.

"I'm going too," I said.

"Your mother will kill you," he said.

He ran up the staircase and hammered on Johanna Seyerstad's door. When he could hear she was standing just inside, he said, "We need someone respectable along, just in case."

"Just in case of what?" she said.

"In case we need someone respectable along."

She opened the door just wide enough to see he was wearing his baked and tattered stump-blasting coat and hat, so she put on her severest and most respectable schoolma'am's skirt and blouse and jacket, and wrapped her scarf around her head like a Hindoo's turban, before coming down to join him on a fender of Dennis Price's tractor. It took her a while to see that I was the one riding up front like a hood ornament on the nose. I heard her whisper, "What's he doing here?" and Taylor whispering back, "In case we need to throw them a hostage while we escape."

They didn't light a lantern. Driving down the road they whispered, as though they thought they might be heard above the tractor noise. When Johanna asked the purpose of this excursion, I could tell they were being evasive. She would just have to see for herself. Nobody objected when I lit one of my cigarettes.

There wasn't much chance of being caught before they'd started. The little church sat in a clearing of its own, surrounded by timber and well out of earshot of the nearest farmhouse. It was no larger than Richmonds' dairy, a squat unpainted boards-and-batten building with a door in the middle of the front, a brow of projecting roof over the door, and a short bell tower perched near the front of the peak.

Taylor had gone down to scout it out, so they already knew that it had been set on a foundation of two solid logs that could serve as a pair of skids, but they'd brought along block and tackle in case they had to drag it up the road with pulleys attached to trees.

"What are we doing?" Johanna asked.

"Hold onto this shackle for a minute willya?" Dennis Price said to me. "I don't suppose you brought a pair of gloves."

"What are you doing?" Johanna asked again. "I don't think we should be doing this!" She unwound her turban, hung her scarf from her neck, and tugged at both ends.

Block and tackle weren't needed, as it turned out. It was enough to attach the tractor to the skids beneath the church with a length of steel rope. The building broke free of its site without a squeak of protest and slid out onto the road.

"I'll lose my job," Johanna accused the man who had thought of this.

Taylor walked alongside the moving church as he might if it were a beast of burden in need of the occasional prod with a stick. I walked beside him. Johanna Seyerstad walked a little ahead, tugging at the ends of her scarf as though they could ring bells to advertise her alarm.

And, right away, the bell in the little cupola started to ring.

"Goddammit," MacKay said. "We'll have everyone out of their beds."

Dennis Price slowed the tractor but the bell kept ringing anyway.

"Charlie, will you ride inside?" Taylor said. "Holler if pictures are falling off the walls. It would be nice if we didn't spill the preacher's wine."

Then he suggested to Johanna that they both ride on the roof. With one foot on a windowsill, he was able to get up onto the little brow above the door. From there, he helped Johanna climb up behind him, and then pushed her ahead of him up the roof of the church to the peak. There he showed her how to hold the bell clapper between her hands, while he sat behind with his hands on her hips. To help maintain her balance, he explained.

I stood in the front doorway as we started moving again. It was something my dad would have liked, only he would have wanted to do this in daylight. He'd have perched on the roof as if he was astride Hannibal's elephant or the Trojan Horse, making sure that everyone we passed was falling in behind to make a parade. I began to think I should write to Matthew Pearson and tell him what we had done.

Old Davy Sanders was out with his rifle that night. He was a bit of a pit-lamper anyway, who thought that since the fire had sent a lot of deer his way where nothing had been touched by the flames, he might as well shoot a few. He was also a bachelor, with no one to tell him a gun should not be in the hands of a man who'd poured half a dozen pints of home brew down his gullet after supper. He heard the growl of something coming up the road. I don't know what he thought it was. Maybe some form of Island wildlife he hadn't heard of yet, but he was willing to kill it anyway.

He crouched behind a tree at the side of the road and waited until he could see the shape of what was coming, something big, something so big that he ought to have run away. But he was used to seeing things adjust their size and shape when he'd swallowed enough of his brew.

Of course we didn't see him. We heard the shot, we heard the tinkling of glass falling inside. Then we saw him scurry out to the middle of the road and brace himself for another head-on shot.

I didn't duck fast enough. A sudden blow to my upper arm spun me back into the church. Slapping a hand to the pain, I discovered my shirtsleeve torn and sticky. I hollered, but of course no one heard.

Dennis Price and Howard Stokes had jumped and rolled free, leaving the tractor to chug up the road on its own. One bullet, then another, clanged off the machine. It took a third to hit something that killed the engine. By then the men had run up the road, keeping well to the side, and knocked Sanders to the ground.

Howard Stokes snatched up the man's gun and pointed it at his head.

They told me later that it was because Sanders was superstitious that he started to scream when The Portuguese grabbed his shirt and hauled him to his feet. "Jesus, Mary, Christamighty, let me go, don't eat me, you sonofabitch, I never did nothing wrong!"

They dragged him down the road and showed him what he'd done. "Take a look at that," MacKay said. "You shot the house of God when all it was doing was travelling up the road. You going to hang it up and gut it next? Butcher it for your table?"

"Who is it?" Johanna called down from the roof.

"Highwaymen," Taylor said. "But we've got them surrounded. You'd better stay where you are."

"What about me?" I shouted from the doorway. "I've been shot!"

They let go of Sanders and came running. Taylor looked worried. I suppose he was thinking of my mother. "You okay?" he said.

"It's bleeding pretty bad," I said. I imagined blood stains on the floor.

By this time Johanna Seyerstad had slid down off the roof. I heard the breath go out of her when she landed on her feet. Now she pushed in ahead of the others. "Give us some light over here."

Dennis Price brought up a lantern and held it over her shoulder while she examined my arm. "It's just a scratch," she said. "Thank goodness." She opened the rip in my sleeve and, with her mouth twisted to one side, tore the whole sleeve free of my shirt. Then she used the sleeve to wrap up my arm.

Taylor ducked and stood up with a long splinter of wood in his hand, its sharper end dark with wet blood. "The bullet must have nicked the door frame."

He looked hard at me for a moment. "You all right?"

I nodded, but Johanna Seyerstad said, "Which you had better be grateful for. Involving a child on a prank like this!" Then she said, "Did you say Sanders? Mr. Sanders's daughter is the school inspector's secretary in town."

"He won't remember a thing," Taylor said. "Even if he does he won't believe it."

Once Johanna Seyerstad was satisfied with her first-aid work, they tossed Sanders's rifle into the bush, climbed back onto the

tractor, and dragged that squat dark building up the Island highway. Mrs. Seyerstad and I rode backwards, sitting in one of the
pews, listening to things rattle and knock around us in the dark.
"This is preposterous," she said. I could tell she was furious so I
handed her one of the cigarettes from my pocket, and took one
for myself, and lit both from a single match. We didn't speak after
that. We passed one gateway after another that led to the stump
farms belonging to the Richmonds, the Barclays, and Herbie
Brewer, and the road to Ahlbergs' tea room and taxi office, before
we came to a stop outside the northern corner of the schoolyard,
less than a hundred yards from the Store.

Dark figures stepped out from behind stumps and bushes and
moved up to peer at the church.

"If it's police you'd better let me take care of this," Johanna said
from the doorway. "God knows you could have handled Sanders
better."

But it was not police. Hueffner and then Leena Hueffner
stepped up, and behind them Nell and Andy Richmond, and the
Reimers. The Martins were there. The Aaltos, even Timo. Even
the Maguires had showed up, though we would never know what
they really thought of this business – the only Irish Catholics in
the settlement.

No one asked what had happened to my arm.

"What can we do to help?" Mr. Aalto said.

Taylor scrambled down off the roof. "Stand back is the best
idea," he said to the others. "You're watching experts at work."

It took most of an hour for the experts to get that little church
settled where they wanted it. I showed Timo my wound, and told
him what had happened, but everyone else was too busy to notice
me there. In their excitement, the people who'd been with me
didn't even seem to remember what a close call I'd had. By the
time they'd finished, the sun had risen high enough to send down
morning heat.

"She's sitting at a bit of a tilt," said Leena Hueffner, standing back to size things up from the road. "The Almighty might of dropped her out of a cloud."

"I seen a church about that size in Panama," said Hueffner. "Ants as big as my hand moved in and gobbled 'er up in an afternoon. Left nothing but a little pile of sawdust in the mud."

We looked at him, waiting to hear that this was how he'd lost his arm, that he'd rushed inside to rescue someone from the disaster and giant ants had eaten their way from his fingertips up to his shoulder before he'd got out.

Maybe he knew. He spat on the ground and started back to the Store.

Leena said, "In Texas they would've made him a hero by now if we'd stayed."

The only response to this was a long low groan that could have been the complaint of a discontented cow. But it came from inside the church.

"Somebody's been using it for a barn?" said Leena Hueffner. "You fools have stole a herd of cows. That's serious!"

A second sound, much higher and longer, was definitely not from a cow. We knew an organ when we heard one.

"Stokes," I said. I could see through the front door that he was bent over the organ keyboard, his big feet pumping the pedals and his greased-up face down close to the open hymnal.

"It's about the right size for chickens," Andy Richmond said, as the opening phrases of "I Need Thee Every Hour" filled the morning air. "If it goes missing again you may find it filled with leghorns behind my barn."

"Does your mother know you've been out in the night?" Leena Hueffner said. "What happened to your arm?"

"He was shot," Timo announced, before I had a chance to say it myself.

Her eyebrows rose up to meet her kerchief.

"We encountered opposition," Johanna said. "But he's fine.

Only a scratch." She was saying this as much to Taylor as to Leena, with a hard edge to her voice. "We'll break it to his mother gently when we tell her. She'll want to put a decent bandage over that. The other fellow's in much worse shape than he is."

Mother did not recover quickly from the shock, even after I'd convinced her I would live. She collapsed in a kitchen chair and tried to keep me from seeing she'd started to cry.

"What's the matter?" I said, pretending the night's excursion had been nothing to get excited about.

"Gallivanting all over the countryside with those foolish men," she said, swatting her hand as though she would send the men flying. "In the middle of the night! And not enough energy to do your chores. D'you think you have no family of your own?" Mother's complexion was always ruddy but today an additional flush ran right up into her hair.

"I'll feed the chickens," I said. "I'll fill the woodbox."

"I'm left to manage everything." I could see this was going to be one of her days for feeling sorry for herself. "Your uncle cares for nothing but them machines, and his stupid forge! He'll have you over there too before we know it, while I'm out there weeding the garden all on my own." She looked up at me, her forehead divided by a severe perpendicular crease, and spoke sharply. "The cows would starve and the garden dry up if caring for this farm were up to you."

People said I was lucky to have Uncle Archie to take my father's place. "And your mother, trying so hard to be two parents at once, when she hasn't recovered from the blow." But they didn't know how quick she was to holler at me, or how often she burst into tears.

She stood up and started slamming pots around in the kitchen sink. "Mr. Sanders!" she shouted. "Mr. Sanders! Wouldn't your father be proud of the company you keep! I'll have the police on Mr. Sanders, we'll see him in jail for your murder!"

I got outside as fast as I could and set about doing my chores, hoping she would forget about reporting my death.

Before he was visited by the police, Sanders had time to cause even more trouble. When he awoke from his drunken sleep he was not as forgetful as the others had hoped. He made sure his daughter knew what the school teacher of Portuguese Creek had been up to in the middle of the night. Then he went on to prove that his experience hadn't cured him of anything. He retrieved his gun and came up the road on his ancient gelding and took a few more pot shots at the church in the schoolyard corner.

His daughter made sure the inspector of schools was told, and before the week was out the inspector of schools would arrange to have a talk with Johanna Seyerstad, making the suggestion that since she was setting such a poor example for youngsters she might consider not returning to the classroom in September. When he'd finished, she would look him squarely in the eye and announce that she was a jump ahead of him. "By September I'll be far from here. So will that lunatic who dragged me into his childish escapade. I hope to see neither him nor you again."

In spite of the sudden change in their plans, Johanna Seyerstad and Wyatt Taylor both attended the Maguires' party, though they arrived separately and did not speak to one another the entire night. Taylor stayed apart, talking only to those who made the effort to stroll over his way, but Johanna circulated through the entire noisy crowd as though to suggest that she was a member of this community while Taylor, after less than a year, was not.

Of course the party was Bridget Maguire's excuse to show off their new house and barn, both of them raised with the help of neighbours. These were exactly the same as the buildings that had burned, but with some of the kinks worked out, as Bridget put it, since they'd had a chance to improve on the original. The meal was plain meat-and-potatoes Irish fare, with soda bread, followed by gooseberry pie, eaten inside by those who got there early enough to hold down a seat and outside by those who came too late and had to eat standing or perched on whatever they could find that wouldn't ruin their clothes with streaks of ash.

Because her brother's health seemed to have improved a little, Maude Pearson had begun to take him out in public occasionally. He sat in his wheeled chair beside her, humming a monotonous tune with his head bobbing this way and that, like a balloon on the end of a willow switch. Of course he was never without the mask that covered the bottom half of his face, but he was probably not aware that people found reasons to come close for a decent look. Some stood at a safe distance and contemplated him. Others knelt beside him long enough to squeeze his hand, and to say a few words of greeting just in case. He was always neatly dressed, Maude made certain of that, in black trousers and white shirt, pressed and smelling of the wash. His pale hair was parted in a ruler-straight line down the middle.

Maude took advantage of these gatherings to encourage people to join the community association, and to get involved in her campaign to make sure a Laurier Liberal was elected from this district in the next election. Nobody who came close enough for a look at Donald MacCormack left without hearing about her attempts to establish a local branch of the Women's Institute.

After dark, everyone moved to the hayloft of the new barn, where they danced to the music of an impromptu orchestra made up of Sven Ahlberg's flute, Fortunat Martin's fiddle, Armus Aalto's tin whistle, Lilly Swift's button accordion, and for a short while Patrick Maguire's whiny trombone that he called a *bazooka*. As Christina Ahlberg said, the only thing missing was Matt Pearson's guitar and "Ye Maidens of Ontario." They hadn't practised together but no one cared about the mistakes except when the mistakes were so bad that everyone stopped in their tracks to holler good-natured insults. The planks underfoot had not been polished yet by wintered hay but that did not prevent anyone from dancing right through the night until dawn.

Nell Richmond had slipped her wartime autograph album into
her purse and brought it out to show off, the first time anyone had
seen it. Some of the wounded soldiers she'd nursed had scribbled
poems. She read aloud to anyone who would listen: "There's
many a boat been lost at sea / Through want of tar or rudder; /
There's many a boy has lost his best girl / Through flirting with
another. Private Reginald Lane, wounded at Guillemont." She
opened the book to her favourite drawing and passed it around. A
man milking a cow, a disgruntled woman saying, "Why aren't you
at the front, young man?" and the man with his hands on the
cow's teats saying, "There isn't any milk at that end."

Christina Ahlberg, normally so careful when she was reading
teacups in her own tea room, set herself up in a corner of the loft
to read palms, foreseeing futures that stood her customers' hair
on end. Bridget Maguire would give birth to three sets of twins
within the next three years if she wasn't careful. Armus Aalto
would receive a large inheritance from Finland but he would have
to swim the length of the Baltic Sea to claim it. Howard Stokes,
who had showed up again in his costume, dragging his chain and
scratching his greasy hide, was promised that he would wake up
one morning soon and discover that he no longer needed the
bearskin rug to be a savage, he would have grown a fine fur pelt of
his own, complete with its own foul odour. She drew attention to
the hair that grew on his nose and inside his ears as proof that the
transformation was already taking place.

Maguire had bought a wagonload of hay from a farm close to
town, and scattered it around the mow, "for the sweet smell," he
said. His cows would get to eat it later. What hadn't been spread
around was still in the wagon, parked in the lower mow. Tanner
and the Reimer boys climbed the wall ladder to the upper mow
and jumped off the edge, setting up such a dust when they landed
in the wagon that it made them sneeze. Timo Aalto and I
watched them for a while, and watched the dancing for a while,
and then went over to sit with our legs dangling from the edge.

My mother had insisted I wear a long-sleeved shirt so my bandage wouldn't attract attention. I rolled the sleeve up as high as I could and pushed a hand up inside to rub against the itch, but nobody seemed to notice. The four little Martins sat further along, dressed in fancy dresses with ribbons in their hair, watching me without saying a word.

Tanner and Thomas Reimer pushed at one another, to see who would lose his balance first and fall. They laughed, teetering on the edge, and grabbed at each other's clothes, and shoved fists of hay down inside one another's shirts. I could tell they'd been drinking. Tanner had already had an argument with his mother, who'd tried to get him to be a little less rambunctious. "Someone could get hurt," she'd said. But Tanner had only laughed.

"Better watch out," he said to me while he stood, panting on the edge, waiting for Thomas to crawl to safety from the wagon. "Lenora Barclay wants you to dance with her."

"I'd rather kill myself!" I said, and pushed away from the edge to fall with legs pedalling down through dusty air to land in a cushion of hay just inches from Thomas's scrambling feet. I spat hay from my mouth, shook hayseeds from my shirt, and crawled as quickly as I could to the lip of the wagon and slid out.

"You crazy bastard," Thomas said. "You coulda killed me."

"Could not," I said. "Don't be stupid."

"Could so," he said. "Go on, you're wrecking our fun."

I looked to the upper mow, where skirts whirled past and swinging lanterns sent light and shadows rocking in the rafters. Timo had disappeared. Tanner looked down on us without any expression that I recognized. Then he folded up his legs, got to his feet, and went off into the shadows where I couldn't see. Thomas made a fist and punched me in the mouth before he ran off.

I climbed the ladder fast and sought out Tanner on the far side of the dancers, and pushed him against the wall. He swung his fist and connected with my chin. He cursed, and threw himself against me, and we both fell to the floor.

It didn't take long before adults hauled us to our feet. When I saw Mother heading my way I decided to get out of there fast, but Johanna Seyerstad put herself between me and the ladder.

"Again?" she said.

I tried to throw myself over the edge above the hay, but she put out a hand and took hold of my arm.

"Charlie?"

Her dark blue eyes knew everything you thought and somehow told it back to you. She didn't have to say anything. I knew why I'd hit Tanner but I wasn't going to say it. I was the one with the right to be mad at my father. I was the one still waiting for him to show up, laughing, to put the world right and allow me to punish him. Tanner was mad at his father even though he still had some hope, while I had to admit I had none.

Mrs. Seyerstad straightened the front of my shirt where a button had been torn off, and went searching through her pockets for a pin to hold it together.

Maude Pearson said that if her son was going to spoil a party with fistfights it was time she took her family home. She tried to make light of it, but Tanner refused to leave. When she took hold of his arm, he shook it off. She took hold of his arm again and lowered her voice to say she was giving him no choice. "Now, march."

"Let go," he said. "You can't make me do nothing."

He pulled away, and climbed up the wall to sit on a crossbeam above us.

Wyatt Taylor spoke up. "You had better do what your mother says there, son."

Tanner looked at Taylor as though he were looking at some cowshit stuck to the walls.

"By God, I'll come up and get you!" said Sandy MacKay.

Maude held up a hand to stop him from doing this. I don't suppose she'd ever before shed a tear in public. When Maude Pearson was angry, she wrote letters. When she was thwarted in her plans she drew on all her considerable moral strength for persuasion. But

it seemed she had no resources for handling Tanner before an audience. She started to call him down from where he sat with his legs
dangling, but her voice caught and she put a hand to her mouth.
Then she slapped away Christina Ahlberg's sympathetic hand and
set about gathering up Donald and Will to leave.

Tanner watched. Then, noticing there were as many people
watching him as were watching his mother, some of them men
who were waiting for Maude to leave so they could come up and
show him what they thought of his behaviour, he climbed down
the wall, hastily rejoined the Reimer boys, and as soon as his
mother and the others had gone, scrambled down the ladder to
head off in bursts of laughter into the night.

There was silence for a while after that. My mother had crept
up behind me and seized my ear in her hand, and whispered that
if I didn't watch my p's and q's she would drag me home as well,
and would twist my ear right off before she'd let me shame her the
way that boy had done to his mother. She gave me a swat on the
head to make sure I knew she meant it.

Mrs. Swift had missed out on the fuss while she was outside
hauling her paintings from her buggy. She started bringing them
in now, and propped them against the barn wall. Then she invited
people to come down and admire them, and, if they were moved
to do so, buy. She spoke highly of them herself. She indicated how
the paintings of Turner had been an influence. She pointed out
that if you looked carefully it was possible to see right through the
fire, as though there were no real substance or lasting danger in it,
to the suggestion of farm and home life going on despite it.

But most of us could see only the trees and buildings engulfed
in flames that did not look like anyone's memory of the fire.
"Not *our* fire!" said Leena Hueffner, screwing up her leathery face.
Anyway, she said, she couldn't see why people would want to look
at reminders of something that had caused them pain. Lilly Swift
should have painted rose-covered cottages or stone bridges if she
wanted people to buy them for their homes.

But when people saw the paintings at the barn dance they
began to tell one another about the fire as if they hadn't all been
there to see it themselves. It turned out that everyone had a different way of seeing it. To some it was a close call that still terror-
ized their dreams. To others it was an adventure, like something
out of a book. To many, it was an opportunity to see themselves
as the central figure in a drama – as comical incompetents, as
confused heroes, as strangers they didn't recognize as themselves.
Articles that were lost to the fire were remembered as "treasures"
and "heirlooms brought from Home." Articles that had been sal-
vaged out of the ashes had become miraculous "souvenirs" – that
new word brought home from the War along with the medals and
German helmets they identified.

Before the night was over they had begun, some of them, to
remember themselves as figures in a ridiculous comedy, scurrying around like frightened mice trying to save their hides. "I lost
every brain I ever had. All I could think of was 'Mother would be
furious if I left her tablecloth behind!' Well, she *would*!" They
tripped over themselves trying to outdo one another. "So there I
was be'ind the wheel for the firs' time!" cried Arlette Martin, her
hands to her face. "*Sacre bleu!* I don' know 'ow to steer this thing!
I will drive right into the firs' tree, I know it!"

Even though it was probably true that the Returned Soldiers
would never get over the War, they hardly ever talked about it.
What they talked about instead was the fire. The Maguires'
dance was the first I'd noticed this. Everyone had a story. Details
neglected in one telling would be reinstated in the next. In the
years afterwards, everyone would tell their own version of the fire
at every opportunity – as their children have done, and now their
grandchildren – like Hueffner with his Panama Canal.

It was little wonder young Macken moved the theft of the
church ahead by a year for his movie, because telling about it had
got all mixed in with the telling of the fire as early as the Maguires'
party. Most people were astonished that, aside from Sanders,

the little community down the road did not kick up any fuss.
Those few who had attended services simply drove the extra miles.
No words of complaint had arrived from the Archbishop of
Canterbury, either, or from the King. It's possible the leaders of
the Church were never told of the midnight miracle that was
meant to give Portuguese Creek its soul.

Not that the squat bell tower on the roof could measure up to
expectations. It was hardly a match for the gleaming spires the
men had seen in the villages of France. In fact, the tiny church
itself was dwarfed and overwhelmed by the grove of second-
growth Douglas firs that soared above it, undamaged by the fire,
keeping it dark in their shade. It was possible to drive right through
the settlement without even noticing the building beside the
road. Eyes that weren't watching the road ahead would be looking
up at the firs.

Sanders would take a pot shot at the church every time he
went past on the highway after that. The men nailed boards over
the little window on either side of the front door and decided not
to replace the glass until he'd tired of his game. This gave the
church the appearance of being blindfolded, hiding behind a featureless mask in the protective shade of the firs, waiting for something more to happen.

(v)

While daisies and cornflowers bloomed across the battlefields,
a late-spring flourish of strangers had begun to appear in every
corner of the countryside. Some knocked on village doors and

asked to be shown the locations of trenches and dugouts –
Liverpool parents whose sons had died, women from Capetown
whose lovers had not returned, sisters from Winnipeg whose
brothers had written faithfully once a week until the eve of a
certain battle, which they had traced, in the face of official resis-
tance, to these particular fields.

"Like Chaucer's pilgrims," Matthew Pearson wrote in his
notebooks, "these survivors were responding to the call of spring,
leaving their homes in search of some great need. You went about
your work while foreigners registered shock at such callousness –
allowing ordinary life to go on when it had ended for so many
others on this very spot. Emile shook his head at this, and smiled
around his pipe. To him, these people were nothing more than
this year's crop of ghosts, haunting the scenes of war."

One morning Pearson came upon a stranger forking manure
onto a wagon outside Emile's barn. The man nodded curtly to
Pearson, but went on with his work. He was dressed in rags,
unshaven, his face ravaged with erupted sores. He could not have
been one of the grieving relatives, but looked as though he might
have come up from the tunnels, one survivor from that pack of
mad men they'd once believed were out with the wild dogs
snarling over the corpses. The air was thick with the rich dark
odour of rotting manure.

"You must be doing pretty well if you've taken on a hired man,"
Pearson said, that evening at Emile's hearth.

But Emile, sunk low in an ancient chair behind a cloud of his
pipe smoke, raised his shoulders for a serious shrug. "There will be
more. Like yourself. Maybe all my life."

So Pearson crossed the fence the next morning and introduced
himself, speaking his halting French as he'd become accustomed
to doing there. The man laughed. "Jesus, mate, with your accent
even I can tell you're no more frog than I am! A Yank?"

"The right continent, wrong country. You're Australian – or
En-Zedder? – come even farther than I have."

"I've come no distance at all. I never left." The man propped the manure fork under an armpit, leaned into it, and regarded Pearson out of a scarred and bulging eye. Reddish whiskers grew in patches around the inflamed eruptions on his face. "Couldn't force m'self onto the boat. Bolted. Been wandering ever since."

"Does that make you a deserter, then? If you were never demobilized."

"Don't know, cobber. They can't even say I went missing in action – just missing. Maybe I'm the unknown bleedin' warrior they go on about. I keep out of the way of the froggy police, in case guests are not as welcome here as we used to be. What's your story?"

Matt Pearson didn't know what his story was. "I thought I'd brought home one good thing from the War but it was taken from me."

The man began again to fork manure onto the wagon. "Bloody amazing, in't it?" He jerked his head in the direction of the fields beyond the hedges. "Makes you wonder if it ever happened." He grunted, lifting a heavy forkload. "Not that I give a damn. I'll just shovel the Frenchman's cowshit for him and then move on."

Later that day, Pearson went out as he often did for a walk across the fields and came to a pond of placid water that he'd thought might be the crater he'd taken refuge in, the morning of August 8. While he'd been stumbling through the thick fog a machine-gun bullet had smacked into his shoulder and sent him spinning to the ground. He had rolled over the lip of that crater and slid down the slimy incline, and found himself face to face with Private Banks. What was left of him. It could have been another crater, of course, he couldn't be sure. Now it was a pond for peaceful cattle to drink from.

The Australian came up behind him through the young hay. "Not much point in just staring," he said, and after shedding his rags ran down the slope and into the pond. He yelled at the shock and threw up his arms but kept on running until the water had reached his thighs, then plunged forward and swam out and turned onto his back. "It's cold as a wowser's smile, mate, it'll wake ye bloody quick!"

Pearson had washed in holes like this before. Washed in them, shaved in them, even swum in them when the grime on his body seemed worse than the mud in the hole. Poets had made much of the swimming hole. And war artists. Pearson had read a few of the poems. You'd think there'd been nothing but beautiful lads in the war, golden-haired and pretty as girls. The English could write such things without squirming, bless them. If those poets were here, what would they do with that hairy-backed Aussie thrashing away like a drowning wombat?

They might not have found much to inspire them in Matthew Pearson either, but the chance to be a boy again was all at once a temptation. When was the last time he had shouted and thrown this body carelessly at the world? He undressed and ran down to the water, but waded in more cautiously than the Australian had done.

"Not recommended for brass monkeys!" the other shouted, and dived under.

Pearson breaststroked the length of the pond, then flipped over and kicked his way back. Grinning foolishly at the sky. Birds sang – he'd never learned to tell one bird from another here. White clouds flew by, inviting him to see shapes. Pigs in sheeps' clothing. There'd been a swimming hole at the bottom of his father's southern pasture. War forced you into middle age when you had hardly lived out your boyhood.

Standing for a moment to slick back his streaming hair, he was aware of shouting from up on the rim of the field. Emile. The two men stood to watch the farmer come peg-legging down across the uneven grass. His excited French in the open air was too fast for either of them to follow. Was he bringing news? Word of some disaster?

It didn't matter what he was saying. His intention soon became obvious. On the slope beside their heaps of clothing he began to remove his own. Then, naked, he sat on the grass and unstrapped the wooden leg.

"Jesus," the Australian said.

Emile hopped on three limbs to the edge of the pool and hurled himself forward, his cry arcing through the air to end abruptly in the thudding slap of a belly-flop. He sank. A pale figure streaked out beneath the surface of the water and did not resurface until it was nearly across. Then he spat and flung his head about and went under again.

Matt Pearson lay back and floated out from the shoreline, occasionally kicking his feet to keep himself moving. He smiled to think of the challenge they would be to the poets now, the three of them slopping around in this cattle pond. A hairy Australian with the whiskery jaw of a Sydney longshoreman. The one-legged farmer with crimson scars on his narrow chest. And himself, with his receding hairline, his puckered shoulder, and the patches of shiny pink skin where burns were still healing. No sign of the beautiful lads.

There had been more than Banks in the hole. There had been two Germans as well. Pearson had fallen across them. He could imagine them down there still, in one form or another, eyes staring up at these three pink men. Why had he thrown himself into this deathly soup? Even if Banks were not below, or those Germans, there were pieces of others rotted into foreign soil. All around them this regenerated flowering landscape was green from the fertilizer of men.

He had to get out if he were not to be sick. But as he thrashed across the middle of the pond he felt a sudden alarming pressure on his belly, the touch of a human hand. Why did Hugh Corbett leap to mind?

He surfaced, splashing, filled with panic, expecting decomposing body pieces to be floating around him. The Australian stood laughing near the shore. Emile rose up like a lean pale breaching whale, both skinny arms raised high. "Sorry, *mon ami*," he said. "I did not know you were so easily frightened."

The water was too cold anyway. Pearson ran out and used his clothing to towel himself, then lay on the grassy slope to let the weak sun finish the job. The Australian followed, and sat with his arms around his furry shins and his chin between his knees. They watched without talking while Emile swam the breaststroke the length of the pond and then turned over to dog-paddle, at a curious tilt, the distance back. He crawled out, and scrambled up the slope to his clothes. All three of them were silent while he strapped on his leg.

"What did you find when you got home?" the Australian said. "I mean, what sent you back here? Your missus gone off with another bloke?"

The thought of Maude with another man was a slap against Pearson's skull. For a moment things went black. The sudden burst of air from his lungs might have been mistaken for a laugh.

"What did anyone go home to?" he said. "Work. Family. Trying to make something out of life. It wasn't any of that."

"Not everyone went home to something so simple," said Emile. He pulled on his drawers and lay back with his hands behind his neck to look at the clouds. "What did the Russians go home to? More bloodshed. You have seen the papers. Their own brothers' blood this time."

"Same with the bleedin' Irish," the Australian said. "Brothers' blood again, mother's and da's as well."

"And the Boche went home to starvation," said Emile. "Who went home to anything better than what they'd left?"

"I hear the Yanks are having a grand old time," the Australian said. "Money flowing down the bleedin' streets. Maybe that's where I ought to be. Whaddaya reckon?"

He stood up and pulled on his ragged underclothes and then his trousers that looked as though they'd been made for someone three times as wide. "You blokes now," he said to Pearson, "you've more in common with us, I reckon, from what I hear. No revolutions, no bloodshed, no orgy of wealth – just getting on with the job."

"So what are you doing here?" Pearson said, stepping into his Penmans. "Do your folks think you were killed?"

"Folks are dead themselves, mate. Long ago."

"And no girl?" said Emile.

"Nobody waits for Bluey Marsden, I can tell you that. Ol' Sydney cares for me about as much as that cow over there." He buttoned his filthy shirt. "It must be the same for our Johnny Canuck or he wouldn't be here. Nobody to care if he's dead or alive, or he'd be snuggled down in the bosom of his family thanking his lucky stars he's not dead or bloody army-surplus like me."

When the Australian had set off up the slope the others got into their clothes and followed, and caught up with him at the top of the field, where he'd waited. "Visitors," he said, a man who had learned to be wary of just about everyone. At the far end of the next field, beside a brick barn whose roof Emile had not restored, a man and woman stood talking. Then one of them – the woman – walked around in a kind of circle, looking down at the ground near her feet, before coming back to stand by the man, who leaned on a walking stick.

"More ghosts," Emile said, starting across the field towards them, though this was not a route back to the village. Matt Pearson followed, while the Australian hung back.

Pearson had formed the habit of keeping his eyes to the ground for what might yet be hidden in the grass. Spring rains had washed the ploughed fields, clearing dirt from the shells and shrapnel and Mills bombs that had worked their way to the surface during the winter, making it easier for him and Emile and the other farmers to find and collect them before the new crops were put in. But there would be others they'd overlooked, concealed amongst the new hay.

The middle-aged couple wore warm tweeds and sturdy boots. The woman, who'd looked alarmed when they approached, explained that they had come from Glasgow, and had spent much of this day exploring the vicinity of the abandoned barn. She wore eyeglasses and a tartan kerchief, and held a Michelin map of the trenches in one hand. Their son Roderick had been killed here, she said, indicating the countryside with a vague sweep of the map. A friend had told them poor Rory had been buried somewhere near this barn, but they'd found no marker. Nor had they earlier found any records showing that he'd been removed to one of the new cemeteries. Her voice was quavery, the flesh around her eyes bruised. Her husband leaned on his walking stick and kept his gaze on his boots. Embarrassed perhaps, or afraid.

"This is my building," Emile said. "My fields. Are you sure this is where they told you?"

"Aye, certainly," said the woman, and stabbed a finger at some scribble on her map.

Pearson could see that Emile was made awkward and somehow nervous by this and would probably rather not be overheard. He moved back a few steps, intending to return to the village alone, but found that the Australian had come up to join him.

"A commercial transaction taking place?" he said.

"What d'you mean?"

"I've seen it up and down the line. I worked for your mate here once before. If this corroboree turns out the way I expect, he and I will be out after dark tonight with spades." His grin suggested that Pearson could not imagine all that he knew. "Those two galahs reckon they'll get their decomposing boy across the Channel. Whether they do or not their money's the same to *notre ami le fermier*. He's just helping the French economy back on its feet."

"I think you're imagining things," Matt Pearson said, and moved away. He'd had enough of this man. At the end of the building he turned the corner and followed a cow trail to an open doorway.

Hugh Corbett was on his mind as he stepped inside. The boy

had been shot against a building much like this – shot for desertion and then himself deserted, left behind in foreign soil while
the rest of them, or some of them, went home. Had anyone gone
looking for his temporary grave, or found his name on some marker
amongst the rows of heroes?

That other building had been some village farmer's abattoir,
but was only a slightly larger version of this barn. It, too, had had
part of its roof blown off, its brick walls shored up with poles. And
a lean-to room at one end that could be locked and barred against
a prisoner's escape.

"Tell them it was a mistake," the boy pleaded, when Pearson
had been permitted to visit the night before the execution. The
guards had given him drink, but not so much as Pearson had since
imagined in an effort to make this bearable for himself. The boy
was far from drunk. "Beg them, sir, for Christ's sake! Dear God,
Mr. Pearson, sir – you can't let them do this!"

Matt Pearson had wiped bits of Fox's flesh from this face. There
were blackheads still, and pimples. A rash from a clumsy shave.
Snot ran from his nose, and was spread by his sleeve across his face.

When the boy had finally been convinced there was nothing
Pearson could do to change anyone's mind, he fell to his knees on
the dirt floor and tried hard not to cry. But he was still a boy, after
all. The twisted face and quivering chin might as easily have
belonged to a six-year-old child.

He muttered something. When Pearson said that he couldn't
hear, the boy looked up. He wanted Donald, he said.

"I'm sorry," Pearson said, thinking he'd meant *now*. But the boy
went on as though he hadn't heard. That was what had happened
out there, he said.

"What do you mean?"

Hugh Corbett put both hands between his knees and rocked
forward and back. Then he looked up to search Matt Pearson's
face for something – Pearson didn't know what. Then he said that
what had happened was something like this: he had got confused

in the battle, his head had started to buzz, there was only the one thing he knew for sure – he had to go and find Donald.

"How could I tell them that?" he cried. "If they knew what I meant, they'd take it as reason enough to shoot me."

"It wouldn't have mattered," Pearson said, kneeling to put an arm around the boy's shoulder. "They couldn't allow themselves to make love an excuse for anything."

For a few minutes they were both silent. Then Hugh Corbett bowed his head over his knees and rocked again, and said that he had messages he wanted to send. Could he trust Pearson to deliver them? Pearson agreed, but could make little sense of the messages he was intended to carry, since they came in fits and starts through bursts of cursing and sudden floods of tears. He knew what was meant, however, and knew that there was little hope of making them understood.

The boy shuddered suddenly, all over, as though some chilled liquid had been injected into his veins. "I can't go out there tomorrow," he said, his eyes wide. "I'll die of fright. I wish they'd shoot me in my sleep."

He was silent for a moment. Then looked to Pearson. "You could do it, sir. If you did it now."

Pearson could not think what to do with his shock. Thank God there were the guards watching from the doorway, who had taken his pistol from him. Maybe requests like this were not uncommon. At any rate, the boy did not seem to expect his compliance. He reminded Matt Pearson that he had been his Sunday School teacher one summer not so many years ago, and asked him to pray.

He could not be sure, now, but it was probably *Thy will be done* that came to him first, for surely whatever *Thy will* might be, it could not possibly be the murder of a confused and frightened boy who had volunteered to fight for his country. He might have recited the words of the Twenty-third Psalm as well, though it was hard to imagine getting past *He restoreth my soul* without breaking down from his own great confusion and need.

When he'd spoken with Hugh Corbett's folks in their small farmhouse in Ferguson Falls, before the move out west, Matt Pearson had mentioned the prayers but not the boy's pleas, nor had he reported that Hugh had not recovered from the loss of Donald.

The father turned his large slow head to gaze out the nearest window without comment. The mother closed her eyes and slumped back in her upholstered chair, so that for a moment Pearson thought she had fainted. But she came round, and got unsteadily to her feet in order to rummage through a cabinet drawer for a piece of paper, which she invited him to read.

It was the letter they had received, quite unexpectedly, as other parents had received "missing in action" letters, but soiled at the creases now from much folding and unfolding. "Sir and Madam," it began. "With deep regret I have the honour to inform you –" He would never forget these words. What this gentleman had the honour of informing the pair of horrified parents was that their son had been tried by Field General Court-Martial in France on the charge of "deserting His Majesty's Service" and was sentenced to "suffer death by being shot," a sentence that had been carried out on such-and-such a day. And the ending: "I have the honour to be, Madam, Sir, Your obedient servant, Frederick Bond, care of the Record Office."

The mother had not taken her pale grey eyes from his face the whole time he read. "What would I say, I wonder?" she said when he'd finished, "if I were to meet this Mr. Bond?"

The cold edge to her voice suggested the man would not be safe.

"Only doing his job," the father said, without removing his gaze from whatever it was outside that held it. "We can't blame the man for that."

The woman snatched back the paper from Pearson's hands, folded it quickly against her breast, and closed her eyes. "I shall never be able to understand how people could do such things to one another." Her eyes flew open again, fierce. "And you, sir. What did you do to stop it?"

"Mother!" the husband cautioned, turning his great head at last to look at her. His hand lifted, but could not reach her from where he sat. "He came to offer comfort."

This had been little more than three years ago. Pearson could recall his own horror on their behalf, as well as a swelling of sympathy for them. But he saw now that he had not been capable of identifying properly with them in their loss, or even fully imagining it. Instead he must have come away from that meeting with a determination he was barely aware of, to shoulder responsibility for protecting everyone who came into his life from now on. He would keep them safe in the future as he had failed so badly to do, both as teacher and officer, in the past.

The guilt that had clung to his bones since the moment he'd crossed the Atlantic with his little girl had not been guilt for the foolish infidelity of a confused and frightened man, nor for the deaths he had brought to nameless aliens, nor for failing to respond to Hugh Corbett's final pleas. It was for the sin of staying alive long enough to crawl out of that hole and then out of this slaughterhouse country altogether when he had failed to keep alive so many who had been entrusted to his care. It was a sickening thought. Of course there must be men all over the world who'd felt and recognized this from the beginning, and somehow sensibly shrugged it off. While he had simply consented, and tried to tidy up the messy world all on his own.

How much more easily could he identify now with that woman in Ferguson Falls, and her quiet husband. And with all the other parents of fallen children, including that distraught couple outside who could hope for nothing better than to find their boy's remains and smuggle them home, against the laws of the Commonwealth.

He had not been aware of kneeling. Perhaps he had knelt without thinking when he'd remembered kneeling with Hughie

Corbett. At any rate, here he was. And might as well assume he had need of it. He closed his eyes, and heard what he recognized as his own tired voice: *Open thou mine eyes. Open thou mine eyes, that I may behold wondrous things out of thy law.*

Seen at close range the barn floor was more than trampled dirt and dried manure. There were bits of hay, and broken brick, and fragments of mortar, and pieces of twigs that birds must have dropped, and small stones, and even here and there a few weeds sprouting. From the powdery soil between his knees a narrow bulge became a piece of wood at such a low slant that dust and kicked-up dirt had all but buried it. A fence slat, probably. Or a bar that had held the door in place. He slid fingers beneath the end, and brushed dirt away, and took hold of the board to shift it from side to side until it slipped out of the earth. It was about thirty inches long, perhaps more, and almost the width of his hand. A shorter crosspiece must have fallen off and been trampled elsewhere into the dirt. He had seen enough of these to know what he was looking at, though any markings had been worn away.

When he stepped outside and went around the corner of the barn, the Australian had gone but Emile was still in muffled conversation with the parents. "The grave they're looking for, could it have been put inside the barn?" He held the dirt-stained slat of wood out for examination. "I didn't find an identification tag, or anything else they might have hung from it."

The woman clasped her husband's arm. Emile's startled eyes rose from the rough board in Matt Pearson's hand to Pearson's eyes and for a moment narrowed with what might have been doubt or suspicion.

"I could give you a hand," Pearson said. To the parents he added, "It may not help, but it seems like something worth trying."

Eventually the parents went off clutching the piece of lumber, having promised to return the following day. When Matt Pearson and Emile had gone a hundred yards or so in the direction of the village, Pearson turned on an impulse to look back. "I didn't know why," he wrote. "There were no human figures in this landscape now. It was the outline of the roofless barn that struck me, dark against the late afternoon sky, its gable ends standing like sharp trowels at either end. From this distance and in this light it might have been poor Hughie's abattoir, as I had imagined it inside. I wondered with a cold shock if it had been Hugh Corbett's building that the abandoned sawmill at home reminded me of, and not the ruined village church as I'd supposed.

"I could not imagine what it meant. I *could* imagine, of course, but didn't want to know. I turned away too abruptly and lost my balance, and staggered upright again before trailing after Emile across the fields to the village."

He was probably ready to come home anyway. The presence of the Australian had made him uneasy. By now he'd done everything he could for the old folks, short of staying on for the rest of their lives. Quite likely my letter only added a sense of urgency to a decision he'd already made.

Dear Mr. Pearson,

I hope that you are well. Mother and I are well too. I think you should come home now. Mother would tell me to mind my own business, and Mrs. Pearson might not want me to tell you this in case it spoils what you are doing over there. Tanner is in the hospital from an accident in a stolen truck but should be out soon. I thought you might want to be here the way my dad would be here if it was me that got into a mess.

Your friend,
Charlie Mackinaw

I did not describe Richmonds' stolen truck, tilted against a black stump on the far side of the ditch closer to town, its right

side crushed and two of its wheels lying a few yards down the road.
Nor did I mention the bottle of rye that Tanner and the Reimers
had stolen from the Riverside Hotel and nearly emptied by the
time they went off the road. It wasn't my intention to alarm him,
nor could I have known that thoughts of deserters and desertion
would be on his mind the day he received the letter. My only
intention was to remind him that there were people at home who
needed him as much as those villagers over there in France.

He left soon after getting the letter, but not before making
arrangements for Emile to take over working the old couple's farm,
turning all harvest and any profit over to them in exchange for
their written promise that he would inherit the property after
their deaths. Whatever he had yet to find out about himself and
his life, he'd come to understand, he would have to find out, like
everyone else, at home.

Maude Pearson decided to wait for him at the farm instead of
going in to town to meet the train. Only Sandy MacKay and
Howard Stokes went in to meet him, riding with Major Burgess
in his touring car. "Don't overwhelm him," the others said. "Let
him come home without a fuss, we'll welcome him at tomorrow's picnic."

I was not willing to be so patient. When I saw Major Burgess
pull in at the Store I scrambled down out of the attic and crossed
the road. "Can I come too?"

"I don't suppose there's any reason why not," said Mr. Stokes,
opening the back door of the touring car with a little bow. All
three men had dressed in freshly washed work clothes, with shirts
buttoned up to the throat, smelling of hot flatirons.

While Major Burgess went into the Store for something, I sat
inside his car to try it out. Behind the lace curtains I would feel
like a prince as we drove down the road, though I could smell and
almost taste the cold-fat odour of the roasts and steaks that

usually rode there. I found no signs of blood on the upholstery, though. From the front seat, Mr. Stokes said that since Tanner had refused their invitation to go along, it would serve him right if I took his place.

But what if Matt Pearson didn't remember me? I wanted to be at the train more than anything else I could think of, but what if he looked at me and said, "Where's Tanner?"

"I guess I won't," I said, and took my time getting out of the touring car in case the men wanted to talk me into staying. "Uncle Archie wants me at his shop." This was the day he intended to show me how to hammer a red-hot horseshoe into shape.

"You'd better help your uncle, then," said Sandy MacKay, as Major Burgess got in behind the wheel. "You can see Matt Pearson tomorrow." Tomorrow was Dominion Day again, another picnic.

So I wasn't there to see Matthew Pearson step down from the train, and would have to rely on what he told me later.

"I'd half-expected to hate whatever I found, Charlie. An ugly burnt-over blackened place, unfit for humans. That's what I remembered. I don't know what I intended to do about it. Maybe I thought I'd talk the family into moving – back to Ontario, or down-Island at least. But I had forgotten the smell of the sea, and the sight of the blue mountains with snow on their sunny peaks this time of year. I'd forgotten the wide sweep of green timber along the base of the mountains to the south of the fire. And that ancient, giant cedar left standing by Richmonds' gate."

He'd forgotten – or said he had – the familiar sight of tall black stumps standing amongst the huckleberry bushes alongside the road – "something you'd never see anywhere else in the world, so far as I know." Or the green fenced-off fields, with cattle grazing, and beyond the fields the snags standing up like scorched bones amongst the singed second-growth fir and the leafy alder. Or the Ahlbergs' well-kept house with Sven's McLaughlin-Buick taxi parked out front. And the unpainted barns that were unlike barns he'd known anywhere else – unique, so far as he knew, to this place.

Because I was sure they would stop at the church I'd parked myself on the front step to wait. Uncle Archie had been so disappointed in my first horseshoe that he'd told me to go home and hoe the peas. I wanted to see Matt Pearson's face when he noticed what had been done in his absence. He would kid me about being shot, much as my dad would have done, and want to know if I'd developed a taste for gunfighting now that I'd survived my first shoot-out. He'd roll up my sleeve and make a face at my wound, and knead his own shoulder while he welcomed me to the club of the Walking Wounded.

But they didn't stop. He didn't even notice the stolen church. If the men had said nothing to draw his attention to it, I suppose it was because they knew he'd be torn between a desire to stop and a need to get home to his family. Let Maude tell him, they thought. He and Maude could drive down together and marvel at the miracle that had taken place in his absence.

He'd been only a little surprised that Maude hadn't gone in to town to meet him, he said, but he was alarmed when he saw that she hadn't come out into the front yard when they drove in. "Is she laid up with something?" he asked the others. "Has she been keeping something from me?"

Hollyhocks were tall against the front wall of the house. Along the verandah posts the honeysuckle was in bloom – not the local flowers of brilliant orange but the creamy, scented species Maude had ordered from England.

Maude was able to look him over from inside the house as he climbed out of the Major's car, crossed the yard with his long strides and nervous grin, and stepped up onto the front verandah calling her name.

Inside the car, the men argued for a moment about whether they should stay, but decided in the end to leave.

He'd got all the way to the door before something stopped him. "Maudie?" It looked, she said, as though he were afraid to come in. He walked the length of the verandah, past empty chairs that faced out to his fields, to stand by sleeping Donald with one hand on his brother-in-law's shoulder, and to gaze out over the pastures.

"Oh, I was cruel!" Maude would admit. "Why did I leave him there, as if he were another invalid set out for the air? What was he imagining?"

He was wishing there was something he might tell his brother-in-law about Hugh Corbett. The name had never been mentioned where Donald might hear. It occurred to him for the first time now that whatever remained of Donald MacCormack's consciousness might have been waiting all this time for Hugh to come home. This might have been all that had kept him alive.

He decided against saying the name. "I'm looking at the spring," he said instead. "Somebody's dug us a pond."

Donald slept on, his head nodding above his folded hands.

"I wouldn't have bought Holsteins myself," Pearson said, looking at the cows in the field, "but they look healthy enough."

He swatted away a wasp that soared in out of the yard and circled Donald's head.

"Somebody's fixed the fences, too. But they've used barbed wire."

"Oh, Matthew!" Maude threw open the door and sailed out, as only Maude Pearson could do, with her arms held wide to gather him in. "Taylor didn't think you'd mind about the wire, after all this time."

They embraced. So hard, Pearson would say, that for a moment they tilted and crashed against the honeysuckle trellis. Maude's feet had risen from the floorboards, throwing them both off balance. He had to grab hold of a verandah post to keep them from falling through to the flower garden below. Laughing, they turned a few circles down the verandah and crashed against the wall of the house.

Eventually Maude stepped back with her head lowered, to look up from under her fierce dark brow. There were tears in her eyes, and her hand was still tight on his arm, but she stood at a distance. "Come in. It's time to consider how things stand."

She led the way in to the parlour, and sat in an armed chair in the shaded corner, beneath her mother's portrait. "We haven't reached seventy-times-seven yet," she said, "but we've come about as close as anyone ought to risk."

But they didn't talk. At least not yet. Matt turned his chair so that he would be close enough to take Maude's hand and hold it between his. They looked at one another, studying features that were as familiar as their own. With his free hand he pushed back a few strands of hair that had fallen across her forehead, then let the tips of his fingers trace the shape of her right ear and down along the pale edge of her jaw to her chin. She pressed the fingers, and moved them to her mouth. He could feel where the two front teeth pushed forward and overlapped just a little. What he saw in her eyes was a remembering.

On her hand the nails were imperfect – some broken, the others uneven. The fingers were stained with the dark lines some vegetables leave in the creases. The long centre finger was bent a little towards the end, possibly from the hours of writing letters, with an indentation where a pen had made itself a resting place over the years. And in the palms, when he turned them over, were small yellowed calluses on the pads of flesh. Yet this hand, he thought, was perhaps the most beautiful hand that he could imagine at the moment. He opened it out so that he might lower his damaged face to its touch.

"The place is quiet," he said. It had been years since he'd run a hand up the naked flesh of her arm in daylight, he realized, somewhat astonished to think so. Nor had she put the palm of her hand on his thigh while sunlight was streaming through the windows – at least not since the earliest days of their marriage. He had never before, outside the bedroom, dropped to one knee and held her face for a long kiss while letting his other hand slip inside the top of her dress – certainly not since the children.

She may have been thinking the same. She stopped his hand with her own. "Will," she said.

"And where is young Will?" he said. He'd thought she must have sent the children to a neighbour.

Will was having his nap.

"Then we should close a door," he said. "Will's a light sleeper."

She put a hand to his mouth, then took it away to kiss him, and then put the hand to his mouth again. "I'm sorry. There is still Tanner."

He knew already that Tanner had recovered from his injuries, and that the Richmonds had not pressed charges, insisting instead that the three boys donate a few days of their time to helping bring in the hay. The boys had been required to hammer out the dents in the truck as well, and to touch up the paint. Matt had learned this in a telephone call he had made from Paris to the Store, where Leena Hueffner presided over the only telephone in the settlement. "He's lucky they didn't chuck him in the *calabozo*. But the Richmonds don't want to make trouble between neighbours. I never seen nothing like it."

"Tanner's been in a foul mood since he heard you were coming," Maude said. She withdrew her hand and stood up, and walked to the window that looked out towards the lane. "Now he's disappeared." She paused, as though she might stop there, but then expelled her held breath and continued. "Yesterday afternoon he left without telling me where he was going. I haven't seen him since. Nor has anyone else that I've talked to."

(vi)

The movie's premiere was held at the twin cinemas beside the newer bridge. The Maple Leaf Theatre disappeared long ago, replaced by dress shops and a bakery specializing in German cakes. The new theatre was a place of thick carpets, rich drapes, and boxed speakers on both side walls. Something else was showing at the same time in the other half but most of the excitement had to do with young Macken's movie. They handed out programs with photos and lists of names, and paragraphs of explanation.

Two rows had been roped off in the centre section, some of them for old-timers like myself who'd been young at the time of the fire. Lise Martin had come from Winnipeg with her second husband. Mackens and Mackens-by-marriage took up most of the reserved seats, but those in the middle were kept for the boy who had written and directed the movie, with his wife beside him, as well as for his father who'd wanted to make movies himself when he was young but had to be content with investing money in this one.

None of the original settlers was there, of course. None of the adults, that is, except for Donald MacCormack and Nora Macken who had outlived the rest. Christina Ahlberg was the most recent to die, after living for years in a nursing home where she entertained the other patients by pretending to see futures for them in their teacups.

Donald, who still lived on the Pearson place with Will and his wife, Lorraine, did not look very much older than he'd looked as a young man. I suppose it was the same mask, with its unweathered and unwrinkled surface and the large black moustache hiding the mouth. His hair had not turned white but had only faded. They said his physical health had mysteriously improved over the years to the point where now in his nineties he was in better condition than he'd been decades before, though it was still unknown how conscious he was of himself or the life around him. He would not make head nor tail of the movie, we assumed, but Will Pearson and his wife liked to include him in things.

Nora was well past the ninetieth mark herself. She came in at the last minute on the boy's arm, narrow and straight and haughty in a long grey wool dress, her thin hair dyed as black as it had naturally been when she arrived here as a young woman. A grand entrance. People turned and whispered, which must have pleased her.

Nora was still a force to reckon with if she took a notion to make herself unpleasant. Having raised her brothers, she'd then sat back and expected them – and now their children, since most of the brothers had gone – to dedicate their lives to expressions of gratitude. From what we had heard, she could make life hell for her nephew Colin, who had bought up both his father's place and the Home Place, which his grandfather and others had spent their lifetimes clearing and his father and others had let go back to hobby farms and Christmas-tree farms and which he was now making a living off through selective logging with a Timberjack. Nora had moved in with him and his family, but apparently nothing they did could ever entirely please her.

The excited chatter took a while to die down. Before anything else, even before the title, the screen was filled to every corner with the arabesques of a giant root mass, the upturned tangled base of a windfall Douglas fir, at least twenty feet high and just as wide, if we were to judge by the size of the boy who sat atop it with his bare heels worked into the gaps in the twisted puzzle. As we moved closer, the roots grew larger and took on the texture and colouring of rain-polished wood, a latticework of coppery snakes and baked vines. Then we were able to look right through the gaps, and could see, as the boy must have been seeing from his high perch, a man on horseback approaching us down a narrow dirt road.

It was possible to hear a murmur of recognition from people who had not even been born at the time this happened but still believed they had been there to see it. Once there was this stranger who rode his horse across the country in pursuit of the girl who'd run away. You could imagine them thinking it. Behind the man on the horse, above the green, timbered mountainside, the sky boiled up rolling clouds of thick brown smoke. Everyone knew what that meant.

He did not look as though he had scorched his clothes in a fire yet, but he did look as though he had stopped somewhere to wallow in a muddy ditch.

The house stood in a small clearing in the tangled jungle of a logged-over plot of second-growth forest, a house that could have been any one of a dozen still standing, with a front verandah, a door between two windows, and a third-eye window in the gable above the verandah roof. But it was actually the house that once belonged to the Richmonds, all of its improvements camouflaged behind a coat of paint the colour of weathered lumber and stapled sections of tarpaper flapping from what was meant to be an unfinished wall, standing in for the Macken house that had long ago developed a sag in its roof, lost half its shakes and even some of its windows, and was used only as a storage shed for Colin's logging equipment. The movie title and the names of actors swam in the hazy smoke-filled air as we travelled up the lane with the horseman to approach the door.

The first spoken lines of the movie were Nora's, but we didn't even need to hear them in order to see that something was different here. The young woman, tall and slender with a crown of dark curls, opened the door and stood blinking into the light as though she couldn't imagine why this man was standing on her father's doorstep. Then, just as we were expecting her to sneer, or ask why he'd followed her across the country like an unwanted dog, it became clear in the woman's face that what she was looking at was more than just the irritating nuisance that we'd thought. She regarded him with a visible mixture of contradictory emotions, as if she were living in a nightmare where the man of her dreams had come at last, making her happy in a way that only increased her misery. We knew already that the boy had chosen to tell the familiar story from a point of view that hadn't had much attention.

We were on familiar ground again when we saw him stripping so she could put his clothes in the oven. We laughed when we saw him stand in her brothers' clothes, which were far too loose for his narrow frame. But we squirmed in our seats when their conversation on the bank of Portuguese Creek began to make it clear that we were looking at a woman who had got herself into a trap that her own nature and the rules of her family would make it impossible for her to escape. Though she couldn't bring herself to say it, you could tell in her eyes that she wanted him to put her on his horse against her will and take her to Owen Sound. It was a relief when she'd finally told him about Herbert Brewer, her voice filled with all that she couldn't say and her eyes filled with messages that no one would ever dare mention aloud. When we got back to the house at last and saw the smoke leaking from around the edges of the oven door, we could slap our hands on the arm-rests, shaking our heads. We were back in familiar territory, at least for a while.

We'd been warned. We would not be allowed merely to sit back and watch a clown from Ontario trying to win the heart of a woman too stubborn and contrary to see what a good catch she was passing up. We would probably have to watch the anguish of a woman so trapped inside the prison bars of her own personality that she could not admit to anyone, even herself, that she wanted to seize this happiness while she had the chance. From the beginning we saw we'd be forced to see the complexity of someone who had lived amongst us as an easily dismissed stock figure for most of her ninety years.

Little time was spent on my father's death. The explosion was shown from Taylor's point of view, not mine, and occurred just as the rider approached the Store in his scorched and still-smoking clothes. So I didn't have to relive it. Still, an uneasy sense of loss settled within me, and continued to grow throughout the rest of the film. Of course I have never stopped missing my dad in all the years since he died. But that wasn't all of it. Once the movie had started putting together a portrait of the Returned Soldiers and their families I began to suspect that I had already lost something important that I didn't even know about, before I was born or soon afterwards. We all had. And had gone on losing even more of it ever since, whatever it was. Behind the colourful parade of this century's gains and losses was a huge absence of something that was neither identified nor regained nor replaced.

Matt Pearson would have known what it was, I suppose, if he'd been here, though I don't know if he'd have been able to tell me. I sometimes doubt he shared his most private thoughts even with Maude, who was impatient with muddle, a believer in action. To her, questions of the spirit were quickly reduced to matters of political right and wrong. I suppose Pearson wrestled with his demons in the privacy of his skull like most of us, knowing that what was important to him could not be resolved by others. If he spoke little of his doubts, or of the insights that came from his reading, this was probably because he lived in a community that thrived (and does to the present day) upon the sharing of nearly everything else – work, joys, disappointments, recipes, machinery, expertise, gossip, good news, and sorrows – *except* for those intimate matters of life and death that, it is suggested in books, people elsewhere in the world debate constantly, or did at one time at least.

Maybe this is another thing about being old. Anything put in front of your face can haul up distant memories so sharp and tangible that they can exist at the same time as the present. We all sat and watched young Macken's version of the Fire of '22 unfold in front of us, but at the same time I was running my own version in my head. While Matthew Pearson up on that screen was taking

Taylor home to the farm he had already decided to abandon (though he couldn't have guessed how he would later do it) I was also thinking of Pearson the day he returned from France, having to go down that lane in Major Burgess's lace-curtained touring car to face Maude. When Taylor and the other men were planning to steal the little church from down the road, I remembered how Elizabeth had been buried for the second time behind it, just a few weeks after Pearson's return.

She was buried in the shade of a Douglas fir whose lower boughs hung over the grave. The mound of fresh clear dirt was spread over with flowers brought out from town, with a small white wooden cross and a polished fieldstone at the head. Most of the community gathered for the brief service, which was conducted by the same preacher who'd spoken at Elizabeth's funeral in town. Burying someone was a way of tying the building to the place, some people said. Now it belonged to us, whether we used it or not.

As it turned out, we wouldn't use it much. Sandy MacKay was to be buried there a few months later, when he was killed in the woods from a tree that bounced off another and came down on his head. The Company closed down operations for half a day so the men could attend the service. The weekly paper did a story on this man they'd earlier made famous for pulling his stumps from the earth without help – "Tree Fells the Bull of Portuguese Creek." Ernie Mitchell was also buried there, killed when a haulback cable snapped. He'd given up a grocery store in New Brunswick to move out here and farm, but he'd died while crawling through the underbrush setting chokers. From the land he'd worked evenings and weekends to clear and tend, he had never made a cent.

They didn't want to be loggers, any of them. There wasn't one of them who came here expecting to work in the woods. They would have been happy if they had never had to cut down a tree that wasn't in the way of a hayfield. They came here to farm but were expected to cultivate land unfit for farming. They were pushed into a lifetime of dangerous labour in the woods in order to give their families more than just the food they could grow themselves. The headstones for Sandy MacKay and Ernie Mitchell had the usual things carved onto them but they could just as easily have been embellished with bitter words.

Elizabeth's headstone said "Beloved Child." Pearson may once have expected to get over Elizabeth's death eventually, but by now he knew he would not. This had nothing to do with Elizabeth's origins, or with his own feelings of guilt, or with the way she died. To get over the pain of that loss he would have had to *imagine* getting over it, and he didn't see how that could ever happen. The only thing that could make this even bearable, he explained to me, would be to discover that Shakespeare had got it exactly wrong: that our little life is not rounded with a sleep but *is* the sleep – a dream, a fiction, an eighty-year-long movie that holds us in its hypnotic spell but doesn't interrupt the flow of real life going on where we don't very often see it. Not harps and clouds and pearly gates, nor flames and cries of anguish, but the unharmed continuing and conscious identity of Elizabeth and everyone else getting on with life out of sight of those blinded, for the moment, by the distractions of this world.

We were not surprised when he gave up trying to make a profitable farm on his land as he'd been expected to do by a government that asked the impossible. Instead, like nearly everyone else, he let his "stump ranch" become just another hobby farm – a couple of cows, a pen full of chickens, a big garden, just enough chores for the family to share. But rather than rejoin the others earning wages in the woods, he took over Johanna Seyerstad's job at the school.

As the teacher, he tried for a while to introduce us to writers he claimed were trying to tell the truth about something, but the poems seemed to be only bizarre and incomprehensible pictures out of what we took to be diseased imaginations. People walking in circles. Corpses planted in gardens. Even he had to admit, eventually, that they may have had less to do with us in this place than he'd thought, at least for the time being. Eventually he began to bring Chaucer and Tennyson and "all those other old fellows" into his classroom again, having gained enough distance, he said, to see them with new and more modern eyes.

He considered the fire an important part of the curriculum, but not his alone to relate. In fact, he preferred to say little about it himself, but formed the habit of inviting people from the community in to tell about it, a different group every year of folk competing to relate the most thorough, dramatic, hair-raising, or comical version of the great disaster. Arlette Martin's account of her first experience behind the wheel of the family truck had developed into something like a cartoon chase, with flames licking at her back tires, burning limbs dropping onto the windshield to obscure her view as she drove madly and blindly down the potholed lane. Up on her toes she went, eyes bulging, hands fluttering about as though sparks and brands were flying around her head right there in the schoolroom. The Winton brothers got over their initial stuttering shyness as soon as one of the students asked if it was true they'd dragged their mother kicking and screaming into the muddy swamp. "That woman was as wild as a bobcat in a gunnysack," John said. "She never spoke a civilized word to us for the rest of her life." And Tom: "Let me tell you what it feels like to hold your own mother's head under the mud while she's trying to get free to where the flames would turn her to ashes in a minute."

Once in a while Matt Pearson invited some of us from the "younger generation" who had come through the fire like helpless creatures in a nightmare. And eventually, of course, he had to start relying on people who had no personal memory of the fire themselves but could relate tales they'd heard a thousand times from their parents. "So my grandmother helped Leena Hueffner throw all the mail into this discoloured ol' tablecloth with embroidered cactuses. She would've killed us for telling this while she was alive,

but the whalebone stays in her corset broke while she was bending
to tie up the corners of the tablecloth and dug like knitting
needles into her ribs all the way into town. Hopping around like
a dog with fleas, my grandpa said. She could hardly wait to get
into one of them tents and strip!"

When the History curriculum dictated that he could not avoid
the Great War, Pearson confined himself to facts and figures, so
that it seemed as dull and distant as the War of the Roses. In his
later years he would sometimes offer opinions, but only those
that had become commonplace by then. "While we were fighting
we said, 'Nobody can win this.' Then we thought for a while that
we'd won it after all, until '39 showed us it wasn't even over."
Eventually he would use the War to issue warnings to younger generations. Now, he suggested, we were beginning to see that the
spirit that drove the enemy in the first place may be winning after
all. The world they'd longed for out of their hatred of the British
Empire with its Victorian certainties about morality, duty, loyalty,
and order, was being created despite their defeat. It was as if the
only winners of that War were the race of savages once rumoured
to live in the tunnels under no-man's-land.

"If my old friend Charlie Sullivan were here he would tell us
we've taken up the cause of the aggressors for ourselves – a world
worshipping the individual, rejecting moral codes, and accepting
propaganda as the equal of truth. Hatred, lying, violence, and
butchery loose in the world. Now let's stop and think if there is
anything you and I can do to combat this." His lessons then
became explorations and discussions of individual responsibilities
and ethics. He led them to no definitive answers, of course, but
it was said that his students went home feeling as though they'd
experienced something as unsettling as war themselves, and had
to sort out what they felt and thought.

I wondered what effect this movie would have upon future
accounts of the War's survivors and the Fire of '22. Was this the
"true" story we were witnessing now in this world of popcorn and

rustling candy wrappers? Would it *become* the true story, erasing from our memories the versions we'd heard a thousand times from those who'd been there and from those whose parents had been there? Had we been honoured and celebrated and immortalized by celluloid, or had something been stolen from us that we would never get back?

For some the movie would provoke a whole new round of remembering, and remembering of earlier rememberings – new tellings of old versions, as well as variations that had not been represented on the screen. We would also witness the young people adopting the movie version as though it were gospel, forgetting the facts. "It shows how times have changed when you think how the teacher ran off with Taylor so quick. One day she's waiting for her husband and then, bang, the fire, and she's running off with this other guy right after that kid's funeral! In those days women couldn't live without a man."

Thinking of matters that still belonged in the future of the story unfolding on the screen did not prevent me from seeing what young Macken was showing us of the past. Everything from the beginning had been designed to fill us with suspense, as we waited for the moment someone would notice that the fire in the hills had come down to the edge of the settlement. We were able to guess early on that he'd chosen to make the fire his film's climax, rather than a turning point or even the true beginning of the aftermath. In the manner of many films, he was more interested in the disaster than in the recovery that followed.

Eventually we'd got all the way through the fire, thinking, "This is what it was like," and were taken into the hospital room where Nora broke the news to Taylor that she would stay with her family. At first it was only the devastated look on Taylor's face that held us, as he absorbed the news that this woman he'd risked his life for was rejecting him in favour of her brothers. When he turned to leave, we thought: *Go. Quick. She doesn't deserve you.*

Then Nora, left alone in the sunroom, began to pick the dead leaves from a potted geranium on the windowsill. Having crushed them in her hand, she dropped the dry brown flakes to the floor. When Taylor appeared below on the pathway, she seemed to panic for a moment, as though she hadn't anticipated this. *What have I done?* She may have been tempted to call him back. She may not have meant a word she'd said to him minutes before.

They regarded one another for a few moments through the glass, she from above and he from below on the gravel pathway. And then he turned away to find where he'd left his horse. Nora gasped and turned as though to go after him, but was met in the doorway by her father. One of the boys had overheard, he said. He wished her to know that he was proud. He said it gruffly, of course. We could see that he was unused to expressing emotions. "Your mother would be pleased."

From the shadow that moved across her face, it was clear that Nora wasn't so sure of this.

"The boys'll have you to thank for the rest of their lives."

She might have been content to leave it at that. But when she turned to the window again, and the row of potted geraniums, and saw through the glass the empty gravel pathway between the building and the cliff that fell away to the bay, she thought better of it. "I would have gone with him." She did not look at her father while she said this, she looked out at the moving current of the bay, fading into the falling night. "I was a fool to leave him in the first place. You better know that. It turned out I loved him after all."

"That makes me even prouder of you, girl."

She didn't tell her father anything more. She saved that for a stranger who could have no idea what she was talking about. When her father had gone to rejoin the boys a nurse came in to see if anything was needed here. A soft, round woman with tight grey curls and spectacles. She joined Nora at the window and took up Nora's hand, whose palm was still peppered with bits of dead leaf. "I'm sorry. I lost my mother too, not long ago. It seems unfair."

Nora might not have heard. "I seen something that even he hasn't seen yet," she told the nurse. Maybe it was because she was a woman. Nora's life had not been rich with women who inspired the telling of secrets. Or maybe she just needed to say out loud what she wished she had been able to tell her father – that this wasn't all self-sacrifice for the sake of the boys. "Trying to win me back had become only a habit for him. I didn't want to think this, but I could see it happening. He doesn't know it yet himself, but he'll wake up one morning and find out I held him off so long I stupidly gave him time to fall for somebody else."

Well, there you are, I thought. Now we knew where the boy had been leading us. There was more to this story after all than we'd believed – or more to the Macken version of the story anyway.

The nurse had no reason to be surprised by what she'd heard. "It's been a terrible day," she said. "Perhaps you'd like something to help you sleep? Nothing will change in the morning, I'm afraid, but you may feel stronger to face it."

Several times before this a subdued disturbance had broken out at the centre of the theatre auditorium. Low grumblings that were quickly hushed. Protests, maybe. I hardly noticed. It was the sort of growling you hear when someone has dropped a ring or a chocolate bar and a neighbour is helping to find it in the dark.

But now the voice rose, indifferent to the chorus of shushing noises from around it. A figure stood up, still talking. Donald MacCormack. The noises he made weren't his usual grunts and groans, he was trying to talk above the voices on either side that were urging him to be quiet. He was also trying to talk above the sound track blasting down from the walls. He *was* talking – I was close enough to know that – though it was the kind of talk that made no language sense.

What was he saying? Indignant protests, maybe, if I had to

guess. We were getting towards the end of the movie now, we'd
started to move through the settlement, observing the devastated farms, and had come to the Pearson farm once more. We'd
seen the house from the outside a number of times already, and
there'd never been a Donald MacCormack sitting on the porch.
We'd gone inside to watch actors eating at the table a few times
too. We'd gone through the entire fire and not seen a glimpse of
Donald MacCormack. It must have occurred to him that we
were never going to see Donald MacCormack in this world. No
Donald MacCormack lived there. That is my guess. If the man
was able to make any sense of what was happening on the screen
he must have thought that someone had erased him from his
own life.

The story continued to unroll before us but I doubt that anyone
paid attention. Donald McCormack would not be silenced by
pleas. Attempts to escort him quietly out of there failed. I don't
know what signals were made, but suddenly the picture on the
screen disintegrated and died, the sound collapsing with an ugly
groan. The house lights came up. Donald stood at the centre of a
group but would neither sit again nor leave with them. He waved
one arm around and continued making sounds in the language of
some race that had learned to talk without benefit of teeth or lips
or maybe even tongues. The hand shot out, jerked back, slapped
at its own face, and shot out again with something it then flung
over the heads of the others.

Will's son leapt over seats to retrieve it. Donald's mask. I
suppose Will and Lorraine may have been the only ones in that
room who had seen behind it. The rest of us had only imagined,
if we had thought of it at all, and we'd got so used to the mask that
it might as well have been his real face. I don't know if it was
Donald or the rest of us the Pearsons thought they protected by
making sure he was never observed without it.

He was observed without it now. It could not be avoided,
though many turned away. Some were later ashamed of being ill,

without enough warning to get to a washroom in time. Courtesy demanded that we look away, but one quick glimpse was enough to imprint the image forever, I think. You don't forget a collapsed hole in the middle of a face where a nose ought to be, or a mouth that falls inward shapelessly like the crumbling entrance to an abandoned coal-mine shaft. It was hard to believe this calamity had been amongst us all these years without our seeing it.

(vii)

He pulled up in front of the blacksmith shop while I was replacing the broken lower hinge on the wide front door. I went out to meet him, nervous and happy at the same time, wiping my hands on the back of my pants. My grin was spread so wide I could feel it stretching my cheeks.

"Charlie Mackinaw?" he said, getting out of the car to shake my hand. He looked pleased enough to see me, but he looked tired and pale and a little jumpy too. I don't suppose he found it easy, seeing people again after being away. "I was hoping Tanner might be with you, son. You any idea where he's got to?"

I shook my head. He could be anywhere, I thought. He could be in jail. He could be drowned in the Strait.

The patches of new skin had faded and blended in with the blurred freckles that gave Matthew Pearson's face the appearance of having been scrubbed of rust or stripped of a growth of lichen. His dark lashes were as long as before they'd been singed. He had that distracted look that adults sometimes got when they were trying not to show how anxious they were. "Well, why don't you climb in and we'll find him. You can tell me all the places you think he could be. Your uncle won't mind."

Uncle Archie would mind if he knew, but he'd gone to town. I didn't much care about finding Tanner, either, but I climbed in anyway, since it was a chance to sit beside the World Traveller on the seat of his Model T Ford.

"Well, Charlie," he said, when we'd started down the road past the school. "You didn't get married or run off to Japan while I was away." He was silent for a moment. "You think Tanner's run off to Japan?"

"I don't know," I said. "I don't see much of Tanner any more."

"I've been up to Reimers'," he said. "The boys said they haven't seen him since day before yesterday." He slowed down for three of the Richmonds' Jerseys that had got out onto the road and couldn't make up their minds which way to go. "It is my fault he's behaved as he has. I should have known. I've had enough experience with boys his age." We passed the laneway into the woods where the little church had stood before we moved it. "If I thought he was just playing games I'd wait and let him come home in his own good time. But I taught school long enough to know how boys can get it into their heads to punish their parents. I wouldn't even mind that, so long as I knew he was safe. You don't think he's run off to Victoria or somewhere?"

"Maybe he's just hiding in the bush to make you worry."

I didn't believe this. In my mind, Tanner had already crossed the Rockies, he was riding a train across the prairies, probably wondering if he should rob it.

We drove past the riverside park where we'd lived in tents for a while, and went over the bridge to town. Tanner wasn't in the pool room. He wasn't in the Five Cent Store or in any of the other stores on the main street. He wasn't in the Maple Leaf Theatre, either, watching the matinee.

"Who else does he hang around with?" Matt Pearson said. "Korsakovs? The Aalto boy?" Until now, he had tried to keep me from seeing how worried he was, but now that we hadn't found Tanner in town he was starting to stir up his hair. The muscles around his mouth were tight.

"He used to hang around with Timo Aalto," I said. "But Timo's my friend."

We drove north in tense silence to the settlement, and turned off at the Store, to follow the old railroad grade towards the mountains. At the river we turned and followed the narrow, rutted tracks past the Prices' and the old sawmill until we came to the Aaltos' little white Finnish house.

Mr. Aalto had brought his truck up to the door, where Mrs. Aalto was about to get in. She stopped, and waited for us to pull up. Timo ducked to attach their wirehaired terrier to its chain.

Mr. Pearson got down out of the car and shook hands with both the adults and nodded to Timo. Mr. Aalto welcomed him back, though you could tell from his voice that he knew there'd be some other reason for the call. He looked relieved when he was able to answer the question when it came.

"Not here, Matt'ew." He turned to his son. "Timo – you seen?"

Timo shook his head and kept his distance. His narrow slanted eyes skittered away.

"You sure?" I said.

He drove his hands down into his pockets.

His father said, "What you know?"

"Nothin'," Timo said.

"Has Tanner been here, son?" Matthew Pearson said.

Timo spat on the ground and looked again at me. "I seen him go through this morning, carrying his gun."

Mr. Pearson looked at me. "Has Tanner taken up shooting?"

"Taylor took him hunting ducks last fall. What would he shoot this time of year? Maybe it was someone else."

"I suppose we could try some of the logging roads," he said as we bounced and rocked along the rutted lane. He fingers were rooting in his hair again, pushing it this way and that and standing some of it on end. When we came to where the abandoned sawmill could be glimpsed through the trees, he stopped and looked hard at it. The whole car quietly trembled while the engine ticked.

"I suppose I ought to trust that he's got the sense to look after himself. Maybe he knows what he's doing." He didn't sound convinced.

"Maybe you should let him come home when he wants," I said.

He looked at me as though he couldn't understand the first thing about how I felt. Or even knew that I felt something. He turned off the engine. "I used to sneer at that building in there, Charlie. It mocked me, I thought, with its shallow pretence at history. I wanted a Spanish fortress, or the ruins of an ancient temple. I'm afraid I despised the absence of such things, and despised this place a little for reminding me of it. Even though we'd come here because of the distance from 'civilization,' I had trouble setting down roots where none had been set before."

He hauled in a deep breath, and let it out slowly, and then got out to step in through the trees. The river rattled over the rocks to one side of me. Crows squawked and hollered down from the branches, and flew to other trees to squawk and holler some more. They didn't like us here.

This was where we'd found him after the fire, face-down across the entrance to that sawmill like some monk before an altar. I got out and pushed my way through the scratchy underbrush and caught up to him where he stood in the clearing outside the doorway. Because we were down-slope from the building, we could not see the machinery footings that looked like the tombs of kings, but we could look up through the young alders that had grown through cracks in the floor, and through the open roof to the sky.

Matt Pearson moved up and put a hand against the cement. "They stood deserters up against walls like this to shoot them, Charlie," he said. "Did you know that? It didn't matter if you hadn't meant to desert. Maybe this isn't something to tell a boy like you."

"Taylor told us at school," I said.

"Good," he said. He folded down to sit on his heels, and draped his forearms over his thighs. He'd rolled his sleeves back to his elbows. "Did he tell you why they did it? To set an example, they said. It was a terrible thing to do, but I suppose they thought they had to."

I moved up and crouched on my heels facing him, with my back to the cold cement wall.

"What they shot you for was this – you behaved as though you lived in a different world from the others and deserved a separate peace." He didn't look at me. He was looking up at the wall and the branches of the trees around us. "You'd acted as if you were the main character in the story and other people could wait until you'd found your own happy ending. This is just the opposite of fidelity, Charlie, I suppose. Tanner could tell us that."

I can't be sure I'm remembering exactly what he said. To tell the truth, I was so pleased with myself for being his audience that I was only half-listening to his words. I was also listening to myself, thinking this was the sort of thing my dad could be telling me now. If he thought I was old enough. My dad would have made some joke out of even this topic, because he couldn't help himself, but he would have sat on his heels in the trees like Matthew Pearson, looking up, and talked to me as if I was part of himself.

"I've seen places where the sun throws stained-glass figures out of stories onto walls like these, to tell us things about ourselves more useful than a firing squad can do." He poked with a twig at the mossy earth beneath us. "Maybe we should worship in roof-less sawmills," he said. "I think we should stand in front of blank walls like this in order to ask ourselves if we have deserted anyone today, including ourselves."

He stood up and stomped his feet to work the kinks out of his legs, and started towards the doorway. "Maybe not you, Charlie. But there are some of us should maybe live in unfinished houses for a while, to remind us of any jobs we've left undone, or the mess we've made of the world. In case that should encourage us to try harder."

"If you need an extra pair of hands around the farm you can count on me," I said.

Matthew Pearson turned back and studied me hard for a moment out of those dark brown shining eyes, his eyebrows drawn down in puzzlement. Maybe he didn't understand. Maybe he thought I was too young to be much use.

"I helped Taylor dig the pond by your well," I said. "I helped him a little with the fences too. I'd rather work for you than Uncle Archie."

He looked alarmed. His face tried one expression, then another. Finally, he laughed – a sort of embarrassed laugh, I think. He'd decided to make a joke of it, but wasn't sure if he should. "What are you saying, Charlie? Surely you don't think I've been scouring the countryside for a runaway hired hand!"

I don't know what I might have said to that. My face was suddenly hot, my arms and legs were cold. But before I could answer he was distracted by something he'd spotted inside the sawmill. "Well, what do we have here! Come look at this. A surprise."

I stepped up onto the concrete floor and followed him across the open space, feeling weak and a little frightened. Small birds exploded up from a wooden table that had been set against a cement machinery footing, with a wooden chair beside it whose green paint was coming away in flakes. A Rogers Golden Syrup tin sat on the table, and some half-empty bottles of preserves. Yellow plums, pickled onions, and peas. Three or four unwashed potatoes lay beside the bottles, and a half loaf of bread set amongst crumbs with its heel up. There was a scattering of coloured pebbles as well, and bits of shell.

"A table in the wilderness!" Pearson said through the sort of quiet, low, rumbling laugh of a man who doesn't need you to understand. I couldn't tell if he was laughing because he saw some kind of joke in this, or because he was pleased at what it probably meant.

Apparently this table acted as a kind of shelter as well, for a heap of gunnysacks and coats beneath it suggested that someone had slept there.

He raised his head, as someone will who believes he may have heard something faint in the distance. He waited, his eyes on a square hole in the floor on the far side of the building, where sawdust or slab-ends were meant to fall through to be carted away. "Tanner?" he said. He put his hands in his trouser pockets and then took them out again. "We've been up and down every damn bumpy road in the country looking for you, son. For the past two hours my heart has been racing so hard in my throat that I nearly choked. You've had me scared. You'd be pleased to know how bad. Now show yourself at least, so we can talk."

He had to wait for a while before there was a rustling noise from down in the hole. And even that might have been a foraging bird. But then the rifle came up, and the hand that laid it on the floor. Then the other hand, which was scored with bloody scratches, I suppose from crawling around in the bushes. Then Tanner's shaggy dark hair decorated with twigs and leaves. And then, tilted up to look, his long awkward face. Angry, or embarrassed, or resentful – you couldn't tell which.

Matt Pearson made no effort to hide his relief and pleasure. "You look like your grandfather. You've even broadened out in the shoulders – Taylor must have put you to work."

Taylor couldn't get Tanner to do a thing, which was why I'd helped when I could.

Tanner had left the rifle on the floor when he stood up, but kept one foot on it. He put one hand against the closest cement block and looked at his father aslant and from under, as though he wasn't willing to face him square on yet. I thought he looked like his mother as well.

"You knew I would have to come here sooner or later. Were you planning to wait?"

"Maybe." Tanner shrugged. His hair was as stirred up as his father's. His eyes flickered my way but shifted to some point on the mossy floor between his father and himself. I moved back against the wall behind the table, not sure I wanted to hear any more of this.

"Were you planning to shoot me, with my own 30:30?"

I could see he was fighting a smile. Aloud, it sounded foolish. His instinct may have been to make a joke of this drama between them, but I guess he knew better.

"I'm not mocking you, son. If you dreamed of vengeance I don't blame you. I'm just thankful you didn't do something stupid."

"I'm not going home," Tanner said. He looked up this time, with some effort, and met his father's eyes. "I've been looking around. There's a shack out back of Evans's I could stay in till they kick me off."

Pearson looked hard at Tanner for a moment. "It will be tough on your mother. She'll drive you crazy delivering food and bedding and furniture she couldn't bear to think of you doing without. She'll ride out in the night and stand guard outside your door. You'll wake up to the smell of breakfast cooking over a fire. I'm afraid you'll have to go farther than Evans's shed if you really want to escape us."

"I might," he said. "I could find a place in town."

"Or you might want to think about this. Your mother told me you refuse to sleep under the same roof as your father. Well, I'd been thinking of sleeping in the toolshed for a while anyway – like Taylor when he first arrived. To tell you the truth, I'd rather you took up that rifle and beat me with it than think I'd driven you from your home."

Tanner looked off to one corner for a while, and then to another, like a dog made uneasy by your watching it. Anyone could see there were long, inspired speeches stuck in his throat, all of them rehearsed at length in his head. But now they were collapsing into heaps of meaningless words that couldn't be said.

"Well," Matt Pearson said, "I can see that if I want to be your father again you're going to make me work for it."

The crows had abandoned the alders and flapped down to line themselves along the top of the sawmill's wall, to scold and complain at the intruders. They might have been eyeing the food Tanner had left on his table, or the coloured pebbles. Amongst these, I noticed now, was a thin blue curve of stone that appeared to have been sharpened into a tiny delicate knife blade. My hand went out, as though of its own will, to touch it.

I heard Tanner's yell before I saw that he was throwing himself across the space between us. He flung his body against me, pushing me hard against the wall and causing the stone to fall to the concrete. He dropped to grab it, and in the same movement was up again to push his opened hand against my throat. His eyes were wet, his red face twisted with something ugly I couldn't put a name to.

His father took hold of his arm and removed his hand from my throat. "What's this? Are you mad at *everybody* now, on account of me?"

But Tanner resisted, tried to pull free from his father's grip. No, it was more than resisting. He fought. He struck at his father's chest with his free hand. Then he pushed against his father's bad shoulder hard enough to send Pearson stumbling against the wall, a look of both shock and pain on his face. *Now* what had I done?

Tanner moved away to stand by his table with one hand on the pebbles and looked defiant. "What's *he* doing here?" He jerked his head in my direction but didn't look at me.

"He's a friend. He's a friend to us both. Who do you think wrote and gave me hell for not coming home sooner? Charlie may be a good deal smarter than I am."

Tanner shot me a poisonous look. "Let *him* move into the house, then. That's what he wants. He could move into my room and take over. You could adopt *him* too!"

Matthew Pearson looked at me with his eyebrows raised and a

half-smile frozen on his mouth, as if he were considering what he'd just heard and didn't know whether to be amused or unbelieving. I felt myself blushing in this attention, as though I'd been caught doing something shameful.

And maybe I had. Maybe I had hoped for something I had no right to. Obviously this was what Tanner believed. His father had called me a friend, but what kind of a friend had I been? When Tanner had turned on me and sent me away nearly a year ago, for all I knew he may not have expected to be taken at his word. When I attacked him in the schoolyard and then in Maguires' barn loft, I suppose he might not have understood my reasons any better than I did. But if he were to see the letter I'd written his father, he would have little trouble recognizing why I'd mentioned the stolen truck, when just telling about the hospital would have been enough to bring his father home.

"You're talking foolishness," Matt Pearson said. "Charlie doesn't deserve this." Then, abruptly, for him it was over. "Now show me this treasure that's so important you're willing to strangle anyone who dares to touch it."

Tanner's hand closed on the stone and slipped it inside a pocket. "Never mind."

"Let's see," his father said.

For a moment they looked at one another, saying nothing. The crows squawked and complained, shifting from one foot to another along the top of the wall. I should have left then but I was afraid to move, even though I felt myself to be invisible and might have walked out of there without anyone noticing.

Eventually Tanner's hand rooted around in his pocket and brought out the stone, but kept his hand folded around it. "I followed along the banks of the creek until I found his cave."

"Whose cave? The Portuguese?"

He nodded. "Goes way back in. There's bottles in there, and old spoons. I crawled right in until I thought I'd find his skeleton, but there was a lot of junk instead."

Now he opened his hand. His father bent close, without touching, to look.

"He might've sharpened it himself," Matthew Pearson said. "Or found it along the creek somewhere. It might be Indians. It might be older than Indians."

"Neanderthals," Tanner said.

"There weren't any Neanderthal here," Matt Pearson said.

"We don't know that."

They were silent, looking down into Tanner's open hand at the thin slice of blue stone – two Pearson profiles tilted forward, dark stirred-up hair falling across their foreheads. I didn't know what they were thinking. Imagining, I guess. Picturing a race of people who might have lived in these woods before anyone we knew about had arrived. Or maybe only aware of one another in a way that could not be talked about between them.

I slipped out of the sawmill and ran as fast as I could towards Timo Aalto's place, my whole body tingling with the heat of emotions I was afraid to name. I would not have minded if the earth had opened up and swallowed me then, or if a new forest fire had swept down and burnt me to a crisp. I set out to follow the cow trails through Aalto and Evans and Winton land, and hoped that something truly horrendous would happen before I got to the Store and had to cross the road to home.

Nothing horrendous happened. I was obliged to cross the road to my home, where I learned from my mother that Uncle Archie was furious I had left the blacksmith shop untended. She swatted me across the ear, and then ran crying to her bedroom. Through the closed door I shouted that Tanner Pearson had run away and I would do the same if she ever hit me again.

I was not surprised when I learned that Tanner had gone back to live with his folks. Nor was I surprised to see later that he got along fairly well with his dad. Of course I didn't know that the minute he was old enough he would find work on the mainland, or that I would seldom see him again once he'd left, and then only briefly when he returned for family occasions. And naturally I could not have imagined then that at this ridiculous age of eighty-four I would feel compelled to sit on my backside day after day for the months it would take me to hammer out these pages, trying to explain to him and to myself what that year of his father's absence meant to me. There may even be an apology in here somewhere, since it's possible I haven't grasped even yet how much harm I may have done. At least I have written him and his father back into the story from which the movie had all but erased them.

The day after we'd found Tanner at the old sawmill, I had little heart for the Dominion Day picnic. I knew what it would be like. People had planned to go down to the beach dressed in their "Wyatt Taylors." Men and women alike would be wearing hats and coats and boots ravaged by fire or cut up and burnt especially for the occasion, just as they would every year afterwards on that date, even to the present day. Later in the afternoon, someone would be named the winner of the Wyatt Taylor look-alike contest.

The Indian woman, still waiting for her criminal husband, would not come out of hiding. Blankets would be laid out here and there on the grass the same as they'd been the year before and the year before that, but you wouldn't know who owned which. Everyone would have gone into the sea – some only standing along the edges to talk, some swimming off towards the mainland, some playing games with a ball, or ducking one another, or paddling convoys of log warships into battle. There would be groups of them everywhere, up and down the beach, families of them, though they wouldn't all be in their own families. From the shore you wouldn't be able to tell who belonged with whom. When they saw the Pearsons arrive they would come out to shake Matthew Pearson's hand, and welcome him back, and invite him to join them for a swim. I didn't want to be there.

Instead, I took my fishing pole and rode my bike only as far as the creek bridge, to see if I could surprise my mother with something for supper. I didn't expect to find Hueffner there. He'd seen brook trout hiding in the shadows, he said, but they hadn't shown any interest in his worms. I moved fifteen or twenty feet upstream to perch on a large flat rock.

A meadowlark sang in the grasses along the bank. *Oh, yes, I am a pretty little bird!* was my mother's idea of the meadowlark's song. The wildlife was beginning to come back. A hummingbird had visited the red climber roses outside our kitchen window. I'd seen two deer that morning, nervously grazing on the grass in our lower pasture.

Creeks like this one ran through every farm in the settlement, most of them dry in the summer, and some of them no wider than a drainage ditch. But all of them wandered through the district ignoring fence lines until they joined with the one they called Portuguese Creek, which ran for a few miles on its own before falling into the river that ran through town.

The creek that wandered across our place was a narrow dry-in-summer ditch, good for nothing except carrying the winter rains away. My dad had built a narrow walking bridge, so flimsy it bounced beneath your feet. "Aye, well, if there's an ogre under there his brains must be shaken up pretty bad by now," he said.

"The man they named the creeks after," I said, "how'd they know he was Portuguese?" I had never thought to ask before. This was the day we went out to blow the biggest stump of them all, while the stranger in the scorched coat talked to Matthew Pearson and the others across the road.

He was about to set off with the boxes of stumping powder under his arms. "They don't. He could have been from Zanzibar. It's just a way of saying he was a foreigner that didna' stay. Maybe he had a premonition of how much work was ahead. Or maybe he missed his bonny lass at home."

"Or maybe he drowned in the creek," I said.

"I lean towards the premonition myself. He knew fine if he stuck around long enough he'd end up clearing land. He saw how thrawn these miserable stumps could be and decided a smart man would leave."

Then he went off with the boxes under his arm and the rolled-up fuse hanging from his belt. He whistled at Dolly and Jim, who'd hung their heads over the gate to watch, and then went down into the hole to shove the sticks of powder into the cave beneath the stump.

What would he think of me fishing alone like this, with only Hueffner for company? Was Al Hueffner the best I could hope for? I watched the slow creek water moving past with a leaf now and then on its surface, dipping in and out amongst the larger rocks, and thought that I, and not Tanner, was the one who ought to run away from home. But run away to where?

Once in a while the bridge rattled from a car or wagon going over it, people heading to the beach. Dust puffed down from its underside, and pebbles dropped between the planks to splash in the water.

"This ol' creek ain't much for someone who seen the world," Hueffner said. He waited for a while, then said, "The Rio Grande, for instance. Or the Canal. The Canal's a hundred times as wide as this and a hundred times as deep, stretched from the Pacific to the Atlantic under a sun that would fry your brains."

Here we go, I thought.

At first it looked as though he only wanted to remind me of the heat and the sweat, working naked under the "blazing equatorial sun" with snakes sliding out of the jungle to strangle you, and mosquitoes injecting malaria into your flesh. I heard again how long it took them to dig the Canal, how many men had worked on her, how much money it had cost. I heard again how a little man from Georgia had dropped dead right next to Hueffner, the victim of an overseer with a grudge against people with lisps. All of this was paid out in lazy drawling bits as if he were talking to himself.

I kept my eyes on the dark dimple where my line entered the water. This would be a good time to catch a fish.

Then Hueffner scratched at his missing arm, the way he did when kids were around, and said, "Dammit, you see that there? It itches like hell and I can't get at it." He waved the stump of his arm around as though the itch might be shaken off. "Every time it happens I curse the sonofabitch that did this. I tell you how it happened?"

"Yes," I said.

He told me anyway. This time it wasn't a jungle beast or a drunken doctor sawing the wrong man's arm, it was a jealous husband. "Caught us billing and cooing in his own front room. I should of knowed better, I guess. The sonofagun took exception. Unfortunately he had a machete in his hand at the time."

"You said it was a crocodile," I said.

He looked into the moving creek water for a moment and said nothing. Then he changed the subject. "You catch a fish, you have to stretch it to feed that multitude down at the beach there, don't forget."

He stood up then, and reeled in his line. Then he picked up his jar of worms and started up the bank. "That crocodile was just a way of putting it," he said. I'd hurt his feelings. "This fellow had tiny yellow eyes and a hide like a croc. Mean when you got him mad."

From the top of the bridge he called, "Well, whaddaya know. Here's the World Traveller, home from the wars."

The Pearson Ford came up from the direction of the beach. When he'd stopped on the bridge, Mr. Pearson got out to shake Hueffner's hand. I hunched down and concentrated on my fishing line and hoped I wouldn't be noticed. I could hear the voices as Hueffner and Mr. Pearson exchanged a few words. Then I could see from the corner of my eye that Hueffner had started away and Mr. Pearson was standing there looking at me. He hollered, "You're not going down to the picnic?"

I shook my head.

He didn't leave. He walked to the end of the bridge and started down the bank. "Tanner decided not to go yet either," he said, when he'd squatted beside me. He was more dressed up today than he'd been the day before. A white shirt with wide blue suspenders and the sleeves rolled back, a tie, and dark wool pants that belonged to a suit. His hair was slicked back, though a few rebel stooks had refused to stay down. "So Hueffner's your fishing buddy now."

Hueffner and Charlie Mackinaw, a natural pair. "I didn't know he'd be here," I said. "He got telling about the Canal again. Does he want us to think he dug it by himself?"

"He probably didn't even get his hands dirty." Matt Pearson smiled. "It was coloured men dug the canal. White men mostly worked in offices."

"You mean he never even saw Panama?"

"Oh, I think he saw it all right. Maybe it wasn't even from the deck of a boat. But if he worked for them he was probably standing behind a counter the same as here. Don't tell him we're onto him, though. He's probably got more stories up his sleeve and we'll never hear them if you squeal." He stood up. "Now you might as well come along. I'm taking a break from the picnic to do Johanna Seyerstad a favour. She and Taylor came down to say good-bye, they're leaving today."

"Together?" I said. He probably hadn't heard the engagement had been off and on again a number of times.

"Together," he said. "If they're still together by the time they reach Owen Sound, they plan to make it permanent. First, though, Johanna wants a stone from one of my fields." He laughed.

"To take with them?"

He shook his head, still smiling. Fingers scratched in the hair above one ear. "Only as far as town. She's decided to do what she didn't do before. It's too late to be part of the cenotaph but she can place it at the base in Tomas Seyerstad's name. I told her any old rock from the ditch would do. She could take all of mine if she wanted, but she's picked out one she's got her heart set on. You coming?"

When we passed by Hueffner, Matt Pearson slowed down and offered him a ride as well, but he waved us on. "So why does he tell them then?" I said. "His stories."

He drove without speaking for the full length of Sandy MacKay's newest field. He wouldn't have seen it before, it had been cleared and planted since the fire. Then he said, "Maybe he's sorry he doesn't have youngsters of his own to make him a hero at the dinner table. Or maybe he's just disappointed he doesn't have something to tell about that's so big he can't bear to talk about it." He waited a moment, maybe sorting out for himself what he'd just said. War, I guess he meant. "That arm, he lost it to a farm machine when he was a boy. You imagine how cranky a thing like that could make you?"

He was silent while the Ford laboured sluggishly up a long hill. Then, once we were on level ground and the car had relaxed to go ticking along the dirt without much effort, he said, "That Nora!" and laughed as though there were some pleasure in just saying her name. "I guess we have to be grateful for honesty, but most of us would just as soon not hear honesty from people who get so much pleasure from it. She'd brought a kitchen chair from home to sit on while she kept an eye on her brothers. 'Them Frenchmen must have figured they mattered more to you than the people at home,' she said. 'Did you think you'd been hand-picked to save them?' What could I say? I told her I was trying to save my family."

No one else had gone out of their way to be rude, he said. In fact, they'd made so little fuss when they saw him he'd wondered for a minute if he'd even been away. "Maybe I'd just come back from an hour in town and didn't know it. I might have only gone east to visit my folks."

In fact, this was not far from the truth. "You know what I did

on my way home from France, Charlie? Once I knew Tanner
wasn't in danger? I stopped to visit my folks. My father and I got
into a terrible row the first day and it took the next three days to
iron things out between us. He couldn't stand it that I'd grown up
and made my life out here, and I couldn't stand it that he'd stayed
behind and got older." We started to slow down as we came up to
the highway. "Looking out from the train as I crossed the country,
I thought of Wyatt Taylor making that solitary journey on horseback because of Nora Macken. We don't know who Taylor left
behind. Maybe he's one of those men who learn young that we
have to become our own fathers."

I wasn't sure I knew what he was talking about, though I was
pretty sure it had something to do with me. Matthew Pearson may
have become a farmer but he had a schoolteacher's way of talking
too much, making sure you knew enough to pay attention even if
you didn't always know why.

"When we go back to the beach, you take a good hard look at
those folks," he said. We turned onto the highway and started
moving past Barclays' farm. "Your father brought you to live
amongst people that turned out strong enough to survive a fire.
Not only that, but strong enough to make something out of what
was only a bunch of strangers that had been badly misled. If he
could have known, he'd be glad he left you with Hueffner and
Stokes and the rest of us to keep an eye on you. You could have
been stuck with worse." He let a few moments go by as we passed
Ahlbergs' and the Store and my own house. Then he added, "You
might want to consider your mother, too."

"What?" I said. "Mother?"

"Maude tells me you may have forgotten you have a second
parent. You know how Mrs. Pearson gets bristly about some things.
Do you think she's right?"

"But Mother is always mad at everyone. She cries."

"She'll get over it. Don't forget she's one of this tough bunch of
hard-to-scare-off settlers too. You could help her."

If this was something else I'd handled badly, he'd saved me from having to think about it right away, since we were already driving down his lane. Wyatt Taylor and Johanna Seyerstad weren't far behind us.

When they drove in to the Pearson farm, Taylor was gripping the wheel of his new motorcar like someone who'd rather be holding the reins of a horse. He was dressed like all the others who'd gone down to the picnic – as himself. You could see when he stepped out of the car that he had some trouble keeping his costume together. Being the original, it had suffered the most abuse. There were safety pins and leather laces to keep his coat from dropping in shreds at his feet. His hat looked as though it had been found on a compost heap in the final stage of decomposition. His boots were turned up at the blackened toes, but luckily the soles had fallen off and he was able to tie the tops on over a new pair. It was understood that he was not to win the Wyatt Taylor look-alike contest.

For travelling, Johanna wore a long black skirt and white blouse, with her scarf wrapped just once around her neck and hanging loose. When she got out of the car, she came around to hang one hand in the crook of Taylor's arm. Her eyes were the blue of larkspur. She slapped a wide-brimmed hat against her skirt and winked at me. "I imagine you think I'm crazy?"

"Yes, ma'am," I said.

Once Taylor had removed his costume and left it in the car, he led us across the first field and the new pasture where he had blasted stumps a year before and then cleared and planted while Pearson was in France. Thick grass grew from soil still black with a shiny film of ash.

Tanner had come out from behind the house when Taylor arrived, but hung back a little, dragging his heels, trying to look as if he didn't care if he was with us or not.

In the farthest corner we came to the last great stump remaining in that field – higher than any lighthouse, wider than any shed. Bayonet spikes stood up from the jagged top. The tree that had once risen above it must have looked like a pillar holding up sky, its branches brushing clouds. Of course you would not have got a good look at it then, because of the dozens nearly as big around it.

Johanna's stone was maybe two feet long and half that wide, flat of face and smooth at the rounded edges, with salt-and-pepper flecks and scattered bits of something shining and metallic embedded in it. It looked the perfect shape and size for a gravestone, but it was tightly wrapped in one of the dozens of surface roots around the base of the stump.

"There are only seventy million rocks on the place," Matt Pearson said, "and you pick the one that doesn't want to leave."

From the way Taylor smiled and brushed a hand against the charred surface of the stump, you'd think he had some real affection for it. "What I thought I'd do is blast this out of here for you," he said. "Free the rock while I'm at it."

I hadn't expected this. This would be the first time I'd let myself get close to blasting since my dad was killed. I'd just as soon not watch but I tried not to let them see. Matt Pearson shooed us back to sit on the strip of grass between the root cellar and the barn while Taylor set to work.

"He had better not damage that stone," Johanna said. She placed the wide-brimmed hat on her head and used her scarf to hold it there, tying it under her chin.

"He won't," Pearson said. "I've watched him. You'd think he was dealing with something alive, he's so careful."

"Shouldn't we go inside?" I said. My stomach told me to expect something bad.

"Oh, I think we can trust Taylor," Pearson said. "You think so, Tanner?"

Tanner was a dozen feet away from the rest of us, sitting against the wall of the shed where Pearson kept his blasting powder. He shrugged, and looked away.

"It took me a while to see what's different about Taylor clearing land," Matt Pearson said. "The rest of us went at it angry, cursing this place for not being what we wished for. He goes at it with that calm and patient respect he brings to everything he does, and the stumps practically pull themselves out, bowing and begging his pardon. I hope some of us have the sense to remember that."

Taylor had done the digging some time before. Now he and Pearson carried the boxes of powder sticks across the dirt to the stump, where Taylor stacked the tubes in the cavity underneath. When he'd set the fuse, Matt Pearson shovelled a bank of soil against the charge.

Johanna sat on a piece of old board I'd dragged over from beside the barn wall, to keep from getting grass stains on her skirt. "I hope they've finished this sort of thing by the time you boys have grown," she said, "so you'll never have to do it."

Taylor came back and sat with us while the smoke hissed down the fuse. Without his hat and coat he looked like someone else, lean and ordinary, a farmhand dressed for travel in dark wool pants and white shirt, with his sleeves rolled high. "Don't take your eyes off 'er," he said, putting a hand on Johanna's.

I watched so hard my body was one tough knot, so tight I lost all feeling. I was nothing but two wide eyes straining to keep the world within my control. The stump rose a little, as I remembered my dad's stumps rising, and settled back into place even before the muffled sound of the explosion reached us. A giant hiccough. Not much dirt sprayed out. Nobody had been killed. But neither had the stump been shattered or split. Even from this distance we could see that nothing had changed.

"Dammit!" Taylor said, and went out to see. He walked around the stump, then stood back and shook his head.

"Maybe he should've worn his coat and hat," Matt Pearson said. "He's lost his touch."

Taylor came back to stand before us, rubbing his hands on the seat of his pants. There were smears of dirt on his face, and streaks on his shirt. "I hate to admit this to you, Matthew, but I tried before. Twice, in fact. But she wouldn't budge." He took his little notebook from his shirt pocket and opened it up, to show us the columns of figures and sketches and arrows. "I thought I had 'er figured out this time, but the tap roots must be wrapped around the furnace pipes of hell."

We crossed the pasture again and saw that Johanna's stone had leapt free and spilled onto the dirt. You'd think it was an egg the stump had given birth to. But after we'd admired it for a while, Taylor and Pearson scooped it up between them and carried it to the pond that Taylor and I had dug beside the well. There they scrubbed it clean, a large grey speckled egg flashing wet lights as it turned in the sun. When they had rinsed it and dried it off with their shirttails, they carried it to the car.

"That's one less to deal with," Pearson said. "If we could find people willing to take the rest of them we might be able to make some kind of decent farm of this place."

"I ought to take just one more crack at that stump," Taylor said, pushing his long hair back off his face. "I'll never feel I've finished things if I don't."

"That's a good way to leave it," Matt Pearson said, placing a hand on Taylor's shoulder to hold him where he was. "Maybe it'll bother you enough to bring you back. For now, I'll thank you for looking after things. The place looks good. Animals are healthy. Family well-fed. I owe you."

"You owe me nothing," Taylor said. "I worked, I ate, I lived like everyone else."

They did not invite us to witness the laying of Tomas Seyerstad's stone. We said our good-byes and backed away from the car. Tanner went to the house, to stand on the steps. Johanna called me over and took my hand in hers. She smelled of violets. "Some of the ladies promised to send me the gossip," she said, "but you could write me about the students."

I promised I would.

Taylor had already started the engine and released the brake, but he yanked the lever again and climbed out and called me around to his side of the car. "I nearly forgot." He removed his roasted coat and hat and the tops of his boots from the floor and handed the bundle to me. "Here you go. Get rid of these. You and Tanner can fight over who gets to toss them onto a donkey-pile and watch them go up in flames. Or wear them to the picnic if you want, next First of July. If they haven't rotted by then."

He got into his car again, released the brake, and drove off, squeezing the rubber bulb on his horn as they bounced and rocked up the lane that separated the Pearsons' two front fields. Then they disappeared into the mess of snags and burnt trees that stood between us and the road. The last I saw of Johanna Seyerstad was the tail of her long white fluttering scarf.

"What do you think?" Matt Pearson said. "If we visit the cenotaph tomorrow will we find it there? Or do you think she was embarrassed to admit she wanted a souvenir – something to remind her in Owen Sound of all that she's given up here?" His laugh was soft, as though there was sadness in it as much as anything else.

"I might keep the hat," I said, "but I don't know about the rest. Maybe Tanner could wear them."

Tanner was already working his way across the yard towards us. I didn't know what it was I could see in his face.

Matthew Pearson used his thumbs to pull both elastic suspenders out, then let them snap back against his chest, like someone ready to turn and get on with things. "You have to wear it all," he said. He put the hat on my head and yanked the rotted brim down to my eyebrows. Then he put a hand under my chin and tilted up my face so I could see his eyes. "We can dig up some rags of mine that look as bad as Taylor's, to throw in with these for you and Tanner to share. Then we can take ourselves back to the beach and the picnic."

I don't suppose Wyatt Taylor cared whether I wore his rags or not. He probably knew I would keep them but he might not have guessed I would never put them on. I would keep them because they were his, and would decide not to wear them for the same reason: they weren't mine. Since I'd been the first to see him ride into the settlement from the wrong direction, I would hang his rags from a nail outside our back door and swear to leave home if my mother or Uncle Archie ever moved them. To someone coming up the steps they could belong to anyone, a visitor inside, or a family member gone out to wander around in the world without a disguise.

Acknowledgements

I wish to offer thanks to the following sources of information and assistance:

The Courtenay and District Museum, for the McPhee collection of photographs and Ruth Masters' scrapbooks; the contributors of family memoirs to *Merville and Its Early Settlers*; the editors and writers of *Land of Plenty: A History of the Comox District*.

Myriam Anderson and Laurent Sagalovitsch; Madame and Monsieur Guy Dassonville of Merville-au-bois; Jeanne Delbaere; Bruno Moynie; Simone Vauthier.

Sarah Harvey; Richard Mackie; Lachlan Murray; Bill New.

Several members of my family, especially Heidi, and most notably my father, who has been generous with his memories; and, as always, Dianne.

The following writers of memoirs and news accounts: Lester Hodgins; Ben Hughes; Gladys Nina King; and Isabel Shark.

And the following scholars and writers for their books: Kathryn Bindon, Norm Christie, John Craig, Sir A. W. Currie, Daniel Dancocks, Modris Eksteins, Marc Ferro, Paul Fussell, Philip Gibbs, D. J. Goodspeed, J. L. Granatstein, J. Castell Hopkins, Lynn MacDonald, David MacFarlane, Desmond Morton, Julian Putkowski and Julian Sykes, Daphne Read, Gordon Reid, Donald M. Santor, John Swettenham, Peter Vansittart, Jay Winter and Blaine Baggett, and Larry Worthington.

Bob Preston

Jack Hodgins was born in 1938 in the Comox Valley, on Vancouver Island. After attending the University of British Columbia he taught high school English in Nanaimo, before teaching at a number of Canadian universities. He now teaches Creative Writing at the University of Victoria.

His first book, a collection of stories entitled *Spit Delaney's Island*, was nominated for the 1976 Governor General's Award, and "did for the people of Vancouver Island what . . . William Faulkner [did] for the American south." (*The Gazette*, Montreal)

His first novel, *The Invention of the World*, published a year later, was hailed as "the major work of Canadian magic realism" (*Canadian Fiction Magazine*), and won the Gibson Literary Award. His second novel, *The Resurrection of Joseph Bourne* (1979), received still more critical praise and won the Governor General's Award. All three works are now in the New Canadian Library.

His later books include *Over Forty in Broken Hill* (about his travels in Australia) and *A Passion for Narrative: A Guide for Writing Fiction*, which has established itself as a perennial classic. He has been awarded the Canada–Australia Prize, among many others, and has received an honorary degree from UBC. He was recently elected a Fellow of the Royal Society of Canada. He is "a writer's writer," greatly admired by his peers, and by an ever-widening circle of readers.

Many new readers were attracted by *Broken Ground*, which hit the national best-seller lists in 1998 and went on to win two awards.

Fragments of poems are quoted from works by Alfred, Lord Tennyson, Gerard Manley Hopkins, George Peele, William Wordsworth, Geoffrey Chaucer, John Milton, and William Shakespeare. The grammar samples are from *An Introductory English Grammar*, by S. E. Lang, M.A., Western Canada Series, Copp Clark. Biblical quotations are from the King James version.